Hearthstones II:
Let the Sparks Fly!

By MaryLee Marilee
and
Sheryl Drake Lawrence

Paper Bridges
Books

Hearthstones II: Let the Sparks Fly!

A Paper Bridges book/February, 2011
(Updated August 2023)
Published by Paper Bridges

Paperbridgespublisher@gmail.com

Disclaimer:

This is a work of fiction. Names, characters, places and incidents are either the products of the authors' imaginations or used fictitiously. Any resemblance to actual people, living, dead (or otherwise incarnate), or to events or locales is entirely coincidental. If you think you recognize someone within these pages, all we can say (as our old, writing professor used to say) is that "it's all grist for the mill!"

Copyright © 2012 by MaryLee Marilee and Sheryl Drake Lawrence

Book design by MaryLee Marilee

ISBN 978-0-9831765-3-4
(Print Version)
ISBN 978-0-9831765-2-7
(e-book)

Paper Bridges
Linking Author / To Reader
771B, S.R. 97
Perrysville, OH 44864
email: PaperBridgesPublisher@gmail.com

DEDICATION

MaryLee Marilee: For the strong women who came before me: Marjorie Miller Johnston, Anna C. Miller (Grandpa always said the "C" stood for "Calamity"), Lilly Eisenman Johnston, and Louise Johnston Roeher-Wilson (Mother, G'Ma, Grandma J., and good ol' Aunt Lou).

Sheryl Drake Lawrence: For the strong women who came before me: Sharon McCarthy Drake, Lawava Slack McCarthy, and Agnes Johnson Slack (Mom, Grandma, and Big Grandma).

Map of Homesteads

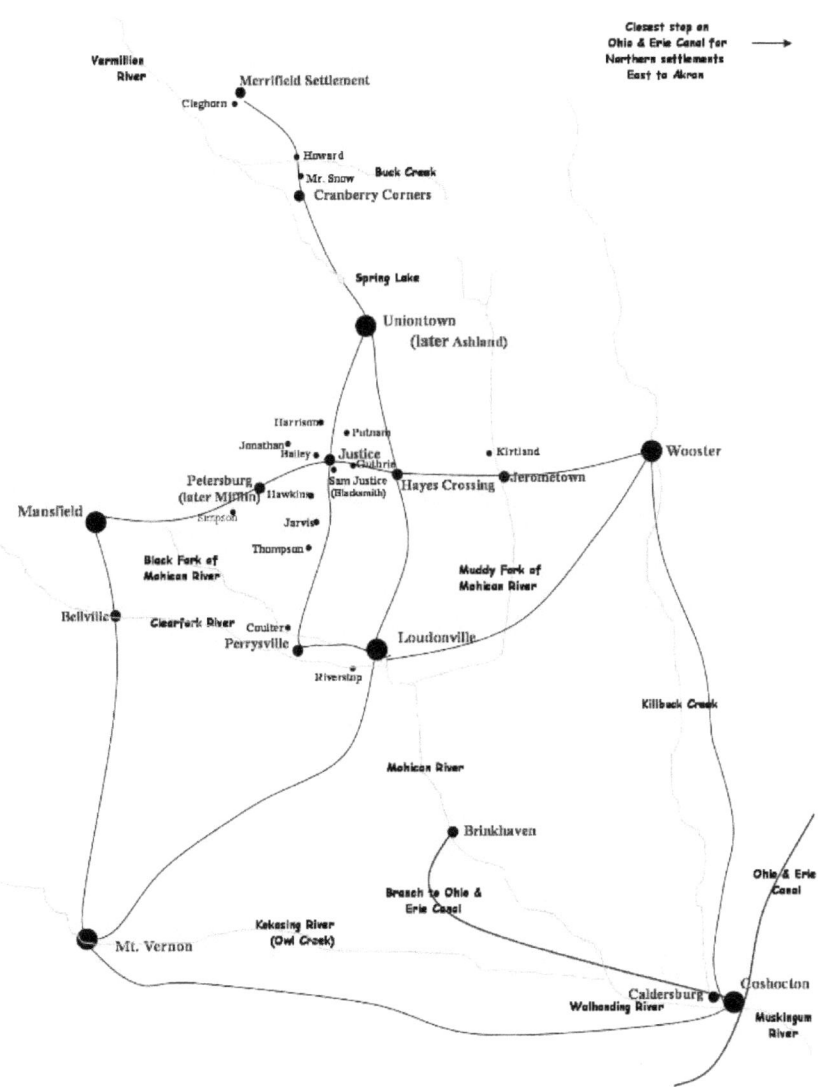

Chapter 1

The Kicking Bee
Justice Settlement, Vermillion Township
Mid April 1818

"You pound that board down good and tight on the end of that wool, now," Emma directed her near-sighted husband, Frank Putnam, as he anchored the last woolen strip fast to the floor of Netta Bailey's cabin. "Sure don't want that cloth workin' loose once we get her all sudsed down."

Frank pounded at the last nail, missing it two blows out of every three. "Dad-blasted hammer! Never could whack a blamed thing with it," he complained.

"If you ask me, it ain't the hammer's fault, you keep missin' that tack," Anson Guthrie teased his best friend. "You didn't ask me, but I'm-a-tellin' you just the same."

Frank squinted his one, good eye to get a better focus on the tack. "I could hit just fine, if I didn't have to put up with so much of your botheration, you red-nosed souse."

"Forget about Anson and finish fixin' them yard goods down," Emma snapped in an obvious huff. "Netta's got three, big wash-tubs full of hot water, all ready for stirrin' in soap suds." The strain of responsibility for organizing this work party was beginning to show on Emma Putnam. Although a good many other township women surpassed Emma when it came to God-given intelligence, she was doing her best to oversee this neighborhood Kicking Bee, since she's the one who'd woven all the woolen goods ready for felting. In spite of her obvious shortcomings, Emma did know how to weave. Once she got past her initial bafflement at stringing up her loom, Emma turned out the best yard goods in the township. Of course, she had the only loom within a 30-mile radius, so everyone expected her unquestioned involvement in this day's festivities.

And festive, it was. After spending a long, lonely winter holed-up in their respective cabins, friends and neighbors from the Justice settlement on the western side of Vermillion Township gathered at the largest, centralized cabin for their work party to felt the woolens woven during the dark hours of the season past.

They accomplished this softening and fulling of the scratchy wool by working warm soap-suds into strips of fabric fastened to the floor. The men would tack down lengths of wool with wood strips, in order to eliminate as much shrinkage as possible, then the women would dump hot, soapy water over the fabric-covered floor so bare-footed men and boys could roll up their pant legs and "kick up" a suds to soften and lock the newly woven fabric.

Hence, the "Kicking Bee."

As with all neighborhood gatherings in any early settlement, necessity dictated that work take precedence over socializing on every occasion, except at a wedding or a funeral. Most other get-togethers revolved around the community's need to accomplish a specific task at hand.

This day's task brought together folks long winter-starved for companionship and social exchange. Men greeted each other with back-slaps and handshakes, talking of crops and weather and politics, while the women rushed to hug one another, ogle over the newest babies, and catch up on all the neighborhood gossip.

As Emma Putnam and Anson Guthrie spurred Frank to finish his tacking task, neighbors continued to arrive at the Bailey place, bearing all manner of foodstuffs for the big party sure to follow the work slated for this day. After all, who could waste a nice clean floor after all that sudsy kicking? It certainly called for a dance, at the very least—and at the most, an all-night frolic to celebrate the new-born spring.

"Haven't you got those yard goods tacked down yet, Frank?" Netta Bailey asked, hurrying to the far corner of the cabin where Frank sat sucking on a thumb with wife Emma scowling down at him. "Oh my lands, you hurt yourself! Let me see that thumb." Netta grabbed his hand to examine the bleeding appendage before he could say a single word. "We got to go soak that thing in cold water right away, 'fore it swells up more than it already has!"

"He don't need no special babyin'," said Emma in disgust.

"Aw, hell. Baby him all you want," piped up Anson. "He ain't much good for nothin' else, no-how."

"Why, Anson Guthrie, how can you talk about your best friend that way? You ought to be ashamed of yourself," scolded Netta. "Come with me, Frank. I got some salve that'll draw the soreness right out of that thumb. Keep it from festerin' on you," she said, pulling him toward her pantry cupboard in the opposite corner of the cabin. "Emma, you better get over there to help Lucy and Winifred stir up suds," she called on the way. "We got to get all that hot water dumped out before it cools down, or it won't do us a bit of good."

She pulled a tin of salve from the shelf and began to swab at Frank's swollen thumb. "I sure do hope more neighbors turn up. We need more men for kickin' up this much cloth," Netta said, coating the wound with smelly salve and measuring out a strip of bandage. "I don't know how in the world Emma ever wove up so much over the winter. She must've sat at that loom every waking hour of the day!"

"Purty near."

"I think I'd go stir-crazy if I had to sit still for so long," Netta rattled. "How can she stand it? Sittin' like that, I mean, doin' nothing but shove those little bobbin doohickeys back and forth all the time? Doesn't it get awful tedious?"

"Hell, sittin's what that woman does best," Frank said. "Ever take a good look at that sitter of hers? Broad as the back side of a southbound mule."

"Why, Frank Putnam! I should wash your mouth out with some of them soap suds, I should. Don't you know it's not proper to say such things in earshot of a respectable woman?"

"Blast it all, Netta, everybody knows Emma ain't no good but for one thing," he said, trying to hold his thumb still while Netta continued to wrap and wrap at it with the long strip of bandage. "On second thought, I 'spect you better make that

3

two," he said with a wink. "She sure can weave up a powerful lot of cloth goods."

By the time Netta finished bandaging Frank's smashed thumb, Edith Hawkins had arrived and taken charge of organizing the incoming foodstuffs. Being one of the oldest women in the territory, "Ma" Hawkins was used to giving orders and having them obeyed, no matter what the occasion.

"Clara, you see nobody touches any pies till after all them yard goods gets taken up, you hear?"

"You can count on me, Mrs. Hawkins," eighteen-year-old Clara Guthrie said, smoothing wrinkles from her crisp, blue dress.

"Mind me, now, girl. If that Reverend Longbottom shows up, you better be double careful he don't sweet-talk you into givin' him a piece or two."

"I promise, I won't let no one touch a single pie," she said, moving this way and that, to set her skirt to swaying.

Edith Hawkins looked her up and down. "I don't s'pose you had brains enough to bring along an apron to cover yourself up with," she said shaking her head. "What in blue blazes possessed you to wear such a fancy frock for a work-doin's, girl?"

"Pa bought it for me... on his trip down to market! I just *had* to wear it, see?"

"Vanity ain't no excuse for poor sense," said Ma, taking Netta's every-day apron down from its peg. "Here, cover that thing up with this extra smock of Jeannette's."

"But Mrs. Hawkins—"

"No buts. Put it on. Can't see compoundin' poor judgment with downright waste by ruinin' that fancy thing," she said, shaking her head.

Clara's eyes began to swim. Dutifully she took the stained apron from Edith Hawkins and tied it over her pretty, store-bought dress, all the while trying valiantly not to cry under the scrutiny of that crusty woman. Thankfully the Harrisons' arrival diverted Ma's attention. She hurried over to check on the Harrison twins and a very pregnant Amanda Jane. Clara turned her face to the corner, giving in to her tears.

"What's wrong, Clara?" Netta asked, coming over and reaching around her to replace the bandage roll back on its shelf above Clara's head.

"Tom won't even notice me now," she snuffled. "Look at me! His own ma made me put this dirty apron over top of my nice, new party dress. He'll *never* look at me now! I just know it!" A fresh gush of tears followed.

"It's not all that bad, Clara. You still look mighty nice in that shade of blue, you know," Netta comforted.

"She don't like me," Clara said with a sob. "She don't like me at-all."

"Now, that's not a bit true," said Netta, patting Clara on the shoulder. "Ma comes across mighty gruff, but she doesn't have a spiteful bone in her body. Not when it comes to womenfolk. If it's a man, though, you're talking a different story altogether."

"But how will I ever get Tom to look at me if he can't take notice of this pretty, new dress?"

"Here, let me trade aprons with you," Netta said, untying the company smock she had on, which covered less of the dress it was meant to protect. "You wear this clean one, and I'll put that every day one of mine back on."

"Oh, thankyousomuch," gushed Clara. "If I can get him to take a good look at me just one time, then maybe I'll have a chance of catchin' that man." While Clara tied on Netta's fresh apron, she looked around the room searching to find the woman-shy Tom Hawkins in the gathering crowd. She spotted him over on the far side of the cabin talking to Jeremy Harrison, but she couldn't catch his eye.

"Willie and me cleared off two more acres last fall," said Tom. "Got it fit up and ready to put into corn."

"I'd sure like to clear another two acres this year," Jeremy said, holding the hand of a wiggly tot. "Five'd be better. But pulling those big stumps is more than one man and horse can manage alone." He bent to pick up 13-month-old Lillian, who'd begun to fuss.

"I'd be happy to come help out, once I get spring plantin' out of the way," Tom offered. "Twixt the two of us, we could clear off two acres, sure. Five if Willie helps out. Mebbe more, if we could keep Harmon home longer than one day at a stretch," he said with a slow smile. "I think he spends more time callin' 'round on sweethearts, than he does deliverin' the mail."

"I 'preciate the offer," Jeremy said. "I truly do." Lillian still wiggled and fussed, despite her Daddy's best efforts to quiet her. "Sadie," he said to his sprightly sister standing nearby, "would you take this little wiggler? She sure don't want her daddy right now."

"Come to Aunt Sadie, you little dickens," she said, leaning in to take the squirming child from her older brother. "I got somethin' that'll keep you busy for a while." Sadie reached into her apron pocket and pulled out a lump of maple-sugar candy. "Look what I found out on that food table... some of Miss Netta's maple candy." She set Lillian down, handed her the candy, and guided the toddler over toward her mama, Amanda Jane Harrison, who still held the hand of Lillian's twin sister, Camellia. When Camellia saw Lillian sucking on something she didn't have, she started to fuss for a piece of her own.

"Here, Millie, Aunt Sadie has some for you, too," she said, leaning down and handing a second piece of candy to the mirror image of the tot she shepherded.

"How many times do I have to remind you to call them by their given names?" Amanda scolded her sister-in-law. "I don't know why you can't seem to remember such a simple request," she said in obvious disgust. The more aggravated Amanda Jane became, the more pronounced turned her southern drawl.

"Just got a short memory, I guess," Sadie shot back.

Amanda looked down at the twins. "Oh my goodness, what in the world have you given them now?" Camellia and Lillian, obviously enjoying their sweet treats, had already managed to get their hands and faces covered with the sticky stuff. "They've ruined their new dresses already. Just look what you've done!

Sticky sugar all down their fronts!"

Amanda struggled to bend down to remove the sugary lumps from her daughters' hands, but before her bulging middle allowed her to do so, the twins took off running right across the stretched-out yard goods, toward Willie Hawkins, whom they'd just spied on the other side of the room.

"Those little scamps know I can't run after them in my present condition," said an exasperated Amanda. "Giving toddlers sticky candy–"

"Let 'em be," Ma Hawkins piped in. "They can run all they want in here today and it won't hurt a thing. An' a sweet treat now and again won't hurt em' a bit, neither... long as they's eatin' proper." She took a hard, scrutinizing look at Sadie. "Looks like you been eatin' pretty good there, girl," she said to Sadie. "You're gainin' a mite in the middle, ain't you?"

"I, ah, think I'd better go look after the babies... make sure they don't get sticky sugar on anybody," Sadie said, making a hasty retreat around the cloth-tacked floor.

"I should hope you would," Amanda called to her retreating sister-in-law following after the twins. They'd reached Willie and begun to pull on his pant legs. "See that they get cleaned up properly, too!"

The two women left standing behind could not see the big smile that lighted Sadie's face as she neared the red-headed Willie Hawkins.

"You take any notice of her plumpin' up some?" Ma asked Amanda.

"I haven't given it much thought. Now that you mention it, she does look a little heavier than she used to."

"She been actin' funny like to you?"

"Funny? I don't know what you mean by funny."

"A might queasy or sick on her stomach mebbe?"

"Not that I'm aware of," Amanda said, rubbing the side of her own distended stomach. "Ooo, this one sure wants to stretch out in there. I swear he must be two feet long already."

"What makes you think it's a he?" asked Ma, touching Amanda's belly to gauge the strength of the baby's kick.

"Ouch. It's kind of sore right there," Amanda said, rubbing her left side after Ma had removed her hand. "I just know, is all. It's a boy." Amanda stood quietly for a moment, seemingly lost in thought. "You know, now that I think on it, I do recall Sadie out of sorts a couple months back. Wasn't a bit like her, either. I wanted Jeremiah to come for some of your stomach powders, but Sadie wouldn't hear of it. Said it wasn't worth bothering you for just a touch of the pips." Amanda stretched and rubbed her lower back. "I can tell you one thing, she hasn't been much help at all with the twins lately. She's always running off with Willie to go fishing or mushroom hunting or some other such nonsense."

"The nonsense part's more my guess," said Ma with indignation. "I guarantee they ain't done much fishin'!" She shook her head in dismay. "I better go have a talk with that son of mine right now," she said, heading toward the back door.

Sadie saw Willie's Ma coming with fire in her eyes, so she quickly guided Willie out the door toward the water pump and wash basin, with both twins in tow. Before Ma could corral her youngest son, Netta Bailey waylaid Edith Hawkins half way around the kicking floor.

"Guess what? Henry said, that Harmon said, that *he* heard that the Reverend might be comin' this way today. Do you reckon we should wait to start kickin' up suds till he gets here? I mean for him to say a prayer or somethin' before we get started?"

"What good's it gonna do to pray over cloth goods?"

"Well, you never know. I mean, anything could happen. Besides, it's just not proper to go startin' up a doin's if we know the Reverend might come, now is it? I mean, we *are* almost ready to pour out the suds. But do you think we should wait till he shows up to call the men in here?"

"No one knows nothin' for sure about that smooth-talkin'

preacher. So you just round up them kickers and get this shindig started, Jeannette. I got no time for nonsense, you hear? I got to go turn a reckless boy into a honest man," she said, brushing Netta aside and continuing toward the back door.

Out at the pump Willie and Sadie each washed a set of sticky fingers, while both twins whined for another helping of the maple candy.

"Do you have to tend these babies all day?" Willie asked with longing in his voice.

Sadie dried Lilly's hands with the drying cloth. "I most likely will," she said, giving the child a drink of water from the dipping gourd beside the water bucket.

"Why don't you send these babies back in to their mama so you and me can go do a little *fishin'*," Willie said with an ornery smile, raising one eyebrow and swatting Sadie on her behind.

"There ain't gonna BE no *fishin'* today," said Ma Hawkins, coming up behind them, "nor any other shenanigans, neither." She gave Sadie another hard look up and down. Sadie held her head erect and met Ma's gaze, not cowering in the least to the older woman's penetrating stare.

Edith Hawkins turned her attention toward Willie. "William Lloyd, I got somethin' to say to you." She stomped off toward the barn. Willie shrugged his shoulders to Sadie, then hurried after his mother.

"Come on, you pretty, little flowers." Sadie knelt down to wipe Millie's hands dry and give her a drink from the same gourd. "Let's go back inside and see what your papa's up to." She stood upright, hesitated for a moment to rub the small of

her back, and shot a concerned look toward the barn. Then she turned to guide both toddlers back into the cabin.

Inside, kicking festivities had gotten underway without benefit of a formal blessing, since no traveling preacher had yet made an appearance. Chattering and laughing females lined the perimeter of the tacked-down yard goods, while bare-footed men and boys kicked and stomped in the center of the floor, as

9

they sloshed warm soap-suds over the newly woven wool.

"Can't you get them feet of yours movin' any faster?" Emma chided her husband Frank, who was doing a half-hearted shuffle over in the corner next to Anson Guthrie. "You two quit your jawin' and get to kickin'."

"You heered your woman, Frank," said Anson, setting his feet into a double-step. "Kick up them heels!"

Frank dutifully followed Anson's lead, working up a funny little hop-step to try and outdo his friend. "You're too old and stiff to do this step proper," Frank teased.

Not one to turn down any kind of a challenge, Anson switched his kick to match Frank's. After falling into a rhythm with his friend, he began a new step-hop-shuffle in an effort to kick up more suds than Frank.

"You two better be careful over there," warned Netta. "We don't want nobody fallin' on their bee-hinds in here today," she said, bouncing her seven-month-old daughter, Rachel, who'd begun to fuss. Netta's toddler, Rosanna, clung to her mama's skirts in fright, for the day's unusual activity in her own cabin had her quite confused. "All I need is someone fallin' down and breakin' their hucklebone."

"Who's that?" Clara pointed toward the cabin door, where several strangers entered, one among them a beautiful, young woman. "Who is that girl?"

"Why, I don't have a clue," Netta answered. "Never saw them before in my life." She tried to walk over to greet the new-comers, but Rosanna kept tugging her back.

"I sure hope Tom don't see that girl. She's so comely! Just look at that blond hair, would you! How can anyone in the world have hair that color?" Clara fussed at her dress, fluffing her skirts and smoothing the bodice over her tiny waist, while looking to see if Tom had noticed the strangers. "Oh, I knew it. I just knew it! He's lookin' at her," she whined. "Now he's *never* gonna take note of me!"

"Stop your fussing, Clara, and let's go meet the new folks.

Here, you take Rachel for me. I need to keep Rosanna from twistin' up my skirts so I can walk." Netta headed toward the door with a toddler hanging onto one hand while extending the other hand in greeting. "Hello there, folks! Welcome to the Kickin' Bee! I'm Jeannette Bailey, but folks 'round here just call me Netta," she said, pumping the older woman's hand. "I don't recall seein' youens 'round about before. You must be new to these parts." She took a quick breath and continued on before the newcomers could get a word in to answer. "I heard someone moved into that deserted homestead outside of Petersburg, down below Jonathan's place. A cooper, I think he said. Might you be them folks?"

"I'm Rebecca Simpson, and this is my oldest daughter Lovinia," said the plain-looking woman, turning to pull the lovely girl forward. Lovinia ushered the rest of the brood inside the cabin. "And these are my other children, Sol, Dora, Jessie, Albert, Paulie and Snooks," she said, pulling each one to her in turn. "Course Snooks ain't this one's real name. His papa stuck him with the same name as his own, Ephriam Alonzo Simpson. But for such a tiny thing, we just took to callin' him Snooks." She mussed the five-year-old's hair. "Besides, it helps to keep things sorted out, with two names the same under one roof."

Nine-year-old Albert and eight-year-old Paulie pushed and shoved each other, so their mother smacked them both firmly on their heads. "Straighten up, you two. Act like company."

"They're all right," Netta said, patting each one affecttionately. "Why don't you boys take off your shoes and socks and

go join the other fellas out there kickin' up suds? That ought to work off some of them orneries."

They looked to their mother for permission, and at her nod, they tore over to the corner piled high with shoes and socks and began to strip off their own.

"Your husband, Ephriam something, you said? Did he come along with you?"

"Alonzo. Ephriam Alonzo," she said. "But we just call him

11

Al. He's out seein' to the horse," Rebecca said, looking around the room. "So, where do you want us to put these vittles?" she asked, pointing to her girls, each holding a basket full of food.

"We have a table all set up back in the lean-to," Netta said, taking a basket from the youngest girl. "Here, I'll show you. Just follow me around to the back door over there," she said, threading her way around the cloth goods and through the crowd. "Careful you don't catch your feet on them tack boards," Netta cautioned. "You never did say, is your husband that new cooper we all been hearin' about?" Netta didn't give the woman a chance to answer, but kept up her jabber all the way through the cabin and out the back door, as the line of newcomers followed her to the food table.

By now quite a suds covered the entire floor, and young boys began to slip and slide around, trying to see who could knock down whom between the legs of the older men. Several of the women lining the perimeter of the cabin held brooms, which they periodically used to sweep escaping suds back onto the yard goods.

Amanda, over to one side, using her broom more as a leaning post than a tool, watched the boys with an amused smile. "Won't be long till you're out there with all those boys, Joseph," she said, giving her middle a knowing pat.

"You're dead certain it's a boy?" Sadie asked with a raised eyebrow.

"Quite," Amanda said. "Grandmother Bently told me so."

Sadie rolled her eyes when Amanda alluded to the dream about her dearly departed Grandmother, who had returned from beyond the grave to predict that Amanda carried a son. But Sadie's attention quickly returned to her charge, as she hurried to recapture the rebellious Lillian trying to make an escape onto the suds-covered floor.

Amanda patted the obedient Camellia until Sadie returned the recalcitrant twin to her side. "You little rascal," Amanda said, leaning down to give the child a befitting swat on the seat. When she straightened up, a sudden movement drew her eyes toward the front door, and her hand flew to her mouth when she saw a lanky man remove his black, broad-brimmed hat.

Amanda's face turned a deathly shade of white.

"What's wrong?" Sadie held tight to both the twins.

A speechless Amanda could do no more than point a shaky finger toward the black-garbed newcomer standing with his back to the kicking floor, greeting folks gathered around him as if they were long, lost friends.

"Amanda? Amanda!" Sadie tried to get her sister-in-law's attention without letting go of either twin. "*Amanda*, what's wrong with you?"

Amanda suddenly dropped her broom, picked up her skirts, and, as well as she could in her gravid condition, began to run across the suds-covered floor toward the back door. She got no more than half-way across when Albert and Paulie came sliding toward her, clipped her from behind, and sent her sprawling to the floor. She landed heavily on her right side, hitting her head so hard, that it knocked the pregnant woman out cold.

"Oh, my Lord! Amanda!" Lucy Jarvis, holding 11-month-old baby, Hank, was the first one to reach her side, with Jeremiah following close behind. "Where's Ma Hawkins? Has anybody seen Ma?" Lucy called.

"Out to the barn," answered Sadie, holding the twins tighter.

"Somebody go and bring her back here quick," Jeremy said, kneeling beside his wife, lying prone in the suds. He cradled Amanda's head and gently patted her cheek. "Mandy? Speak to me. Mandy!" He eased Amanda up, into his arms, then carefully rose to his feet, just as Netta burst through the back door.

"What's goin' on? What happened? I heard someone holler."

"She fell down," Clara whispered, still holding Rachel tight. "I don't know how it happened, but all of a sudden, there she was, feet flyin' every which-of-a-way, and they went right out from underneath of her. She went down hard, too."

"Oh, my lands. I just *knew* if we didn't say a startin' prayer, something like this was bound to happen," Netta babbled. "Where's Ma? Has anyone gone for Ma?"

"A fall like that will put her into labor for sure," said Anson's Guthrie's somber wife, Winifred, with her usual doom-and-gloom conviction.

"I need a place to lay her down," Jeremy said, to Netta.

"Upstairs. Put her in my bed upstairs." She moved swiftly toward the door that opened into a steep set of steps leading to the loft bedroom above.

"Ohmylands, why did this have to happen today?" said Netta, turning to Lucy, who followed close on Jeremy's heels. "Where *is* Ma? Did anybody go to fetch her?"

Lucy turned to Netta before following Jeremy up the stairs. "You keep things going down here. And make sure Ma comes up the minute somebody finds her." She handed baby Hank to Netta. "Would you keep an eye on him for me? Don't let anyone else up here, *just Ma.*" She closed the stairway door behind her, and her long legs took the narrow steps two at a time.

"All right, all right, people," said Netta, attempting to gain the milling group's attention. "Let's keep them kickers workin' up more suds over there. We've got a lot more cloth to put down after this batch gets all kicked and rinsed. And we sure can't put dinner out till all that cloth gets kicked up." She shifted the chubby Hank onto her other hip and attempted to keep Rosanna from tangling her skirts. "And forheavensakes, don't nobody else fall down!"

In the flurry of activity that followed, no one noticed the lanky, black-garbed Ephriam Alonzo Simpson—who bore a striking resemblance to the circuit preacher, the Rev. Harold P. Longbottom—take his two, high-spirited sons firmly by the ears and pull them outside the cabin.

* * * * *

"You hear what I'm tellin' you, Willie? You're gonna be a papa. I got no doubt about it, neither."

Willie stood before his mother, dumbfounded by her startling pronouncement.

"William Lloyd, you better be makin' some marryin' plans

with that Harrison girl, and you better be makin' 'em quick. I judge she's more than half way done growin' that young'un already."

Willie shook his head in wonderment. Then a broad grin began to fill his face. "I'm gonna be a papa? *Me*? You mean it?"

"I didn't call you out here for a friendly jaw and a back-slap. If that gal ain't took a notion to tell you, then you been a blind fool, not to mention a downright careless one," she said, with a shake of her finger. "Now that you're takin' a man's pleasure, you're obliged to uphold a man's duty. So it's high time you look after that unborn offspring of yours… and his mama, too."

"*His* mama? You mean I'm gonna have a boy? A son?"

"I ain't *said* it'd be a boy," she huffed at her youngest, happy-go-lucky son. At the sudden creak of a door hinge, they both turned to see who had entered the barn.

"You're needed up to the house," Luther Bailey said in his simple, direct way, as the tall, buckskin-garbed form stepped into the shadows of the barn. "Accident."

Edith Hawkins didn't wait to hear any of the particulars, given that Luther had little inclination to relate anything but the most basic of information, anyway. She hurried toward the house without saying another word to Luther or to Willie.

"What's goin' on up there?" Willie asked.

"Woman trouble."

"Who's in trouble?"

"Harrison woman. Fell in the suds."

"*Sadie*?" Willie nearly hollered the name.

"Nope. The Mrs. Out cold."

"I better go see if I can do anything to help."

"Best thing us bucks can do is stay out the females' way."

"But what if Sadie needs me to help with the twins?"

"Do what you have to. I aim to stay put rit'chere." Luther went to the far corner of the barn, grabbed a handle in the floor and, in a swoosh of straw and dust, pulled up a trap door. He disappeared into his root cellar below.

Willie took off running for the cabin. As he reached for the latch string, the door swung inward and nearly pulled him over. "Oh, Willie! Thankgoodnessit'syou. Your mama wants her birthin' bundle out of the wagon," Netta said, all in a fluster. "*Now*!"

"But I gotta see if Sadie—"

"Right *now*, Willie! She told me, 'Send Willie to fetch that birthin' bundle out of the wagon *right away*!'"

"But—"

"Go *NOW*, Willie, or she'll have both our hides!"

With a helpless shrug, Willie spun on his heels and made a beeline out behind the barn where the neighbors' wagons stood in a line, horses tethered here and there in shady spots around the barnyard.

* * * * *

"You'd best get Jeannette to gather up all the clean beddin' she can spare," Ma instructed Lucy, "and tell her to set one boilin' pot to simmer with no suds in it. They'll have to make do with one less pot for suds," she said, taking the cloth from Amanda's head and dipping it once more into the basin of cool water. "This baby aims to come now, ready or no."

Lucy headed down the steps, but before she reached the bottom Ma called out one more order.

"You make sure *nobody* else comes up here, neither."

Lucy pushed the stairway door shut behind herself.

"Last thing I need is a bunch of busybodies pokin' their noses into this birthin'," Ma mumbled under her breath. "Specially that hair-brained Jeannette. Gonna be tricky enough to keep the noise down up here, without that blabbermouth carryin' tales down to scare young girls."

"You think we should take her home, Ma?" Jeremy asked. "I'm not crazy about the whole neighborhood being privy to what's going on up here."

"Too dangerous with pains already started. She sure don't need to be bouncin' around in no wagon, on top of a bad fall."

"I'm staying with her, you know."

"Men don't belong at birthin's," she began to grumble, looking up to meet his steady gaze. "But in your case... well... I never figgered any different," Ma answered knowingly. "You done proved yourself back at Ben's birth... not to mention catchin' one of them twins all on your own."

"Thanks for your vote of confidence."

"Well, don't let it swell your head," she grumbled. "I still say men are always in the way."

"Jeremiah?" Mandy roused from a short rest between contractions, which were coming at fifteen-minute intervals.

"I'm right here, Mandy. Everything's gonna be all right," Jeremy crooned in as reassuring a tone as he could muster.

"I think something's wrong, Jeremiah. The pains feel different than they did with Little Ben or the twins."

"How different?" Ma asked. "Tell me how they feel."

"In my back. A kind of pressure I never felt before. And here," Amanda gingerly touched her left side. "A sharp, knife-like pain whenever a contraction starts. It doesn't go away when it stops, either. Keeps... right on hurting... all the time," she panted."

"How did she fall, Jeremy?"

"Two little boys came up from behind–"

"I don't mean what made her fall. How did she *land*?"

"On her right side, I think. Pretty hard, too."

"Hmmmm." As the contraction eased, Ma's skillful fingers explored the same area that Amanda had complained about in their earlier conversation downstairs. She tried not to inflict any more pain than absolutely necessary.

"Oooph! That's the spot!"

"Hmmmm."

"What's wrong, Ma, "Jeremy asked with concern.

"You notice any bleedin' in the last week or so?"

Amanda nodded her head in the affirmative.

"Much?"

This time, Amanda shook her head no.

"Something *is* wrong," Jeremy insisted. "What is it?"

"Could be somethin'. Could be nothin'."

"Can't you be a little more specific?"

"Not at the moment," she said with a veiled nod toward Amanda. "We'll have to wait and see what develops here."

"But Ma–"

"No time for explanations now," Ma answered curtly, noticing an increasing amount of bloody show since the last contraction and expertly moving herself between Jeremy and Amanda, so as to conceal it from him for the moment. "You go down and see what's keepin' Lucy. I need them clean bed clothes... and quick," she said, dabbing at the steady trickle of blood with a corner of the soiled bed sheet. She made sure to push the bottom edge of the counterpane that covered Amanda away from the business end of this birthing bed. "I'd bet my eye teeth Lucy needs a stern man to shut off Jeannette's blatherin'."

"Is Mandy going to be all right?"

"Go on, now! Do as I say. And get yourself back up here quick as you can," Ma instructed. "Bring a pot full of that boilin' water with you, too."

As Jeremy hurried down the stairs, Ma turned her attention to the tiny woman nearly swallowed up by the huge, rope bed. "I know you an' me's gone through this business before, girl. An' I don't doubt you think you've seen the worst childbed has to offer a woman. But I got to tell you, I believe this time we've got us a serious problem."

"I knew it. I just knew it would come to this. God is punishing me. He had to."

"I don't know what you're goin' on about, but you listen to me, now. I didn't want to say nothin' to the Mister just yet. Not till I had a chance to let you know in private what we're up agin'," she said, shaking her head. "Are you payin' attention?" Ma patted Amanda's hand to make her look up. "Look at me, girl. Focus right here. Good. I think part of the birth sack tore away from the womb too quick. Might've started a while back, but I reckon that fall you just took done the worst damage."

"The baby's going to die, isn't he."

"Now, we don't know that. There's a good chance you'll both come through this fine. Long as a part of that sack sticks tight where it belongs, the baby'll get all he needs… till he's out here a-breathin' on his own," Ma said. She took a deep breath and forged ahead. "But you need to know goin' in, there's apt to be a lot more blood this time. Pain's likely to be worse than anything you felt before, too." She laid her hand on Amanda's arm. "You also gotta know this baby ain't facin' the direction he ortta be, neither. If I go reachin' in there to try and set him to rights, I'll likely do more damage than if we just let this little feller come into the world back-asswards."

"Save my baby, Ma. *Please* save my baby!"

"We gotta work together to get this one here safe, girl," Ma said with true concern showing in her tone for the first time. But she recovered her brusque demeanor the next instant, so as not to alarm this laboring mother any more than necessary. "I ain't lost a single babe I helped another woman give birth to yet," she said with conviction. "And I don't aim to lose this one now."

Edith didn't bother mentioning the loss of her own first, five babies, all born prematurely and unattended in a dirt-floored cabin back when this Ohio country was still a territory barely open to settlers. To this day, she never attended a single birth without reliving her losses all over again. *I swear I'll never sit by and watch another woman go through that kind of sorrow, not if there's ary a thing I can do to help,* she vowed. *I just hope my help is enough to bring this babe through safe.*

* * * * *

Downstairs, a haze of suds covered the entire cabin floor. Despite the drama unfolding above, neighbors talked and laughed and continued to have a high old time kicking up more suds on the second batch of woolen cloth, now tacked on the floor.

"I wish I knew what was goin' on up there," Netta said to

19

Winifred, out behind the cabin. The women busied themselves rinsing suds from the long lengths of wool that had been felted in the first batch. They worked together to twist and wring as much water as possible from each piece, before hanging it to dry on the line Luther had strung up between big trees in back of the Bailey's cabin. "I just can't understand why we don't hear somethin' out of Lucy at least. What in blazes can be takin' so long up there?"

"Can't be nothin' good, you can bet your topknot on that," said the sour-faced Winifred Guthrie. "Here, now, watch what you're doin'. Keep the tail of that piece out of the mud, Netta."

"Oh, my, I almost did it, didn't I. If I lost this one we'd have to rinse it all over again," she said, retrieving the twisted end of the cloth that dangled from under her arm. "I do believe I'm about as soaked as these cloth goods. Just look at me!"

"You be careful you don't take a chill a'fore you dry off," Winifred said, busy snaking a piece of wet wool along the clothesline and pegging it with wooden pins every few feet to hold it tight. "It may feel like spring, but this breeze still has a bite to it, if you ask me. And you didn't ask me, but I'm-a-tellin' you just the same." She pushed two more clothes pins onto the line. "Can't be too careful, this time of year. You know how easy it is to take the ague in this kind of weather. And a'fore you know it, it'll turn right into the red cough and put you six feet under."

"Oh, don't be so gloomy. There. That's the last piece from the first batch all rinsed out," Netta said, dumping the suds-sullied rinse-water around her lilac bush and leaning the tub against the woodshed. "I'm goin' in to dry off by the fire." Netta headed for the cabin door muttering with every step. "Can't understand what's takin' so long. Only took me a few pushes to bring my babies into this world. Heavenly days, it's been hours, and not a single word from anybody up there, except to stick a head out the door and shout orders to 'Bring more beddin',' or 'Get another bucket of boilin' water'." She grabbed a piece of cornbread on her way past the food table and stuffed it in her mouth, before she opened the back door and stepped into the swirl of activity.

"They almost got this next batch ready to take up," Clara said, meeting Netta at the door. Clara clutched Rosanna by one hand and held Rachel on her opposite hip.

"Thanks for watchin' my little sweeties, Clara," Netta said. Rosanna grabbed for her mother's legs and nearly tripped them both, getting all twisted in Netta's soggy skirts. "Come on, Rosanna. Let's go over by the fire and get us a sip of hot tea."

By now, the crowd had thinned out a bit, since the men had begun spelling one another at the kicking chores, as they finished kicking up the last of the wool. The thirstier ones made trips back and forth to the barn, where Luther had already broken out several jugs of corn juice from his root-cellar stash.

"I think we best get this last bolt finished, while we still got some men who can stand up," said Rebecca Simpson, nodding toward the few left out on the kicking floor. She held Paulie and Snooks by their shirt collars. "Simmer down, now. Just stand here and dry yourselves off. Time you two settled down before dinner." Snooks tried to make a break for the kicking floor, but Rebecca caught him by the shirttail. "Sit, you!"

"We've got the food all laid out, Mama," Lovinia Simpson said in her lilting, child-like voice.

"You get those pies cut into nice, even pieces?"

"All cut up, just like you wanted, Mama."

Clara sneered at the flaxen-haired beauty, then huffed past 13-year-old Dora Simpson, who bounced little Hank on her knee near the hearth, while she tended him for Lucy. Clara threaded her way around the kicking floor, trying to make her escape out back. But as she neared the stairway door, it flung open nearly knocking her backward.

"Clara," Lucy said, sticking her head around the edge of the door, "Can you go find Sadie? Jeremy's asking for her."

"I think she's out by the water pump, washin' the twins up for supper. Food's all laid out. Almost ready for the big feed."

"Go get her. And be quick about it."

"I'll fetch her right away," Clara said, thankful for a legitimate reason to leave the cabin, where Lovinia Simpson stood relishing the looks of admiration her golden locks drew from all males in the room—eligible or no.

Sadie stood by the water pump, holding the dipping gourd up to the lips of Camellia, who drank with loud, dribbling smacks. Willie held her squirming, kicking twin tightly under his arm. "But why didn't you tell me about that little tadpole you got swimmin' around in there, Sadie?" he asked, giving her middle a hesitant pat.

"I don't know what in the world you're talkin' about, Willie Hawkins," she said, swatting his hand away.

"But my ma *told* me you're... well, you know," he turned a lovely shade of crimson. "That you're... settin' on the nest. So we *got* to get married, now. That's all there is to it!"

"I never heard such foolishness in my whole life."

"But *Say*-dee!"

"But Sadie nothin'. I can't marry you, Willie. I told you that four hours ago, and I'm tellin' you again for the ump-teenth time, No! I can't do it. I *won't* do it. And that puts an end to it."

Willie took a deep breath to once again protest his sweetheart's stubborn stance, but before he could utter a word, she softened a bit at his hang-dog look.

"Oh, Willie. Don't you see? Amanda's up there... maybe dyin' this time, and I'm pledged to help Jeremy take care of these two babies–"

"You ain't told me nothin' I don't already know," he said with a huff. "You got a duty to your brother. So what... I can live with that. But you still ain't give a straight answer to my very first question. Are you havin' my baby or not, Sadie Harrison?"

"Sadie! Oh *Saaay*-deee!" Clara called, hurrying toward the two bickering love-birds, squared off at the water pump. "Jeremy wants you upstairs. An' Lucy says you better get up there *quick*!"

"Would you watch the twins for me–"

"OfcourseIcan watch them. Now GO!" Clara whisked Camellia away from Sadie, who hurried toward the cabin, leaving Willie standing with a confounded look on his face, and Lillian still kicking the air as she dangled from his arm.

Sadie met Lucy at the bottom of the steps, with little Hank back in her arms after a long afternoon apart from his mama. "Jeremy wants you to come up. But you got to know it's not a pretty sight. There's a lot of blood this time."

"I can handle blood."

"Well, she's beginnin' to get... I mean, she's not quite–"

"I can handle that, too," Sadie said with a nod.

"How did you know?"

"She's been addled before."

"But how–"

Sadie had already bounded half-way up the steps before Lucy could finish her question, so she turned and closed the stairway door in front of herself, then sank onto a step, where she could sit her lanky frame to nurse little Hank in solitude—as much for her own comfort as for his nourishment.

"You can't push yet, girl. That babe still ain't locked into the birth canal, proper. Jeremy, get your face right down into hers, and breathe with her. *Show* her what she has to do through the next pain. And the next one after that," said a stern-faced Edith. "Keep her breathin' *through* these pains. If she starts pushin' too quick, that sack's gonna tear clean away, sure as I'm a-standin' here with blood near up to my armpit."

"Jems." Sadie came up behind her brother and laid a hand on his shoulder. "Maybe you better let me take over here for a while. You're lookin' awful peak-ed."

"I can't leave her, Sadie. Look at her, she's dyin' right in front of my eyes!"

"She *ain't* dyin', mister. You keep them thoughts to yourself, now, you hear!"

Ma's glare made him shake his head in remorse. "I'm sorry,

Ma. I know I shouldn't even think such a thing, let alone say it."
He ran his hands back along both sides of his head, then dropped them into his lap in frustration. "But look at her, she's not hearin' a single word we say to her."

"She may not let *on* she's listenin', but you better believe she *can* hear us," Ma answered. "She ain't wastin' energy on needless talk," she said, trying to reassure Jeremy, as well as herself. "So you keep right on tellin' her what a good job she's doin', and that she has to keep *on* doin' it if she's gonna bring forth this babe."

"Why don't you go downstairs and have a cup of tea, Jems. Maybe eat a little supper while you're at it," said Sadie to her weary, big brother. "I'll help up here till you get back."

"But how can I leave her when she–"

"Go. She'll be fine," said Ma. "We'll see to that." She gave Sadie a hard, steady look. "While you're goin' down, dump that bucket and bring some more boilin' water up here when you come back," she instructed Jeremy, as she continued to hold Sadie's unruffled stare. "Clean is more important this time than it ever was," she said by way of instruction to the young girl about to witness her first, human birth.

Sadie nodded to Ma in understanding, then gave her brother a friendly nudge. Jeremy reluctantly rose to his feet and plodded down the stairs. When he reached the third step from the bottom, where Lucy still sat nursing Hank, he hesitated. "I'm sorry, Lucy. I don't mean to disturb you, but–"

"No matter," she said, pulling her sweater closed to cover herself and the baby, then rising and turning sideways to allow him to pass on the narrow stairs.

Jeremy took the last two steps, then turned back. "Lucy, I want to thank you for all you're doin' to help us."

"No need," she replied. "I'm so sorry this had to happen."

Jeremy took a deep breath, then opened the door into the hubbub of a neighborhood meal.

"Jeremy, what on *earth* is goin' *on* up there?" Netta nearly attacked him the instant he made his appearance downstairs. "Is she all right? Nobody's told us a thing down here! Did that baby come yet? Why won't Ma let me up there? I can help out, really I can."

Jeremy took a deep breath and heaved a weary sigh. "I'm sure you can, Netta. But, I could really stand a cup of hot tea right now," he said. "Would you mind?"

"Oh, my lands, ofcourseyoucanhavesome tea. How could I be so thoughtless?" she gushed, turning to the hearth and lifting the kettle to pour out a cup. "You've got to be purely tuckered after all this time."

"Not half as tuckered as Mandy is right now."

"Well, no. Of course not. I mean, we all know the childbed brings a terrible sufferin'. That's just the way of things. But what *IS* goin' on up there? I mean, it's been hours and we haven't heard a sound! No screamin', no baby cryin'. *Nothin!*"

"Mandy won't ever cry out, if she can help it. That's just her way," Jeremy said, taking the steaming cup Netta handed to him. "An' with all the neighbors down here… well, that just upsets her even more. She's workin' awful hard to stay mum."

"I have noticed she keeps things to herself a lot. Won't let on a bit when she's feelin' poorly. I took note of that about her right off," Netta said, putting the kettle back on the hearth. "But how in the world can she keep from hollerin' out when she's givin' birth? How *can* she? Why, I hollered my fool head off with both my babies. Nearly drove Ma right out of this cabin, it did. My lands, did she ever get agg-ervated at me!"

"Mr. Harrison, can I get some supper for you?" asked Rebecca Simpson, coming in from out back, where folks filled their plates from the pans and crocks and bowls full of food-stuffs spread out on the big, plank table in the lean-to.

"I'm not really very hungry–"

"But you've *got* to eat. Keep your strength up," Netta said, butting right back into the conversation. "Luther ate like a horse when I had my babies. I think all my hollerin' made him jumpy. He always eats like a horse when he gets upset."

"Here, take this full plate," Rebecca said, handing hers to Jeremy. "I'll go fill up another one."

"Why thank you. Mrs. Simpson, was it? I'm obliged." Jeremy accepted the wooden trencher of rabbit stew, cornbread and pumpkin pie she extended to him.

"Folks usually just call me Becky," she said with a warm smile. "Think nothin' of it. You're more than welcome." She turned and headed back outdoors.

Clara leaned in close to Netta, so no one else could hear. "Look at her. Acts just like she owns the place," whispered Clara. "That daughter of hers is out there actin' the same way— like *she's* the one who made every single pie on that table," she added with an obvious huff. "Wouldn't you know, Tom had to try every one *she* dished up, too."

Back up in the loft, Ma queried Sadie. "Did Amanda eat before you got here?"

"Just a little porridge and a cup of tea. Not really much to speak of."

"You better fetch that crock and hold it up to her face. Won't be long, till her stomach turns inside out," Ma instructed.

Sadie laid the damp cloth aside and did as she was told. "Does that always happen at a birth?"

"Gener'lly, if the mama ate anything recent-like," answered Ma. "You'd best mind close what happens here, girl. I reckon you'll be the next one lyin'-in."

Sadie didn't say a word, just nodded in agreement.

"How far along you figger to be?"

"Nearly five months, I judge."

"Tell your brother yet?"

"I haven't told anyone. Not even Willie."

"He knows it now."

"Thanks to *you*."

"Well you *ortta* be thankin' me, girl. And marryin' that boy in a big hurry, too."

"I'm obliged to my brother's family," she said, with a nod toward the laboring Amanda. "I can't think about marryin' anybody right now."

"We'll see 'bout tha–"

"Papa... Papa," Amanda moaned, when the next contraction began to tighten its grip. "Papa, help me, Papaaa–" the word came to an abrupt halt when Amanda wretched into the crockery bowl Sadie held close to her face.

"How long has she been out of her head?" Sadie put the crock aside after Amanda finished vomiting and obligingly wiped her face with the damp cloth.

"Long enough."

"This pain is sending her over the edge again, isn't it."

"Hard to tell. Leastwise not till it's all over," Ma said, taking a fresh cloth from the stack of bedding to dab at the bloody trickle, now beginning to flow a bit harder with each contraction. "I got a feelin' there's a heap more than birthin' pain troublin' her right now. But if we don't get this bleedin' slowed down, it ain't gonna matter."

"Papaaaaa! Oh, God, get him away from me, make him *stop! NOOO!"* Amanda let out a shriek as the next pain gripped her hard.

"*Breathe*, girl. Breathe through it," Ma commanded. "Things'll pick up, now," she said to Sadie. "Pay close mind to what I tell you, no matter what comes out of her."

"Why? What's she been saying? Anything that could explain what set her off last fall, when she got so addled for that long stretch?"

Ma rolled another soiled cloth in a ball and tossed it on top of the heap of bloody linens already piled in a basket over in the corner. "She had a bad spell 'fore you come out here, too, you know... after that fire when she lost her first baby, Little Ben." Ma paused, as if in careful thought. "She did speak of that slippery Reverend, but your brother judged it to be no more than foolish talk brought on by the pain. Said to pay it no heed." She pulled another new cloth from the clean pile. "None of them words matched up to make any kind of sense in my mind, no how."

"What did she say, *exactly*?"

"Somethin' like, 'You can't do it Reverend. Not this misdeed.' Then she got to moanin' on again, about how the Lord had to punish her."

"You don't suppose... it was him that night?"

"What night? What are you talkin' about?

"After the huskin' bee last fall. Don't you remember? The Reverend left early, before the doin's even got a good start."

"Never did trust that slippery devil. Gave some lame excuse, as I recall. About havin' to rest up for preaching the next day, or some such of a thing, wasn't it?"

"Don't you see, that next morning after the doin's is when I found her in a heap by the fireplace, all addled and crying for her papa," she said, dipping the cloth in cold water again and wringing it out tight. "All this time I thought it was my fault she lost her senses... 'cause I stayed out so late with Wi–"

"I know who you was with."

"Well, I thought leavin' her alone for so long is what did it. But I'd bet my eye teeth it was him! *He* did something to push her over the edge," Sadie said with dawning comprehension. "I found two dirty teacups that next morning when I was setting the house to rights." Sadie wiped Amanda's face tenderly. "I never gave it a whole lot of thought at the time. But I couldn't figure why there'd be two. One was in pieces all over the floor."

Ma stood shaking her head in silent understanding, eyes locked with Sadie's.

"Noooooo, Reverend! *Don't!*"

This time Amanda's outcry carried all the way downstairs, and in practically no time Jeremy came bounding up the steps with Lucy and Netta hot on his heels.

"No... no... I can't, Jeremiah! Get him off me! Please! Help me, *Jer-ri-miiiii-ah!*"

"I'm here, Mandy. I'm right here." He slid to her side, nearly sending Sadie tumbling from the impact, as he bumped her away from the bed at his sudden entrance.

"Oh, my Lord! Whatintheworld is goin' on up here?" Netta shrieked after climbing the stairs and taking a look at the bloody

cloths piled over in the corner. When she noticed the crimson spectacle at one end of the birthing bed, she nearly swooned from the sight. "Heavenly days, she's dyin' right there in my own bed. She's *dyin'*!"

With one look at Netta, Ma hollered a string of commands. "Jeannette, get yourself back downstairs. *RIGHT NOW!* Lucy, go get blankets hot, ready to receive this babe. Sadie, when I give the say so, you knead on her stomach *hard*. You got that?"

"Yes ma'am. Knead hard."

Lucy hurried down the steps with baby blankets in hand. Netta stood like bug-eyed statue, unable to move an inch.

"Jeremy, go push that piece of baggage down them steps if you have to, but get her out of here!"

"I won't leave Mandy again. Not for anything in the world," he said from his position beside his wife, where he held both her hands firmly in his own.

"Dad-blast it, Jeannette. Move your carcass! Go do somethin' useful. Send them folks on their way. Tell Anson I want no fiddle-playin' nor dancin' in here this night."

"No, no! Don't *do* it, Reverend!" As Amanda let out another screech, Sadie made a quick dash to the top of the stairs where Netta stood, still rooted. Sadie took her by the shoulders and firmly spun her around, the motion of which finally roused Netta enough so that she bustled down the steps as fast as her stocky legs could carry her. She emerged from the stairway silent, a condition quite out of character for Jeanette Bailey.

"Netta, what's wrong? What's happenin' up there," Clara asked. "Lucy wouldn't tell me anything."

Before Netta uttered a word, her hand went to her throat, then to her mouth; she stood shaking her head as words began to pour forth. "Ohmylands, she's dyin' up there, Clara. I swear

29

Amanda's *dyin'* right there in my very own bed! She's bleedin' to death and rantin' on somethin' terrible about the Reverend!"

"The Reverend? You sure?"

"Certain sure."

"Well if she's callin' for the Reverend, then she *must* be fixin' to die."

"No, she wasn't callin' *for* him, Clara. More like she was tryin' to get *away* from him."

"What can we do?" Rebecca Simpson asked, cutting the gossip short as she came in from her self-appointed station at the food table.

"Ohmylands, where's Anson? Ma said to tell him no square dancin' tonight. We got to tell Anson to take his fiddle back home. And we got to send *everybody* home," she said, beginning to search the crowd. "Clara, where's your pa? Did he go out to the barn with Luther? Where in blazes is that man of mine? Prob'ly out in that hole of his drinkin' stump juice again. He's never around here when I need him. Always takin' off just when a calamity breaks out." She hustled about, continuing her mindless chatter while she tried to figure out what to do next.

Rebecca Simpson, seeing the need for someone to take matters in hand, began to set folks about cleaning up and gathering belongings to head for home. "Dora, get that mess cleaned up over there," she instructed her younger daughter, pointing to the over-turned plate that had clattered to the floor when Jeremy bolted for the steps at his wife's shattering scream. "Lovinia, you get the boys rounded up. And send Albert out to the barn to fetch your father. Start him hitchin' up," she said, handing her Paulie's shoes.

"You mean we won't have any dancin' tonight?" Clara whined to her mother, Winifred, also busy with the clean-up work at hand. "I was *so* lookin' forward to the dancin' part. How am I *ever* gonna get Tom to notice me, now, with no dancin' to set this pretty skirt a-twirlin' so's it'll catch his eye?"

"Clara Marlene, you stop your fussin' this minute," Winifred scolded. "Don't you know it's bad luck to be in a house when a woman dies in childbed? Puts a curse on every female who ain't yet borned a child of her own."

"Not even one single dance in my new store-bought dress, Mama?"

"I aim to get you away from this place, quick as we can pry your pa out of that whiskey jug," Winifred said with her most sour-faced scowl. "Mark my word, I see death hangin' over this house tonight. Ever'one of us had best be high-tailin' it as far away from here as we can get."

"Is she really gonna die, Mama?"

"Be a downright miracle if she *don't* die, right along with that unlucky babe."

* * * * *

By sunset, most of the neighbors had said hasty good-byes and departed for respective homes, leaving a heavy gloom hanging over the Bailey cabin. Henry and Lucy Jarvis remained, along with Willie, who struggled to keep the twins out of trouble while the rest of the Harrisons were otherwise occupied upstairs. Netta had her hands full managing her own two daughters, as well as Henry and Lucy's little Hank, while she directed Luther and Henry's efforts to move her furniture back inside the cabin.

"That table goes over there, by the hearth," Netta instructed. She held Rachel on one hip, Hank on the other, and Rosanna hovered around her skirts. "No, maybe it should be over that way, a little farther for a change."

Luther obliged, moving the table to the spot Netta indicated.

"Oh dear. I think it takes up too much room there. You best move it back where it was."

"Make up your mind, woman."

"There. I like it right there!"

Luther let the table drop with a thud, and Henry, with his trussed-up arm, carried in one chair at a time, putting each at its appropriate spot by the table. Before Netta could change her mind again, Luther disappeared out the door, with Henry right behind him, to go fetch the cradle and Rosanna's bedstead.

31

"Come back here, you little minx." Willie made a quick grab for Lillian, who had nearly scampered out the door after Henry. "Gotcha!"

The cabin door closed behind the two men just as Lucy reappeared from the stairway. She headed straight for the fireplace to retrieve the baby blankets she had put in the Dutch oven where they warmed on the hearthstone.

"Any news yet?"

"Not yet. Baby's real close, though." Lucy hurried back to the stairway and disappeared into the loft, leaving Netta and Willie hugging the babies and toddlers in their care.

"Them blankets good and warm?" Ma asked Lucy, when she came back upstairs.

"Nice and toasty," said, Lucy taking the last two steps in one long-legged lunge and holding the blankets out to Ma. "Here."

"Hold 'em tight to yourself, so they keep warm," Ma instructted. "One last push ought to do it. Sadie, get ready to mash on her stomach... real hard, hear?"

"Won't that hurt her?"

"Hurtin's the least of her worries just now," said Ma, using her expert fingers to help stretch Amanda's tender flesh so it wouldn't give way in a nasty tear. The baby's backside presented itself with a large bulge. "Kneadin' on her belly will make the womb pull down," Ma explained quickly. "Let's hope it'll pull down tight enough to get this bleedin' stopped quick."

A sober-faced Sadie nodded her understanding.

"Come on, Mandy. Just one more push," Jeremy coached. "You can do this." His own big paws totally engulfed Amanda's tiny hands. "Pull on me, Mandy. Pull hard and bear down."

"You heard him, girl. Now *push*."

Struggling to do as instructed, Amanda had trouble focusing on anything but the intense pain. "I... can't... I ca–"

"You can, girl. And you *got* to," Ma instructed. "Push now!"

At Ma's command, Amanda bore down with all the strength she had left, and as she did so, the baby—still in its birth sack—

was forced into this world. But only his back half made it. His head stuck in the birth canal, with a large portion of the afterbirth, which had already pulled away from the womb.

"Open up that blanket and get ready to take this babe. I gotta work fast." Holding him firmly under the arms with one hand, Ma snaked the fingers of her other hand behind his head, moving around the lump of placenta, to encircle his skull as best she could. Then she gave a firm pull. At her tug, Amanda screamed when the baby's head broke through, making a ragged rent in her tender tissue. The remainder of the birth sack came along with him, followed by a large gush of bright, red blood.

"Mash down on her belly *now*! And keep mashin' till I tell you to stop," Ma said, placing the motionless, gray baby on the warm blanket in Lucy's arms. In one, swift motion Edith Hawkins pulled the birth sack away from the baby's face and laid it aside on the bed. She worked quickly to clear his airways.

Nothing.

She covered his tiny mouth and nose with her own mouth and blew. Then she pressed on his tiny chest and blew again.

Nothing.

Without hesitation, she took him firmly by the legs with one hand, held him upside down, and smacked the side of him that had entered this world first.

Still nothing.

"He's not gonna make it." Jeremy said. He continued to hold Amanda's hands in his own. She'd passed out shortly after the baby's entrance into this world, so at least she didn't have to feel the pain of Sadie's essential task.

"Don't give up on him, yet," said Ma. "Lucy, get that knife and cut the cord. Quick."

Lucy picked up the knife as well as a dry cloth, so she could staunch the spray of blood she expected. But no blood-spurt followed the knife's blade, when she cut into the baby's birth cord. Nothing more than a trickle of dark blood presented itself.

"I don't like the looks of that," Ma said, taking the baby by his legs and hips and twirling him around in an attempt to let

33

centrifugal force clear the remaining mucus from his airways. After making several, swift circles, she came to a stop, laid the baby back in Lucy's arms, and again, she blew, and pushed, and blew into that tiny body.

The baby boy did not respond.

"Ma, you got to look after Mandy, she's still bleedin' like a stuck pig," Jeremy said with alarm. "For God-sakes, *help* her!"

"I ain't about to give up on this babe." Ma snatched the baby from Lucy, gave him a quick, head-first dunk in the now cold bucket of water sitting at the foot of the bed, then she laid him back in Lucy's arms and repeated the blow, push, blow routine to try and stimulate his breathing.

Still no response.

Ma did the whole thing again. Dunked the baby, blew into the tiny lungs, pushed on his chest, and blew.

"He's dead, Ma. He didn't make it," Jeremy said with a stern tone. "Stop all that and come help my Mandy. Now! At least she still has a chance."

"I ain't lost a single babe, and I ain't about to–"

"Let him *go!*" Jeremy jumped from his place at Amanda's side and swept the baby into his arms in one, swift move. "You can't save him. But you *can* still save Mandy."

Ma dutifully turned her attention to the tiny woman-child, not yet out of her teens, who lay stock-still in the crimson-stained bed. Sadie stood over her, tears streaming down her face, faithfully kneading on Amanda's belly with all the strength she had to give this grisly task.

Ma eased Sadie aside and took over the kneading duties herself, being careful to feel exactly how small the knot of the womb had become by now. "You done a good job, girl," she said in a throaty tone, completely out of character for Edith Hawkins. She continued to knead for a moment, then she commenced the job of sewing up the jagged wound, to stop the last source of bleeding.

And this gnarled, way-weary midwife, who felt nothing but contempt for religion of any kind, began a silent prayer to all she held holy, that this empty-armed mama might be spared.

Lucy walked over to Jeremy and laid the other blanket over the tiny body lying motionless in his arms. She took an edge of the blanket and wiped away tears that had fallen onto his bushy beard, shedding some of her own as she did so. "I'll take him, Jeremy. Let me go clean him up and get him wrapped for burying." But as she reached to take the tiny, silent infant from his papa, Jeremy turned toward the window and gave in to sobs that shook his entire, stocky frame.

No one had noticed Sadie slip down the steps. She stood at the bottom of the stairway with her head leaning against the door, sobbing her heart out as she hugged her own, swelling middle. After a few moments, she took a deep breath in an effort to compose herself, opened the door, and walked straight into Willie's arms. "I'll marry you, Willie Hawkins," she said, as another sob caught her off guard and brought a catch to her voice. "I'll marry you right away."

April 12, 1818
Jerometown on the
Muddy Fork of the Mohican

Dear Libby,

Greetins to you. Hope you and yours kept safe and warm through the cold times.

I bet that Bud who turned out not to be a rosebud is growing like a weed. I have seen the change in my grand daughter Josie over these dark months. I am so thankful I was let out of the whooscow in time to have Christmas with her and her mama and daddy. Help out my son Jason some. And I got to see his wife Mary Sue through her second confinement.

Sister Edie's middle boy Tom come over last week. That is the first body we have seen all winter but for each other. Wished he was more of a talker so I might know how Edie has faired and hear all the news from Justice. His older brother Harmon is the talker. He has girls all over the territory. Tho he supposes just to take them the mails. And Willie the youngest. He is friendly and talkative too. But Tom is the shy one of my nephews. He brung me my trunk from over at Edie's. Sure is nice to have my spare drawers back. And all your letters. I missed reading them over again and again.

Tom is keeping my mule for a bit longer. Needs my Lucifer to break more new ground. He kept the beast for me while I was locked up in the pokey. He did say one of the neighbors in Justice borrowed that mule last fall and ended up with his arm in a sling for the trouble. Tom is the only one apart from me who can handle old Lucifer. He should of knowed better.

I got to say it one more time. Thanks for standing by me Lib. You been a good friend. What with me being jailed for a murderer and all. I ain't likely to forget it. Some certain folk believe it still. And that would be Harvey and his new woman. I do not guess he will ever forgive me for the death of his son. Even though the judge declared me in defense of my own self. And as Harvey has put a new woman in my kitchen not to mention my bed, I got to let it go at that.

In truth it haunted my nights over winter. I still see Theodore. Not as he was that day. Mostly growed and the worse for drink. I see the child I was raising as my own. Then there he is coming at me with that knife like some crazed animal. If I had not kicked that knife over the edge of the hay mow I know he wouldda used it on me. You know I never meant him to fall on it Lib. But I did not aim to let happen what he had in mind neither.

Sometimes I dream of him laid out on the barn floor so still. But in my dream when I walk by he reaches out and grabs my ankle as I pass. Wake up in a sweat I do. I feel bad the boy had to come to such a sorry end. But he turned so wild. Was no help for it.

I can not be sorry for how things turned out over Harvey in the end. Nope. Even if it did cost me another man a home and a hearth. I wouldda paid a bigger price to keep them than they was worth. Which is my self-respect. Course Harvey would never see it that way. All he seen was his son dead. And the blood on my hands.

Still it sure does sting to find some floozy in my kitchen and wearing my own good apron to boot. I heard he picked her up at a tavern on the way home from Mt. Vernon. And blast it. Those are my sheep in his pasture. I brung them from right here where I am staying now. My old homestead that son Jason is farming.

Least I can be grateful my girls did not end up in the middle of the whole sorry mess. Being as Johannah rode off behind that stranger on a bay horse. And Katrina went back to Penna with my ma soon after. Flora Jean is still keeping school at the Coulter's in Perrysville. The only one of my girls still in these parts. For the first time I am glad they left.

Now I got to quit looking back. Needs must I look ahead instead and make new beginnings. Speaking of which. I did not tell you of the new beginning we had here in March. I got me a new grandpup. A boy. They named him Harley J. Kirtland. Harley after Mary Sue's daddy. With the J. standing for Jason.

A good name I think. After such a hard confinement he came into the world easy enough last month.

Now I offered up the name Gabe for them to chew on. But Mary Sue thought naming her babe after the Angel Gabriel a bit uppity. I thought it fitting enough as he was born about nine months after that revival we all attended. Remember when I told you there would be more births nine months hence than a hound dog has fleas? I did not know that I bespoke my own kin when I said it!

I still can see that river-running scallywag Zeke. When he stepped out of them woods at sunrise in his birthday suit. Light hitting him. Making him look all gold and shimmery. The screech of his bagpipe striking fear into grown men and boys. Folks startled awake expecting the fires of damnation they heard tell of all week. I think it was Emma Putnam shouted out how the Angel of the Lord surely had come to take us all home.

Zeke MacTavish as the Angel Gabriel. Laugh my fool head off every time I think of it.

Josie loves her new little brother. Calls him He-He. It is a cute sound she makes like a laugh. If we tell her to go give He-He a kiss she puts her mouth on his head and says, Bwaaa. Sounds like a kiss to me.

I have prized this time with the babies. But I am in a hurry to get on with my own life. Whatever that may be. Mary Sue is fit as a fiddle again. Riding herd over Jason and the tykes with no help needed from me. She is a corker sure enough. Tries to make me feel needed. Acts like my cooking is better than her own with the same foodstuffs. She will say, Ma, what did you do to this stew? Mine never comes out this tasty. That sort of a thing.

Mind, I do value it. But I am feeling like a third leg here.

I do have a scheme in mind, friend. Which should be no surprise to you. It come to me during my time in hiding from Harvey. Down on the Clear Fork feeding the river men like I was. I saw a empty place downstream of Perrysville. Needs a little work for sure. Most of the old roof fell in. But it would be a dern good spot for a hardy woman to make her own way. In style with a proper hearthstone and all. Stead of working over a cookfire in the out-of-doors.

Mary Sue asked me to take back my favorite cook pot and frying pan from that other life of mine. Back when I lived here with Jason's daddy. Says she don't need all these pots as she already had her own she likes better.

Before long I aim to set out for that cabin on the river. Get to work on repairs soon as the prospect of snow is past. With some help from Jason I think I could get it fixed up and running in no time.

That Mary Sue even claims she is up to heavy cleaning if you can credit that. The Riverstop I aim to call it. Around the next bend in my life.

Take care friend. And let me hear from you.

>your friend
>Ellie Mae

Chapter 2

Wedding Bells
Early May, 1818

"I can't do it, Jems," Sadie told her older brother, standing before him with hands on hips and a stubborn edge to her voice. "I won't do it. I won't leave you to fend by yourself. So don't even try to make me go through with any of this wedding nonsense."

"But the Justice of the Peace comes today! You can't back out now."

"Oh yes I can."

"Willie and Ma will have something to say about that, you know."

"They can't *make* me get married. So, quit trying to change my mind."

"Look at yourself, Sadie. You're with child."

"I know that, Jems."

"How could I have been so blind? Not to see it before Ma spilled the beans. Don't you see? You've *got* to marry Willie right away."

"No I don't."

"What do you mean you *don't?*"

"Hush, you. Keep your voice down. You'll wake the twins. I had enough trouble getting them to sleep for naps today."

Jeremy's frustration at his sister's headstrong attitude toward this day's hastily-planned nuptials had begun to get the best of him. "How can you not get married when you're having a baby?" he asked in a softer voice, letting his need to shout come through in a forced whisper.

"Simple. I just don't say 'I-do'."

Jeremy shook his head. "Let me try this all over again. Sadie… you need to give that baby a father."

"He already has a father."

"Why are you making this so hard?"

"Because I won't even think about leaving you all alone with two toddlers and a crazy woman, that's why!"

"She's not crazy!" he said with an angry glare.

"I'm sorry, Jems. I didn't mean to say that. You got me so agitated, it just popped out of my mouth before I had a chance to stop it," she said, laying her hand on his arm. "It's just that... well, we've been down this road before. And none of us knows how to bring her back to her senses."

"She came back to me before, and she'll come back to me again. I know she will," Jeremy said, beginning to pace. "She's *got* to."

"But how long will it take *this* time? Tell me that. We already tried everything we can think of, Jems," Sadie said, turning toward Amanda, lying on a blanket beside the warm hearth, curled up in a fetal ball. "Look at her. She's worse this time. Lots worse. I can hardly even get her to drink a cup of tea or take more than a couple bites of soup in a whole day."

"She's still weak from losing so much blood. That's all."

"Eating worse than a little bird won't make her any stronger, Jems. It's a lot more than being weak in body after that birth. It's her head," Sadie said, taking a blanket from the back of a nearby chair and laying it over Amanda, tucking the edges carefully around her shoulders. "Every time she gets addled like this, it seems to take longer and longer for her to come out of it. Ma says so, too. An' she's the one ought to know."

He kept pacing the floor, shaking his head, unwilling to admit to the obvious.

"I'm not leaving you to take care of her, *and* the twins, *and* the animals, *and* the farm all by yourself, Jems. That's final."

"Hello the house!" The sound of horse hooves and creaky wheels accompanied the booming voice. "The bridegroom has come to claim his bride!"

"Willie's here," Jeremy said, walking to the door and pulling it open. He sauntered onto the porch. "Afternoon, folks."

41

Willie had already bounded down from the cart and stood helping his mother descend. "Is that bride of mine all ready to tie the knot?"

"If I was you, I'd give her a wide berth for a while, Willie."

"Did she go and change her mind again?"

Jeremy simply nodded.

"Well, I got a thing or two to say about that," Ma Hawkins said, smoothing her skirts and reaching back up under the seat to retrieve a bundle she had stashed there. "I'll be dad-blamed if that grandbaby of mine is comin' into this world without a legal Papa to fend for it."

"Let me talk to her first, Ma. She can't say no to this face, now can she?" he said, flashing his most winning smile.

"I hope you got your tongue greased up, Willie, cuz you got some fast talking to do, if you aim to win over that bullheaded sister of mine." Jeremy stepped down from the porch and headed toward the Hawkins' rig. "Go on in. I'll tend your horse."

"Fetch that basket back there, first, Willie. Take it inside while you're goin'," directed Ma. "Be careful with that. Mind you don't upset it, now, you hear?"

Willie picked up the large basket, being mindful to hold it steady, then he made a beeline for the cabin.

Jeremy took the horse by the halter to lead him toward the barn. "Tom and Harmon not comin' today?"

"Harmon ain't made it home from his mail run to Mt. Vernon, yet," said Ma, following along with Jeremy to give the lovebirds a little more time to themselves. "He left three days ago, so he shouldda made it back here by now. I *told* that wanderin' fool he better get his carcass home in time to stand up for his brother," she said with a huff. "Tom's givin' him another hour or so. Then if he don't show up, Tom aims to head on over here and stand up for Willie his own self."

Jeremy pulled the cart to the side of the barn and began to unhitch the harness.

"You're awful quiet," said Ma, studying Jeremy more carefully. "How's Amanda? Any change yet?"

"Not yet."

"How's she eatin'?"

"Sadie said she gets a little more nutriment into her every day," he said, giving the horse a pat. "I do believe she's beginning to look a mite better."

"Well, I'll keep my peace till I get a good look at her."

Jeremy led the horse around to the barn door. "I'll go put Freddie inside with Patsy and throw down a little hay," he said, disappearing into the barn.

Deciding she'd given the ruffled lovebirds enough time to smooth their feathers, Edith Hawkins began to make her way up to the house.

Back in the cabin, Willie and Sadie stood toe to toe. "What in blazes has got into you?" Willie asked, taking her by the shoulders and trying to pull her close.

Sadie wiggled free and gave him a push. "Get away from me, mister! I'm not about to let you sweet-talk me into changing my mind again. I aim to stand firm."

"But what about our baby?"

"What about it?"

"Don't you want to give him a papa?"

"You *are* his papa, Willie. Whether I marry you or not won't change that."

"But I *want* to marry you, Sadie. I want us to be a real family," he said, giving her his most pathetic, hang-dog look.

"Oh, Willie. You know I want that too. More than anything in the world I want to be your wife," she said, coming back to him and touching his cheek lightly. "But look over there," she pointed to Amanda. "Take a good look at her, and then tell me how I can leave Jeremy to manage two babies and her and this place all by himself."

Willie nodded his head in understanding.

"It's not that I don't want to marry you, Willie. I just can't leave here right now."

"Then you *will* marry me?"

"You hard of hearing? I just told you I *couldn't* marry you."

"No, you told me you can't leave your brother."

"Well isn't that the same thing?"

"I never asked you to choose between us, Sadie. We can get hitched and stay right here. All of us."

"You'd do that?

"Of course I would."

"You mean you wouldn't expect to take your wife back to your own place?"

"I'd sure like to have a place of our own someday. But with everything so whopper-jawed right now, it don't make a whole lot of sense. 'Sides, I only have Ma's place to take you back to."

Sadie stood shaking her head in disbelief. "You'd marry me and stay here?"

"I just *said* I would, didn't I," he boomed, beginning to get frustrated with her all over again. "I think maybe you're the one who's goin' daft, woman," he said, giving her braid a yank.

Just as Sadie opened her mouth to make a smart-aleck reply, Ma Hawkins walked through the cabin door.

"All right, , that grandbaby of mine needs him a lawful daddy. I won't hear no more about calling off this weddin'."

"But–"

"No buts about it. I aim to see you go through with this hitchin', if I have to take a rope and tie you two together my own self!"

"We don't nee–"

"After I went and made Opal Ann promise to keep her sorry, excuse-for-a-Justice of-a husband sober today and drag him all the way over here afore eventide, you ain't about to back out now."

"But Ma, she already said she wou–"

"I don't care what she said, she's a-marryin' you. And that's that!" Edith Hawkins said, throwing down the bundle she had tucked under her arm with a thud. She pulled off her shawl and tossed it over the peg beside the door. "'Sides, after I went and stirred up a spice cake special, I don't aim to waste it on the neighbors for no good reason." She walked over to the basket Willie had parked on the puncheon table.

"You made us a spice cake?" Sadie asked in wonderment, knowing how hard spices were to come by way out here.

Ma raised the basket lid to make sure the cake still sat upright.

"You haven't made a spice cake in years," Willie said, rubbing his hands in anticipation. "Did you put sweet maplein' on top, too," he asked, reaching into the basket to snitch a taste.

"Get out of there, mister," Ma said, taking a swat at her youngest son.

Willie licked at his finger with an ornery smile.

"Go on. Get yourself on out of here. Don't you know the groom ain't supposed to be sparkin' the bride a'fore all the I-do's gets said on their weddin' day? Shoo!"

With a shrug of his shoulders Willie gave Sadie a helpless look, then took his leave from the cabin.

"Now we got that mess all straightened out, I need a good look at Amanda," Ma said, walking straight to the blanketed heap lying by the fire. She knelt beside the skeletal woman and stroked her hair. "How you doin', gal? You back among us yet?"

Amanda lay unmoving, uttering not a sound.

"She takin' any rations?"

"Not much," Sadie answered. "Maybe a cup of tea and a little soup now and again. That's about all I can get into her. Only thing that seems to give her much comfort is lying by the fire." Sadie tucked the edge of the blanket tighter around Amanda's chin. "She slumps over after a short spell if I put her up in the rocking chair. So mostly I lay her on that blanket. Keep the fire goin' for her all day, whether it's cold out or not."

"She said anything in the last week? Moved around on her own yet?"

"Only moves when I help her. Hasn't said a word since... well, since she came to after the birth," Sadie said with a shiver, remembering the ungodly screech that tore forth from Amanda when she found out her baby boy had never drawn breath.

"I don't like the look of this," Ma said, shaking her head. "I don't like it at-all."

Jeremy had left Willie to greet the neighbors, now beginning to straggle in for the afternoon nuptials, and he entered the cabin, going immediately to the two women kneeling beside his motionless wife. "I think she's looking better. Don't you, Ma?"

"She ain't a bit better than she was last week. Nor the week afore that. And don't you try to tell me any different." Edith Hawkins lifted Amanda's hand and pinched the skin on her forearm. "She's losin' flesh. I can see that plain. An' she don't have a bit to spare, neither."

"What else can I do to help her?" Sadie asked her mother-in-law to be.

"We tried everything I know," Edith said with a helpless shrug. "Even the potion that brung her around last time ain't done a blasted thing. I got nary a tonic nor elixir left in my poke of remedies we ain't tried," she said, easing Amanda's arm back under the blanket. "If she don't turn around pretty soon and put some meat back on these bones, we'll likely be diggin' another bury hole right beside both her unlucky babes," said Ma, shaking her head at Jeremy. "You and me got us some hard talkin' to do after this shindig gets done with," she said, waving a finger in his face. "Right now, we better see her upstairs and tucked into bed. Sure don't need no blabbermouth neighbors gapin' at this poor soul," she said, moving from her kneeling position and hoisting herself to painful feet. "Hard enough we got to hold this weddin' business here, on account of her helpless state. But she sure don't need to be sittin' out for public eye-ballin'."

"Sadie, you want to get the door for me?" Jeremy asked, bending down and easing the feather-weight bundle of skin and bones and blankets into his arms. Sadie opened the door to the stairway, and he disappeared into the loft bedroom above.

"Now, young lady. Let me take a good look at *you*," Ma Hawkins said, turning to her future daughter-in-law. "I know you been shoulderin' enough burdens here without havin' to knit up a young'un of your own to boot. How are you holdin' up?" She walked slowly around Sadie, eyeing her up and down. "You look fit enough. How you been feelin'?"

"I'm feeling fine."

"Anything painin' ya anywheres?"

"No pains. I'm *fine*. Really I am."

"You eatin' proper, so that grandbabe of mine gets all the nutriment he needs to grow stout?"

"Great gandersnipes, do you browbeat all your mamas with so many questions?"

"Just the ones givin' me grandbabies."

At that moment Lucy Jarvis pushed open the cabin door. "Sounds like we got a bride in here with a bee in her bonnet," she said, balancing the chubby Hank on one knobby hipbone and holding out a bouquet of purple-and-white lilacs in a man-sized fist. "I brought these along for you, Sadie, in case you didn't have time to fix yourself a wedding nosegay."

"Thanks. I never gave a thought to flowers."

"Looks like you didn't give much thought to wedding duds, either."

"Here, let me have Hank," Ma said, reaching for the one-year-old. "I'll leave you two gals to fuss with flowers and such. Never have been much good at that sort of thing, myself." She set the toddler down on unsteady feet and helped him wobble his way to the cabin door, then on outside to where the closest neighbors had begun to gather in the sunshine.

"Maybe we could fasten your hair up on top with a flower or two in it," Lucy said, fingering the one, thick braid fraying loose that hung half-way down Sadie's back.

"I never wore my hair up before."

"Then I'd say your wedding day seems a good time to try it out. You got any hairpins?"

47

"Nope. Amanda does, though. I'll get 'em." Sadie went to the shelf above the wash stand to fetch her hairbrush from its perch beside Jeremy's shaving mug and straight razor. He seldom used them anymore since growing the bushy beard that covered his scars, after his little mishap with that bear at the last, big surround-hunt. She opened the small box that held Amanda's prized brooch from her grandmother and removed a handful of hairpins from inside.

"Here." Sadie handed the pins and brush to Lucy.

"Sit down, and I'll brush your hair out," Lucy said, pulling a chair away from the table. "We'll get you looking more like a real bride."

Sadie sat, as instructed. "I haven't had time to even think about all this wedding business," she said, fussing with her apron strings as Lucy untied her hastily made braid and began to brush the light, chestnut hair with firm strokes. "What with the twins, and chores, and caring for Amanda and all, I haven't had time to think about anything, except what needs done next."

"Is she any better?"

"Ma says she's got to put some flesh back on if she's ever gonna turn around. But I can't get her to eat more than a little-bitty bird."

"What's Jeremy going to do, once you're hitched to Willie? Can he manage all this on his own?"

"Willie said he'd move in here with us... for the time being, anyway. I wouldn't agree to marry up with him, otherwise. So he said he'd just have to take me, passel and all," Sadie smiled. "To be truthful, I'm powerful glad. Some days it's almost more than I can manage around here. At least this way, I can stay on to help Jems, and Willie will be here to help us both out."

"Sounds like a workable solution to me."

"I've got to be honest... this marryin' business has me awful jangled," said Sadie, still twisting her apron strings. "Not that I'm afraid of marrying Willie, exactly. It's just that... well, the whole thing's pretty scary if I study on it for too long."

"Marriage is a big step for a girl."

"Jeremy's right, though. I do need to think about this tadpole," she said, giving her middle a pat. "And truth be told, I haven't had the courage to study on that very hard, either."

"Hallooo-oo!" Netta Bailey called out, as she swept into the cabin with a food basket over one arm and a wrapped bundle under the other.

"Shhhhhhh! The twins are still sleeping," Sadie shushed. "At least I hope they're still sleeping."

"Oh, I'meversosorry," Netta said in a loud whisper, as she set the basket down beside the table. "I didn't think about wakin' babies. I left mine out in the wagon. Both of 'em fell asleep on the way over here, so Ma said she'd keep an eye on 'em till I get back out there." She laid the bundle down on top of her basket and began to remove her bonnet. "Where's Amanda? Is she doin' any better?"

"She's upstairs, resting."

"Well, I brought her over some of my sweet biscuits. I heard she needed fattenin' up, so I figger'd what's better than some of my sweet biscuits?" She opened her basket. "I'll just take 'em on up to her and see if she needs anythi–"

"Why don't you set 'em over on the sideboard, Netta," instructed Sadie. "Ma said no one's to bother Amanda today. She needs her rest."

"Well, I just wanted to save someone else the trouble of climbin' up there and checkin' on her. But if you think it's best, then I guess–"

"Let her be, Netta," Lucy chimed in. "Just let her be."

"Well, all right. But I know these sweet biscuits will help plump her right up. Why just look at me, if you don't think so! Luther says I got to quit eatin' so many, but I just can't help myself. Once I get started eatin' 'em, I can't seem to quit," she said, placing the biscuit bundle on the sideboard where Sadie had indicated. "Besides, when my Luther's gone I don't have much else to do but eat, once I tend to the chores and my girls, that is. Just can't help myself when it comes to sweet biscuits."

49

"Did Luther come with you?"

"Oh, heavens no. He took off into the woods right after that kicking bee, and he hasn't showed back up yet. That's Luther's way, you know. Takes off for weeks at a time, and then comes back home totin' the softest, tanned buckskins I ever did see. He can't stand to be around sociable doin's much. Why he only hung around for the kickin' bee 'cause I threw such a big hissy fit. Soon as he set the cabin to rights after we kicked up all them yard goods, he disappeared very next day. I *did* hope he'd get back in time for this weddin', but I have to tell you, I really didn't expect he would. Even if he did find out about it out there in them woods. Matter of fact, he prob'ly aims to stay out till the party's over—if he does know about it, that is. Luther always did hold that weddin's was for none but womenfolk and fools."

"I can tell you, I sure do feel the fool," Sadie said. "All this fussing for nothing more than a couple of I-do's."

"Well it's your *weddin'* day, forheavensakes! Of *course* we're supposed to fuss over you," Netta gushed. "Oh, that reminds me, I brought something for you, Sadie." She dug around in the bottom of the basket, searching through its contents. "Here it is," she said, waving a flowered handkerchief in the air. "It's my weddin' hankie. You *got* to have a weddin' hankie, you know," she said, handing Sadie the linen kerchief, delicately embroidered with red and pink roses. "My Grandma Rosanna gave it to me on my own weddin' day. The roses stand for her, Grandma Rosanna, you know. She gave it to my own dearly departed mama on her weddin' day, too. So I figger'd you could use it for the 'somethin' old' you got to have. 'Somethin' old, somethin' new, somethin' borrowed, and somethin' blue,'" Netta recited. "It's bad luck if you don't have all of them things."

"Thank you."

"Oh! I just thought of somethin' else! That hankie can serve you for *two* of them rhymes. The something old, and the something borrowed. I do want that hankie back when the I-do's are all done with. Cuz it's from my Grandma Rosanna, you know. And I aim to save it for my own little Rosanna, for the day

50

when she stands up to be wed her own self," Netta said. "Do you have somethin' new and somethin' blue? It really is bad luck if we can't find somethin' to suit for all four of them rhymes."

"We'll manage," Lucy answered, as she twisted at the long locks. "Hand me some pins, there, would you Sadie?" she instructed.

Just then Clara Guthrie poked her head through the door. "Netta?"

"Shhhhhh! Sleepin' babies," Netta whispered loudly, pointing to the other room.

"Your own babies are stirrin'. Ma sent me to fetch you."

"All right, I'm comin'," she said, grabbing her bonnet to tie back on as she hurried out the door.

"Can I come in to see the bride?" Clara still stood only halfway in the door.

"Come on in. We're fixin' Sadie's hair up," Lucy said softly through the pins she held in her mouth.

"I never saw you with your hair put up before," Clara said. "It sure makes you look like a real lady."

"Thanks."

"Tear off a piece of that white lilac for me, please Clara?"

"Sure." She picked up one of the stems and pinched off a large twirl of blossoms.

"You look mighty nice today, in that blue dress of yours," complimented Sadie.

"Why, thank you! I sure hope Tom gets here, so he can take notice of me in it," she said, twirling the fragrant flower in her fingers. "Pa brought it back special, you know. From New Orleans. Just so's Tom would take a good look at me."

"Don't worry, he'll show up in time for weddin' vows," Lucy answered. "He's not one to stand around jawin' beforehand when there's work to be done. Hand me a few more pins there," she said, extending her big-boned hand to Sadie.

"I hope that piece of Simpson baggage don't darken the door

way here today. I can't stand to lay eyes on that hussy," Clara hissed. "Ain't natural to have hair that color. Just ain't natural."

"Why Clara, I do believe the green-goblin's got a-hold on you," Sadie smirked.

"I don't reckon you'll have to worry your head over her today," Lucy said, putting the last pin in Sadie's hair. "Here, hand me that piece of flower, now." She took it from Clara and tucked it in on one side of Sadie's topknot. "I think we need another one over here, too," she said, touching the other side of Sadie's hair. "Tear me off some more, Clara."

"Don't you think the Simpson's will come?"

"I reckon just family and the closest neighbors will show up for this marryin' day.'"

"I can't imagine *anyone* missin' a weddin' shindig, can you? Specially that Simpson gal. Oh, I know she has her cap set for Tom, sure as I'm standin' here a-twirlin' this posy. I can *feel* it."

"Well, I don't think Tom has taken mind of *any* woman yet," Lucy answered. "And if it's left up to him, I doubt he ever will."

"What do you mean?"

"I mean, that's one man who's gotta be told what he wants, when it comes to pullin' heart strings."

"Really?"

"Really. I'll take that other piece of lilac." Lucy held out her hand, as Clara stood pie-eyed, lost in thought. "Clara. You in there?"

"Oh, o' course. Here." She handed the flower to Lucy and looked hard at the portion of stem she still held in her other hand. "This piece don't look too good all tore up... to put back in that nosegay, I mean," said Clara. "You mind if I tear off these last pieces and use 'em myself? Might make it easier on Tom to look at me, if I was prettied up some like Sadie."

"Fix yourself up any way you want, Clara. It's no skin off my nose," Sadie said.

"Halloo-ooo? Is that bride all ready yet?" Emma Putnam waddled through the door, carrying a large food basket, with a blue bundle rolled snuggly under one arm.

"Hi Emma. We just got Sadie all fixed up. Don't she look real nice?" said Clara, primping herself in the cracked mirror hung over the washstand. She fussed with the sprigs of flower on one side of her head, then the other, having trouble deciding.

"Them posies up in her hair make her look like a bride for sure," Emma said, setting her basket by the rest. "That dirty apron don't do much for her, though."

Sadie took a good look at her attire. "I didn't aim on getting married when I got dressed this morning," she said, wiping her hands across the front of herself, which made her swelling belly more noticeable.

"Looks to me like you *better* be gettin' hitched," Emma said, "and mighty quick, about it, too. Here, now, you take that every-day thing right off," Emma instructed. "I made this up last night," she said, unrolling the blue bundle. "Wish't it could be a pretty, new, marryin' dress, but you'll have to settle for this here smock, instead," she said, holding it out to Sadie. "I used up every bit of blue goods I had left over to make it."

"Why Emma, it's beautiful! Thank you!" Sadie doffed her everyday apron, hung it over the back of her chair, and took the new, company smock from her chubby neighbor. "I never had a blue smock before. I never even saw one."

"My, don't you look a fittin' site, now," Clara said, turning from the mirror to show off her own flower-bedecked hair. "Would you just look at the two of us? We match up real purty, don't we? Both of us in blue. And white lilacs in our hair!"

Clara's mother, Winifred Guthrie, now stuck her head inside the cabin. "Opal Ann and the Justice just pulled up. Time to get this weddin' under way." She stepped inside. "Clara Marlene Guthrie what in blazes are you doin' lookin' like the bride?"

"I just put a few posies in my hair, Mam. That's all."

"Well you take 'em out right now. You got no business lookin' like you's the one gettin' hitched."

"Oh, Mam. Do I *have* to?"

53

"Do like I say, now. Don't you know it's bad luck to out-shine the bride on her own weddin' day?" said Winifred. "No shame intended," she said, nodding to Sadie. "My gal can't help herself, bein' how she's such a looker to start with."

Clara resentfully pulled the flowers from her hair, but she tucked them carefully into the pocket of her skirt, so as not to crush them.

All the talking and commotion had finally roused the Harrison twins in their bent-twig cribs over in the adjoining room, and they began to fuss at the sound of strange voices in the house.

"I better go tend to Lilly and Millie," said Sadie.

"Don't bother yourself. Winifred and I will get 'em up," Lucy said, heading for the babies. "We'll see they're tended for the rest of the day, too. So don't you worry your head over them anymore."

"But–"

"No buts. You got a man out there waitin' to make you his wife. I reckon that's more important this day."

"Is she all ready?" Netta came bouncing back inside with Rosanna and Rachel in tow. "Ohmylands, just look at you. You found somethin' blue after all."

"Emma made it for me. Isn't it nice?"

"So it's something blue *and* something new? Then you're all ready and set to get hitched up proper. Oh, I just love weddin's, don't you?" she asked of no one in particular. "Willie's lookin' kind of skittery, with all those fellers back-slappin' him and pokin' fun. I think you better get out there an claim that man before they spook him so bad he runs right off. Don't you forget that pretty nosegay," she said, shifting Rachel to her other hip and taking her toddler by the hand. "Don't twist my skirts, Rosanna. You'll make me fall right down if you keep it up. Come *on* now. Jeremy says we got to get everybody outside. With the sun shinin' and all, this day's just made for a outdoor weddin'."

"Did Tom make it yet?"

54

"He's here. So's Harmon. Both of 'em just rode up on Harmon's horse. They wouldn't dream of missin' their own brother's weddin', now, would they?"

"What about them Simpsons? They haven't showed up, have they?"

"No sign of 'em," said Netta. "But I don't reckon they'll come, do you? Bein's they're so new here, and all, and no relations. Willie's Uncle Jonathan just walked up, though. And so did Sam Justice. Now who'dda guessed Sam would show up? Didn't figger him to leave that forge for a weddin', of all things. But there he is."

"Don't you know he never misses a chance to pay court to Ma Hawkins, if he can help it?" said Clara. "Mam tells that he's been sweet on her for years. But she won't have ary a thing to do with him. Nor any man. 'Ceptin' her own sons, of course."

"She's a hard woman," Emma agreed.

"What about Willie's Aunt Ellie? Do you think she'll come?" asked Sadie.

"Ain't too likely she'll set foot this close to Harvey's place," Netta said with a sober look. "Luther says it's best she lays low a spell longer."

"Sad thing, losin' that boy like that," Emma said.

"Terrible. Just terrible," Netta said, shaking her head. "Makes me shiver every time I think of poor Theodore that away, all laid out with that knife stickin' out of his chest. Nary a soul who could budge it till Harvey come home. Can you imagine, coming home to find a dead son and his own wife to blame for the deed?"

"You *know* it was an accident, Netta," said Sadie. "There's no blame to it. The judge said so."

"Far as Harvey's concerned, it warn't no accident."

"Why so many long faces in here?" asked Lucy, coming back into the kitchen with one of the twins. "A wedding's supposed to be a happy day. What happened to all the smiles?"

"We was just talkin' about Willie's Aunt Ellie and how she

kilt Harvey's Theodore. Sad. Real sad," Clara said.

"You women folk ever comin' out? Or do we have to hog-tie and drag that bride out here to meet her mister?" Jonathan Johansen called, sticking his head inside the cabin door. "Afternoon, Lucy," he tipped his hat. "This Justice ain't apt to stay standin' upright too much longer, if you know what I'm-a-sayin'. So we'd best get this hitchin' business done with, whilst he can still spit out the right words to tie up a knot proper."

"We're comin'. We're comin'!" Netta turned and swept out the door with Rosanna clutching her skirts. Lucy and Winifred carried the twins, and Emma lumbered her way out the door, following right behind.

As soon as her mother had exited the cabin, Clara pulled the lilac spray out of her pocket and quickly stuffed it right back into her hair, just above her ear. "Who's gonna stand up with you, Sadie?"

"I guess Jems will."

"It should be a gal, you know."

"Well, Amanda's sure in no shape to stand up with me."

"Oh, let me do it, please? Then you and me can march out there just like them big-city brides do, with a proper bridesmaid to lead the way. Would you like that?"

"I don't need to carry on so uppity, Clara."

"Oh, pleeeease? *Please* let me do this. Then Tom will *have* to take notice of me, at least for a minute or two. Please?"

"Go ahead. Suit yourself."

Clara smoothed her dress, tucked the loose ends of her hair back up, then slowly began to move her hips back and forth to set her skirts to swaying.

"Hurry up, in there! We ain't got all day!"

Sadie gave Clara a push, which got her to put one foot in front of the other and slowly move toward the cabin door, all the while making sure that her skirts still swayed in time with each step.

"Here comes the bride, here comes the bride," she sang out

in a squeaky voice, *"here comes the bri-ide to meet with her groom!"*

As soon as Clara reached the afternoon sunshine, Winifred Guthrie began to fuss at her only daughter, sashaying out there for all to see, with those flowers sticking right back up in her hair. But before she got more than a few words out of her mouth, Anson gave her a poke with his bony elbow. "Keep your peace, woman! Let her be. 'Tain't frettin' a soul but you."

"It ain't proper," she hissed back at him. "It just ain't proper for a young gal to outshine the bride."

"Daughter Clara looks mighty good, if you ask me," he said with a spit of tobacco juice out the side of his mouth. "And you didn't ask me, but I'm-a-tellin' you just the same."

By the time Clara and Sadie had reached the Justice of the Peace, listing a little to starboard as he stood underneath the big maple tree between the cabin and the cistern pump, the whole crowd had pushed in close, so they could be sure to hear all the "who-gives" and "I-do's."

"We're a-gatherin' to tie up this here man with this here gal," said the Richland County Justice of the Peace, Ranson Newell. "I got to say, it's a mighty good thing, bein' it looks like these two's gonna get blessed right quick," he said winking at Willie.

"First one can come any time. After that they all take near nine month," hollered Harmon from his place of honor beside the groom.

The whole crowd laughed at that, except for Winifred Guthrie. "Bad luck comes of tormentin' a bride," she muttered. "Bad luck all around."

"Now bein' as these two aim to get theirselves hitched up proper, I got to know who's standin' up with 'em, to make it all legal."

"I stand for the groom," said Harmon.

Jeremy made a move to go stand by his sister, but before he could push his way through the company, Clara called forth, "I bear witness for the bride!" She beamed so, swaying her skirts a bit as she said it, that Jeremy shrugged his shoulders and went to stand out of the way beside the apple tree.

He leaned against the trunk and stared at his baby sister—the one he'd raised from a tiny, little-bit-of-a-pup—and marveled at the grown woman now standing calm and confident with the man she intended to marry. *Who'd believe she started out no bigger than a mite, with no mama to suckle her,* he thought, remembering the squalling babe he'd managed to pull through when their mother had died in childbed. After bearing twelve sons, she never got the satisfaction of knowing her only daughter. *Look at her standin' there, so proud and hardy. She'll make Willie a wonderful wife.*

"State your given name, son," the Justice said to Willie.

"William Lloyd Hawkins."

"William Lloyd, do you take this here woman to be your lawful wife?"

"I do."

"And what's your whole name, girl?"

"Sarah Elfrieda Harrison."

Willie gave her a curious look, and she shot back a glare that said, *"don't you even snicker, boy."*

"Sarah Alfree-da, do you take this here man to be your lawful husband?"

Sadie hesitated a moment, looking around for Jeremy with a panicked look. When she found his eye, he gave a nod to reassure her. *It's all right, Sadie. Go ahead,* said his broad smile.

"Do you take this man, missy? Or do we haf'ta dig us up another bride?"

"I do. I do. I really do."

"Well that's a ree-leef. For a tick, there you gave this groom a good scare," Justice Newell said, wiping his hand across his brow. "Now I gotta ask you both a mite more, afore this here knot-tyin's official," he said, turning the page in his leather-bound handbook. "Willie... ah, William, do you take this woman in sickness, and in health, in plenty and in want, givin' up all other women but her, till death comes atwixt?"

"I do again."

"Good. Now Sadie, ah, Sarah. Do you take this man in sickness and in health... "

As the Justice's voice droned on through the obligatory vow-taking, Jeremy pulled a handkerchief from his hip pocket and blew his nose. *In sickness and in health,* he thought. *Mandy, my little yellow bird, will you ever come back to me, happy and whole?* Jeremy's mind wandered back to his own wedding in the little church in Pennsylvania, with no one but Sadie and their brother Michael to stand up for the nervous couple—virtual strangers to one another. Mandy looked so tiny and helpless, all decked out in her yellow finery like a skittery little canary, clutching onto that letter from her Papa like it was hope itself. Not a single person she knew could brace her up on her wedding day. If it hadn't been for the child of violence she carried, Jeremy would never even be standing here, on his own place, watching his little sister become a bride herself.

"By the legal power that comes with this here office of Justice o' the Peace, I declare you two tied up steadfast and proper," said Ranson Newell.

"Well, whattya waitin' for?" Harmon said, giving his brother a poke in the ribs. "Go on. Kiss your bride!"

Willie grabbed Sadie and planted a big smooch, square on her lips, as everyone sent up a loud cheer.

"You know," drawled Justice Newell, once the noise had died down, "it seems a real shame to waste this here gatherin' on just one hitchin', now that I'm all warmed up good. Be there anyone else we can tie up to get double duty from this here party, whilst I'm in the hitchin' mood?"

Clara didn't waste a second. *"I will,"* she called out, holding up her hand and moving hastily forward. "Tom Hawkins, I aim to marry you, do you hear? So get yourself up here and do right by me," she said in no uncertain terms, taking her place in front of the Justice and smoothing at her skirts. She waited calmly for Tom to join her.

The crowd hummed with surprise, and over to one side, Anson Guthrie knelt by his passed-out wife, waving his hat in her face in an effort to try and bring her to.

"Your folks got anythin' to say about this, gal?" the Justice asked Clara.

From his place on the ground Anson shouted, "'Bout time she got herself hitched up," he said between waves of his hat. "You best be quick about it, though, a'fore this woman of mine comes to and puts the royal ky-bosh on it."

"What do ya' say, Tom? Only chance a hairy goat like you's gonna get to claim hisself a bride," said Harmon, pushing his brother forward. "If I wuz you, I'd jump at that looker."

"Go on. Get up there," Ma Hawkins said, giving her shy, middle son a poke in the back to push him along. "Ain't much substance to that one, but she does have gumption, I gotta give her that. Likely she's ten times better than anythin' you're apt to drag home, if'n it's left up to you."

Tom hemmed and hawed, moving forward all the while by well-meaning pushes and shoves and back-slaps from the neighbors. Presently he found himself standing beside a beaming Clara Guthrie.

"'Bout time you got here," she said, giving him a big, toothy grin.

"Here, Clara," Sadie said, pushing her nosegay of lilacs into Clara's hand. "Hang on to 'em tight so your hands don't shake," she whispered to the second bride this day.

"I ain't shakin' a bit," she said, accepting the bridal bouquet. "Don't know why I didn't think of this long ago."

* * * * *

"Here you go, Sadie," Lucy said, handing her a piece of spice cake from the table full of foodstuffs. "You and Willie get the first pieces. Then Tom and Clara."

"Make mine a big one," Willie said in eager anticipation. "Can't wait to get a piece of that in my mouth.

Sadie didn't waste a moment as she put a big fork-full of her own cake right into Willie's mouth, smearing maple topping all over his face in the process.

"Hey! Look at Willie a-wearin' the cake!" Jonathan said, pushing up right behind the bridal couples in order to get his own piece directly from the hand of Lucy. "Sure improves your looks considerable, too," he said with a big smile in Lucy's direction.

Netta and the Justice's wife, Opal Ann, stood near the cistern pump keeping an eye on all the toddlers and babies playing on the ground at their feet. "Would you look at the way Jonathan's makin' cow eyes at that Lucy Jarvis? Why you'd think he was sweet on her. And her a married woman with a young'un, to boot," said Opal Ann.

"He's always been sweet on her. Didn't you know?"

"He has? Then that husband of hers better keep a close rein on that one. I ain't seen him about today. Where is Henry?"

"He stayed home. Said he had too much corn to hoe. But I know the real reason."

"What is it? You can tell me, Netta."

"Well, the way I heard it, he won't have nothin' to do with a weddin' frolic if a baby's already on the way," whispered Netta. "Says the proof of the sin's bad enough, without makin' a party of it, to boot."

"Blazes, half the folks Ranson hitches up are already settin' on the nest. I don't see the fuss in that."

"If you knew Henry you'd understand. He thinks only a preacher can tie up a proper weddin' knot that'll stay tied tight."

"Well, what in tarnation makes him so all-fired holy?"

"That's just Henry. Any travelin' preacher comin' around here always seems to take to him right off. Usually makes Henry a prayer leader, or some such, till he gets 'round again on the next circuit."

"How does Lucy take to all that holier-than-thou business?"

"She don't say much. Just goes about doin' what she thinks

is right," Netta said, noticing a ruckus starting up between toddlers. "Rosanna, what on *earth* are you doin'? Give me that thing right now," she said, taking a stick away from Rosanna, who was about to hit one of the Harrison twins with it. "You tell Millie you're sorry. Go on!"

"I'm not Millie. I'm *Lilly*," the other toddler said in no uncertain terms, with a stomp of her foot.

"I never can tell you two apart. Go on, Rosanna. Make amends."

"Sorry."

"All right, now, you girls play nice," she said giving both little bottoms a swat and boosting them away. "Mind you don't torment Hank like that no more, neither." As soon as Netta turned back to her gossip with Opal Ann, both girls gave each other an ornery look, then picked up sticks and went after Hank Jarvis, wobbling his way to the group of men standing over by the horses.

"You do know how Henry kept Lucy a-waitin' to marry up with him, don't you? After she come out here as his mail-order bride?" Netta said.

"Her? A mail-order bride?"

"Oh, yes. Scandalized the whole township, too. Why, I figger'd you already heard this story, Opal Ann. Course, with you livin' over Mansfield way, it ain't local news to you. End of July it was, in 18 and 14, Lucy Peterman showed up, holdin' onto Henry's want ad and ridin' right up there behind Harmon, like the parcel of mail she was."

"No! She just showed up?"

"Sure did."

"Well what did Henry do?"

"What else could he do? He married her! But not until the old Reverend Blankenship came on his circuit a month later. Lucy took up residence in the cabin, and Henry moved out to the barn. No Justice-o-the-Peace hitchin' would do for Henry. That's why they never came to see youens. Had to have him a real service done by a real preacher. So he asked Jonathan to bunk with him, till the preacher came... just so's folks wouldn't get any notions about unseemly shenanigans goin' on betwixt the house and the barn."

"And that's when Jonathan got sweet on Lucy?"

"I think so, too. Course, he never said a word. Just kept on a-living' with those smelly hogs and that worthless dog o' his. Prowls the woods between here and back East like a shiftless man lackin' a good woman. Mark my word, I know that cow-eyed look when I see it," Netta said, looking around to check on her girls. "Rosanna! You put that thing right down!" She scuttled over to take another stick away from her toddler.

Folks had mostly finished eating the light refreshments laid out by the women, and up near the porch the new Clara Hawkins' curiosity had begun to get the best of her. "Ain't you gonna open your presents?" she asked the only bride and groom folks had anticipated for this day.

"I don't think we should, seein' as how you and Tom don't have anything to open," Sadie answered.

"Why, that don't bother me a bit," said Clara, twisting the now bedraggled lilacs she still held. "I already got me the best present of the day anyhow," she said with a blush, watching Tom sidle his way over to where the men stood by the barn, talking weather and crops and politics.

"Open up the gift I brought over," Netta called, coming forward with Rosanna in toe. "It's somethin' I made special."

Sadie took the bundle, untied the piece of whang and carefully began to unroll the soft buckskin that wrapped Netta's gift. "Oh, my lands, Netta. They're beautiful!" She held up two, rose-embroidered tea-towels, woven of pure linen. "Since there's two of these nice towels, and we've got two brides, would you mind if I shared one of these with Clara?"

"I was sure hopin' you'd say that, cuz' when Clara surprised us all like she did, well, I just didn't know what to do! I don't have a single piece of linen left to make another set of company towels for Clara and Tom," Netta babbled. "I used up the last of my red thread for makin' those fancy roses, too. Every scrap I had left! Oh, I hope Luther comes home pretty soon. My larder's runnin' clean down to the dregs, it is."

"You need someone to make a trip up Uniontown way for supplies? I'd be happy to oblige," Jonathan said, tipping his hat in Netta's direction.

"If Luther don't show up pretty soon, I might take you up on that. I just might! Come on, Rosanna," she said, shooing her toddler dancing ahead. "You need a trip out to the backhouse, and right now."

Sadie picked up the other bundle that Ma Hawkins had left beside the wedding cake. "I think this one's from Ma. Has anyone seen her lately?"

"She took to the cabin with Jeremy a while back," said Harmon through the piece of cake stuffed in his mouth.

"Maybe we should wait to open this one, then."

"Oh, go on. Open it now," Clara urged. "She already knows what's in it."

Sadie began to unfold the package wrapped up in a square of homespun goods, carefully laying back one side, then the other.

"Oh, how precious! Baby things!" Clara couldn't help the blush that rushed to her cheeks. "Hold 'em up, Sadie. Let's see what all's in there."

Sadie held up a knitted cap, two sacques, and a receiving blanket made from the finest of linen fabrics to put against a newborn baby's skin. She looked more closely at the homespun wrapping, and, turned over, discovered it was a baby comforter.

"Leave it to Ma to think of somethin' for our little Tadpole," Willie said with a wink, holding up a tiny pair of knitted booties, that had lain underneath all the rest.

* * * * *

"We got to do somethin' for this girl, if you aim to keep her this side of heaven," said Ma Hawkins, standing beside Jeremy, who sat on the edge of the bed beside his emaciated wife.

"I didn't think you believed in heaven, Ma."

"Never said I didn't believe. Just can't stand good-for-nothing preachers," she muttered. "Waste too much time with their God talkin', instead of pitchin' in to do what's needed out here."

"Sometimes talkin' to God's the only thing we can do, Ma."

"Poppycock! There's *always* something a body can do. I still say them that's strong and able don't need a God. Them that ain't, don't belong out here," she said with a scowl. "And this here tender little thing never did belong out here, Jeremy. She ain't cut out for countrified livin'."

"I agree with you there. But since her own family kicked her out, she *is* here. That makes this the only home she has left."

"Well she ain't gonna have it for long, if she don't turn aro/. und mighty quick."

"I've tried to get through to her, Ma. God knows I've tried. But I don't think she hears a single thing I say," Jeremy said, stroking Amanda's cheek as she stared at the ceiling. "And you've already given her all the herbs and potions you have. So I guess prayin's all that's left to me."

"The time to pray and talk is done! We got to *act*. And NOW! This girl needs the kind of doctorin' I don't know nothin' about."

"Are you sayin' we should send down to Mt. Vernon for Dr. Bradley, then?"

"Don't you *ever* repeat that man's name in front of me again, mister!" Ma stomped her foot indignantly. "You ain't sendin' for that quack, not while I got ary a breath left in me, you ain't! He *kills* babies! Even let his own mama waste away for her lack of hard cash to pay the bill," she said with a fire in her eye.

"I do have a little something saved back. You *know* I'd give everything I have in the world to get Mandy on her feet again."

"You got acorns in your ears, man? If you send for that snake charmer, you better start makin' her bury box right now," she said, shaking her head. "She needs a *real* doctor. The kind with school learnin' behind his shingle like old Doc Latham back in Philadelphee. Not some sorry, old goat, play-actin' with leeches and a bottle of jalap."

"So if we don't send for Dr. Bradl–"

"Watch your mouth, man. I done told you once!"

"Well what in hell do you want me to do? Take her clear to Philadelphia?"

Unaccustomed to hearing swear words escape from Jeremy's mouth, Ma stood astonished at his vehemence. "Not quite that far. I was thinkin' just east of here, to the big river. To Mt. Pleasant. Jonathan passes through there when he drives his hogs to market. He's got right friendly with the Quakers settled in them parts. Says they've built 'em a big meetin' house and just put up a real hospital, too. Them Quakers might be a funny bunch, but at least they put their backs behind their conviction."

"Could they help Mandy?"

"That's what I'm a-countin' on," Ma said with a nod. "Jonathan says a new doctor just come to town from that Quaker lunatic asylum up north of Philadelphee."

"Mandy's no lunatic!"

"*I* know that. And you know that, but I'm a'feared she don't know that, son," Ma said with a pat on Jeremy's shoulder. "Jonathan says this new doctor aims to set up a piece of that new hospital for treatin' addled souls beat down by this harsh land. And if there's ary a soul more addled than this poor child, or more beat down, I'd sure hate to meet her, myself."

"Could Mandy stand a trip like that?"

"Hard to say one way or t'other. But I can tell you one thing, sure. She ain't gonna last much longer, wastin' away here."

"Then I'd better start packing," he said with firm resolve, standing straight and slapping his sides. "I better go speak to Willie. See if he'd mind staying on here to tend the farm till I get back."

"Them two lovebirds already got that all figger'd out."

Dear Ellie Mae,

I have your letter and am so glad to hear that you wintered pleasantly with your son's family. You amaze me, friend. All that you have endured, to remain so undaunted still. A new adventure, indeed. I am sure that your Riverstop will prove a great success.

Surely you do not mean it, when you say you are glad to have your daughters away. I look at these two of mine— budding Lizzie, who will be a woman wed much before I can bear it, and my sweetest Leesha. I know that a mother can never be happy at such departures. And here is my own baby, toddler Elijah, showing our Buddy how to clap his hands very loudly. It is a contest, with a winner hard to declare, as both are quite deafening. Do such as these make me old or keep me young, Ellie? At least Elijah has gotten over his jealousy of Caitlin's new babe.

Can you credit how many bodies warmed this cabin the winter through? It seemed full to the rafters last winter with but my own seven children. That was before the arrival of my baby sister Zannah and niece Caitlin, not to mention Cait's little passenger who turned out to be Buddy. Would that Sister Rose could have seen this, her very first grandchild.

But now I must speak of disturbing matters.

It is beyond the powers of my mind to comprehend it, though the proof is before my eyes. I shy away from the horror of the realization. My sister, Zannah, a child of mind but woman in body, is in a family way. How could this be? What manner of person could do such a thing to this simple soul?

How long was this knowledge in my mind before I could look upon it and truly see it? I have spoken to my husband today, taking him well away from the cabin, and his reaction was as I imagined. At that moment I was glad to be ignorant of the identity of the scoundrel, for there was blood in his eye.

I convinced him not to go to her in that state, but to let me talk with her quietly.

It was for naught, as she seems to know less about her circumstance than do we. I am not sure she took the meaning of my words at all. But she wanted so to answer in order to please me. "God makes the flowers and the trees and the buds," she said, smiling her innocent smile. It sickens me to think of it, that someone could be so evil. Would that she had stayed at home in Connecticutt and never come to me after dear Sister Rose's passing.

Zach goes on about how her innocence has been betrayed and blood must be let, but it is Zan and the babe we need think of now. I must stop my mind from compiling these lists of neighbors and passersby. I loathe myself for some of the thoughts which have crossed my mind. Under the circumstances, I have no idea when her time will come but can only guess that it will most likely be middle to late summer.

On a happier note, our oldest son Nate has asked for the hand of Miss Chastity Cleghorn. My first boy is to wed! I believe I had mentioned to you that he was calling on a young woman at the Merrifield Settlement. We had her family to dinner on Sunday last to discuss plans for a June wedding.

They are constructing a church there, preparing for the arrival of a new pastor. This will be the first wedding in that structure after it is completed. The girl is strikingly beautiful, but so quiet that I know not what to make of her. I fear that she is dimwitted, as she has not said more than a dozen words in my presence. Nate seems content to look into her eyes and bask in the glow of her smile. Zach assures me they speak volumes by this method.

The rest of her family seems of normal intelligence, so I should put this idea aside, says he. In truth she has an older sister who seems quite quick-witted and clever of tongue. Ivy is making the wedding gown her sister will wear and most everything else for the occasion, being quite clever with her fingers.

My husband is full of a new project, a thing which does bring a distracted look of satisfaction to his face of late. He and the boys have drawn plans for a lumbering mill on the river, using the water power and the saw blade that brother-in-law Garth brought us from back east (along with sister Zan and his wayward daughter, Caitlin after losing our dear, sweet Rose).

Nate is to be instrumental in the building and running of said mill. The other boys are not happy with the idea that they are to do the farm work while Father and Brother work elsewhere. If it has water, Simeon would be there, as you recall of my second son, whose manners you did admire. Christian, in his turn, would be tied to nothing, choosing to wander and explore merrily, as did my rambling, Irish "Da." My Levi, however, I dare not let far from my sight in any endeavor, lest he find new mischief and bring harm onto himself.

I wonder how Garth's sons do without their mama Rose to watch over them, to help shape the men they are growing into.

And there, I come back again to my dear, departed Rose. All roads lead me there of late, friend. Is my sister looking down on us, happy with the child I helped her Caitlin bring into this world? Would that I could chide her on her erroneous prediction that our Buddy would be a girl child. And now, is she seeing what has befallen our special little sister, the one we vowed to protect from those who could not understand her condition of mind or those who would not care?

Garth, while he has his sons for comfort, could he have protected Zannah better than I? If not for Caitlin's embarrassing situation, child on the way and no husband, their journey here might never have taken place, and our trusting Zannah might yet be unmolested. But, then, we would have never known our little Buddy.

I cannot puzzle it out but only know that all loss ultimately balances against gain. In that way the scale does not tip. And so, mayhap, Rose is smiling at things I cannot yet see.

Zach says that we shall come down your way soon. Mr. Snow has asked him to retrieve that ram, as Harvey is refusing to pay the balance owed on the beast. He claims it is not of an acceptable quality, having done his ewes no good whatsoever. Zach is to bring back either the animal or the monies due. It was that same animal which first brought us together, Ellie Mae, after I arrived in this wilderness, having left behind all that was familiar to me but husband and children. I was so afraid on that day of our cabin-raising. And there you were, a person with all the confidence and knowledge I needed to keep all seven of my children alive in this new land. If you had not been north looking for a ram on that fateful day, we might never have met, you and I.

I will travel with him, Ellie, and we shall help you with your new venture! Daughter Lizzie can see to things here for a short while. Zach will help to work on your repairs, while you and I can set things to rights inside. We are to meet again, friend! I hardly can wait for the day to arrive!

Yours,

Libby

Chapter 3

Working on Riverstop
May 1818

"Can I trust you girls to get a little work done, or are you gonna hold a gabfest all day?" Zach Howard teased his wife Libby and her dear friend Ellie Mae from atop his horse. "Once I get all this ram business tied up, I aim to hightail it right back here and start on that roof." Zach gave his wife a wink, then he turned and headed his horse northwest. "Make sure you get all your gossip out of the way before I get back."

Ellie Mae and Libby stood at the doorway of a ramshackle cabin near the banks of the Clear Fork River and gave each other's hands a squeeze, as they waved goodbye to Zach. From all appearances, the cabin had been long abandoned.

"Don't you worry your head about us," Ellie hollered to his disappearing back. "Me and Lib'll have this place spit-shined before you make it across the Black Fork."

Libby turned and walked into the cabin to survey the extent of the rubble facing the two women. "If you plan to have this whole mess cleaned up in one day, my friend, I don't think we'll have time for any distracting conversation whatsoever."

"Oh, Lib, I was just joshin' with your man," said Ellie, kicking at a pile of rags. Her kick dislodged something alive ensconced in the center of the ratty mess. A furry body appeared, scurried across the filthy floor, and disappeared into a hole gnawed through the cabin's south corner.

"Godalmighty, we got us some live occ-y-pants!" said Ellie, grabbing for the broom. She started pounding at the pile, and as she did so, five more little fur-balls began to run helter-skelter around the cabin. "Grab that shovel and start kabongin', Lib! We got us a whole litter!"

"Oh, my heavens," Libby danced, trying to avoid all the little creatures scurrying at her feet. She glanced around the dingy cabin in search of the shovel, keeping one eye on the floor at all times to make sure none of those creatures tried to run up her limbs. Spying the shovel, she picked it up, closed her eyes gave a tentative smack at the floor.

"Over there, Lib! There goes another critter! Get him! Pound it a good one!"

Libby put as much power into her swing as she could muster. But when she felt the dull thud of her shovel finding its mark, she dropped the handle and ran for the doorway. Ellie Mae, busy whacking at furry rodents with her broom, didn't even notice her friend's escape from the filthy cabin, astir with baby chipmunks.

* * * * *

Zach had hit the trail at first light in order to arrive at the Thompson farm before midday, where he hoped to find Harvey at his nooning table. He didn't want to waste precious time hunting him down in the fields, for Zach intended to expedite this errand for his Cranberry Corners' neighbor and head right back to Ellie's Riverstop, so he could get to work on her collapsing roof before too late in the afternoon. With the feel of rain in the air, he had no intention of camping out in the open for another night.

After finding the Thompson place in such neglected condition on his trip down the previous September, when he made delivery of the Merino ram for Vern Snow, Zach wasn't too sure how he might find conditions this time. At least the corn liquor should have given out by now, so that fact alone ought to have caused Harvey to emerge from his grief-driven, drunken rampage after the death of his son.

Life does, after all, go on. And if a body intends to survive in this back country, spring means time to plant.

"Hell-ooo the house!" Zach rode his mount to the Thompson porch and dismounted. He heard a scuffling of chairs inside before a mousy-looking woman stuck her head out the door.

"Is Harvey to home?"

"Why he's... ah... out behind the barn... last I knew," stammered the woman, squeezing her buxom body out the door opened just a crack. Quickly she closed it behind herself.

"Guess I'll head back there, then," Zach answered, tying his reins to the porch rail. "Got some business with the ol' boy."

"Ain't you the one who come by here last fall bringin' that mean buck sheep?"

"That was me. Looks like you cleaned this place up since then," Zach offered.

"Damn that critter! Comes runnin' up from behind and tries to kill me every time I get anywheres near him, he does."

"I didn't notice any lambs running around in the front pasture when I rode up. That buck did earn his keep, didn't he?"

"Can't get near that damn buck sheep. Guards those ladies of his so close, a body can't even take a bucket of feed into the pen without fearin' for her life!"

"How many lambs did he throw?"

"Too many to count, that's for sure. And twins to every female but one, on top of it. Blasted buck sheep–"

"That's all I needed to hear," said Zach, heading around the corner of the cabin toward the barn.

Once he disappeared from sight, the cabin door flew open and Harvey stormed out, grabbing the woman's arm. "Why did you yabber on about lambs? Don't you know he's here to collect for that goddamn buck? When are you gonna learn to keep your trap shut, woman?" he said, raising his hand above her head.

Before he could land the blow, he heard Zach returning. "Thought I heard voices back here," Zach said, stepping out

from beside the cabin and up onto the porch corner. "Good to see you," he said, offering his hand to Harvey and waiting there for the other man to accept his greeting.

Harvey's grip on the woman's arm eased and his touch appeared to change into a caress of sorts. "Well if it ain't Zach

Howard in the flesh," he said with a big grin, taking the other man's hand and pumping it hard. "I come in a mite late for noonin'," he said, doffing his hat and swiping his arm across his brow. "Just finished plantin' a piece of corn yonder," he said, pointing his hat in the opposite direction from which Zach had emerged. "Cleared it late last fall. Ought to produce a bumper crop on new ground. Make another five, six gallons of corn juice, at least," he said with a snigger. "I'd offer you a snort, but I'm plumb out till after harvest," he said, replacing his hat.

"I can't afford the time to sit and jaw right now," said Zach, reaching into his pocket and pulling out a piece of paper.

"So, how's life been treatin' you an youren?"

"Fair to middlin'. We stayed warm enough through the cold months and had sufficient food laid by to line our stomachs. I'd say we came through winter in respectable shape."

"Glad to hear it," said Harvey. "Glad to hear it." He watched Zach carefully unfold the paper he held. "Say, why don't you come out back and take a look at the bull I got loan of to service my heifers," Harvey said, taking Zach by the shoulder with the aim of steering him toward the barn. "I'd like your opinion. He's a big 'un, he is, and hung lower than any bull's got a right to be. But I'm thinkin' he might be too much animal for a first breedin' heifer. I'd like to hear how you judge him."

"I think you know more about breedin' bulls than I do," said Zach with a smile. "Besides, I got a roof that needs fixin' before rain sets in. By the look of those clouds, it don't appear I have time to spare for studying livestock," Zach said, handing the paper to Harvey. "Vern Snow asked me to stop by and give you this while I was in the vicinity."

Harvey scowled and looked over the bill of sale.

"He expects me to bring back the full amount you still owe on that ram," Zach said, "provided you were satisfied with the offspring he threw."

"Well, that does raise an in-ter-estin' question," said Harvey, scratching at his ear. "Seems that ram up and died on me, before he got all my ewes serviced. So he didn't prove to be much of a bargain at all, now, did he."

The woman began to shift her weight from one foot to the other while she twisted at her apron strings with both hands. Harvey saw her movement from the corner of his eye. "Sophie, go inside and fetch us a drink from that gourd hangin' by the mantle." He looked over at Zach and gave a wink. "I do have a little straight Kentucky bourbon saved back for special."

Sophie made a beeline for the door, closing it firmly behind herself as she disappeared inside.

"Don't bother wasting your good whisky on me. I've got a roof to climb yet today," Zach said, leaning his foot against the porch rail. "Now we were talking about that ram of Vern Snow's. From what your woman told me, that ram must have been around long enough to service a good number of those ewes," Zach answered. "And to my way of thinking, one that threw mostly twins ought to satisfy any man into seeing the value of such a sire—whether he's still alive or not."

"Can't argue with that kind of sense, now can I," said Harvey turning on a charming smile. "Oh hell, come on in, Zach, I'll dip into what I got saved back for a new plowshare to settle up my debt with Snow," he said, smacking Zach firmly on the back in a gesture of friendship. "Least I can do for a friend like you who come all this way to collect, now, ain't it?"

The two men walked amicably through the door and into the darkened cabin. "Say, what kind of roofin' job did you get yourself bamboozled into clear down in these parts?"

"Old friend of mine took over a homestead by the river. Needs a hand with some of the heavy work," he said giving a vague enough answer. He noticed that a nearly empty stewpot hung at the hearth, and the dishes sitting on the table showed signs that they'd already held a meal for two. "I've got my own planting to finish up, too, so I don't have a lot of time to waste,"

Zach said. "I'd be grateful if we could get this collection business done with so we can both get back to our work."

Harvey pulled a sack from under the bed, counted out a number of bills, then handed them to Zach.

Zach took a hard look at the currency, turning over each bill to scrutinize the writing on it. "Don't know as the bank that put out this paper is a going concern any longer," he said with a steady look. "So many of 'em are goin' belly up these days, you can't trust any kind of paper. Most of it ain't worth the ink that printed it." Zach handed the money back to Harvey. "Besides, Vern asked me to bring back the ram or hard cash. Nothing else'll do."

Harvey grabbed the fistful of money, shoved it back in the sack and threw it underneath the bed. Then he flung back the bed-ticking, ripped open one end, and retrieved a smaller money-pouch that had been stuffed inside the mattress. He grumbled under his breath the entire time, as he carefully counted out the precious silver coins. "Here's your *hard cash*," he said with a surly edge to his voice. "Better count it up again, so we both know we're all settled up square," he said with a broad sweep of his hand. "Hell, we don't want a measly thing like a few dollars to come between friends, now, do we?" he said in a sarcastic tone.

Zach deftly counted the coins, dropped them into an inside vest-pocket, and gave Harvey his hand. "We sure enough wouldn't," said Zach. "And I'll shake on it, too, *friend*." He turned to leave the cabin, but before exiting, he stopped and tipped his hat in a parting gesture to the woman hovering by the dirty table. "Afternoon, ma'am."

Zach strode across the porch, then swung up, into the saddle. The animal turned and headed out the lane before he even had himself firmly settled in both stirrups.

Harvey hurried to the edge of the porch, hesitating at the top step, then he smacked his hat against his knee. "Goddamn blabbermouth. Now I'm out a new plowshare till next year." He continued to mumble under his breath, then, as if making a sudden decision, he stood straight and headed back into the cabin. "Woman, get some vittles ready for travelin'. Fast! I don't aim to turn another acre with that worn-down excuse for a plow," he said, grabbing his gun, powder horn, and lead pouch from their hanging places over the door. He headed toward the barn. "I'll track after that bastard and wait till nightfall if I have to," he mumbled. "He's got to sleep sometime."

* * * * *

Zach balanced himself carefully atop the ridgepole at the far end of Ellie Mae's roof and hoisted up a bundle of the wooden shakes he'd brought along for fixing her cabin. "You girls get another pallet ready to tie on down there. I want to close in this end I got stripped off before dark sets in good," he said, unfastening the bundle of shakes and dropping the rope back down to Libby and Ellie Mae. "Looks like we might be in for a storm. And I *don't* aim to sleep with a pot over my head to keep off the rain."

The girls caught the returning rope, fastened on the second pallet of wood shakes and watched as Zach hoisted it up and balanced it carefully between cross beams. "Sure glad we didn't have to replace all these beams," he said. "At least they're still good and stout." He lowered the rope once more. "I need another rib pole, now, Lib."

"You be careful up there Zachary Howard," Libby fussed at him from below. "I do not intend to raise fatherless children."

"Don't you know I'm half squirrel, woman? Why I could jump from beam to beam up here if I had a mind to," he said, feigning a half-hop.

"Noooo! I can't look!"

"Lib, why don't you go on back and tend to that fire. He's just tryin' to get a rise out of you, you know," said Ellie Mae, fastening the rope to a long pole that would hold the shakes securely down on the roof. "I'll keep helpin' Zach over here." She watched her friend amble back toward the fire, mumbling under her breath as she went.

77

Libby gave the fire a tentative poke with a long stick, then she threw on a few more of the rotten pieces of the old, bark roofing from the refuse heap. Smoke billowed as she did so, and she stepped back, wiping a sooty hand across her forehead.

Back around the other side of the cabin Ellie Mae hollered up, "Hey Zach, you want me to climb up there and give you a hand'?"

"We don't need any ol' woman falling off a roof, do we?"

"Who you callin' old? I can climb good as you can. Good as any man!"

"Don't doubt it for a minute, Ellie. You're spry as any woman I know. But I think it's best if you girls stay down on the ground. I can do what's needed up here," he said, unfastening the rib pole and laying it beside the shakes. "If this weather takes a notion to break sooner than I expect, I just might take you up on that offer, though," he said. "I would be obliged if you'd send up a drink of water, Ellie. This job works up a powerful thirst."

"Comin' right up." Ellie made a beeline for the river and filled a bucket half full. She set a gourd dipper inside, then carried the bucket back over to the rope and tied the bail on with a tight knot. "Haul 'er up, Zach. Water on the way."

After he pulled the bucket up, he stood tall and gazed across the adjacent clearing while he took a long, cool draught. He watched for movement in the underbrush along its border. About an hour before, Zach had spotted Harvey Thompson trying to conceal himself over there. Rather than confront the man, he intended to concentrate on the task at hand and get this part of the roof finished before nightfall or storm—whichever came first.

"Ellie, I want you girls to stay close to the cabin till I get down off this roof."

"Gettin' jittery up there all of a sudden? You ain't plannin' to fall off, are you?"

"Just mind what I said. I've got my reasons for keeping you

two close." He lowered the bucket back to the ground. "Thanks for the drink."

Ellie untied it and headed to the porch, where she deposited the bucket and dipper beside the door. "You makin' any headway with that burn pile, Lib?" she hollered to her friend back by the trash fire.

Libby stood in a trance-like state, staring at the flames.

"Libby. Hey, Lib! You in there girl?"

"Hmmmm? Oh, goodness, I must have been dozing on my feet. Forgive me, Ellie, I do believe I'm about done in."

"I thought that husband of yours wasn't skittish up high."

"He's not. He's fearless where heights are concerned."

"Well for someone who's fearless, he sure is actin' mighty curious."

"How do you mean?"

"Told me we both better stay close to the cabin till he comes down off that roof."

"I'm sure he has his reasons," Libby said, trying to smooth back hair that had escaped from her bun. In doing so, she managed to smudge even more soot across her face and neck. "I must look a fright," she said, anchoring the fly-away hair. "A nice, hot bath would certainly feel wonderful about now."

"I'm afraid all I can offer is a dunk in the river, Lib. But it's god-awful cold for bathin' in this time of year."

"Do you suppose we could put a pot of water on to heat, so we can at least wash up a bit before we retire tonight?"

"Only got the one big pot. And it's full of supper stew right now. But once we've et, I'll heat us up some washin' water."

"Just look at me." She tried brushing away ashes that had landed on the bodice of her dress, which itself served as a nighttime chemise underneath her skirts. But since removing her apron earlier, after she'd spilled spirits of turpentine all over it while scrubbing clean the hearth, she had no protective covering left to shield her clothing from grime. In trying to wipe off the soot, she only managed to make her chemise even dirtier. "How can I sleep in this, now that I've gotten it so dirty?" she asked her practical friend. "Wouldn't you know, I didn't think to bring another thing along. I guess with just one apron and one night-dress I didn't plan very well for a work party, did I."

"Don't fret your head over it, Lib. I got a spare bedgown you can wear, once we get ourselves cleaned up for sleepin'," said Ellie, giving her friend a pat on the shoulder. "I got to admit, I'm powerful tired myself. But we still got an hour or more of work left, before we can eat and take to our sleepin' pallets."

"I suppose I had better go check on our stew," said Libby. "Should I mix up some corn cakes to go with it, do you think?"

"Good idea. Got me some fresh-ground meal just last week. Ol' Zeke brought it by. It's in that keg by the table. I reckon I'll have to use them kegs for stools, till I can get some proper benches and chairs built."

The girls remained busy tending to dinner preparations and feeding the trash fire, while Zach continued work on the roof—all the while keeping one eye cocked toward the edge of the woods.

* * * * *

"Can't remember when I ever had such a tasty dinner," Zach said, pushing himself away from the table while he picked at his teeth with a sliver of wood from a shingle. "Mighty fine stew, Ellie. Mighty fine." He moseyed over to the window and stood looking across the meadow, as the girls cleared the table and cleaned up the dinner mess. "River-runners in these parts will sure have a good thing with you on the job. That's a fact." He could make out little through the darkness, straining to catch any hint of movement in the underbrush.

"Why, Zachary Howard, I could take that comment to mean you have not had tasty meals at my table," Libby said with a seemingly hurt tone in her voice.

"Lib, that's not at all what I said, and you know it."

"Why do you assume that Ellie made that stew and not I?"

"Because, my little cinder, I've never known you to make a venison stew with garlic in it, since I told you I didn't like the stuff. But I have to admit, it tasted better that way than I ever thought it could," he said, giving her a little swat on the behind.

"Guess I got used to putting garlic in everything Harvey ate," Ellie explained. "Got to be so's it's habit to use it, now," she said, washing up the last dish. "That Harvey did like his garlic." She handed the bowl to Libby, who dried it and stacked it inside the other bowls sitting on the shelf Zach had mounted for her beside the cabin's only window.

Libby gave the towel a shake and carefully smoothed it over the piece of sapling attached to the edge of the wash stand. "Why did you call me your little cinder?"

"Take a gander in that looking glass, and you'll know why," he said, pointing to the piece of broken mirror that hung above the wash stand.

Libby had to rise on tiptoe in order to see, since they had mounted the mirror high enough for Ellie's use. "Oh my goodness, I do look a mess," she said, wiping at the sooty smudge across her cheek.

"I'll put some more water on to heat, now that we got supper cleaned up," Ellie said, tossing the dirty dish water out the door. She picked up the bucket of fresh water still sitting there, poured some into the cook pot, then went to the fireplace and hung it on the trammel hook. "I'll bank this up a might, so's it'll heat faster," she said, giving the fire a poke and throwing on another log. "Then we can have us a real good wash."

"While you girls get yourselves fixed up for sleep, I believe I'll take a little mosey around outdoors," Zach said, stretching his arms to their full length and giving a big yawn. "Got a few things to check on out there, before we bed down for the night." He walked over to the door. "Make sure you spread those sleeping pallets out on this side, where we've got a solid piece of roof over our heads," he said, pointing to the newly shingled third of the cabin. "It looks like that rain might break anytime, and I sure don't cotton to sleeping in a wet bed."

He exited the cabin and closed the door behind himself, but not before he took his rifle from beside the door and carefully checked the load.

The girls busied themselves shaking blankets and smoothing out beds, while they waited for the water to heat. "Sorry I don't have a proper bedstead for you and Zach," Ellie said. "Guess we'll all have to make do sleepin' on the floor."

"No excuses are necessary, my friend. Nary a one," said Libby, fluffing up the feather pillows she had brought Ellie Mae for a house-warming gift. "Why, after the condition we found this place in, I can scarcely believe we got it cleaned up enough to eat in here, let alone make up our beds." Libby stood up stiffly and rubbed at the small of her back. "Ouuuuu, I must say, I certainly do feel my age this evening, though."

"You wait here. I got just the thing for aches," Ellie said, heading for the door. "Maybe tomorrow we can tote the rest of my crates out from under that covered-up cart and stash 'em in here with the rest o' my belongin's." She ducked outside.

While she was gone, Libby pulled the pot away from the fire and tested the water temperature with her little finger. Evidently satisfied, she carried the pot over to the wash stand,

removed her skirts and began to undo the ties of the stomacher, which held her cumbersome breasts in tightly.

A few moments later Ellie returned with a little crock jar in her hand. "Got this stuff from Sam Justice a few years back. Claims it's good for healin' cuts and easin' soreness in man or beast," she said. "Here, rub a little of this in and see if it don't help. Mind now, a little bit goes a long way." She handed the jar to Libby, who held it up to her nose and gave a sniff.

"Oh, my lands! It does have quite a smell," she said, wrinkling her nose.

"Believe it or not, Harvey always had a likin' for that smell."

"I think learning to like this would take getting used to."

"Give it a try. You'll be surprised how good it feels after it sinks in."

"If you say it'll help, then I guess I have nothing to lose... except perhaps my husband, once he gets a whiff of this balm." She squeezed out the wash cloth, relishing the warm water as she did so. After washing herself within the modest confines of her chemise, she took a very small amount of the ointment and rubbed it into her low back. "Why, I think I can feel it beginning to work already!"

"Told you. It's good stuff." While Libby washed, Ellie walked over to her trunk, sitting just inside the door, and shuffled through its contents. "Here, Lib. I found that extra bed gown. She handed it to Libby, who held it up to herself. "Looks too long for you. But we can tie it up at the waist if you want. Make it a mite easier to walk."

"There's no need. I don't intend to do much walking this night, unless I happen to walk in my sleep... Heaven forbid," she said, slipping out of her filthy chemise and quickly pulling the clean gown over her head, sliding her arms into the long sleeves. "This is beautiful handwork, Ellie. Did you do this embroidery?"

"Nope. Was a gift from my sister Tabby, when I took up with Harvey. She sent it clear from Philadelphee. I always thought it too fussy for a plain woman like me, but Harvey sure had a hankerin' to see me in it," she said, closing the trunk. "Course, I never did have it on long if he had anything to say about it." She removed her apron and readied to take a wash herself.

"How in the world can you even talk about Harvey after all that's happened between you two?" Libby asked, carefully removing each hairpin from her bun to let down her hair.

"T'ain't easy gettin' a man out of your system after livin' with him so long, you know," Ellie said, squeezing the washing cloth in the warm water and wiping off her face and arms. "Just 'cuz he turned so hateful and quit lovin' me, don't mean I quit lovin' him."

"Heavenly days! You mean to say you still have feelings for that man? He had you put in jail, Ellie Mae!"

"I know he warn't perfect by a long shot, but he did have his good points," she said with a smile. "Course not too many folks could see 'em for all his blusterin' ways."

"Why, I do believe if he were to walk through that door and make amends," Libby said, waving the hairbrush she'd been using toward the cabin's entrance, "it sounds as though you'd actually take the scoundrel back!"

"Don't know as I'd go quite that far," Ellie said, rinsing the cloth out once more and giving it a final squeeze. "But I got to admit, times I sure do miss havin' his strong arms 'round me." Finishing with her wash, Ellie gave her chemise a good brushing with a damp towel, then she proceeded to let down her hair in preparation for sleep.

They heard Zach stomp up onto the porch and give a firm knock on the door. "Everybody decent in there?"

"Sure enough are," answered Ellie, "and we got clothes on, too," she sniggered.

"That was good, Ellie Mae, very good," Libby giggled and lowered herself to the sleeping mat she and Zach would be sharing this night. "You know, I think that ointment has helped already. It's feeling quite warm."

Zach thumped into the cabin, then closed the door firmly behind himself, making sure to pull in the latch-string. "Don't want any uninvited callers this night," he said, walking over to the pallet his wife occupied. He purposefully laid the rifle next to the blankets on his side. "God almighty, what is that odious smell?" he asked, sniffing all around till he zeroed in on Libby. "Don't tell me that stink is comin' from you, Lib?"

"All right, I won't tell you."

He came closer and gave another whiff. "Did you tangle with a polecat?"

"It doesn't smell *that* bad now, surely."

"Who are you callin' Shirley?" he teased.

"I give Lib some salve to smooth out the soreness in her low back," Ellie explained. "Sam Justice swears by the stuff. Says it's good for whatever ails a body… man or beast, and I got to agree with him."

"Maybe I should send her out to sleep with the beasts, then," he said, sitting down to untie his boots.

"Zachary Howard, you wouldn't!" Libby sat up and tucked her arms indignantly across her ample chest while he slowly removed each boot and sat it carefully beside his gun. "You're making a mountain out of a molehill. This ointment does not smell *that* bad," she said, beginning to fuss with the blankets. "I think I might even develop a fondness for this pungent aroma."

"I suppose a body could get used to just about anything… given enough time," said Zach, pulling off his gallowses, one shoulder at a time. "You can put that candle out now, Ellie, unless you're waiting for a peep show when I drop these britches.

"Wouldn't be the first time I seen a man in his birthday suit." Ellie stretched over and blew, putting the cabin into darkness. "'Sides, if you seen one, you seen 'em all," she said, lying back and getting comfortable in her bedding.

Zach removed his pants in the darkness, deliberately laying them out beside his boots. He gave his shirt a cursory brush down, then snuggled in beside Libby, who still hadn't moved from her sitting position. "You gonna sit up all night, woman?"

"Only until you apologize."

"Apologize? What do I have to apologize for?"

"For insulting me."

"Insulting you? When did I insult you?"

"When you said I smelled like a skunk."

"Oh, Lib, you know I didn't mean anything by it," he said, rubbing the small of her back softly with his big hands. "Come on down here now. That's it. Right next to me."

"You won't put me out with the horse?"

"I won't put you out with the horse… 'less you want to go

out there to get some privacy," he whispered.

"You two gonna carry on all night, or are we gonna get some sleep in here?"

"We're all settled down now, Ellie. All's forgiven." Zach gave her backside a pinch.

"Ooooo! Zachary Howard! Now you quit that!"

"Mebbe *I* should go out with the beasts," said Ellie.

"You'll do no such thing," said Libby, giving Zach a swat.

"All right. We better get some sleep. Morning comes quick enough as it is." Zach rolled over and pulled the blankets tightly up to his chin with one hand, and with the other he gave his rifle a pat, pulling it closer to his side.

"Good night, Ellie Mae."

"Good night, Lib. Hope you can keep that man of yours in line over there."

"It is a trial. It certainly is."

"If either of you girls hears anything unusual, let me know right away, hear?"

"You did make certain that trash fire was out properly, did you not?" Libby asked.

"Just a pile of smoldering coals now, Lib. Nothing to fret over. Besides, it's gonna start raining soon."

After more adjusting of covers and a few coughs and yawns, they listened to rumbles of distant thunder, as the three, weary friends fell into an exhausted slumber.

* * * * *

Libby coughed herself awake to the acrid stench of smoke and thought immediately of the trash fire. Hadn't Zach assured her it should be out by now? Men! If you wanted a thing done right, you had to do it yourself. That was a fact.

Her back rebelled, as she struggled to sit. "Zach, wake up." She shoved at her husband's shoulder. "Zachary Howard, I have need of you. I am asphyxiating here," she said with a cough.

He gave a snort and rolled over, still sound asleep, sticking his nose into the pillow.

"Ellie? Are you awake?" She heard not a peep from her worn out friend, also apparently dead to the world on her night-time pallet. Libby hoisted herself up from her own sleeping mat and gave Zach another push, hitting his leg with her foot as she stood. She staggered toward the door in the murky darkness, tripping over the too-long bedgown.

He continued to sleep soundly.

Extending her hands in search of something to guide her, she walked only a few steps before stubbing a toe on the corner of Ellie's trunk. "Ooouch! That door has got to be close by here somewhere," she muttered, fumbling until at last she found it and lifted the latch bar to pull it open.

Finally, cool night air. She pulled the door open wide and sucked in a cleansing breath. As she continued to breathe, standing there in the doorway, it began to dawn on her that something felt amiss. She detected no noxious cloud of smoke out where she assumed the trash fire still smoldered. Strange. Why would it be smoky inside and not out here? The night felt cold and damp, with a haze of rain clouds blotting out all sign of moon or stars. Was she sleepwalking, perhaps? Was this really a dream? Is that why Zach and Ellie wouldn't waken? Her hand went to her face, feeling the chill of a slight drizzle. "How can I be dreaming if I'm getting wet?" she mumbled to herself.

She turned around to reenter the cabin and go check on her husband and best friend, when an arm reached out from the darkness, wrapped itself around her middle, and jerked her off her feet in one swift motion.

She froze only an instant, then called Zach's name in a blood curdling scream, just as another hand clapped over her mouth and face. Her screech came to an abrupt halt, with nothing more than a muffled squeal escaping lips clamped shut by filthy fingers.

"Keep yer peace, you good-for-nothin, murderin' Jezebel," said a bitter voice beside her ear.

The arm around her middle squeezed tighter, and, with hair flying forward into her face, she felt herself being carried away from the cabin. She hung like a rag doll, in the clutch of a ruffian, too terrified to kick or to put up any kind of a struggle.

"Didn't bargain on findin' you, when I come to reclaim my silver," said a voice with a growl that sounded suspiciously like Harvey Thompson's. "You may feel a mite chunkier, but I'd know that smell and that bed gown anywheres." Harvey pulled his mistaken victim behind Zach's buckboard, parked down beside the river where it still held the remainder of the new, wood shakes. He threw Libby to the ground, intending to tie and gag her with the harness until after he'd recovered his hard cash.

But as soon as Libby hit the ground, she opened her mouth to holler for Zach. This time she got the entire word out, before the giant hand smacked her into silence. The force of the blow came as such a surprise, it rolled her backward, and when she bumped up against the wagon wheel, she immediately reacted by rolling underneath the buckboard to try to evade further assault.

Back in the cabin the smoke grew thicker from the fire Harvey had ignited on the remainder of the old rooftop. In spite of a constant drizzle, the rotted section that Zach had not yet rebuilt burned readily. As pieces of the decayed and flaming shakes began to fall inside the cabin, Zach and Ellie finally awakened to the stench of burning bark and the sound of Libby's nearby screams in the darkness.

"Zachary! Zachary! He's trying to kill me!"

In his haste to reach his wife, Zach grabbed for nothing but his gun and ran.

"What in blazes?" Also in bare feet, Ellie stumbled her way toward the door, trying to avoid chunks of flaming bark as she hurried after Zach into the sodden night air. When she came to the clearing adjacent the river, the clouds parted just long enough for her to see Zach running toward the silhouette of a lanky man, reaching for a gun propped up against the wagon. "Good God, that's Harvey!"

Zach sprinted toward him at a dead run, swinging his gun around and holding on to the barrel with both hands. Before Harvey could hoist his own gun up to shoot, Zach overtook him, and with one powerful swing, he caught Harvey in the side of the head with the butt of his rifle.

The blow knocked Harvey off balance with such momentum he keeled over sideways and plunged into the spring-swollen river.

Ellie didn't wait to see if he rose up from the raging torrent to continue the fight; she ran for her terrified friend cowering underneath the wagon. "You all right, Lib?"

"He wanted to kill me, Ellie! I mean he wanted to kill *you!* He thought I was you!"

"Oh, Lib, I'm so sorry you got mixed up in this."

"He recognized your bedgown and the smell of your ointment on me, and he thought I was you! He wants to *kill* you, Ellie Mae! How can he even *think* of doing such a thing? How *can* he?"

"Got a powerful devil drivin' him, that's how," she said, rocking her best friend in her arms, both women sitting in mud beneath the wagon.

With the moment of crisis now past, Libby began to cry, and Ellie did her best to comfort her distraught friend. "It'll be all right, Lib. Honest. Why, you shouldda seen your Zach give him what for! Sent him ass over teacup into the drink, he did."

"Oh my Lord! Zachary! Is he all right?" she asked through a panicked sob.

"Don't fret about that man of yours. He can damn sure take care of his own self."

Libby looked down at herself and then over at Ellie. "Will you look at us out here in our night clothes? Your beautiful bed gown's a muddy mess. Look at it!" she said, wiping at the mud smeared down the front. "I ruined it for you. I just ruined it!"

"I don't give a Sam Hill about a blasted bedgown, when I almost lost my best friend in the whole world out here tonight!"

Ellie pulled Libby closer, nearly squashing her with a stranglehold of a hug and began to add her own tears to Libby's, now flowing freely once again.

A cleansing cry gave necessary release to both women, while they sat clutching one another, contemplating the "could-have-beens" of this night's ordeal. After a few minutes they both settled down, wiping at teary eyes with the backs of mud-smeared hands.

Then, without a word, they both looked at each other again and started to giggle.

"You look just like a black-eyed raccoon," Libby said, pointing at Ellie's mud-streaked face, giggling all the harder.

"You should talk," Ellie said, making a face, which caused them both to laugh so hard, the tears began to flow once again.

"Well, I'm glad someone has found amusement in this evening's altercation," said Zach coming up behind them.

"Oh, Zachary, you're all right! Is it safe to come out now? Is Harvey gone? Did you kill him? What happened?" Libby babbled, out of sheer relief.

"He won't bother anybody else tonight," Zach said, extending a hand to help each woman up in turn.

"You walloped him a good one. Yesss-siree Bob!"

"He never did come back up for air," Zach said, making sure he kept Libby between himself and Ellie Mae, since he finally realized he stood there in nothing but his night shirt. "I followed down the river a spell, but I found no sign of him anywhere."

"I don't *ever* want to go through anything like that again in my whole life," Libby said, clinging to Zach, and starting to cry all over again. She began to shiver from the dampness and the cold.

"We all lived through it. That's the main thing," Zach reassured. "Looks like you're gonna end up with a cracker-jack shiner, though," he said, touching the side of his wife's face with a gentle paw.

"Well, I reckon we got more cleanin' up, come mornin'," Ellie said, with a wave of her arm toward the cabin. The rotted section of roof had practically all fallen in by now, leaving the new, greener section intact, with nothing more than a few smoldering spots at its edges. "At least we got some cover left."

"The rain ought to put the rest of that fire out, soon enough," Zach said, looking up at the clouds, now beginning to pour their contents out with harder force. "By the looks of you two, I think you better get out of those wet gowns and into something dry before you both come down with the pips."

"Come on, Lib. I still got a clean house dress and one chemise left in that trunk, if the trunk's still in one piece, that is."

Libby tried to take a few steps, but her legs buckled underneath her. Before she could hit the ground Zach scooped her into his arms and carried her toward the smoking cabin. "I feel so foolish," she said, laying her head on his shoulder.

"Think nothin' of it, girl," Ellie tried to console. "You been dragged through a knothole backwards this night, you have."

"I don't understand how you can collect yourself so quickly to carry on, Ellie Mae. How can you do it?"

"Don't have much choice, way I see it," she said with resolve. "Got to give up or go on. And I sure ain't about to give up yet. Not by a long shot, I ain't!"

Dear Libby,

Thanks again for helping me with The Riverstop. You got to
thank Zach for me some more, too. He did so much hard work.
And for no better pay than a thank you and a couple good
meals. You told me to stop saying it but I can not leave it be.
You dern near come to harm in my stead. And at Harvey's
hands to boot. I do not like the idee of losing the best friend I
ever did have. Can not believe I still pined over that man.
Makes me spitting mad to think of it. He has not been seen in
these parts since he went into the drink. So I will waste no
more spit on him.

After you and your mister dropped me at sister Edie's I
spent but a day visiting round Justice. I sent Harmon over to
Harvey's. To see if that scoundrel found his way back home.
That woman of his give Harmon a earful, she did. Said she had
enough of farm life with a man who could not even see fit to
stay put. She lit back out for the tavern she come from. Over on
the Mt. Vernon Pike.

I caught up on all the Justice gossip while I was at Edie's.
Mostly about what went on at a kicking bee a couple months
back. Also found out I missed the wedding of my own nephews.
Willie and Tom, that would be. Willie wed the Harrison girl who
will make him a daddy right soon. And somehow Tom got his
self tied up with Clara Guthrie that very same day. Come as
quite a shock to everyone. Specially Tom.

On a sad note, it seems Amanda Harrison really has lost
her mind this time. She never did come out of this last strange
spell after losing her baby. Day of that kicking bee it was. I
guess you did not know about that. Now you do. She fell on the
suds and started laboring early. Babe come out a pasty gray
color. Never even drawed breath. Funny thing, Edie told me it
had webbed toes. Said she never saw such a thing before in all
her born days.

Edie had to make Jeremy see no one round here can help

that poor girl no more. He aims to take her to a nut house somewheres south along the big river. Quakers started one up for poor souls like her. Ones this hard land has sent round the bend.

There is also talk of that Rev. Longbottom dipping his wick in unlikely wax pots. Come out that he might of pushed Amanda into unseemly deeds while her husband was away to market last fall. She went daft for a spell after that Longbottom passed through on his last preaching round. Did nothing but stare into the fire for weeks. Would talk to no one. My sister said weeks after her mister finally come home she just woke up one morning and commenced to making flapjacks. Just like she had not missed a few months in between at all. Could not recall ary a thing after her man left home for New Orleens. Some say the herbs Edie give her finally did the trick to bring her back to her senses that time.

Jeremy was holding out hope she would do the same thing this time. Snap right out of it with one of Edie's potions. But my sister found Amanda wasting away so. She said something had to be done right quick before the poor thing withered away to nothing.

Now Lib, I got to say it. I know you do not like to think of a preacher doing evil deeds. But with this feller Longbottom there is no getting round it. Something struck me about one of your old letters. So I went back and read over them till I found what I was looking for. Your little nephew Bud got christened about the same time that egg likely got put in Zannah's nest. More even than that. When you asked her how it got there, I think you miss-took her reply. Seems to me she said God makes the flowers and the trees and the Buds, like your little Buddy there. Not like the buds of trees and flowers. Would be just like that Reverend to plant such a idee in her simple head. God putting a Bud of her own in her belly, she loved that boy baby so.

It is a hard thing. But it does have the ring of truth to it.

I did find out why Jason did not show up to help us out with the roof. Seems he went down with the grippe for over a week.

He is up and about again. Doing fine. I sent word for him to go get my sheep from down at Harvey's. By now they are likely back to my old homestead. Where they come from in the first place. Where they rightly belong. Along with that new ram what brought you and me together to start with.

Morning of the next day after youens left me at Edie's, I saddled up old Lucifer and rode my mule back here to get this Riverstop up and running. I was right grateful for you and Zach wanting to look out for my well-being. By taking me to my sister for safe keeping and all. But I am a business woman now. So I could not stay away from my Riverstop for long.

Business is good. I am feeding anywheres from 2 to 10 men most every day. Maybe Harvey will show up again where he is not wanted. Knowing him it would be when least expected. But I will not let fear of a varmint like him keep me from living my life. I choose to look ahead. Not quake in my boots over maybes and what ifs or dwell on the past.

Things are going good for me now, friend. I am a happy woman. It is a strange feeling. One I ain't had in a good long while. Got my mule back with me. Got my sheep back where they belong. Got the trunk of all my worldly goods. Got a fine business started. There is nary a soul who can reign me in.

Here comes some of my regulars. Back to work for me.

Your friend,

Ellie Mae

Chapter 4

Brother Michael
June, 1818

Jeremy slumped on the seat atop his creaky farm wagon, as he neared the familiar stretch leading to his father's farm in Fayette, County, Pennsylvania. But brother Paul ran the place now—likely a worse tyrant than Father had ever been.

Three, short years, and so many changes. Yet, no matter how humiliating the circumstances, Jeremiah felt he had to go back home. With Amanda committed at the Quaker hospital in Mt. Pleasant, and sister Sadie starting a life of her own, he needed help to run his farm and care for his twins. He needed Michael.

But would Michael come? That question repeated itself over and over.

"How can I convince him?" Jeremy mumbled the question.

No one heard but the horse.

What can I say that would make him give up his apprenticeship? Could a life in the wilderness appeal to someone with his talents? Someone with such a promising future building mansions and court houses and the like? Jeremy clucked to Patsy, urging the tired beast into a faster gait. He wanted to get this leg of his trip over with as soon as possible. After the emotional upheaval of leaving Amanda at Friend's Asylum, he did not relish the prospect of dealing with Paul in order to acquire Michael's release from the master stone mason who'd been training him for the past two years.

As head of the family now, Paul would have final say in the matter. Undoubtedly, he'd insist that Jeremy take their youngest brother John, or one of the twins, perhaps. He couldn't see Paul ever parting with one of the brainless brutes—Homer, or Brandon or Ezra. He depended on their strong backs and weak minds to do the grunt work around the farm. Paul couldn't begin to replace such pliable laborers at his bargain price of all they could eat and the day off to sleep on Sunday.

"I can't even think about taking one of them back," Jeremy spoke aloud. "A man needs his wits about him every minute just to stay alive out there."

Jeremy rounded an unfamiliar bend in the road and gazed over the valley spread before him trying to get his bearings. "Looks like the creek changed course again. Someone built a new bridge here." He climbed down from the wagon, stretched with a loud yawn, then moved forward to take Pasty by the halter and lead her across the bridge. Before he stepped out, he tested the flooring with a firm stomp. "Appears sound. All right, girl. Let's go," he said, giving the horse a tug. "We're almost there. Let's hope we can get back on the road to home by this time tomorrow."

Home. How could he face going home without his Amanda there. "Will you ever come back to me, my little yellow bird?" he whispered. His footfall on the bridge resonated with a dull thud, like the door at the hospital swinging closed behind him— the sound which haunted him still…

Five days earlier

…"Can you help her, doctor?"

"All I can tell thee, friend Harrison, is that we shall do everything possible to restore this poor soul to herself."

"How long will it take?"

"No one but the good Lord has the answer to that question."

"You will write as soon as she comes around, won't you?"

"Regular posts will inform thee of her progress. Keep in mind, these things do take time."

"I have two babes waiting for their mama to come back to 'em," Jeremy said to the bearded man in plain garb. "She has to get well. She just has to."

"All I can promise thee, friend, is that we shall give her the very best of care," said Dr. Kirkheiser, gently patting the hand of the emaciated woman curled up in the bed beside him. "The rest we must leave in the hands of the Almighty...."

...After crossing the bridge, Jeremy hoisted himself back onto the wagon seat and gave the reins a sharp flick. "Michael has to come home with me. He just has to."

* * * * *

"I don't know what to tell you, Jeremiah," said Melinda Harrison to the brother-in-law arriving on her doorstep just after supper. "Paul left for the stockyards in Pittsburgh early this morning," she said, patting the baby against her shoulder. "He's not likely to get home till late next week."

"I can't wait around that long," Jeremy said shaking his head. "Shouldn't have taken the time to come this far east as it is. But I didn't know what else to do." He twisted the hat he held in his hands. "I have to find some help."

"Come in here and tell me about it," Melinda said. "Did you have supper yet?"

"Just a few Johnny cakes a while back."

"The boys finished up all the potatoes and ham, but I have soup left. Would you like some of that?"

"A bowl of hot soup would hit the spot. I'd be grateful."

"Make yourself to home, while I put my little sweetheart down to sleep. I'll be right back," she said, making her way to the adjoining room, where Jeremy saw the corner of the same crib he'd used for Sadie.

"The place looks good," Jeremy told her when Melinda re-entered the kitchen. "You've made some changes, I see."

"A little touch here and there to make it feel more like home," she answered, bending to give the soup pot a stir, then pushing it back over the coals to reheat.

"It looks real nice. I like the curtains."

"Thank you. The boys didn't seem to mind, although Sadie had a little trouble adjusting to some of my changes."

Jeremy chuckled. "Why am I not surprised."

"We managed to work out our differences without too much trouble," Melinda said with a smile. "How has she done with you? Hasn't she been help enough?"

"Sadie's been a God-send," he said. "She's worked her heart out for us. But I can't impose on her any longer. She's married and expecting a child of her own. So, I can't ask her to stay on to keep looking after my twins. She needs to make a life with her own family, now."

"You have twins! How wonderful! And to think, Sadie actually found herself a man? I hardly can believe it. I shouldn't be surprised that someone from the backwoods would find her ways charming. I always did think her too straightforward for the men in these parts." She dipped a ladle full of soup into a bowl and set it on the table in front of him. "It would appear sending her west worked out well all around."

With his mouth full of soup, Jeremy didn't say a word.

"Who did you have a mind to take with you? Frankly, I don't see any of your brothers having the patience to care for children."

"I don't need anyone to take care of my girls. I can do that myself just fine," he said. "I raised up Sadie, didn't I?"

"Yes, you certainly did that." Melinda turned away and rolled her eyes.

"I was thinking Michael might consider coming west... to help with farm work for a while. After Mandy gets back home, he could strike out on his own. It's a whole new country out there. Before long, all the towns will be wanting fancy, stone courthouses and such laid up. It'd be a great place for a man of his talents to make a life for himself."

"I see," she said, busying herself stacking dried dishes in the cupboard. "Did you consider asking one of the older boys?"

"I thought about it. To be honest, I'm not sure any of the brutes really have what it takes to survive out there. No doubt you've seen how dependent they are on Paul."

"I certainly have, that. But if you want my opinion, I think he relies on them more than they depend on him, truth be told."

"In my mind, that just leaves Michael."

"Not one of the younger boys?"

"What do you think?"

"No, I suppose you're right on that account, too."

"How often does Michael get back home, here?"

"He generally shows up for dinner every Sunday. And eats like a horse when he does, I can tell you that. They don't feed him too well over at the Caspar's. Annabelle always has been on the stingy side, when it comes to portions for the help."

"What day are we in?" Jeremy asked, taking the last bite of soup. "After so much time on the road, one day blurs right into the next and you lose track."

"This is Tuesday. Tomorrow's market day up in Uniontown. You could take the baked goods up to sell for me and go see Michael at the same time, if you've a mind to. That way you could head home before week's end."

"What about Paul? The decision about Michael is his."

"I can take care of Paul. Just leave your big brother to me."

* * * * *

"Jems!" What in the world are you doing here?" Michael gave his long-lost brother a big, bear hug.

"Melinda sent me to town with her breads and cakes."

"I thought you were happily settled out West, in Ohio."

"I was. I mean, I am. But everything's turned upside down, right now."

"What's wrong?"

"It's Mandy. This whole thing has been too much for her, Mike. Too long a story to bend your ear with right now."

Michael swallowed hard at the mention of Amanda Jane. He could still see that tiny, yellow-draped figure, standing up so bravely, waiting to wed his older brother. At the time Michael had longed to be the one taking her as bride. But at 17, he understood Jems' point. She needed someone older and more capable of taking care of her.

"It comes to this, brother," Jeremy said. "I need help. Would you consider coming back to Ohio with me for a spell?"

"How did you know I was getting squirrelly here?"

"I didn't. Just figured you coming with me made the most sense all around."

"When do we leave?"

"Just like that? No questions, no hesitation? You're ready to go so fast?"

"I'm more than ready."

"Don't you have to get Mr. Caspar to release you from your apprenticeship?"

"Believe me, that will NOT be a problem."

"How long do you need to deal with your affairs and get packed?"

"Give me a day. By this time tomorrow I'll be saddled up and ready to ride!"

* * * * *

While Jeremy spent the rest of the day helping Michael tie up the loose ends of his life in Uniontown, PA, back at the Harrison farm, Melinda had been making some hasty preparations of her own. She'd sent a message to her cousin Violet (twenty-two, single, already considered an old maid) to come over and help her make strawberry preserves the following day. The only child of a domineering father and long-deceased mother, Violet spent her days trying to please a man incapable of satisfaction with anything in life—most especially his daughter. Melinda knew she had to try and rescue her cousin from a life of hopeless despair. Violet's father had made it known quite plainly around the community that his daughter would not be suitable for marriage—not now, or ever.

By the next morning, Melinda had her scheme in place. "Have you finished your breakfast, Jeremy?" she asked, gathering plates from the table. The three brutes and John stood by the mud-room door, pulling on overalls and boots, after finishing their morning meal. Food always came first with the Harrison boys, even before morning chores.

"Yes, "I'm done," Jeremy said, wiping his mouth with the back of his hand. "You can have this one, too." He put his plate atop the stack. "You want help with dishes?"

"I wouldn't hear of it," she said, plopping the stack of dirty plates into the sudsy pan on the sideboard. "Why don't you go spend a little time out there with the boys? You haven't had much of a chance to visit with any of them since you got here."

"I might do just that, if you're sure there's nothing you want me to do in here," he said, pushing himself away from the table. "Michael won't be here till after noon, so I may as well give the boys a hand with chores… and whatever else they have lined up to work at this fore-noon."

"Go right ahead. We'll have lots of female talk going on in here, anyway. Violet's coming over to help make preserves this morning. Getting out with the boys will give you a good excuse to escape all the 'women's work'."

Jeremy raised his eyebrows. "Then I'll take one more cup of coffee and get out of your hair," he said, refilling his mug from the big pot simmering over the hearth.

"Off with you, then. Oh, I forgot to tell the boys that noonin' will be a little later today, what with cooking preserves, and all. Would you let them know?"

"Happy to," Jeremy said on his way outside.

"Tell them I'll ring the dinner bell when I have everything ready," she said. Then, as an apparent afterthought she called, "Send John back in here around 10, would you? I'll have a job for him then."

"Will do." Jeremy walked out the back door toward the barn, just as Violet knocked on the front door of the parlor.

"Door's open," Melinda called from the sink. "Come on in!"

Violet timidly stepped through the entry, as if expecting someone to pounce from behind the door. She took a look all around, then stepped back out on the front porch and picked up the two buckets full of strawberries she'd already picked, carrying them carefully into the kitchen. She set them down next to the kitchen table, where their heady fragrance immediately filled the room.

"You picked already? Lordy, what time did you get up?"

"Pa eats his breakfast at five. So I figured we could get a head start if I went right out and picked. Maybe get finished up early. That way I can get back in time to fix Pa's noon meal," she said. "He doesn't like to eat late, you know."

Melinda dried her hands and turned to give her cousin a big hug. "Oh, my dear, dear Violet! Don't you worry your little head about that old tyrant anymore! Today we open the door of your prison for good!"

"What in the world are you talking about?"

"I'm talking about you... starting a new life, with a new husband in a new land."

"You've *got* to be kidding. You *know* Pa would never hear of such a thing. I'm bound to look after him for the rest of my days. You know that as well as I do."

"Not if I have anything to say about it, you don't."

"I don't understan–"

"I have a *plan*. Today, we get you ready for your wedding!"

"You mean we're not making jam?"

"No, we're not making jam.

"Then what about all these berries?"

"Well, we'll just make strawberry short cake for your wedding party, that's what. Because, this afternoon you're going to marry Michael."

"Michael?" Violet squeaked.

"He doesn't know it yet. But by tonight, you'll be Mrs. Michael Harrison, and on your way to a new life in Ohio, before that father of yours even has an inkling."

Violet began to look a little pale, so Melinda pulled out a chair. Violet sat down with a thud. "Ohio?"

"Ohio. You'll be free of that old geezer forever."

Violet breathed heavily through a veil of tears, "I think I need a cup of tea."

By the time Violet regained her composure, Melinda had laid out the whole plan to her. She knew Violet had pined after Michael for years, never daring even to hope she could escape her prison, let alone win his heart. So Melinda had taken matters into her own hands to play matchmaker.

For the next hour, as the girls cleaned strawberries, Melinda talked, while Violet listened. By 9 a.m., when baby Pauline awoke from her morning nap, the berries sat in three bowls, cleaned, sliced and ready to spoon atop cake. Violet had the first pot full they'd cleaned, simmering over the fire, so at least some preserves found their way to her father's table. In her own mind, she still had to justify her morning's time and labor.

While Melinda nursed the baby, Violet stirred up two short-cakes. Once in the reflector ovens at the hearth, she began cleaning up the mess.

"I'll finish getting things ready here," Melinda said as she changed Pauline into a dry saque, "then you can head back home to gather your things. I'll send John over with the cart to bring you back here before noon."

"No. Pa will be coming in to eat by then, and if I'm not there he'll get suspicious. Let me fix his dinner and see him back out to the fields. Then you can send John after noonin' time." Violet had a nervous shake in her voice. "Oh, what if he finds out!"

"Get hold of yourself, Vi. Don't you dare let on you're up to anything out of the ordinary or you'll never get another chance at your own life." She gave Violet a hard glare. "You deserve this. You've more than earned the right to live your own life."

"I'm not sure this is going to work."

"If you're not certain about it, then it won't work!" Melinda said with authority. "Do you want this, or don't you?"

"I do. You know I've always loved Michael," she answered, "even though he is two years younger." She took a deep breath.

"But how in the world are you going to convince him to go along with this crazy plan?"

"You leave that up to me," Melinda gave her a sly wink. "Now *go*. Pack what you can't bear to leave behind. But not too much, mind. Fix your father's dinner, if you feel you must. Carry on as if nothing different is going on. And for heaven sakes, do not, under any circumstances, breathe a word of this to anyone!"

* * * * *

Two hours later, Violet had her mother's faded valise packed with her most precious possessions: her Bible and Sunday dress, the gold locket handed down from her mother's mother, and the silver-plated hairbrush, which had also belonged to her mother. She carefully wrapped the last, china teacup to have escaped her father's tantrums into the folds of her extra chemise. Then she added two sets of drawers, two pair of stockings, her extra apron, and the roll of rags she always used to manage her unpredictable monthlies. On top of all, she laid her hooded cloak, then snapped the valise shut tight. She pushed it underneath her bed, all the way back against the wall, so as not to have anything appear amiss.

When her father arrived from the field for his noon meal, she had his usual soup and corn cakes, sausages and potatoes all hot and ready to serve, just the way he liked them. She also set a dish of fresh, strawberry preserves next to the pan of corn cakes.

With nothing more than a cursory acknowledgement of her labors, he dug into his food with the gusto of a starving man. After sopping up the last of his soup with a corn cake—her strawberry preserves never touched—he pushed the empty bowl aside, pulled over the platter of sausages and the bowl of potatoes, then, after filling his plate to overflowing, circled it with a protective arm. To look at him, one would think he had to keep a hoard of ravenous vultures from stealing every bite.

After emptying his plate, Violet served up a big wedge of apple pie, along with a steaming cup of black coffee. She proceeded to wash the dishes at the dry sink with her back to him;

he never noticed the tears sliding down Violet's cheeks. He pushed his chair back, propped his feet on the table, and lit his pipe for a leisurely smoke before returning to his work.

"Aim to finish plantin' the far north field by sundown," he said, more to himself than to Violet.

"That's good, Pa."

Not another word passed between them. When he finished smoking he knocked his pipe out against the leg of the chair, strewing ashes on the clean floor, tucked the bowl back into his vest pocket, then headed outdoors with nary a backward glance.

Violet sank to the floor where she stood.

* * * * *

Melinda had a flurry of activity stirring around her at the Harrison farm. She'd sent John to Uniontown to fetch back the twins, Matthew and Mark. As soon as they walked through the door, she had them all moving parlor furniture against the walls to clear the main area for a wedding. Then she set them to work making a small arch from willow branches, which she decorated with roses from the bush climbing outside her kitchen window. The bride and groom would stand beneath that fragrant arch, over by the parlor stove. And the Justice of the Peace would officiate from his spot, here, in front of the grandfather clock. Everyone knew weddings needed to take place on the up-swing of the minute hand, otherwise bad luck might befall the couple.

By 1 p.m., after feeding John and sending him for Violet, Melinda rang the dinner bell to call the brutes and Jeremy in to eat. She had a light lunch of soup, cheese, biscuits and fresh, strawberry preserves at the ready.

"You boys be sure to wash up good and proper before you set foot in this clean kitchen," she called from the back door.

"Michael get here yet?" Jeremy asked, wiping his hands dry on a feed-sack towel, as he came through the kitchen.

"Not yet," Melinda answered. "I imagine he'll ride in any time, though. He always has a way of showing up just when the food gets put on the table."

True to her words, they heard a horse trot up to the hitching post out back. Michael swung down, tied the reins, and headed for the cistern pump to wash up.

"Michael!" The brutes mobbed him as if they hadn't seen him for a month of Sundays, shaking hands and smacking shoulders all around. The gang trooped into the kitchen and took their places at the trestle table beside Matthew and Mark.

"I'm ready to ride, Jems. When do we leave?" Mike asked.

"Soon as we fill our bellies. The sooner we get on the road to home, the better."

"Perhaps you might like to wait until after your wedding," Melinda mentioned casually, as she ladled soup into bowls and handed them all around. "Pass the biscuits around there, Ezra, would you? I made fresh preserves for them, too."

Michael choked on the spoonful of soup he had just taken. "My what?"

"Wedding. Justice Wallace should pull up any time, now. So will your bride."

Michael sat stock still, another spoonful halfway to his mouth.

"Bride?" Jeremy asked. "Is there something you forgot to tell me, Mike?"

Melinda jumped in before Michael had a chance to say a word. "I took it upon myself to arrange for my cousin Violet to accompany you two along to Ohio, seeing as you'll have no one to cook and clean and care for those babies back there, Jeremy. And since she's putting her life on the line to do this—you all *know* what her father's like—you better do the honorable thing and marry the poor girl and get her as far away from that tyrant as possible, Michael. It's the only way she has any hope for a life of her own," Melinda explained. "The way I figure it, we don't have any time to waste beating around the bush about all this. You've got about six hours before that old man of hers finds out and comes barreling over here with blood in his eye."

Not a single Harrison brother took another bite. They all

stared at Melinda, as if she stood there with two heads.

"Eat up, boys. We need to get this meal finished up, so you can all have fresh, strawberry-short-cake after the nuptials!"

Before anyone could say another word, Violet hesitantly walked through the kitchen door, wringing a hankie in her hands, with John two steps behind, carrying her faded valise.

Michael rose upon her entrance, his chair clattering to the floor. He tried to talk, but not a sound escaped his lips.

"You don't have to marry me, Michael," Violet jumped in before he could protest. "I'm committed to running away now, but you don't have to get involved in this if you don't want to."

Michael turned and walked into the parlor, with Jeremy fast on his heels.

"What am I supposed to do?" Michael asked when they reached the other room.

"As I see it, you have two choices, Mike. Walk away and leave that fragile thing to fend for herself. Or be the bigger person here and marry the girl. Give her a chance at a decent life," Jeremy said. "Father and Ebersol may have been friends, but knowing that bully the way I do, I can only guess at what Violet's suffered at his hands."

Michael stood thinking.

"If you've given any thought to finding yourself a wife out there in the wilderness, I can tell you there are precious few marriageable gals to be had in Ohio country. You'd likely do a lot worse than Violet." Jeremy added. "At least she knows how to cook!" he said, in an effort to lighten the mood.

Michael paced the room, thinking.

"In case you didn't know it, she's pined after you for years."

At Jeremy's comment, Michael stopped dead in his tracks.

"For *me*?"

"Frankly, I don't know what she sees in you, myself," Jeremy said with an ornery smile and a slap on Michael's shoulder, "but in her eyes, you obviously have some redeeming quality."

Melinda walked into the parlor, with her arm around Violet's shoulder, and at that same moment a knock at the door announced the arrival of the Justice of the Peace.

"Well, brother," said Jeremy. "What's your verdict?"

"I'd like a word with Violet... alone, if you all don't mind."

Violet began to shake, but stood her ground valiantly. "It's all right," she addressed her cousin, "We do need to talk."

"Mr. Wallace, why don't you come in and have a cup of coffee," Melinda offered, ushering him into the kitchen, as Jeremy followed, leaving the couple alone.

"Michael, I–"

"Before you say a word, I've got something to say," Michael barreled in. "It's just not fitting for any wedding to take place before there's a proper proposal made."

"I know all this has come as quite a shock, bu–"

"A man needs to have a *say* in his future," he cut in, "not feel bamboozled into one of the biggest decisions of his life."

Violet began to cry softly. "I told Melinda this would never wor–"

"Are you going to let me get a word in edgewise, woman?"

"I'm sorry about all this, Michael. Really I am–"

"Violet. Look at me." He raised her chin so her eyes would meet his. "There's something I need to ask you." At this he dropped onto one knee. "Will you do me the honor of becoming my wife?"

Violet stood rooted, tears streaming down her face. Unable to say a word, she nodded her head in the affirmative. She blew her nose into her hankie, then took a deep breath. "I aim to make you a good wife," she said in a shaky voice. "You won't be sorry, Michael."

Melinda stuck her head through from the kitchen. "So, are you two ready?"

Michael put his arm around Violet's shaking shoulder. "Let's get this knot tied up good and proper, so we can get this party on the road. And I do mean *on the ROAD!*" he bellowed. "Time's a wasting! We need a head start before the Ebersol posse comes chasin' after us!"

Melinda took Violet's hand and gave it a squeeze. "Come with me, Vi," she pulled her toward the downstairs bedroom she and Paul occupied. "I have something special for you," she whispered. Then she raised her voice enough for everyone else to hear. "We'll just be a minute, boys. We have to get the bride ready for her groom."

While the girls conferred in the bedroom, Jeremy took Michael into the kitchen to ask, "Do you have any kind of ring you can give that girl?"

"Hells bells, Jems, you think I can pull one out of thin air?"

"What about mother's ring?" Ezra asked.

"Paul gave that to Melinda, remember?" Brandon gave his brother's head a slap.

The brothers shuffled around, searching pockets and drawers and windowsills for something usable to substitute for a wedding band.

Nothing.

Then Homer got an inspiration. "Hey! I got it!" He made a quick exit outside.

"What do you suppose *he's* apt to come back with?" the twins asked one another, of the brother they considered the most thick-headed of the bunch.

As the rest stood talking weather and crops with Justice Wallace, Homer made his return, beaming proudly. "Here!" He held out a small, twisted wire.

"That looks like a chicken band," Ezra observed. "Violet's no chicken. He can't give her that."

Michael took the band from his simple brother. "At least you've come up with some kind of solution, Homer," he said, giving him a pat on the back. "Thank you. We'll make do with this till I can get her a proper wedding band."

Meanwhile in the back bedroom, Melinda had taken down a

box from the top shelf of her wardrobe. She opened it to reveal her wedding gown, neatly folded with a lovely veil resting atop.

"This was my mother's," Melinda said. "She gave it to me when I married Paul."

"Oh, I couldn't wear your wedding dress," Violet began to fuss. "It's not righ–"

"We don't have time for changing into fancy clothes, Vi. You need to travel fast, once we get finished with all the 'I-do's'. But at least you can wear my veil. That'll help you look and feel more like a real bride." She shook out the veil, and placed the simple circlet of pearls upon Violet's head. Then she began to fuss with the festoon of lace twisting down her back, straightening out wrinkles as she worked her way around the veil. Melinda took one layer and began to fold it forward, over Violet's face.

"Oh, no. You can't *do* that," she said, pushing it back. "You know what that means. And you *know* I have no right."

"You know, and I know, but no one else in the whole world needs to know, Vi. You've never had a real man love you. Your Pa's cruelty doesn't count a bit, far as I'm concerned."

Silent tears trickled down Violet's cheeks.

"Here, take this new, blue hankie. Dry your eyes," Melinda said, holding out a lovely blue handkerchief embroidered with violets. "I made it special for you a long time ago, Vi. To use on your wedding day."

Violet broke down and sobbed onto her cousin's shoulder. When she finally got control of herself, she blew her nose on her old hankie, tucked it in her pocket, then accepted the beautiful creation from Melinda. "Thank you," she said, "for *everything.*"

"Think nothing of it. I'd do anything to help you."

"It's likely you'll have to face down Pa, you know."

"You leave that worry to me," she said, "I have a whole army of brutes behind me, don't forget." She replaced the lace over Violet's face. "Today you become Mrs. Michael Harrison, with a new husband, a new home, and a new life," she said, giving her a hug. "Don't ever look back. From now on, focus on what lies ahead." Melinda placed a small bouquet in Violet's hand. "I'd have picked you violets, but you know they're all gone by now. I hope you don't mind the scent of roses."

"They're lovely. Thank you."

"Turn around. Let me have a look," Melinda instructed. "Something old and borrowed, new and blue... you're ready!"

The girls opened the bedroom door, stepped into the parlor, and Melinda placed the bride's hand into that of the groom. Once she had everyone else in their appointed places, with Jeremiah standing up for his brother, and she, herself, standing up for her cousin, the Justice made short work of the wedding vows.

As he instructed Michael to kiss his bride, the grandfather clock struck two.

"We made it before the hand started to fall," Melinda whispered to herself. "They have a chance."

Dear Ellie,

I have received your letter of June and am glad to hear that all is well with you, and that the Riverstop is a success. I see you still as we left you at your sister's, back in May, waving to us, with a smile covering your face bigger than any I have ever seen you wear.

As to the other intelligence imparted in your last post, I am dismayed and know not what to think. Surely there is some misunderstanding and all will be put to rights. The person in question is, after all, a man of God. But poor Mrs. Harrison. To lose a baby is always difficult, but she certainly has endured more than has ever been required of myself in all these long years. (Though they seem but shorter all the time, friend.)

I passed that letter to my husband to make of it what he could, and he seems to have no such qualms as mine, as to how matters stand with that Reverend Longbottom. In fact, after reading the information you conveyed, Zach seemed more than a little upset. I told him we have no proof of such a possibility in our Zan. But that did little to assuage his ire.

The way events have transpired here, of late, my head is still awhirl.

Upon arriving home from our visit with you, I threw myself into preparations for Nate's wedding, with much help from Lizzie and from the bride's sister, Ivy. Alas, the church was not to be completed in time, as we were pounded with heavy rains up here early in the month. Therefore the new pastor would likewise not be arriving as scheduled. So it was decided that the ceremony should take place instead at the Cleghorn home, a real two-story with stairs for a bride to walk down and decorated so prettily by the girls.

A justice was found to perform the ceremony, though he was of an informal sort. By this I mean that when he announced to the assemblage that he was about to begin, it sounded something like, "Are you all ready for this here

112

funeral?"

I do not mean to make it sound a dismal scene. The morning had dawned with a heavy haze which burned off to become a beautiful afternoon. My dear ones stood round with shining faces and hair bullied into place. Zach and I exchanged proud glances as we surveyed our brood. I saw my first-born son standing nervously beside his brothers, shifting from one foot to another.

Friend, you will not credit this next part. Ivy came down the stairs and walked right by me as I spoke to her. Now this I found strange, as she and I had become quite companionable during all the preparations. I saw her go to her mother with a very closed and angry expression on her usually open face, and the two exchanged words in hushed tones, after which Mrs. Cleghorn looked quite ill. Mrs. Cleghorn then spoke to Mr. Cleghorn, who in turn went charging up the stairs. Zach gave me a shrug of the shoulders to say that he had no clue as to what was afoot. We all waited some long moments for enlightenment.

Burt Cleghorn came back down much more slowly than he had gone up, and at the bottom of the staircase, spoke to the company. "There will be no wedding," he announced, "as Chastity has run off with the boy from the livery." At this point the guests were astir with gasps and whispers. Mrs. Cleghorn swooned, being caught half up and half down by her elder daughter. Zach helped seat the poor woman while Ivy fanned her with a pillow. I went to Nate, but he merely stood with slack mouth and blank expression.

At this point, the justice spoke up. "Well, folks, seems a shame not to have a weddin' as we are here, decked out and all. Any other gal here want to claim this man?"

There were some nervous titters at that, of the kind that bubble up at strange moments, and then a voice spoke up. "Yes, I'll take this man."

Ivy's voice rang out clear and strong. "Nate Lawrence, I love you, even if you were fool enough to want my empty-headed sister. I promise that if you take me for your wife, I will make you happier than she ever could with her selfish ways."

All eyes turned to her, then toward Nate who stood motionless by my side. His mouth did open and make as if to speak, but no words issued forth.

"She's a good woman, son," I whispered in the direction of his ear above my head. "The better of the two by far."

Just as Ivy's gaze began to waiver, I heard him take a breath. Her chin dropped to her chest. Then he spoke. "Ivy Cleghorn, I would be most honored to take you as my bride."

I let out my breath as the room filled with voices and a smattering of applause. Mrs. Cleghorn recovered herself and came up from her seat, helped by her husband, to embrace her daughter. Several men clapped Nate on the back. The justice said, "Shush now, and let's get to it before either one of these two decides to weasel out."

And so, Ellie Mae, I have a new daughter-in-law, but not the one expected. This one is much more to my liking. Of course more important is that she be to Nate's liking. But I have no doubts on that score after seeing them together these past weeks, shy with each other at first, but now obviously past that stage. It is a good match.

As it turned out, Mrs. Cleghorn had the foresight to acquire materials for wedding attire, but the daughter who had a wedding dress made did not wear it, and the other daughter married without the chance to make a white gown for herself. But Ivy looked lovely in her pale green bombazine with eyes aglow and cheeks full of color.

I hope that all goes well with your new venture, Ellie, as it does with Nate and Zach's.

Always your friend

Libby

Chapter 5

Michael & Violet
Late June 1818

Nearly two weeks on the road gave Michael and Violet the chance to get acquainted. After the first few days of uneasy tension—half expecting her father to catch up with them and make trouble—they began to relax and enjoy the trip. Jeremy tried to keep himself as inconspicuous as possible, although spending hours at a time together in a small wagon did present its restrictions.

The couple found they had more in common than either one realized. Both had lost mothers at an early age and suffered at the hands of oppressive fathers, and both had kept their hopes alive by living on dreams.

Michael visualized impressive stone buildings—cathedrals, court-houses, and such—laid up by his own hands. He possessed the basic skills. Now he need only hone and put those skills to work, to reach the level to which he aspired. Violet harbored more modest dreams: home, hearth, and a family of her own. Nothing out of the ordinary for most women, but most assuredly out of reach for her, she'd thought—until now. She could hardly believe she actually had a husband of her own, the two of them heading West to make a new life together.

Most days Jeremy drove Patsy over the hilly countryside, and the newlyweds sat in back, talking and talking and talking. Michael would take an occasional turn at the reins, to give his brother a rest. At those times, Violet usually napped, giving the brothers a chance to converse.

"Seems you two found a lot to talk about," Jeremy observed.

"I *like* her, Jems. Never thought I would, but I do. The girl does have spunk," Michael said. "All those years she seemed so shy, so ordinary. I never really took notice. She sort of blended into the woodwork, you know?"

"Maybe she did that on purpose, Mike. Avoiding undue attention to keep things from getting any worse at home," he offered.

"That old man of hers sounds like a beast," Michael said. "She hasn't told me all that much, but what she has mentioned sounds worse than being stuck in a prison."

"No wonder Melinda took matters into her own hands. I don't blame her a bit for doing what she did," Jeremy said. "That poor girl deserves a chance, and they jumped at the only one likely to come along that'd take her far enough out of her father's reach."

"I sure felt put out at first. Being taken in that way. But now we've had a chance to get to know each other a bit, I'm beginning to think this marriage just might work out after all!"

"I'm glad to hear you say that, Mike. I've had my doubts about all this, too."

"Can I tell you something I never told a soul?"

"You know you can tell me anything."

"You might not like hearing this, Jems."

"Why don't you let me be the judge of that."

"Here goes. Back when Amanda showed up with that letter, expecting to find a husband from our family, it's her I've had stuck in my heart ever since."

"I remember how you begged to be the one she married. I just figured it was puppy love," Jeremy recalled. "You weren't anywhere near ready for a wife, let alone a child." *As if any of us were,* he thought to himself. "Mandy's another girl who deserved a chance."

"She expected a child? Geehosephat, I never knew that!"

"I know. Father aimed to keep you younger boys far removed from that part."

"Then, maybe it *was* all supposed to work out this way," Michael considered. "Yearning after Amanda these past months has kept me from looking at any other gals. If I had looked around, I likely wouldn't be here for Violet, now, would I."

"That's a good way to look at the whole thing, Mike."

"I've decided I want to make this work, Jems. I really do."

"Good. Just remember that, when things get tough," Jeremy said. "I can guarantee you, they *will* get hard out here in the wilderness, brother."

They sat in silence for a few minutes.

"Speaking of 'hard'," Michael said with a sly grin, "I've been so hard for these last three days, I can hardly stand it! What *am* I gonna to do about it? I never... well, I'm not sure how... I mean, I–"

"Don't worry. Give the girl a little time to get used to the idea of all this. When the time is right, you'll know what to do."

"Are you *sure?*"

"I'm sure. Took Mandy and me quite a while to come to our marriage bed, too," Jeremy said, remembering her reluctance at the whole idea of intimacy, after the terrible ordeal she'd been through—not to mention her unwanted pregnancy. "Since we're swapping confidences, I have to tell you, after we finally *did* get there, it still took her a mighty long time to get used to the whole thing. But once she warmed up to me... well, let's just say nothing's more joyous in this world than the willing love of a good woman."

Jeremy went silent for a spell, longing for his shattered wife to come back to him.

"Jems? I'm sorry things turned out the way they have for you."

"Thanks."

The two rode for the next few miles in silence, with Jeremy nodding off on occasion, until the wagon would hit a rut, bouncing him awake. After several stops every now and again to rest the horse, twilight began to fall. Time to find a campsite and bed down for the night. So far, they had come across an occasional stagecoach stop along their journey, where they could obtain a simple meal of soup or stew. But most nights, they made do with nothing more than journey cakes, hard tack, and coffee—the coffee so graciously contributed by Melinda. All relished the prospect of a real, home-cooked meal.

Three more nights on the road ought to bring them close to Justice—and home.

"Would you like another cup of coffee?" Violet asked the men, as she rose from her kneeling position beside the campfire.

"I'll take a refill," Jeremy said, holding out his tin cup. "You know, you don't have to serve us, Violet. We're quite capable of pouring our own coffee."

"I have trouble getting used to such things," she answered with a nervous smile.

"No more for me," Michael said, swishing the last of his cold coffee around and giving it a pitch outside the camp circle.

Jeremy watched the precious coffee hit the ground. "One day soon, you won't waste that last swallow, cold or no," he told his brother. "Extras like coffee come mighty dear out here."

Michael shrugged his shoulders.

Jeremy knew his brother had a lot to learn.

"I'm ready to hit the hay... or in this case, the ground," Michael said with a stretch and a yawn. "I believe it's our turn to take the ground, and yours to have the wagon bed tonight, Jems."

"I don't mind the ground, if you two want to take the wagon again."

"We do fine on the ground underneath," Violet jumped in. "Besides, I feel safer, somehow, having the wagon over my head. Makes me think I'm tucked in a cozy cocoon."

"I'll put out the fire," Jeremy said, rising from his spot. "You two go ahead and get yourselves settled for the night."

Jeremy checked the hobbles on Patsy, then took a stick and stirred the coals of the fire apart, kicking dirt over the dying embers. Meanwhile, Michael and Violet pulled a bed of dried leaves under the wagon. They covered it with the quilt, crawled on top, then pulled a thick comforter over themselves, tucking its sides under the quilt to make that cocoon Violet so enjoyed.

As they made themselves comfortable below, up in the wagon bed, Jeremy folded the last blanket in half, and tucked himself between its folds. In minutes, he slept soundly.

"You think he's still awake?" Violet whispered.

"I hear snoring. I'd guess that means he's out." Michael put his arm around Violet's shoulders and pulled her closer.

She stiffened for a moment, then took a deep breath, consciously forcing herself to relax against Michael's side as much as she dare. She wasn't ready to willingly snuggle against him, yet, but these past nights had given them the opportunity to get accustomed to lying beside one another. With his brother in such close proximity, Michael had attempted nothing more than a good-night kiss. Though they never discussed consummation of their marriage, it seemed they'd silently agreed to wait for that deeper intimacy until reaching their final destination.

Truth be told, both found themselves scared spitless at the prospect.

"Is my arm all right like this?" Michael asked. "It's not too lumpy for you?"

"No. It's fine," Violet said. "I'm just not used to lying so close to someone, yet."

"Are you sorry you did this? Run off with me?"

"No. Not a bit sorry. Just a little… unsettled, if you know what I mean."

"I know exactly what you mean," Michael said. "I am too." He gave her a squeeze, then leaned closer to give her a kiss. "Nite, Violet."

"Good night." She took a deep breath, closed her eyes, and willed her heart to stop racing. *Breath in. Breath out. S-l-o-w down. He will not hurt me in the night. He won't. He won't. He will not hurt me.*

It took them both a good while to fall into a fitful sleep. After a time, they slept soundly enough that neither heard the rumble of distant thunder. Only when Jeremy joined them beneath the wagon to avoid the downpour did they realize it was raining.

"Sorry to bother you two," Jeremy said, pulling his cover in behind himself, "but it's getting wet up there." The couple scooted closer together, to make room. Jeremy rolled up in the blanket with his back against Michael's back.

"Let's hope it stops before morning," Michael said with a yawn. He wrapped himself around Violet in a "spoon."

Violet tucked into a fetal ball, clutching at her middle. The first twinges of cramping announced her long-overdue nemesis. Since her monthlies never had come at regular intervals the way most women's did, Violet came to assume that hers never would. She half expected this sometime along the trip, but she'd hoped it would hold off until the end. With all three huddled under the wagon to stay dry, there was nary a thing she could do about it tonight.

Morning greeted them with a foggy mist. At least the downpour had come to an end. By the time they folded up bedding, made coffee and hitched up the horse, the sun had begun to peek through the remaining clouds. The day looked promising for travel, even though they'd now have to slog through mud. With the end of their trip in sight, the men hurried to get on the road. But the prospect of another three days of bumpy riding made Violet cringe. Her bleeding had increased, and she knew something didn't feel quite right.

After a half day of being jerked and jolted around in the back of the wagon, Violet was grateful for the noontime stop. She excused herself immediately and headed for the bushes with her roll of rags tucked between folds of her skirts. At every stop to rest the horse, she repeated the same exercise. Before the day came to a close, she'd already used up half the roll—a supply which normally lasted her three or four days. Violet hated to mention a word to the men, but how long could she keep this bleeding from them, if it continued on so heavily? *Maybe it'll slow by morning.*

Another night of cramping, and another night of sleeping on the ground didn't rectify the situation. When Violet awoke the next morning at Michael's side, she lay in a pool of blood.

"My God, Violet! What's wrong?" He panicked at the sight.

"It's just my monthlies," she replied, trying to act unconcerned. "I don't recall bleeding quite this badly before, though." Violet tried to extricate herself from the bedding without sullying it further. "I guess bumping in the wagon hasn't helped any. I'll go rinse this out, before it stains."

"How can you lose so much blood and still be cheerful?"

Violet didn't let on how much it worried her. Instead, she cleaned herself up, rinsed out the bedding in the little creek they'd camped beside, and did the best she could at spreading blankets to dry over the wagon's sides as they continued on their way. After another day of bouncing, Violet's bleeding had not slowed at all. Michael could no longer hide his worry.

"We need to stop," he told his brother. "She can't keep losing blood this way!"

"We're only one day's ride from home, Mike. If we push on through tonight, we likely can make it by morning. I think Patsy can handle it, if we breathe her often enough."

"What do you think, Violet? Want to ride through, or stop?"

"I think we'd better get there quick as we can," she said, now beginning to show concern of her own. She'd gone through all her rags, and now she sat upon the oldest blanket Jeremy had used to make the bed for Amanda's long trip to the asylum. It already appeared to be half soaked through where she sat.

"You heard the lady. Make tracks, brother!"

* * * * *

By the time they reached the outskirts of Justice, sun's rays filtered through morning mist; Violet appeared nearly comatose. Michael cradled her in his arms, willing the horse to hurry.

"I aim to stop at Ma Hawkins'," Jeremy told Michael. "She handles most of the doctoring in these parts," he explained. "We'll reach her place before our own, anyhow. Let's hope she's not off somewhere delivering a baby."

They pulled up to the Hawkins' hitching post, hollering for

Ma. She stepped off the porch with a stiff gait, took one look in the back of the wagon, then began issuing orders.

"You, carry that girl inside," she addressed Michael. "Lay her on my bed. Clara! Put water on to boil. Tom, see that Jeremy's horse gets rubbed down good. Looks like that poor beast is ready to drop in its tracks. You don't look much better yourself," she told Jeremy. "Who is that girl?"

"My new sister-in-law, Violet," he explained. "That's my brother Michael."

"What on earth happened? Someone shoot that poor thing?"

"She says it's her monthlies. But it don't look like any monthly Mandy ever had."

"It's not." She hurried inside after Michael. "Easy, now. Lay her over there, on that bed," she directed. "Here, let me put this old coverlet down first." She pulled a worn blanket out from underneath the bed. "Always keep one handy—just in case." She pulled the divider curtain across the corner of the cabin to hide the bed.

By the time Ma had given Violet a cursory once-over, Clara had chased the men outdoors with cups of steaming chicory. They sat out on the porch, sipping the strong brew, eating hot sausage gravy and biscuits, and worrying.

Inside, Ma busied herself cleaning Violet up enough so she could get a good look at what was wrong. It took her most of the next hour to evaluate the situation and get the bleeding slowed enough to do some much needed stitching. By the time she joined the men out on the porch, they were both beside themselves with worry.

"Jeremy, I got some hard things to say to your brother, here. Seein's we ain't been properly introduced, we better get that task out of the way. I'm Edith Hawkins, boy. Who might you be?"

"Michael Harrison, Ma'am," he said, extending his hand. "Jeremy's brother."

"He already told me that. Now tell me something I don't know. What happened to that girl in there to get her torn up so bad inside? What kind of fool are you, anyways, to get a gal with child when she's in such frightful shape to start with? "

"You mean she's going to have a baby?"

"Not no more, she ain't. Lost the poor thing," Ma said, shaking her head. "Likely it was just tryin' to get a good hold. It's a wonder you didn't lose the mother, too."

Michael sat down hard.

"This comes as quite a shock, Ma," Jeremy said. "These two just got married the day we left for home. Haven't even had a chance to bed down proper, yet, what with all the hard traveling we had to do."

"Well, it's clear she bedded down with somebody."

Michael sat in a stupor, unable to talk—barely able to breathe.

"Whoever did this to her don't have a brain in his head, that's for damn sure."

"Who–?" Michael squeaked.

"Did she say *anything* to you, Mike?"

"Not a word. I assumed she was still..., well, you know... innocent, and all. Sure seemed that way to me. She hasn't acted ready for any kind of... ah... closeness. Except maybe a little peck on the lips, now and again."

"I ain't surprised, seein' the injuries she's suffered. Seems you two have some hard talkin' to do," Ma turned to re-enter the cabin, and Michael rose to follow her. "Not now," she said, turning back to him. "She's sleepin'. Let that poor thing rest." She closed the door behind her, leaving the two men standing in bewildered silence.

After their long night's push, they'd fallen asleep on the porch for the remainder of the morning. Noontime came, and Clara fixed a simple lunch for the men. They welcomed the steaming, rabbit stew Clara offered, eating it down hungrily, then wiping their bowls clean with the last of the cornbread.

"I should head on home," Jeremy said, pushing himself away from the table. "I bet the twins grew a whole foot while I was gone."

"You ain't fixin' to move that girl out of that bed, are you?" Ma asked with a glare. "She won't tolerate no more bouncin' till she can heal up some." Ma gathered up the dirty bowls and clattered them into the dish pan for Clara to wash. "Leave her with me for a few days. Let her gather some strength."

"Maybe Michael should stay on, then, seeing how she's new here an' all," Jeremy said. "She'll likely be upset to wake up in a strange place."

"He's welcome to stay, if he sees a need to," Ma said with a sour look, "but I don't see any call for such, myself. Just be under foot, like men always are."

Michael shrugged his shoulders at Jeremy. "I'll go hitch up the horse," he said heading out the door.

* * * * *

By mid-afternoon, Violet finally awoke from a fitful sleep—confused, disoriented and more than a little upset at finding herself in a strange place among strange people. Ma, taking

matters in hand as always, comforted the girl, then explained what had transpired over the last day.

"I lost a baby?" Violet squeaked. "But that can't be!" she said, ringing her hands and getting agitated all over again. "I only got married two weeks ago," she objected. "My monthlies came late, is all," she insisted. "They most always do. Even skipping a month or two oft'n times. That's when I have big bleeds like this… only this one was worse than usual, seeing I skipped three months this time."

"I never knowed any woman to go that long, 'lessin' she had a seed planted in the melon patch," Ma said.

Violet gave her a blank stare.

"Well, you know well as I do how they get planted, now, don't you?" Ma said in her no-nonsense manner. "From the look of things, that garden of yours' been hoed mighty hard," she said, nodding.

Violet looked even more confused.

"You mean to tell me, you don't have a clue about what's been happ'nin' to you, girl?" Ma asked incredulously.

Violet only gave her a blank stare. "A *baby?*"

"Yes, a baby. 'Bout two, three months along, I'd wager."

"A Baby." She shook her head in disbelief.

"Well, not no more, it ain't," Ma said. "Shape you're in, it had damn little to hang on to in there. Lay back down, now, and rest. Gather your strength. You're gonna need every ounce you can muster for livin' out here." Ma tucked in the comforter, then headed through the curtain to the main cabin, where Clara worked at making a raspberry pie for supper.

"Don't understand such ignorance," Ma mumbled, walking to the side cupboard. "Don't understand it at-all." She took down her tea tin, put a spoonful of her favorite herbal blend into the tea pot, then picked up the kettle from the trivet at the edge of the hearth and filled the pot with steaming water. While she

waited for the mixture to steep, she pulled out her chipped mug, wiped it out with the corner of her apron, and set it on the table. "How can any gal past the age of twelve *not* know where babies come from?" she asked the cabin. Ma seldom talked to Clara directly, but on occasion Clara would answer, anyway.

"Maybe she's simple."

"Well, my stars," Ma said, shaking her head. "You might have a thought there."

Clara beamed. It didn't happen often that Ma would actually listen to something she had to say. Clara took heart and forged ahead. "I even heard tell some simple gals can carry a child to full term and still not know what's goin' on," Clara offered.

Ma didn't say a word. She poured her tea, then sat down and held the mug with both hands, relishing its warmth.

"You could amount to somethin' yet, girl."

Clara hardly knew how to handle a compliment from her mother-in-law, backhanded though it may be. Rather than risk

125

raising her ire by saying anything more, Clara kept her peace.

Before Ma had her tea mug emptied, they heard a horse trot up to the porch. "Hello the house!" called a feminine voice.

"Sadie!" Clara dropped the lump of pie dough she stood patting and ran to pull open the cabin door, wiping hands on her apron as she went. "Sadie, it's so good to see you!" Clara gushed. "I been wishin' for some female company."

"What am I, girl. Possum pie?" Ma harrumphed. She pushed against the table, rose stiffly, then placed her mug in the dish pan with a splash. "Let me take a look at you, Sadie," she said, eyeing her daughter-in-law over sharply. "You keepin' that grandbaby of mine growin' proper?"

"We're doing fine," Sadie said, giving her swelling middle a pat. Jeremy says I have a new sister-in-law here. Is she awake?"

"She's headin' for sleep, again, last I looked," Ma said. "You know that gal?"

Sadie nodded her head.

"Is she a simpleton, or just plain stupid."

"Violet? Stupid? Why would you even ask such a question?" She gave Ma an incredulous look. "She's one of cleverest people I ever knew. You should see some of the hand-work she does. Always one to help other folks out when there's a need."

"I ain't askin' about her sewin' skill nor her charity," said Ma with a grunt. "I'm askin' how can a woman who's had such hard use, *not* know where babies come from."

"Wait a minute. Just exactly what are you talking about? What's going on here? Jeremy and Michael told me Violet took the trip awful hard, so they left her with you to rest up and recover some strength. I don't follow what you want to know."

"That gal's just lost a baby, along with a whole lot of blood," Ma said matter-of-factly. "Going to take her some time to build strength back up after such a bad bleed."

Sadie stood in disbelief. "I thought they just got married!"

"You know well as I do, that first babe can come any time,"

she said, shaking her head at Sadie and eyeing her middle." Maybe she married your brother right recent, but if he ain't the one done this to her, I'd sure like to meet the low-account pole-cat who did," Ma said with blood in her eye. "I'd give him a piece of my mind, I would, right along with *takin'* a couple pieces of him, so's he'd know how bad such misuse can feel."

"What *are* you talking about?"

"That girl in there's tore up so bad inside, it's a wonder she ever got pregnant in the first place," Ma said, shaking her head. "Looks like somebody took a pointed stick and started hackin' away at her. No mystery at-all that poor babe couldn't hold on, what with all the scarrin' she has inside."

"I don't understand. How could Violet get pregnant? She's never had a single man court her. Her pa wouldn't let any buck within ten miles of her." Sadie said, with consternation.

"Your brother managed, looks like."

"Michael told me all about that. The day they left for home, Melinda... that's our oldest brother Paul's wife... she up and sprung it on Michael. Had a Justice there and everything, ready to tie the knot and send them off, before Violet's father caught wind of the whole thing."

"Her pa?" Ma asked.

"Violet's ma died years ago... she was, I don't know, nine, ten... something like that," Sadie offered. "She took over caring for the house and looking after her pa ever since. He's always been a hard man to please."

"Hmmmm... in more ways than one, I'd wager," Ma muttered with dawning suspicion. "She have any women relatives to explain things to her? About monthlies and babies and such?"

"No one I know of, except maybe Melinda," Sadie offered. "They'd spend a lot of time talking whenever Violet came to our house. Never could stay long, though. She always had to get back to fix a meal or such for her pa. She was awful scared of him. Never wanted to rile him if she could help it."

"It's beginnin' to add up."

"What is?" Sadie asked.

"Neveryoumind, girl. Go peek, an' see if she's still awake. Maybe you can get more out of her than I could."

The cabin door opened before Sadie had a chance to check on Violet. Luther stood there, calm as you please.

"Blazes, Luther. You always got to sneak up like a in'jun?"

"You're needed over to the Guthries," he said. "Anson's down." Then he turned and headed back outdoors after his simple declaration.

"Ohmylord!" Clara started to panic.

"Get a grip, girl," Ma ordered. "Don't go gettin' yourself all worked up till we know what's wrong."

Clara took a deep breath and tried to calm down.

"Get my bag," Ma directed. "Sadie, I need you to look after Violet while I'm gone. If the bleedin' starts up again bad, pack her good with those clean rags till I get back. I reckon she should be all right with what sewin' I already done."

"We'll be fine," Sadie said with confidence.

Clara reached for her mother-in-law's healing bag atop the side cupboard and gave it to her with shaky hands. "Can I go along?"

"You stay put right here. I'll have my hands full enough with that sour mother of yours," Ma said with finality.

Clara knew better than to argue.

Dear Libby,

So your son is wed. You have your first daughter-in-law. Hope she is to you as kindly as Mary Sue is to me. You tell that Cleghorn girl that was, if you scratch a dog where he can not scratch his self, he will never run away. Not that I am one to go giving advice on matrimony. Seeing the hard end I came to with both my men.

But I have to say, I still ain't give up on the breed as a whole. As I see it some few bad ones do not have to ruin the whole barrel. Edie does not agree. She never did see much good in any man. Excepting for that Jeremy Harrison. I still can not figure why she holds such a high opinion of him when she thinks so poorly of most.

Speaking of Jeremy. I hear tell he brought out more of his people. Jonathan come by on his way to Mount Vernon the week past and brung me all the news from Justice. Jeremy took his misses to the nut house. What with his sister being married to my nephew Willie and about to pop a babe of her own soon, he brung back his brother and his new wife to help him out. Michael and Violet that would be.

Seems the girl had a mighty hard trip though.

While Edie was tending her Luther showed up to fetch Edie over to the Guthries. He had found Anson walking in circles out in his barn, blathering nonsense. Right arm warn't working at all. And his right leg did not want to move much, neither. He ain't talking sense to no one yet. His wife Winifred never did. So maybe they will get on better now.

Edie figured Anson had him a stroke. Will not be able to tend to his farming no more. So my nephew Tom moved over there to the Guthrie place. You recall Tom married Clara. The Guthrie girl that was. Being as she is the only living child of Anson and Winifred it just made sense. Her and Tom moving in there. With Jeremy's brother and new wife at the Harrison place now Willie and Sadie felt free to move over to Edie's. So

Willie can do the farm work at the Hawkins place. Seeing as Tom ain't there no more. Sadie says she wants to help Edie with birthins, too. Edie seems to think the girl has promise.

With Anson down we do not know who will fiddle for dances at neighborhood doin's no more. Sure will miss that man's music. The more he drank the faster he could fiddle. Too bad. Maybe someone else will pick up that fiddle and carry on in his stead.

Well that is all the news from these parts. Lots of young people hitching up and moving round about and popping out babes this year. Sparks flying ever-where!

Sure hope this finds you and yours doing well up there in them Fire Lands. Hope Zach's mill business is growing fast as my river business. I am feeding more and more river men all the time. Keeps me right busy. Sometimes too busy. I ain't complaining mind you. Just reporting facts.

Take care Libby. Sure hope we can meet up again before too many moons go by.

Your friend

Ellie

Chapter 6

Celebration!
July 4th, 1818 (Saturday)

"Here, take this basket," Sadie told Willie, handing it down from the wagon seat where she sat. "I'll climb down myself."

"But Saaay-deee," he protested. "I'm s'posed to help you!"

By the time he set the basket aside and turned back to reach for her, Sadie already stood on the ground beside him.

"Blast it all, woman. When are you gonna learn to let me *help* you?"

"You do help me, Willie," she said. "But I'm not one of those mamby pamby kind of gals who needs to look helpless just to make a fella feel manly." She gave his cheek a pat. "You're plenty of man for me. 'Sides, when I can't manage a task, you step in and help me just fine."

Willie melted under her touch. In his eyes, Sadie could do no wrong. He still could hardly believe she'd actually married him and would soon give birth to their very own babe.

"Would you take that basket over to the tent in front of Sam's? I need to make a trip to the backhouse. The way this Tadpole sits, it won't give me five minutes relief."

"Are you sure you're all right?"

"I'm fine, Willie. We've got at least one more month to go," she said, patting her cumbersome middle. "I just never figured on so many trips to the outhouse, in this condition, that's all."

While Sadie made a beeline behind Sam Justice's blacksmith shop, Willie carried the picnic basket over to the table, where most of the women from the area had already gathered to set out foodstuffs for this Fourth of July Celebration. The men milled around Sam's forge, cold for the day of frivolity, and took turns spelling one another in the shed, where Sam kept his best stump juice.

The little settlement of Justice looked forward to celebrating this young country's independence. To be honest, folks looked forward to most any excuse for a celebration—especially one without work involving music, dancing, food, and corn juice.

"Hey, Willie! Where's Sadie? Did you leave her to home?" Clara called, when she saw him walking toward the food table with his basket.

"She's here. Had to make a quick stop out back, is all."

"Let me take your vittles. I'll set 'em out for you," Lovinia Simpson said, stepping up and reaching for Willie's basket. She flashed him a winning smile as she took it from his hand."

Clara leaned over to Lucy and whispered, "Guess that yellow-haired piece of baggage don't know Willie's taken already. Look at her flutter those eyelashes at him. Makes a body want to gag."

"Clara, you can at least try to be charitable toward that girl now," Lucy pointed out. "After all, you're the one who ended up with Tom."

Clara hung her head. "You're right. I know that. But I still can't help feeling ruffled when she's around."

"Focus your attention on something cheerful. You got no call to bear a grudge."

Lucy leaned down to pull Hank from under the table. "Come out of there, you."

"Lucy…?" Clara had a question she couldn't quite put into words.

"What is it, Clara?"

"How do you get… I mean, how long does it take till…"

"Spit it out, girl. It can't be that bad."

"How do you get a man to get you with child, if he don't even give you a kiss or… or nothin'?"

"Tom's shy?"

"Shy ain't the word for it. Scared seems more like."

"Don't worry, he'll warm up to you, Clara. It just takes some men longer than others," Lucy said. "Henry didn't come to my

132

bed till four months after I got here. Course, the first month of that he spent waiting for the minister to show up. I guess the rest of those months he had to work out his own fix on the whole idea first."

"Well, how can Tom warm up to me, if he ain't even sleepin' in the same bed?"

"You have to admit, you *did* take him by surprise. Maybe he's working up his courage to take you by surprise."

"I never thought of that," Clara said with the beginnings of a timid smile.

"You slept in the same house with his mother for the first month or so, right?"

Clara nodded.

"Well no man's going to jump his wife with his mother listenin' on!" Lucy shook her head. "Do you have a private spot to bed down at your folks' place?"

"I'm sleepin' up in the loft where I always did. Tom comes up to get his clothes and such, but he usually goes back out to the barn to 'check on things,' he says," Clara explained. "Never does show back up till mornin'."

"Seems to me, maybe the man's waiting for you to come to him."

Clara stood dumbfounded. "I never thought of that!"

"Follow him out to that barn some night and check on things yourself."

Just then Sadie rounded the corner of the smithy, rubbing the small of her back.

"Sadie!" Clara called. "Sadie, we're over here!" She waved a dish towel in Sadie's direction. "Look at you! That apple looks ripe enough to drop any minute!"

"Clara, I still have more than a month to go," Sadie said with exasperation. "I wish folks would stop saying such things!"

"You can't blame us for bein' eager to meet the newest little Hawkins, now, can you?" Clara came up and gave her new sister-in-law a big hug. "I'm glad you're here. I didn't think you'd come at all."

"Ma didn't want me to. But I told her 'I'm goin', and that's that.'"

"Great gandersnipes, how can you talk to her that way?"

"She's no different than any other woman. Just more direct than most," Sadie said. "Folks back home always did say I spoke out too plain for a woman. Maybe she respects that."

"I could *never* talk to her that way," Clara said, wringing her hands. "She scares the stuffing out of me."

"Give her time—and maybe a grandbaby—and you can bet things will change."

"That's just what Lucy and I was conversatin' about," Clara said. "How to get a man to get you with child."

"You don't know?"

"Of course, I *know*," Clara said. "Tom just ain't warmed up to the whole idea yet."

"Maybe you need to be the one doing the warming," Sadie said with a smirk.

"That's just what I told her," Lucy added. She shifted Hank to her other arm and gave Sadie a big hug. "You're looking wonderful. Feeling all right?"

"I'm fine. Things are just getting a little tight in there," she said, rubbing the sides of her belly. "Sometimes I wonder how this Tadpole doesn't pop right out, with all the squirmin' around he's doing."

"Last month's the hardest. I think it must be Nature's way of getting you used to doin' without much sleep for after the babe gets born."

"I sure will be glad to get this wiggler here," Sadie said with a great sigh.

"You heard anything after Violet?" Clara asked. "I wondered if we'd see her today."

"I don't think that's too likely," Sadie answered. "She's still not very strong. I imagine she'll stay home, even if Jeremy and the girls do decide to come. Michael, on the other hand, wouldn't miss a doin's for all the bacon in the smokehouse."

"I take it he's the sociable kind," Lucy stated.

"Charmer's more like," Sadie said of her gregarious brother. "Nothing pleases him more than telling a good story to a willing crowd. He could always make us laugh back home."

"You think he'd come without Violet?"

"Right now, I gather he and Violet don't spend all that much time together," Sadie said. "They've had a mighty rough start. Mike pretty much leaves her alone, so she can heal up and gain strength. Spends most of his time out workin' with Jems."

"Did you get any more out of her? About how she got with child?" Clara asked.

"She wouldn't say a word to me the whole time we were getting her moved in to Jeremy's upstairs room," Sadie offered. "Jems said she and Michael should have the private quarters for starting out a marriage. With Amanda gone, and me and Willie moving over to the Hawkins' place, he took his things down to the old part of the cabin by the twins' cribs." Sadie rubbed the small of her back. "He's sleeping in the old bedstead he built after the fire. Said it worked out better all around that way."

"Who do you think did it?"

"Did what?"

"Got a baby on her!"

"Long as she and Michael work things out, isn't that what really matters?"

"What does Ma say?"

"She keeps to herself," Sadie answered. "She asked me a lot of questions about Violet's father, though."

"Her father?"

"Terrible man, Vi's pa. Not many people scare me, but he always has."

"Maybe I should pay her a call and see if I can cheer her up some," Clara offered. "Boy, I sure am hungry. When do they aim to start the speechifin'? I'm hoping pretty soon!" She snatched a sweet biscuit from the nearest platter.

"Don't we have to wait for Ma to show up first?" Lucy asked. "You know Sam won't start a thing till she gets here."

"Is he really sweet on her?" Sadie asked.

"Has been for years. But she won't give him the time of day."

"He'll have to wait a long time for her today," said Sadie. "She went down South yesterday to deliver a baby. Willie'll tell Sam."

"Where do you suppose Netta got to?" Clara asked. "She's always one of the first to show up at a doin's. It's not like her to be so late."

"Maybe she's hoping Luther will come with her," Lucy mentioned. "I'd guess he's due back home pretty soon."

"Since when does she ever wait on him?" Clara huffed.

"I bet she misses him," Sadie offered. "What about Emma? Is she here yet?"

"She went over to stay with my ma," Clara said. "She knew Ma and Pa wouldn't go out, what with Pa still so confused, an' all. I can't make heads or tails out of anything he tries to say. But Ma seems to understand him just fine," Clara confessed. "Emma asked Frank to drop her at our place for the day, and he came on over here with Tom and me… to fiddle in Pa's stead."

Lucy gave Clara's shoulder a pat. "We're all prayin' for your pa, you know."

A tear trickled down Clara's cheek.

"Enough with the gloomy faces," Sadie said. "We're here to *celebrate*!" Her voice raised considerably at the last word, and people standing around began to cheer.

"Hip, hip HURRAY!" The crowd picked up the chant.

"What's everyone hollerin' about, Sam?" Henry asked.

"Derned if I know!"

"Maybe they want to get this shindig started so we can EAT

today!" Willie said. "My stomach feels like it's rubbin' a blister on my backbone."

"What?" Sam asked, cupping a hand over his good left ear.

"We're HUNGRY!" Willie shouted. "They want to EAT today!"

"I guess we can get this jamboree off the ground, then," Sam relented, wheeling his home-made blunderbuss around to face the woods south of Justice. "I was hopin' to wait till everyone got here, but looks like the natives 'r' gettin' restless."

"If you're waiting for Ma, you'll wait a long time," Willie shouted to Sam. "She headed South last night to deliver a baby."

"What?" Sam asked, turning his head back toward Willie.

"Ma ain't comin'," Willie hollered. "Delivering a BABY!"

He shook his head in disappointment. "Then hand that powder keg over here, Henry," he directed. "Willie, fetch one o' them cannon balls. Hold on to that a minute, boy," Sam said. "Henry, you pour a good charge down in there, first." Henry pulled the cork, poured the black powder, then stopped. "Keep on pouring. We want us a BIG bang," Sam instructed. Henry poured in some more.

"Now?" Willie asked.

"Now," Sam instructed. "Set it right down in there. Just like that," he said, picking up the ramrod. "Now shove it down good and tight with this."

Willie did as instructed.

"You boys head back yonder, by them women 'fore I shoot this thing off."

"Can't I shoot it?" Willie asked.

"What?" Sam turned his head in an effort to hear.

"Let me shoot it," Willie hollered.

"You want to be deaf, boy, well as daft?" Sam said. "I done already lost my hearing. You beat it back over there by your little misses and hold her ears back tight, now, hear? Make sure everyone's standin' a-way behind me."

Willie dutifully shuffled toward the rest of the crowd, motioning them farther back, and settled in next to Sadie. "He said it's going to be loud," Willie said. "You all right with that?"

"I'll be fine." Sadie said. "Don't know how this little Tadpole's apt to take it, though. Guess we'll find out, won't we."

Sam turned to face the crowd. "I ain't givin' no long-winded speech," he shouted. "Just shootin' off this here cannon to celebrate our liberty." He turned back to his blunderbuss, took a long puff on his celebration cigar then held it to the fuse set into the flash pan. "Ready!" He dropped back holding his ears tight.

Ka*BOOM!!!!*

The acrid smoke from spent black powder wafted over the crowd, as people coughed and sputtered at the stench. Children hollered, babies cried in fright, and a large roar went up as the company sent round another loud cheer.

"You all right?" Willie asked Sadie.

"Wow!" She said, eyes wide in wonder. "You shoudda felt this Tadpole jump!"

Just then loud shouting rolled up from the area beyond Sam's cannon.

"Who in Samhell's shootin' at a unarmed woman?" The unmistakable voice belonged to Ma Hawkins. "Sam Justice, you

old fool," she said, coming up to him with fire in her eye, "you like to kilt me with that blasted field gun of yours."

"Edie! You're here!" Sam ignored the fact that she seemed to be miffed.

"Didn't you hear what I told you? You shot that thing off right by where Harmon and me come out of the woods!"

"You say you want me to take your arm and come get some food?" Sam snuffed out the cigar against his heel, stuffed it into his shirt pocket, and reached for Ma's arm with a big smile on his face. She gave his hand a whack.

"What kind of dimwit are you, man?"

Sam winked at Harmon and tried to usher Edie over to the

food table. "Let's get us some vittles,. I got me a powerful hunger."

Ma Hawkins stomped her foot, turned on her heel and walked straight over to Sadie and Willie, muttering under her breath the whole way. "Crazy as a shikepoke and deef as a back-assward fencepost... not a lick of sense to his name." By the time she reached Sadie's side, the crowd had swarmed the food tables to begin dishing out the celebration dinner. Blankets covered the ground, and families sat around, eating, visiting, and enjoying the warm, summer afternoon.

As the last folks settled in for a leisurely dinner, the first ones to fill their plates got back in line for second helpings. Before the serving dishes had been scraped clean, a flurry of activity announced the late arrival of Netta Bailey and her girls.

"Look, Netta's finally here!" Clara pointed toward the hitching post by Sam's smithy. "Who's that with her? It sure ain't Luther."

"Wait till she makes her way over here. Then we'll find out," Lucy answered. "Here, Hank. Let's clean up your plate. You need to eat these last few bites."

"He sure is a good eater," Clara crooned to the chubby little tyke sitting on Lucy's boney knee. "He's almost big enough for you to start thinkin' about gettin' him a little brother or sister, ain't he?"

"You have nothing but babies on your mind," Lucy noted. "If I have any news about another one on the way, I'll be sure to let you know."

"I'm sorry. I know I'm way to nosey. Just can't seem to help myself these days."

"You better get in the family way, soon, Clara, so you can get your mind on something more practical... like making baby things," Sadie said.

"You got enough laid by for a little one?" Lucy asked Sadie.

"With all the clothes Jeremy gave me from the twins, I hardly had to make a thing. 'Course, if it turns out to be a boy, I'll have to work on some other kind of clothes, once he outgrows the sacques."

"I have some things from Hank you're welcome to use," Lucy offered. "No sense having them sit there in the trunk."

"Thanks. That would help out a lot."

Clara stood, waving her dish towel. "Netta! Woo Hooo! We're over hee-er!"

Netta gathered up the hand of her toddler, ushering along her friend, holding 10-month-old Rachael. She hurried over to join her friends.

"Girls, girls, you'll never guess who's come to visit!" Netta called, making her way past blankets filled with families finishing dinner. When she reached the group, they gave hugs all around, squishing babes in between each hug. "I didn't think we'd *ever* get here today. Looks like we made it just in time to clean out the food bowls!"

"Who's your comely friend?" Clara asked, eying the willowy newcomer with a critical eye.

"This is, Luella, my cousin from back East. She came all this way just to see *me!* Can you believe it?" Netta caught a breath. "I been writing for *years* tryin' to get her to come out here, an' she never did say she'd come. Then what do you know, but up she pops! Just like that!"

"You came out all on your own?" Clara asked in wonder, as she offered a tentative hand in welcome.

"Heavenly days, not on my own!" Luella answered. "Luther came to fetch me. So I could hardly refuse, after he'd come all that way." Her voice had a beautiful lilt.

"Isn't it something! Luther goin' all the way to Virginia to fetch Luella here, just so's I'd have company! I can hardly believe he did such a sweet thing. Who wouldda thought? Luther thinkin' of somethin' so nice for *me!*" Netta babbled. "He knows I get awful lonesome when he's gone out in the woods, doin' whatever it is he does out there. Lord knows, I tell him often enough. But can you believe he was truly listening? I'da never guessed it!"

"He's a good man, Netta," Lucy offered. "Just because he won't say much, it doesn't mean he don't care."

"I know, I know. It's just sometimes I get to longing so much for another grown-up voice to talk to, I can hardly stand my own self blabberin' away like I do." She grabbed a breath. "So he brought me Luella! What a thoughtful man!"

Clara leaned over and whispered, "He did it to save wear and tear on his own ears, I'd sooner guess."

"Clara, be nice," Sadie scolded. "Give the man the credit he's due for thinking about something his wife truly needs. Someone in the house to *listen* to her."

Ma came up with raspberry pie on her plate. "Welcome, gal," she said. Who might you be?"

"Luella," she answered. "Luella Witherspoon, Jeannette's cousin."

"Luther brought her, Ma. Isn't that somethin'? He went back East to fetch her."

Netta's girls began to fuss.

"Here, give me them girls. They're hungry," Ma handed her pie to Sadie and motioned for Luella to hand over Rachael. "Let's go get you two somethin' afore the vittles is all." She took Rosanna by the hand and marched her to the food table, while the other women continued to talk.

Over beside Sam's smithy, where a temporary, puncheon dance floor had been laid out for the day, a motley crew of men began to blow on jugs of various pitches, taking a swig every now and again to adjust for tone. Frank did his best to tune up Anson's fiddle, while a group of boys gathered spoons, sticks, washtubs and various other pots and pans to serve as a make-shift rhythm section. Harmon pulled out his juice harp and added its distinctive "twang" to the mix.

"Sounds like they're fixin' to dance," Clara said.

"Sounds more like they're workin' on a death dirge," Sadie said with a wince. "But give 'em time. Maybe they'll come up

141

with some real dancing music before the day's out."

"I hope Tom will dance with me," Clara whined.

"Well don't wait here a-wishin'," Lucy said. "Go and *ask* the man!"

"You know, I think I will, at that." Clara smoothed out her blue, store-bought party dress and marched over to where the group of men sat finishing their dinner.

"Tom, you come on over and dance with your wife," she said with authority.

Tom dutifully obeyed, taking her hand and walking her over to the dance floor where other couples had begun two-stepping to the beat of the music as best they could. With no square dance caller, they managed what steps they could on their own.

"Look at them," Lucy said, nodding toward the dance floor. "I think Tom is actually smiling!"

"Maybe there's hope for those two, yet," Sadie said.

Chapter 7

Tadpole
August 4, 1818 (Tuesday)

The day dawned with a murky haze hanging over the eastern horizon. The night had been so hot and sticky, Sadie and Willie slept out on the front porch, since they could barely stand the heat and confinement of the loft. With Ma gone Mount Vernon way on another baby call, the two lovebirds had the whole place to themselves.

"Think we'll get any rain, Willie?"

"Looks like cloud cover rolling in. Maybe it'll bring us a little relief."

Sadie struggled to rise from the tick they'd laid at the back corner of the porch. "Give me a hand, would you?" She held both hands out to Willie, who gave a tug, lifting her to her feet. "Sure would be nice if this babe decided to get here today. I'm gettin' awful tired of haulin' him around this way," she said, rubbing her back.

"Don't say such things with Ma gone!" Willie said with the start of panic in his voice.

"Relax, I'm just fine," Sadie said, patting his head. "You sure are jumpy lately."

"I'm going to be a *father*! Any *minute* now!!"

"Well not in the next few minutes, you won't," she said, stretching as best she could. "A nice, cold glass of milk would sure go down good about now," she said. "Would you go get some?"

"I'll fetch a pitcher full," Willie offered. He jumped off the porch, then turned. "Don't go nowhere while I'm gone!" He flashed his orneriest smile, then headed toward the spring house next to the barn, where they kept the milk cooling in the ice cold water.

Sadie struggled to fold up the feather tick and haul it back into the cabin, laying it behind the ladder leading to the loft. Accomplishing that task, she pulled the leftovers from last night's dinner out of the side cupboard and laid a table for their breakfast, consisting of cold corncakes and fresh blackberries. Sadie loved blackberries and had especially craved them of late. She and Ma managed to find a wild patch down by the edge of the little pond, and she'd spent hours picking every berry she could, most days eating more than she saved. Even so, she'd managed to save enough to dry a whole bag full for winter and still have some left for eating fresh.

Willie returned with a dripping pitcher. "Here's your milk." He sat it on the table and took the seat Sadie indicated.

"Thanks, Willie." She gave him a peck on his forehead. "You know I love you."

"I love you too," he said, giving her a hug around the middle. He put his ear against her belly and addressed the babe, "and I love you in there, too, little Tadpole."

Sadie took a cold, corn cake, crumbled it into a bowl, then added a handful of blackberries on top. She picked up the milk pitcher and poured a goodly portion over the top, handing the finished concoction to Willie. As he dug in, she filled the other bowl up with the same thing for herself.

"This tastes good," Willie said with a full mouth. "Cool for a hot morning."

Sadie ate her bowlful in silence. When they'd finished, she took the dirty bowls and spoons and put them over in the dry sink. "I'll wait to wash dishes till after lunch. No sense making it hot in here to boil water for no more than this." She retrieved the broom from behind the door and proceeded to sweep out the cabin. Unable to bend over to clean up the pile of dirt, she looked around, then swept it over to the door and gave a great heave to push the mess over the threshold and out, onto the porch. She continued sweeping the porch, till she came to the other end. "Willie, you still here?"

Willie poked his head out the door. "I was changing to work pants," he said. "I'm heading out to do chores, soon as I get these suspenders hooked up right." He fussed with the button, but had trouble making it hook over the loop.

"Here, let me do that," Sadie said, turning him around and fastening the last button. "What will you do when I have a baby to dress? Still expect me to dress you too?"

"Saaay-deee, you know I dress myself," he said with an obvious huff.

"I'm just joshin' with you, Willie. What happened to your sense of humor?"

"It went down to Mount Vernon with Ma," he said with a smirk. "If you got to know, I'm awful nervous about bein' here all by ourselves with this babe so close. How could Ma go and leave us at a time like this?"

"I told her to go, Willie. She'll be back in plenty of time to meet our Tadpole."

"You sure?"

"Sure as any woman can be," she said, crossing her fingers behind her back. Two days ago, despite Ma's misgivings, Sadie had insisted that she go off to deliver Mrs. Crittenden's daughter of her very first grandbaby. Sadie had a feeling things might move along faster than she'd originally thought, but she still figured this babe would hold off a few more days, at least. "We'll be fine, Willie. Go and do your chores."

Willie did as instructed. Half way down the path to the barn, he looked back with a hang-dog expression. "Smile, Willie," Sadie called after him. "I'm fine."

But she wasn't fine, and she knew it. She'd felt a shift during the night, and ever since, the babe had lain more quietly than usual. She hoped Ma would make it back before nightfall. Things could get real interesting by then.

The morning haze burned off into a hot, muggy day, with barely a breeze to stir any air movement. Sadie had little energy to tackle housework, so while Willie stacked up the last of the dried hay he had down in the front field, trying to beat the coming storm, she sat against the beechnut tree out back in the only piece of cool shade she could find.

"If you aim to get here today, little Tadpole," she talked to her stomach, "you better do this thing fast and easy." She laid her hands across the sides of her belly and held on as the muscles tightened. When the contraction released its hold, the babe only flinched a little kick here, an elbow poke there. She felt none of the big flip-flops she'd experienced over the previous weeks. "I sure would like to get you here right quick, but I don't know if your daddy can handle this task all alone."

Sadie tried to think whom she might send Willie to fetch back here to help. Guthries lived the closest, but she surely did not want Winifred's doom and gloom ushering her innocent babe into this world. Nor would Clara's self-centered ignorance do at a time like this. Lucy wasn't all that much farther off, and she could no doubt be a great comfort. But the only one Sadie really wanted with her was the closest person to a mother she'd ever known: "Jems."

She dozed on and off for the next hour or so, with only an occasional, light contraction disturbing her rest. When she felt the first raindrops on her face, she roused herself enough to roll onto her side, then used the tree as leverage to get to her feet. By the time she made the front porch, the rain pounded so hard, she was already soaked to the skin. She met Willie at the front step, as he ran in from the front field. They gave each other big, sloppy kisses and reveled in the cool shower they shared.

"Willie?"

"Hmmmm?" He held her close and smoothed the wet hair out of her face.

"I think you'd better go fetch Jeremy."

"I already got the hay stack finished."

"I don't mean to help with your hay. I mean to help me."

"What do you need your brother's help for, Sadie?"

"Oh, I thought maybe I'd make soap today and he could leech out the lye for me," she said with an ironic edge to her voice."

"Soap? In weather like this?"

Sadie stood there, tapping her foot, giving him a disgruntled stare.

After a moment, Willie's eyes began to widen, and he finally understood what Sadie had asked of him. " The baby? It's *coming?*" he stumbled over the words. "You're having the… You want Jeremy to help deliver the BABY?"

"Relax, Willie. The pains just started. We have plenty of time," she said, cupping his cheek in her hand, then patting his forearm. "You go on and fetch Jems back here. I'm going to go get out of these wet clothes. Make myself a cup of tea."

"Who's gonna watch you while I'm gone? Will you be all right by yourself till I get back? Why isn't Ma here to do all this woman stuff…" Willie kept rattling question after question into the rain-soaked air.

"Just go, Willie. I'll be fine till you get back. Saddle up Dinah and bring Jems back here before supper."

"I'm on my wa-aaayy!" Willie hightailed it for the barn and grabbed the bridle off the fence post, swinging around it with one, wild jump. He flung open the gate of the horse's stall, pushed the bridle over Dinah's nose, then grabbing a handful of mane, swung up on her bare back, and took off at a gallop.

Sadie stood on the porch with a big smile, shaking her head at the man she loved. "Well, Tadpole, for the time being, looks like it's just you and me."

The trip to the Harrison homestead took about half an hour at an easy trot. Willie tried whipping Dinah into a gallop for portions of the trip. But the old horse fell back into her slow, shuffling trot at regular intervals, frustrating Willie to no end. "I can run faster than this on my own two feet," he muttered to the horse. No amount of kicking or prodding could coax old Dinah into hurrying any faster. "Why did Ma have to take Freddie? I could have been there twice on him by now." By the time Willie reached Jeremy's cabin, he had himself worked up into such a state, he could hardly talk.

"Willie, what brings you here in the middle of the week?" Michael asked, greeting him at the front door.

"I'm come for... I mean, Sadie needs... Sadie's having the baby! I need Jeremiah! *QUICK!*"

"He's clear out back, working on a drainage ditch to feed the pond he wants to put in. I just got back up here to check on Vi and the girls, and to fetch us a jug of tea."

"Well go *get* him! Ma's gone, and I'm gone, and Sadie's home doin' this birthin' business all alone!"

"Geehosephat, Willie. Calm yourself down!"

"Calm down? Calm *down?* How can I calm down when Sadie's facing death all by herself to bring forth our little babe?"

"Death?"

"Ma says you never know about these things. Every woman faces the prospect of her own death when she brings forth new life. That's what she always told us boys," he said with authority. "It made us clear out of her way right quick, I can tell you that."

"Get down off that horse and give it a drink, Willie. Looks like you need one yourself," Michael said.

At the sound of voices, Violet stuck her head out the door, with a twin holding on to either side of her skirts, peering around to see who'd come to call. "Unka Willie!" they called together. At seventeen months, they weren't talking a whole lot, but they always lit up whenever they laid eyes on Willie. They dropped Violet's skirts and rushed to grab Willie's pant legs, nearly tripping him where he stood.

"Hi, you little flowers! Uncle Willie can't play today. I've come to fetch your Papa right quick."

"Can I help?" Violet asked in a shy voice.

"Sadie sent me to bring Jeremy. I better do what she asked."

"I understand completely," Violet acquiesced. "No doubt he's closer to her than anyone... except you, of course, Willie," she said with a blush.

After watering his horse, he tied her reins to the hitching post. "Come on, Mike. Take me to Jeremy." He started out at a dead run toward the back woods.

"The other way, Willie!" Michael hollered after him.

Willie did a quick about-face and started running in the other direction.

"I'd better go catch that boy before he runs clean to Union-town!" Michael gave Violet's hand a squeeze, then he picked up the tea jug and bounded after Willie. "Wait up! I'm right behind you!"

* * * * *

After Willie had ridden out, Sadie busied herself changing into dry clothes, making a small fire to warm the kettle, and laying the table for an early supper. Since Willie took off without a single bite of lunch, she knew he'd be famished by the time he got back. She put a pot of vegetable soup to simmer over the small fire. Every now and again she'd stop dead in her tracks for a few moments, holding on to whatever prop happened to be most handy, until the contraction of the moment relaxed its grip.

They came at ten minute intervals now, growing ever stronger. Things seemed to be moving along faster than she remembered at Amanda's last birth. 'Course this little Tadpole seemed more than ready to make his grand entrance than did poor, little Joey, who'd never drawn a breath. She mustn't think about that now. *Focus on something positive.* She pictured Willie holding his very, own, red-headed son, and that made her smile.

"That's it, Tadpole. Come meet your daddy," she crooned to her rock-hard belly. "He's the most loving man in the whole, wide world, and you get to call him Pa."

Sadie took down the birthing tea Ma kept in the buckskin pouch hanging on the side of the cupboard. She measured out a goodly fistful and put it in the teapot. Then she turned to lift the kettle off the trivet sitting on the hearth. "Oooph! This one's different!" She took in a quick breath and held her side. The next contraction tightened with an iron-like grip, surpassing anything she'd experienced thus far. She felt an overwhelming urge to throw up, which she managed to swallow back down. "I think we're too late for tea," she said to no one but the hearthstone.

Sadie set the teakettle back down, made her way over to the corner, and held on to the post at the foot of the bed. With the next contraction, her water broke. "At least we kept that mess off the bedclothes," she muttered. When that contraction eased, she pulled the old birthing blanket out from underneath the bedstead, spread it over the wet puddle, then eased herself down, with her back propped against the wall, and her knees drawn up on either side of her belly, feet flat on the floor. She fashioned a little pouch in the blanket to cushion her babe's head. The urge to push overcame her with such force, she gave in to its primal power.

* * * * *

By the time Willie returned with Jeremy, an exhausted Sadie lay rolled in the birthing blanket, cradling her squirming, carrot-topped, baby boy. "Come say 'Hello' to your son, Willie," she said in a ragged voice, as the men opened the door.

"You did it all by yourself? You did it by *yourSELF!*" Willie rushed to her side and pulled his wife and newborn babe into his arms.

"We did it by ourselves," Sadie crooned. "I asked him to make it fast and easy, and dog-goned if he didn't do just that!"

"You all right?" Jeremy asked, coming up behind. "You need any stitching up?"

"I think everything's all right that way, Jems," she said with a breathy grin. "That little head popped right out, and the rest of him just swam right along," she said. "I wrapped the afterbirth in that sack, over there in the corner."

"Violet sent along some clean rags for packing yourself, to help manage the bleeding," Jeremy said, holding out the pack. "She figured with all she used up over here, it was the least she could send."

"Thanks."

"I'll get some hot water goin' to clean you up," Jeremy said, heading over to the hearthstone to poke up the fire. "What's this, you laid supper out already?"

"Gave me something to do while I waited on Tad to get here."

"Tad?" Willie asked.

"Yeah, well, I thought since we've been calling him our little Tadpole all these months, we might as well name him Tad," she said. "What do you think?"

"I like it."

"I suppose we should make it something more important sounding, though... for when he gets all grown up, don't you think? How about 'Thaddeus Jeremiah Hawkins'?"

"My little Tadpole!" Willie said with a huge grin. "Give me that boy, let me get a good look at him."

As Sadie handed over the baby, the cabin door burst open, and there stood Ma, taking in the whole scene before her.

"I missed it!" she groaned. "I just *knew* it'd happen today. I missed deliverin' my own grandbabe!" She hurried over to Sadie and took a good look. "You all right, gal? Babe all right? Who caught this little carrot-top? You, Jeremy?"

"Not me."

"Don't tell me you did it, Willie!"

"Me, neither, Ma."

"You mean to tell me you left your wife all alone to have this babe on her own?"

"She sent me for Jeremy!" Willie protested. "I didn't know he'd come so quick!"

Sadie sat there with a big grin. "Tad and I managed all by ourselves," she said, crooning to the baby. "We did it just fine."

"I'll see about that my own self," Ma said. "Here, give me that babe."

Willie handed Edith Hawkins her first grandchild. She unwrapped the boy and gave him a good looking over. "Good job cuttin' the cord, girl."

"Thanks."

"Here, wrap this boy up tight and keep him good and warm," Ma said, handing the baby back to Willie. "Let me get a look at you," she said, kneeling down to where Sadie still lay propped on her side on the floor. "Jeremy, get us some hot water so I can get this girl cleaned up."

"That's what I was just doing," he said, pouring the water into a washbowl from the kettle. "Thaddeus Jeremiah Hawkins," he repeated with a proud smile. "I like it."

Dear Ellie Mae,

We gave up our little Bud a few weeks past. Mr. Will Skillicorn, who had grown to near legendary status in this household, so often has my niece spoken of him, appeared at our door one night. Her love was a small, skinny youth with hair the color and texture of straw and a smile that lights up the world. I had barely opened the door and seen aforementioned smile when I found myself knocked aside and pressed into the doorjamb as my niece launched herself at this stranger, leaving little doubt in our minds as to who had come to call.

Zan, excited at this display of happiness and the high-pitched bubbling noises coming from Caitlin, ran up and began hugging the couple as closely as her swollen middle would allow. The bubbling noises seemed to be some form of communication, and though I could make neither heads nor tails of it, Mr. Skillicorn seemed to understand what Cait was saying, as he would nod his head and say, "Yes. I know. Same with me." And then, "I came for you."

This declaration sent up a wail from Caitlin who seemed undone, and her wail was met and matched by one from Bud, awakened by this commotion. All heads turned toward the cradle near the fireplace, which Nate had made and our Buddy had nearly outgrown. Our cherub sat up, a tear glistening in the firelight as it moved down his chubby cheek.

Will disengaged himself, walked to the crying child and picked him up, holding the baby in the air and looking into his eyes with an expression not of wonder, but more like, "Yes, just as I thought." And Buddy who loves people, looked down, smiling, and began to drool onto his father. Caitlin moved to join her men, and I must confess to you, my friend, that I have not seen a prettier sight in an age. With this, the tableau in our cabin broke and everyone was released from the spell of the young lovers, who were then mobbed by the children, as Will was plied with questions from them and from Zach.

I came to my senses, closing the door, and proceeded to find food and drink for the traveler. As I took the last of the rabbit stew that was our meal from its pot and unwrapped the cornbread, I listened to tales of travel and adventure which all left my mind when the young man revealed that he was on his way to take up farming in Pennsylvania.

His uncle, it seems, had need of a strong, young man. Said Uncle has ten children, the first eight of whom are girls with sons yet in diapers, and a small farm. The opportunity had come for him to acquire a larger, neighboring farm through the unhappy circumstance of his elderly neighbors passing on, but as he barely can farm his own parcel without any help, he sent for his nephew. There was an empty farm somewhere in Pennsylvania, and here in Ohio, we had a small family ready to fill it.

All this comes of my interfering with fate. Had I not forwarded news of the birth and of Caitlin's deception, revealing her obvious love for the young man she drove from her parents' home, so that he might follow his dreams, Buddy would still be with us. But by the same token, Buddy would not now have a father, my niece would not be with her true love, and that young man would still believe her to be a very jaded young woman, dallying with a young man she cared for naught.

Though there was no time for a proper wedding, I at least made sure that a hasty nuptial was performed. We held the service out-of-doors, as it was the perfect summer day, sky filled with fluffy, white clouds. When the Justice Zach brought home asked for any reason why these two should not be joined, Buddy let out a big whoop. Our little assemblage was vastly amused. And the smile he gave in satisfaction to a job well-done, getting the attention of all present, eyes alight, is the way I see his face still.

They were such an excited little party as they left, all smiles and high color. You would have been impressed by the cheery sendoff I gave them, not giving in to my tears until they were out of sight, and I was behind closed doors. Lizzie cried with me, and seeing us, Zan began to sniffle as well, but all were saved by a little witness who pulled out his hanky and said, "It's all right, Mama. You still have me."

You may imagine that I held him a little too close then, but Elijah did not complain, merely tried to wipe my face with his dirty hanky which stopped my tears quite effectively. We all laughed, then rejoined our now smaller family outside. Zach patted my shoulder to say that he knew it was hard. He smiled approval that my cry had been brief. Elijah joined Leesha in looking at a group of busy ants in the dirt, and life went on, as it is wont to do.

We are putting up new stores and getting wood in as autumn approaches (I sent a good deal of the provisions we had put by for winter with the travelers for their journey). Lizzie is starting a pair of mittens for her little brother as a Christmas gift, and the plan is that Zan will embroider them with bumble bees and butterflies and all manner of interesting insects with the last bits of her colored threads. Both are excited over the project.

Zan is huge with child, and we expect the new bundle most any moment.

Now, friend, I must close and return to the garden where I am waging war against some very ugly insects who seem determined that we should do without this winter so that they may glut themselves today. I also note that they are not attractive enough to earn a place on anyone's mittens.

Your friend,

Libby

Dear Libby,

Well, that is something now. You helped to settle some of your people in happy homes. Helping Nate pick a fine gal this spring. Getting little Bud settled proper with his daddy and Cait with her fella this summer. Off in time to nest before the cold sets in. Good piece of work, Lib.

You feel a mite lonesome with all them goodbyes. I know how it is. Remember what you told to me? Back when Katrina went east with my ma. And Johannah rode west with that stranger fella. We do not know who could turn up next.

You shore hit that nail right on the head, friend.

My Katrina is back with me. She traveled home with Jonathan after his last trip East to market. Seems she got fed up with city life. Says the fellas was too stuck on their selves for her taste. So here she is. Working beside me these last weeks. My work load and my heart have got lighter. It was like you said, Lib. Never can tell what is ahead. Course I wouldda never guessed I could land in the whooscow, neither.

Business is booming. So it is double good to have Katrina back. I was not too sure how she would handle this rough sort we get here. She puts them in their place. But in a way that leaves them laughing. Her voice is firm and sure while her eyes smile. I think my girl has come home a woman grown.

And there is more even than that. I have had word from Johannah! Seems a stranger come by Harvey's old place looking for us. Being it was deserted with a tree come right down through the roof he stopped off at the Jarvis place to ask after us. I heard it from Henry Jarvis when he brung me the note. The fella had met a young couple in his travels. When they heard he was headed back to Ohio the girl begged him to carry a letter for her. Johannah that would be. Justice was out of his way a goodly distance. But seeing how much it meant to the girl, he obliged.

Henry said Lucy filled that man to the brim with hot food

156

before he left. And what he could not eat she packed up for his saddle bag. Now I sure do welcome that fella's effort. But truth be told, that letter had been wetted through and smeared and tattered till a body could barely make it out. Could not even read the name of Johanna's man. The jist of it seems to be that she is happy. That is all I need to know. Not properly settled yet. She will send word when they are. And Libby, the fella said they had a little one. A baby girl they called Mae. Can you beat that? I got me another grandbabe! Named with a part of my own name, to boot.

My sister Edie has got her a grandbaby, too. Her first one. Willie and Sadie's little boy. Name of Tad. Sadie delivered the bundle by her own self. Seeing as Edie was down Mount Vernon way on another baby call. Henry says Edie is right put out with herself for going off when Sadie's time was so close. But she is mighty proud of the way Sadie handled the whole thing. Willie calls the boy his Tadpole. Who wouldda thunk that when them Harrisons come out here, I would end up related to them!

Well, Katrina tells me that I am loafing and she needs help with a crowd of hungry varmints what just wandered in.

Write me again before snows come if you can. I want to hear the news about Zannah and her confinement. Sure hope all goes well. Goodbye for now.

your friend,

Ellie

Sept. 18, 1818
Cranberry Corners, Fire Lands

Dear Ellie Mae,

We have lost Zannah and the child. Zach went for help, but it was clear from the amount of blood she was losing that there would be no help for her in this world. We tried to staunch the flow, Lizzie and I. Before it was done, every bit of cloth we own was sopping. Lizzie is having terrible nightmares, for which I blame her not. A nightmarish sight it was. She launders and launders, but finds naught clean enough.

The child was a boy, as perfect of form as was his mother, except for one curiosity: he had webbed toes. The poor babe never drew a breath. My only consolation is that Rose went on ahead and will look after them both in Heaven, as I must look after the rest left us here. Once again, needs must I look only forward. I have written my two remaining sisters. That is Abigail back in Connecticutt, our schoolmarm, and Hattie in Virginia, if you recall.

Everyone feels the loss, but we have our faith or we have nothing at all. It binds us together and lifts us up. And then we have each other to do the same.

Shortly after Zannah and the babe's funeral (we laid the beautiful boy in her arms) Zach took a trip south, "on mill business," so he said. The week before he left, he kept muttering on about webbed toes and how retribution was about to be reined down upon the accountable. I never did understand his rantings but attributed it to the upheaval of the entire household over the previous days. During his absence we did manage to reclaim a semblance of normalcy. He returned after a fortnight, satisfied at the apparent success of his endeavor. We welcomed him home with delight.

I am gratified to hear that you have your daughter back with you, friend. Enjoy her as you can, for at her age it mayn't be long until another sort of change is likely. (Though mayhap it will be of a happier nature.)

Zach and Nate have come in this evening to announce to

all that the mill is up and running. A celebration is in order. You would not credit the enthusiasm of Simeon, Christian, and Levi at this news, unless a little bird told you that those three have done all the farming work here these past months while Father and Big Brother have been otherwise occupied. I see no love of that work in these boys and would go so far as to say that any one of them would as leif play dead as play farmer. If Zach intends to continue with the mill next year, we may well starve to death.

And here is next year's plan. We are to have a new house! My husband says that ours will be the first house built with the milled lumber. It is to be a smaller replica of my home back in Connecticutt. Need I share what tears of joy spilled at this telling?

Fourteen years we spent in that house, in that kitchen, in that bed. And it's sorely missed.

I remember still that day we left. It was a hard thing, but once I turned my back, it went easier. Mama's mantel clock made by Mr. Eli Terry and her Sheffield plate did not make it over the mountains of Pennsylvania. My pewter, all but three spoons, is in the Monongahela River yet, which we took as far as Pittsburgh to the Ohio River. Of each thing lost past the border of our own Connecticutt, I said to myself, "At least it was a some-thing and not a some-one." Having made it with all seven children, I know that we fared better than many. And these seven of mine are living and breathing still.

How goes life for you, Ellie? I understand that your days are filled with your new enterprise, but I long to hear that all is well with you and yours. Please find time to pen even the briefest reply before the weather turns.

Libby

Dear Lib,

 I was sorry to hear that sad news about your baby sister. I just can not get out of my head that the Lord only meant her to be on this earth as a child. So He called her back before she could be a mama. Now I do not of usual do much thinking on such things, but that is how I see it sure.

 As for the one who brought on these troubles. I think he was more like sent from the devil than from the Lord. The varmint whose name does not need mentioned here, got his just desserts in the end. Though it would seem not soon enough to avoid so much hurt all round.

 I overheard some river men talking about a reverend with webbed toes who was found washed up down river a few weeks past. They said his pants was wrapped around his ankles and some of the original parts God give him got took back. You can tell Zach ain't nobody looking for the one who done the deed neither. And that is all I will ever say on the matter.

 Only the good Lord knows what other damage got done in His name by that sinful one. Besides your witless sister, poor Amanda Harrison is now daft on his account. Sister Edie said Jeremy got a letter from that Quaker hospital down by the Big River where he left his wife last spring. It took them doctors many months to put some meat on her bones and get her back on her feet again. Still she does not speak a word. So they shipped her off to another crazy house farther back East to see if doctors there can get her to talk.

 I do not rightly know if that poor thing will ever come back to her senses. Meantimes, those babes of hers keep growing and may not remember their mama. Even if she does come home. Guess they have taken to Michael and Violet right strong. That gal had a rough start out here. But she seems hardy. She does a fine job keeping house for Jeremy and her new husband. Michael Harrison that would be.

Flora Jean brought the Coulter boy out here to pay a call week before last. She is my oldest girl who is teaching school down in Perrysville. I could see right off how things stood with them. They plan to wed at Christmas. She is still living on at the Coulters. But of course she will no longer keep school once they tie the knot. I expect it will not be long till she has her own children to fill up her days. Which means more grandbabies for me.

And talking of babies. My nephew Willie's wife. Sadie that would be. She says that Clara and Tom Hawkins expect their first child come spring. I say it took those two long enough to figure it out.

What good news to hear that Zach will build you a new house! Now you have many plans to lay over the long days of winter.

Katrina and I aim to close up Riverstop for the coldest months and stay on with Jason and Mary Sue. Until the river thaws again in early spring we can help out over there and keep each other company for the dark days of winter. And I will get to take pleasure in my grandbabies.

Hope you and yours stay warm and well fed this winter. Lord willing we will have a mild one.

Your friend

Ellie Mae

Chapter 8

Asylum
Late November 1818

She shuffled along, concentrating on the pair of feet in front of her. Keeping in step with those feet became the most important task in the world.

"Stop dawdling, Amanda Jane. Thou art falling behind. "The black-and-white-garbed attendant gave Amanda a little nudge to get her back in line with the rest.

Startled, Amanda stumbled, then regained her balance. Never saying a word, she kept watching the feet in front of hers, trying to match their exact step with her own. Mar-ching, marching, mar-ching along...

She bumped into the body attached to those feet.

"Watch it, honey, 'r I'll punch yer lights out," said the owner of the feet.

Confused, Amanda looked up to see an angry, withered face staring into hers.

"What's the matter," Mabel the attendant asked, coming forward from the end of the line.

"This youngster keeps a-followin' me closer 'n a hound dog after a bitch in heat."

"Thou art all in line, Mabel. She's supposed to follow thee."

"Oh. Well, I reckon it's all right, then." Mabel turned and continued walking, but Amanda stood rooted to her spot.

"Keep moving, ladies. Thou must not be late for dinner, or the Matron is apt to make thee go without." The attendant gave Amanda another nudge and got the rest of the line moving again, but this time she stayed close to Amanda Jane.

Once more Amanda focused on the feet ahead of her. Step, step, step, step. Walk-ing along. Foot, feet, step, foot, step-step.

The sound of marching feet, echoing in the vaulted, stone hallway, preceded the 26 women as they neared the female dining hall.

"Here they come. You ready?"

"Ready as I ever be," said Gertie, giving the stew pot a stir. "I hear we got a new gal. That right?"

"Little-bit-of-a-thing," said the head cook, as she put bowls in a stack next to the stew pot. "Need to feed her up, if we can."

"What's she here fer?"

"Not sure. You'll have to ask the Matron." "

"I ain't gonna ask. You do it," said Gertie.

"Naw. She's too stiff for me."

"Shhht. Here she comes. She don't like us talkin' when them gals come in here." Gertie stirred harder, aiming to look busy as the cook counted out bowls.

Abigail Tetherwood, head matron at the Friends' Asylum in Frankford, Pennsylvania, halted the line of women entering the dining hall.

"Thank thee very much, Friend Preston," said the Matron to the attendant. "I shall take over from here."

"Keep an eye on Mabel. She's feisty today."

"How is the new girl doing?"

"Can't say for sure. Hasn't uttered a single word yet."

Mrs. Tetherwood took the set of keys the attendant handed her, then turned to face the line of women. "All right ladies, thee may walk through the serving line, one at a time, please. Then proceed to the tables in an orderly fashion."

The line of women inched forward. The head cook handed each one a bowl and motioned her toward the next stop, where Gertie Simmons ladled a small, but adequate, portion of stew into each bowl. The Matron stood at the end of the serving line, making sure each woman found her assigned seat at the tables.

Amanda shuffled ahead in line, still concentrating on the feet in front of hers. She jumped when someone thrust a crockery bowl into her hands, and only then did she look up. Kind eyes smiled into her own. The head cook motioned Amanda ahead, showing her how to hold the bowl to receive her portion. Gertie scooped a generous ladleful into Amanda's bowl and nodded her on. But Amanda stood stock still, cradling the warmth of the bowl in her hands while she watched steam rise.

She felt a firm hand on her arm, pulling her ahead. "Come along, dear." The Matron guided her to a table. "Sit here by Mrs. Mueller. This will be thy dining place from now on. Understand?"

Confused, Amanda stood helplessly rooted, while Mrs. Tetherwood took the bowl from her hands, put it on the table, then sat Amanda firmly in her place. She strode back to the serving line to oversee the rest.

"My name Lottie," said the plump woman sitting to her left.

Amanda stared at her bowl.

"What your name is, please?"

Amanda did not answer.

"Maybe she don't talk," said a woman sitting across the table.

"Why sure she talk," said Lottie. "She have trouble, maybe to understand my accent. I talk ze English nicht so goot. Sprechen ze Deutch, leibchein?"

"Maybe she don't want to talk. Did ya' think of that?"

Amanda stared at her bowl of stew.

"You gonna eat, that?" asked the skinny woman to Amanda's right. "I'll eat it if you ain't gonna eat it." She reached for Amanda's bowl.

"Not to take her food," Lottie rescued the bowl as the skinny woman grabbed for it. "So tiny like a bird, she is. She need her own food."

"I'm still hungry. Look at her, she ain't gonna eat it."

"Eat more bread." Lottie passed her portion of bread to the skinny lady. "Here, leibchein," Lottie put the spoon in Amanda's hand and guided it to the bowl, as if she were teaching a child to use a spoon for the first time. "Open up. Eat."

Amanda chewed as Lottie urged her on. But after two bites, her spoon slumped to the table.

"How are we doing here?" the Matron asked, checking on each table.

"We do chust fine," Lottie answered.

"Amanda Jane, why art thou not eating?"

"She slow to eat," said Lottie.

"Thou must not dawdle, dear. We have a schedule to keep." The Matron turned and moved on to the next table. A single tear slipped down Amanda's cheek.

* * * * *

Amanda lay awake long into the night, listening to the rhythmic breathing of the other seven women in the room. She tried to remember when she had last slept, shifting nosily on the lumpy mattress. Corn fodder—had to be corn fodder—a straw tick would not feel this lumpy.

How long had it been? Weeks? Months? Years? For want of sleep—that blissful state of unconsciousness that continually eluded her—she walked through her days in a constant daze. When did it all start? This sleepless state? What the cause?

"Fuzz. It's all full of fuzz in here," she said, holding her head. The tiny words echoed in the vaulted room. She listened to the clock, ticking its methodical course around the night. Tick, tock, tick, tock, goes the clock, ticking away the tick, tock.

"Jeremiah, the clock needs winding."

No one answered.

"Jeremiah. Did you hear me?"

Still no answer.

Amanda folded the covers back and slipped out of bed. Her bare feet hit the marble floor, but she felt the cold only momentarily as she paddled quietly into the hall and came to a stop beneath the huge, wall clock on sentinel duty. She stared up at the clock with a contorted face, as if the effort of trying to remember something caused her excruciating pain.

Tick, tock. Tick, tock, goes the clock; tick tock.

"What art thou doing out here in the middle of night, child?" asked the attendant on her hourly rounds. "How long hast thou been standing in this hall?"

Amanda stared ahead with a confused expression.

"Come, dear," the woman gently turned Amanda around. "Thou art cold as ice, Miss. To bed with thee." She led Amanda back to the ward, guided her into her bed, and pulled the covers up around her chin. "I shall tuck thee in tight to stay put, child." She pulled a large tie-down from under the mattress, folded it over the bedclothes, and secured it tightly to the bedposts at either end of the bed.

Amanda lay in the restraining cocoon without moving a muscle.

"Sleep now. Morning comes all too quickly here." The night attendant left the room and continued on her rounds.

Amanda closed her eyes. "Fuzz. It's all fuzz..."

...a large hand held her tight. But she couldn't escape, no matter how hard she struggled.

"No, don't. Please!" Tears soaked the blindfold tied around her head.

She fought harder, trying to strike out with her fists, but more rough hands pinned her wrists over her head.

Another hand reached between her legs, groping. Then a hard jab, and another, while something big and hot poked at her most private parts. At the hardest thrust, ripping flesh sent bolts of pain through her, and she let out a sharp cry. Amanda wavered at the edge of semi-consciousness as bright lights flashed inside her head...

...water trickled across her face, and she didn't know where she was. Tears? She felt her own tears—and the long-ago touch of someone wiping them away...

"...There, there. Let it all out, Mandy dear," Rev. Long-bottom crooned in his most sympathetic tones. "You've harbored that pain for much too long. It's time to let it all out and be done with it," he said, patting her shoulder softly as he eased her head onto his shoulder. "If anyone in this world deserves a good cry, my dear, it certainly is you."

"I... I never... never let... myself... cry like this before... over... over...Little Ben!" Her tiny frame shook with uncontrollable sobs. "I killed my baaabyyyy!"

"Give your grief to me, dear one. You've born this burden far too long. Let me carry away your heartbreak. I'll help you forget everything in this painful world." His breath brushed her ear as an oppressive weight bore down upon her. Amanda wrestled to free herself, but outweighed by a good 100 pounds, her struggles came to naught...

...Waking from a fitful sleep, Amanda felt herself drenched in sweat. She tried to move, but the constricting tie-down held the bedclothes tight.

* * * * *

Jeremy re-read the well-worn letter explaining why the Board of Friends had made the decision to send Amanda to their parent hospital near Philadelphia. He folded it carefully, returning it to its place on the mantle behind the clock. Mandy, my little yellow bird, will you ever come back to me?

He couldn't remain mournful for long, when two, boisterous toddlers ran to him, attached themselves to his legs and began pulling at opposite sides of his pants in an effort to elude one another's grasp. "Hey, you two," he said, lifting Lilly up into one arm, then Millie into the other. "Who's your best friend?"

"You, Papa!" Camellia stated with authority.

"Unka Mikey!" Lilly said with an ornery twinkle in her eye.

"Uncle Mikey? Really?" Jeremy gave her a big sloppy kiss, ending with a raspberry tickle on her cheek.

"You, Papa! YOU!" Lilly loved the game they played every evening after supper.

He set them on their feet. "Go, now. Let Aunt Vi get you ready for bed." He gave them each a swat on their bottoms and sent them off to the other room where Violet had fresh night-gowns laid out. But first Millie chased Lilly around the table, around the rocking chair, then followed her under the table in an effort to catch her twin.

"Enough, girls," Jeremy said with his that-ends-it tone. "Lilly, come out of there, now." Lilly obeyed. Before Jeremy could say another word, she streaked toward the other room, with Camellia at her heels.

He shook his head with a chuckle. "Those two keep this place alive."

"You say something to me?" Michael asked, turning from the dry sink, where he had just rinsed the last plate in the basin.

"Those girls. I don't know what I'd ever do without them, Mike."

"They definitely keep us on our toes around here." He dried the plate and sat it on top of the stack on the shelf. "Jems, I got a question."

"Shoot."

"Is there anywhere around here I can get a real wedding ring for Vi?"

"Hmmmm," Jeremy mused. "I never gave that kind of thing much thought."

"She's been wearing that chicken band long enough. It's turning her finger green, for heaven's sakes," he said, flicking the towel at his brother. "I told her to take the blasted thing off, but she won't hear of it."

"I reckon it means a lot to her, knowing she belongs to someone other than that tyrant of a father."

"I finally got her to talk about that some," Michael said soft-ly, so Violet wouldn't hear. He listened for a moment, and hear-ing loud giggles coming from the other room, he continued on in a low voice. "Took her long enough to trust me. I can hardly believe what all she's told me."

"He's the one who put the babe on her, isn't he."

Michael nodded his head in the affirmative. "From what she said, he'd been 'hurting her in the night' for years. That's how she put it. And that's all she'd say."

"Makes you appreciate how hard it must have been for the poor girl, doesn't it."

"How could he do such a thing to his own flesh and blood?"

"It's beyond me," Jeremy said. "I look at these tykes of mine and wish I could protect them from all the pain of this world forever. It'd kill me to be the cause of any hurt comin' to 'em."

The brothers stood in silence before the fire for a few moments.

"I sure would like to surprise Vi for Christmas, if I can find something suitable."

"I'll ask Jonathan. He gets around. I'd bet he'll know where to find you a wedding ring."

"Thanks."

Two little night-gowned girls, short braids flying, streaked in from the other room for their nighttime kisses. "Night Papa! Night Unka Mikey!"

The men scooped up little girls, one each, and gave nite-nite hugs and kisses. They switched girls, repeated the process, then carried them toward the other room, where Vi stood in the doorway, beaming at the sight.

"You'll never know how much good it does my heart to see a Papa love his little girls so," Violet said softly to Jeremy, as he passed her in the doorway.

Jeremy gave her shoulder a squeeze on his way by. When Michael reached her, he leaned down and gave her a peck on the cheek. "You're just beginning to see what real love can be," he whispered in her ear.

Jeremy and Michael tossed the girls into the big bed Jeremy

had put in the opposite corner from his own bedstead in the old part of the cabin. The twins had outgrown their bent-twig cribs, and now that they no longer needed nighttime diapers, Jeremy deemed them ready for their "big girl bed."

"Sleep tight, you two," he said, tucking the covers in snugly. "No wrestling, Lilly, you hear?"

"Yes, Papa."

The three adults retired to the other room, leaving two, wiggly toddlers trying to wind down for the night.

Jeremy took his pipe from the mantle, opened the tobacco pouch, and carefully filled the bowl, tamping it down to just the right firmness with his thumb. He stuck a kindling stick among the coals till it flamed to life, then held it to the pipe while he drew in easy breaths until the tobacco glowed. Waving out the stick, he carefully laid it beside the stacked wood to use again. Then he took a seat in the rocker, gazed into the fire, and sat there rocking, enjoying his evening smoke.

Violet removed her apron and hung it on the hook next to the pantry. She retrieved her knitting basket from the bottom shelf, pulled out the chair at the end of the table, and sat down to resume work on the stocking she had begun the night before.

Michael poked up the fire, adding another log, then lay down on the hearth rug, hands behind his head, and watched Violet's hands fly. "How in the world do you know what to do to make a sock?"

"It's not hard," Vi answered. "I've been making them since I was six years old," she said, throwing over the yarn for another stitch. "It's the last thing my mother taught me before she died," Vi said in a quiet voice. "Makes me feel closer to her, somehow, when I'm knitting."

The three had come to enjoy a companionable silence in the evenings, with an occasional comment here and there to interrupt their quiet ease. Jeremy usually excused himself to bed down early in the other room, as soon as the twins had fallen asleep, leaving the hearthside to Violet and Michael. Tonight's activities followed the same, familiar routine. Jeremy tapped out his pipe over the fireplace, laid it back on the mantle beside his tobacco pouch, then stretched with a long, tired yawn.

"Guess I'll go turn in," he said.

"I'll bank the fire before we bed down," Michael said. "See you in the morning, Jems." He pushed the burning embers together, added another log to the pile, then moved the ashes close around the base, so the fire would smolder throughout the night.

"Night, Jeremy," Violet said with a smile. "Thanks for a lovely day."

After Jeremy left the room, Michael walked around behind Violet's chair, leaned down and snuggled against her ear. "You feeling tired yet?"

She laid the knitting back in its basket and turned to him. "I believe I am, husband of mine," she said with a knowing smile.

Michael pulled her up from the chair and gave her a long, deep kiss. He felt her relax and melt into his arms. "Let's take to our bed, wife," he said with a wink. Before she knew what happened, he'd lifted her off her feet and was taking the steps, two at a time, up to the loft bedroom they shared.

Christmas 1818

Two beribboned little girls jumped up and down, eagerly awaiting the arrival of Aunt Sadie and Uncle Willie, who'd been invited for Christmas dinner. This would mark the first time in four years that Michael, Jeremy and Sadie had been together to celebrate the holiday.

"They coming! They coming!" the twins took turns hollering, as the girls hopped on and off the bench sitting below the cabin's south-facing window. Jeremy had finally managed to replace the greased-paper with real glass this past fall. Ever since, the girls spent a goodly portion of their days with noses plastered against it, enamored with the novelty of being able to see outdoors from inside the cabin, wavy though the world looked through that windowpane.

Michael opened the door to the young couple, welcoming

them in for the long-awaited celebration. Amid hugs, kisses and all manner of boisterous noises emanating from the little girls and a tightly swaddled four-month-old Tadpole, the family doffed coats, hats and mittens, and settled in for a heartwarming day of fun.

"Here, Millie, would you put this under the Christmas tree for Aunt Sadie?" Sadie handed the tot a wrapped parcel and aimed her toward the decorated bough Jeremy had set up in the far corner of the cabin's addition. Millie dutifully carried the bundle over to the tree and laid it gently underneath.

"Me too! Me too!" Lilly jumped up and down, demanding equal duty.

"Here, you can take this one over, Lilly. But be careful with it." Willie handed her a package that stood almost as tall as she did. Lilly pushed and shoved at the large parcel, trying to move it over to the tree.

"Too big!" she stomped her foot in frustration.

"Here, let Uncle Willie help," he said, lifting the package while Lilly held on to the string. Together they set it underneath Jeremy's tree. "Thanks, Lilly. That was heavy! I couldn't have done it without you."

Lilly began to pull at the package string, only to be stopped by her daddy. "Wait a minute there, little girl. We have a dinner to eat before anyone opens gifts."

Lilly stomped her foot again. "Want my present NOW!"

Jeremy stood, staring down at his headstrong daughter with an uncompromising gaze. "Lilly, is that any way to act after your Aunt Vi cooked up such a nice dinner for everybody?"

She hung her head at his gentle authority. "No, Papa. Lilly bad."

"Lilly's not bad," he said, reassuringly. "Just all wound up for a special day of fun, that's all." He reached down, picked her up, and gave her a great, big hug. "Come on, Pipsqueak," he said, using Sadie's old nickname for the daughter who reminded him so of the baby sister he raised long ago. "Let's get you and

Millie up in your chair." He plopped Lilly into one side of the high-legged, double chair he'd made for the girls, then reached down and picked up Millie, placing her beside her sister. He tied them both securely with the fabric strip that kept them from escaping.

"I hope everyone likes turkey," Violet said with a broad smile. "Michael shot us a big one, and I've been cooking it since last night. I do hope it's not too tough."

"I been smelling that bird basting on the string for hours," said Michael. "I can't wait to get a taste."

Sadie and Willie took places on the bench Jeremy had moved over from beneath the window, with Michael sitting at one end of the table, and Jeremy at the other. The girls' chair sat around the corner from Jeremy, with a place for Violet next to them. Before she brought the serving dishes over from the sideboard, Jeremy asked to pray.

"Dear heavenly Father, we thank you for this time together as a family. Being here in this hard land makes us all realize how much the people closest to us really mean. Thank you for Sadie and Willie, and for Michael and Violet, who have all enriched my life beyond measure. And a special thanks for the little ones You sent us. Without them, our lives would be mighty empty." Jeremy swallowed. "Dear Lord, please send a special angel to help my Mandy, to touch her and make her whole so she can come back home to us. Make our family complete."

Lilly started to kick at her sister, causing Millie to whine.

"And Lord, please give two little girls the daddy they need to keep them from getting into too much mischief while they're in my care."

The girls stopped kicking at each other and dutifully folded hands and bowed heads at their daddy's one-eyed stare.

"Thank you, Lord, for the Christmas dinner we are about to receive, and the loving hands that have prepared it. Bless it to the strengthening of our bodies and spirits. We pray all this in our Savior's precious name. Amen."

"Amen," came a response from around the table. "Let's EAT!"

Violet rose and moved to the sideboard, where she had the feast laid out in serving dishes for the occasion: roast turkey and gravy with cornbread stuffing, squash swimming with freshly churned butter, shelly beans with side pork, fried apples, and special, blueberry ebelskiver, made with a generous portion of Sadie's dried blueberries.

Violet handed each dish to Jeremy, in turn, who first fixed little girls' plates, then offered the repast to his honored guests. The room rang with the clatter of dishes, ooos and ahhss at each taste of a new gustatory delight, as well as giggles from little girls, wound up tight on this special day of days. Tad, lying on the hearth rug, fast asleep, would enjoy his own, liquid feast later in the afternoon.

By the time the crumbs from the last ebelskiver scraped clean the last dab of turkey gravy from the last plate, everyone glowed with full stomachs and overflowing hearts. Kicking at each other once again, the little girls clamored to escape from their chair and open gifts.

"All right, you two," Jeremy said, releasing them. "We can open presents now. But we'll all help Aunt Vi clean up the dishes after we finish with gifts."

Lilly raced Millie to the tree, grabbed the biggest package, and started to wrestle with the string that wrapped it tight.

"Wait just a minute there, Pipsqueak," Jeremy pulled his overzealous daughter back away from the parcel. "How do you know that one's for you?"

"Unka Willie *told* me!"

Willie affirmed her declaration with a nod of his head.

"All right then, have at it."

"Here, Millie," Sadie said, handing the more bashful twin the smaller package. "This one's for you to open. But *both* gifts are for you girls to *share*, understand?"

Millie nodded her head in acquiescence. "Share," she stated simply.

Lilly finally managed to extricate her package from its binding string, then folded back the blanket that concealed a miniature baby cradle.

"Uncle Willie made it for you girls, Lilly," Sadie said. "Wasn't that nice of him?"

Lilly wrapped herself around Willie's leg and hugged tight. Meanwhile, Millie carefully pulled string loose from around the other gift, unfolding a matching blanket that revealed two, rag dolls sized to fit the baby cradle.

"Aunt Sadie made the dolls and blankets for you, too," Willie told the girls, still trying to disentangle the boisterous Lilly from his leg. "You better give her a big hug."

Both girls swarmed Sadie, dutifully giving hugs and kisses.

"All right, you two," Jeremy said. "Go play with your dollies for a while and let the adults have a turn." He picked up a small parcel from behind the tree and handed it to Michael. "Here, Mike. I didn't know what to give you that would let you know how much I appreciate all you've done to make my life easier over these last months," he said, holding out the pouch. "This is for you and Vi."

Michael took the leather pouch, unfolded its cover, and pulled out an official-looking paper. He studied it for a moment, then gave his brother an incredulous stare.

"I deeded over half the farm to you, Mike. It's the least I can do to help you two get a start of your own. Next year we'll put up a cabin for you."

Michael stood speechless, pulling Violet to him with one arm; she shook her head in disbelief. "Half the farm? For *us*?"

"You deserve it, after all the clearing work you've helped with around here this year, Mike. Not to mention all the other thankless labor you've both put in."

"But this is way too much—"

"No arguments. You two need a start, and that's that."

Michael grabbed his brother and hugged him tight."

"Hay-de Ho, Jems! Good for you!" Sadie chimed in. She winked at Willie, who squeezed her hand in answer. That morning, the two of them had received a similar gift from Ma Hawkins, who'd signed her farm over to Willie and Sadie. With Tom now officially installed at the Guthries, and Clara being the inheritor of the Guthrie Place, Ma figured the time was ripe for her to pass her acreage to her youngest son. The footloose Harmon had shown no desire whatsoever to settle down to a life of farming, so Ma considered her choice well made.

"Can't say as I have anything quite so earthshaking for you and Willie," Jeremy said to his sister. "It's more of a responsibility than a gift, really. Here," he handed a similar pouch to Sadie. "This is for you two."

Sadie accepted it with trepidation, carefully peeking inside to find another official looking document. She read in silence, with Willie looking on over her shoulder.

"I had a paper drawn up by that new barrister up in Uniontown. I want you and Willie to be the guardians of the twins, if anything should happen to me," he said with a thick voice. "Since we don't know when Amanda will come back, I thought it best to have legal guardians set up to take care of the girls."

"Jems, you *know* I'll always take care of them," Sadie said with force. "I've taken care of them since they were born, haven't I?"

"I know that. But I wanted to make sure it's all official."

"We're honored to be trusted with those two precious charges," Willie said.

"We'd never let anything happen to them, Jems," said Mike.

"I know that. But I'm not asking you and Vi to give up any more of your life for me and mine. You've done so much already. You two deserve to make a life of your own together."

"Good grief, are you planning to kick the bucket on us, Jems?" Sadie asked.

"Lord willing, I aim to have a good, long life," he said with a smile. "But we've all found out you can never be too sure about anything in this hard land."

"All right, all right. Enough with the doom and gloom," Mike shouted. "We're here to *celebrate*!" He took a small package from its hiding place among the branches of the tree and handed it to Violet. "It's nothin' fancy, but it's given with all my love," he said, handing her the tiny box.

She accepted it with her usual shyness, then carefully lifted the walnut-inlaid lid. Nestled inside on a small piece of soft wool, lay a golden wedding band. "Oh, Michael!" she breathed in surprise. "It's a wedding ring!"

"Long overdue, I'd say." He lifted it out. "Don't you think it's about time you threw out that ugly chicken band?"

Violet removed the rusted band and tucked it into her pocket for safe keeping. That chicken band would always remain a special keepsake. Michael slipped the new wedding ring gently on the third finger of her left hand. "For my wife," he said. "May you always wear it with pride."

Tears slid down Violet's cheeks, and she impulsively threw her arms around Michael's neck and gave him a big, squeezing hug. When she realized what she'd done in front of everybody, her face turned several shades of embarrassed red.

Willie smacked Michael on the back, "Well done, brother-in-law!" he said with an ornery wink. "Keep surprisin' 'em and they'll always have plenty of hugs to spare!"

Violet held her hand at arm's length, treasuring the sight of her very own wedding ring. "Oh, Michael. I don't have anything nearly so glorious to give you," she said with eyes lowered. "But I do hope you get as much joy from this small token as you've given me." She handed him a package she pulled from her other pocket.

Michael took the gift, untied the string, then folded back the piece of cloth. In his hand lay two, tiny baby booties. "A baby?" he asked, incredulously. "A *Ba*-by!"

Violet nodded her head in affirmation, face glowing red

once more.

"Are you sure it's safe?" Mike asked with sudden concern.

"I'm feeling fine… really," she said, taking his hand and giving it a squeeze. She eased it onto her middle, over to one side, and Michael's eyes lit up in wonder as he felt the slight flutter beneath his fingers.

"It *moved*!"

"I wanted to wait to tell you until I felt life," she whispered. "I had to be sure."

Sadie lunged toward them both, giving them a big, group hug. "Congratulations! What a wonderful Christmas this has turned out to be!"

Chapter 9

Angel Visit
January 1819

Dear Lord, please send a special angel to help my Mandy, to touch her and make her whole so she can come back home to us and make our family complete.

With that one, simple prayer, Jeremy loosed the power of heaven in the life of his confused and hurting little wife. Although he believed in the influence angels can bring to bear over earthly affairs, he never dreamed how far their wings would reach.

Most often, those ethereal beings of light do their best work where no human eyes can bear witness. On rare occasions, however, they appear as real and as solid as Aunt Sadie's loving hug.

That's what Amanda needed now—an angel hug with skin on. And that's exactly what she found in the big-boned, big-hearted Lottie Mueller.

No one at the Friends' Asylum had heard Amanda utter a single word in the eight weeks since she'd come to them. From the time everyone awoke at 5 a.m., until the bell echoed in the long hallway giving the lights-out signal at 9:30 p.m., no one had heard a peep from Amanda Jane Bently Harrison. She followed along like a lost puppy, as the women marched through their daily routines.

The night attendant had reported hearing soft noises, on occasion, coming from Amanda's ward during the wee hours of the morning. But she could never tell whether those noises had come from Amanda or from one of other women talking in her sleep. By the time the attendant reached the room, all within had always quieted.

The days ticked by without incident in Amanda's sheltered, regimented world. Breakfast, 6 a.m.; medicine powders and examinations, 7 a.m.; exercise, 8 a.m.; morning chores, 8:30 to

11:30 a.m. The main meal came at noon. After dinner, the patients had a brief rest period at 1 p.m., then resumed their daily chores at 2:00. They ate a light, evening meal at 6 p.m., followed by indoor recreation from 7 to 9 p.m. At nine o'clock, they attended evening vespers, then the attendants administered sleeping powders to the most agitated inmates, and everyone prepared for bed. By 9:30 p.m., lights went out, and all the asylum lay tucked in for the night—some more firmly tucked than others, with Amanda still among their number to keep her from wandering the halls.

Daily duties of the more able-bodied patients varied by wards. Each ward assumed a particular task in sequence: one week wash dishes and help with light kitchen duties, the next week clean floors, the third week do laundry, fourth week tend the garden, in season—and so went the rotation, eventually including all the household duties that kept Friends Asylum running smoothly. The men's wards saw to the more physically demanding of tasks, such as tending the farm animals, planting and harvesting during summer months to help keep the inmates fed, and in winter seeing to the heavier maintenance chores, like hauling wood and shoveling snow.

Men and women alike had small tasks to perform during the first hour of their recreation period each evening—mending, polishing, patching, spinning—anything that could be performed indoors during the waning hours of evening light, in separate 'amusement rooms,' of course. Inmates could then spend the second hour of their recreation time reading, writing letters, or praying, if they so preferred. Most of them simply sat, exhausted from the days' demands and the effects of their individual hells. Those unable to work quite often had to be restrained, or undergo 'treatments' for their various conditions.

On the Sabbath, of course, everyone rested.

Amanda performed the tasks demanded of her with no fuss. At first someone had to show her how to do every job, taking her step by step through each basic chore. The more patient of the attendants, accustomed to leading many an addled soul through such exercises, took time to show Amanda how to spin and weave and then to sew a simple apron.

Some of the inmates even helped to teach her uncomplicated tasks on occasion. No one realized that Amanda had known few of these skills before she came to the asylum. The staff assumed that, as a settler's wife, she already knew how to do such chores. They had no way of comprehending the previous life from which she'd come—a life where servants would see to her every need.

In the course of the asylum's daily routine, Amanda came to learn the very skills she should have known to help her family survive on the frontier. As the days turned to weeks, and the weeks turned to months, Amanda began to gain not only valuable competence and experience, she also gained a trusted friend in Lottie Muller.

Since the staff had no clue as to what really troubled Amanda, they continued to treat her like a helpless child, leading her through each day's activities, convinced that sticking to a regimented routine would help the most tormented of souls find a measure of peace.

But Lottie had a feeling that inside this tiny, woman-child lay the troubled mind of a complicated woman who eventually would respond to kindness. Having lost her own children to scarlet fever, Lottie mothered anyone who appeared a likely recipient for her thwarted maternal attention. She took Amanda under her wing and tried to shield her from the more 'troublesome' of inmates.

Though not mentally unstable like a majority of patients at Friends Asylum, Lottie Muller suffered from epileptic seizures. Medical science at that time understood so little of the brain's intricate inner workings, people feared the 'falling sickness.' Its victims often found themselves locked up right along with lunatics and the insane.

Lottie's husband had 'put her away' five years before, when he could no longer cope with the anguish of watching her 'have a fit.' During the ensuing years, Lottie's seizures had become fewer and farther between, but each one grew progressively more severe. The seizures she'd experienced in the past six months required that the attendants restrain her in order to prevent injury whenever she convulsed. In the two months since Amanda's arrival, Lottie had suffered only one seizure, and that at night, so Amanda had never seen Lottie in her incapacitated state.

"Look, leibchein, you pull against spindle so, to twist," she demonstrated. "Keep tight and squeeze. No lumps... see?"

Amanda tried to mimic her example.

"Good. You learn."

Without a word, Amanda proceeded to pull and twist, pull and twist, as she wound the growing length of yarn around the spindle.

"That one'll never git outta this place," said old Mabel Winterstein. "Ain't hooked up right," she pointed to her head and made a face. "Cain't talk at-all."

"She talk when ready. Not before," Lottie answered. "Be patient, vershtain?"

"I say she cain't talk ev'n if she wanted to, so there." Without another word, Mabel took a length of the wool she held, shoved it in her mouth and began to chew.

"She more right in head than you," Lottie mumbled.

Amanda continued to spin, undisturbed by the conversations and people around her. Lottie kept pace with Amanda's progress, pointing out missed lumps here and there, showing her over again, how to pull them out smoothly. As they progressed together, Lottie kept up a one-sided conversation, telling Amanda all about her life before the asylum.

"Did I tell you where I come from, leibchein? My Mutti, she come from the Swartzwald, the Black Forest in Deutschland. My Papa was clock-maker. Made good clocks for rich people who come to Swartzwald on holiday. My Rudi, I meet in Heidelberg. Where Papa send brother Franz to school. Rudi become friend to Franz—help him find flat to live in, work to do for money. Wonderful times together they had." Lottie paused to give Amanda the opportunity to talk, but when she didn't say a word, Lottie continued.

"At Weinachten—you call Christmas—Mutti and I so miss our Franz, Papa take us on trip to Heidelberg to make visit. First time to see big city for me! Was *wonderful!* Franz introduce us to friend Rudi. Right away I feel deep in bones, he to become mein man. His eyes, Achh! When he look at me, mein knees to water they turn!" Lottie lowered her head and spun quietly for a time. "He take me dancing to Heidelberg Castle. We laugh, and we dance—on special wood floor. Right on top of giant wine barrel! Such fun!" She raised her hand to wipe away a tear.

The days passed, one after another. Each day, Lottie stayed close to Amanda, telling her more pieces in the puzzle of her own life, sharing friendship without expecting a thing in return. She told Amanda about her wedding; how she and Rudi came to live in Philadelphia, in America; about the birth of her four children and how they each grew. And she told how she'd nursed them through all manner of illness and injury, only to lose all four to the scarlet fever six years ago. Not once did Lottie tell how she came to live in the asylum; not once did she mention a word about her condition.

Even though Amanda made no outward indication that she heard any of the information Lottie imparted, she'd taken in every word. The quiet, acceptance Lottie demonstrated over her life of heartache and pain made a lasting impression on the hurting Southern girl, who'd never been taught how to handle the harsh realities of this world. Amanda came to love and respect the courageous woman who had been revealing the very strength of character she, herself, needed to survive. She began to understand that in spite of sorrow and anguish, she did have the capacity to endure.

February 1819

Wind howled through cracks under the cabin door, pushing puffs of powdery snow around its edges, onto the floor. Winter had settled in hard and cold this year, and the Harrisons did their best to keep the bodies and souls within the confines of their cabin warm, fed, and secure. They'd put up plenty of stores to see them through until spring, and with a hefty wood pile stacked outside, they had no fear of want nor winter's chill.

With only the basic of barn chores to carry out during the short days, Jeremy and Michael spent many an hour indoors. Jeremy kept himself busy cleaning guns, making new lead bullets, oiling harness, and shelling seed corn, while Michael had taken it upon himself to face the simple fireplace in the kitchen addition with new, cut stone. He also worked at fashioning a bread oven right in the stonework itself—quite the novelty on the frontier. Violet could hardly wait for him to finish, so she could bake the first, official loaf of real bread.

She'd grown tired of corncakes, and, in her advancing pregnancy, she craved a slice of crusty, whole-wheat bread. She'd been budding a yeast starter for that very purpose. With their babe growing and kicking under her breast, she beamed at the prospect of coming motherhood.

"You're looking mighty happy these days," Michael observed, hard at work on the stone. "You have a glow I've never seen before."

"I *am* happy," she said with a contented smile. "For the first time in my life, I have everything I ever wanted, and to be honest, it almost scares me."

"You have a right to be happy, Vi," he said. "I'm going to keep telling you that until you believe it."

"What do you think this little one will be like?"

"If he's anything like you, Mike, he'll be an ornery son-of-a-gun," Jeremy piped up from his spot under the window, where he sat rubbing oil into Patsy's harness.

"And if she's anything like you," Michael said with a nod toward Violet, "she'll be the most beautiful little girl in the world."

"I can hardly wait," Violet said with a sigh. "Three more months seem like an eternity until we meet this little person."

"It'll pass. Just you wait and see." Michael tapped away at the stone he was shaping, being careful to keep the chipping mess on the blanket he'd spread to catch shards of stone. He warned the girls to play with their dollies over on the other side of the cabin, while he wielded his mallet and chisel over here. Michael had closed up the back of the fireplace, so they could keep it burning warmly in the main part of the cabin. For the time being, until he finished this new side, Violet moved all her cooking activities into the other room,.

The last time Jeremy had checked, the girls sat playing with their new dolls on the floor near the warm hearthstone, a protective barrier shielding them from the fire. Unbeknownst to him, they now sat at the whistling front door, playing in the little drifts of snow that had blown in underneath.

"I'd better check on our stew," Violet said, laying her knitting aside. She'd been working on baby things since Christmas and had a respectable layette ready to welcome her coming child. When she stood up from the rocking chair, she felt a solid kick that took her breath away. "Oooph, you surely are an active little one," she said, holding her middle. She walked through the doorway to the other side of the cabin and immediately saw the twins smearing snow on one another's faces. "What *are* you girls doing over here?"

"Washing!" Lilly answered. "Millie has dirty face."

"Come away from that drafty doorway this minute," Violet said, hands on hips, which accentuated her swelling middle.

The twins dutifully obeyed, walking to her side with heads hung low. Violet took their hands in her own. "Your fingers are cold as ice! Come warm up by the fire before you catch your deaths." She shooed them to the hearth and sat them down. Then she leaned over the fire shield so she could stir the venison stew. Judging it nearly done, she added a little hot water from the kettle sitting on the nearby trivet, gave another stir, then replaced the lid and swung the trammel back over the glowing coals.

"You two sit there till your hands warm up, you hear?" she

185

instructed the girls. "And don't you dare move any closer to that fire."

They nodded in the affirmative, sitting as still as two toddlers could manage.

Violet went back to the other room and collected her knitting basket. "I'll be around by the fire," she told the men. "I need to keep a closer eye on those two till they warm up. They were playing in snow drifts by the door. They're ice cold!"

"It's about time to lay them down for naps," Jeremy said. "Let me know when they get warmed up, and I'll come over and put them down. You don't need to be lifting those girls any more, you know."

"I know. I've been very careful about lifting things, just like Mrs. Hawkins told me," Violet answered. Ma had warned Violet to be extra cautious, since she feared the girl's poor, abused womb might not be able to carry a child to full term. With all the scarring and the history of miscarriage, which Violet in her simple ignorance had misinterpreted as irregular monthlies, Ma had her misgivings about this, or any, pregnancy for Violet Harrison.

"The stew will be ready shortly. Why don't you let the girls have a little dinner first, then you can put them down for the afternoon," Violet suggested.

"Sounds fine to me," Jeremy said, rubbing a finish cloth over the harness, to wipe dry the last of the oil.

Outdoors, the wind picked up and whipped around the cabin, causing a loud moaning sound. Daylight faded to a gray, foreboding haze, full of the prospect of coming snow.

"Feels like we're in for a big storm," Jeremy observed, rubbing at his aching shoulder. "I'd best go check the animals before it hits. Get them settled in for the duration."

"I'll help," Michael offered. "I need to move around, after sitting hunched over these stones all morning." He laid his tools aside, then stretched his arms over his head with a loud yawn. "We'll be back in directly to eat, Vi," he called on their way out the front door.

Wind pushed the door wide open, whipping more snow onto the floor. "Pull that door closed before you freeze us to death in here!" Violet called from her seat by the fire. The sudden draft stirred the coals into flame. With a loud slam, the wind sucked the door shut just as violently as it had blown open. "That's some nasty weather!"

"Nasty! Nasty! Nasty!" the girls called. "Snow! Snow! More snow!" They ran for the new drifts blown in the doorway, grabbing handfuls of the powdery fluff and stuffing it into their mouths with glee.

* * * * *

After checking things in the barn and seeing all the animals fed and secured, the Harrison men returned to enjoy a leisurely, early afternoon meal, as the coming storm wound itself up to near blizzard-strength. With the girls tucked in for naps, the adults took advantage of the time for a little rest of their own. Jeremy lay down on the hearth rug beside the twins' bed, soaking in the warmth of the nearby fire. Michael and Violet snuggled together on Jeremy's bed in the opposite corner of the main cabin. Before long, all occupants slept soundly.

Along about four in the afternoon, the temperature dropped, and the wind took on a heart-rending moan, as snow began to blow nearly horizontal from the northeast. Violet awoke, terrified at the haunting sound.

"Michael! Wake up!" She shook him frantically. "It's awful! Just awful!" She began to cry against his shoulder. "I had a terrible dream! Blood everywhere. It wouldn't stop!"

He pulled her closer, crooning softly in an attempt to ease her trembling. "Shhhhh, it's just a dream. "Everything's fine." He stroked her hair, her cheek, and folded her more tightly into his arms. "The wind has you upset, Vi, that's all." They lay there, listening to the storm bluster around the cabin. "Can't say as I ever heard wind sound quite that mournful before."

"It's a sign. I know it is."

"It's just a winter storm," he said, snuggling her even closer.

187

"Don't listen to it. Here, listen to my heartbeat instead." He guided her head to his chest, where she lay against him, trying to concentrate on any sound but that shrieking wind. "Listen," he said, "it's beating for you... I love you, Vi... love you, Vi... love you, Vi...."

He managed to evoke a smile from his apprehensive wife.

"Thank you, my love," she said with a sigh. "You always manage to make me feel better."

"Think nothing of it. I'm here to serve, you know."

"Michael?"

"Yes?"

"Promise me something."

"Anything, Vi."

"Promise me you'll always love me the way you do today."

"I can't do that."

"What?"

"I can't love you the same way, because every day, I love you more."

Violet melted against him, her quiet tears wetting his chest. She no longer heard the blustering storm, only two hearts beating as one.

* * * * *

The storm raged on throughout the night, snow piling half way up in drifts outside the door. Jeremy snuggled with the twins in their bed, while Michael and Violet had taken over Jeremy's. With the temperature dipping well below zero, and the kitchen fireplace temporarily out of commission, precious little heat made its way to the bedroom above the addition, so everyone slept in the main cabin, sharing in its warmth. Jeremy and Michael took turns feeding the fire, to keep them all snug.

In the wee hours of morning, Violet awoke in a cold sweat. Something felt amiss. She listened for a moment. Silence. Finally! That unsettling wind had stopped its disconcerting wail. But something else didn't seem right. She lay there, as her greatest fear began to tighten its unrelenting grip: cramps. "Lord, no," she whispered.

She shook Michael awake.

"Hmmmm?"

"Michael, something's wrong!"

"It's just the storm, Vi. Go back to sleep." He tried to snuggle her into his arms, but she resisted.

"Michael!" she cried with growing alarm. "Something's *wrong*… with the *baby!*"

He snapped fully awake, sitting straight up in the bed.

"Light the lamp, would you?"

Michael did as she asked. When she folded back the covers, they stared in shock at the crimson pool in which Violet lay.

"Oh my Lord, what are we going to do?"

"Wake Jeremy," Violet instructed. "We need to fetch Mrs. Hawkins."

Stumbling across the room in stocking feet, Michael tapped his brother's shoulder, trying not to awaken the twins. Thankfully, youngsters sleep soundly at this growing stage of life.

Jeremy roused at his brother's touch. "Hmmm? What is it?"

"Vi's bleeding. We need help."

"I'll go for Ma." Jeremy eased himself out from tangled arms and legs, making sure to cover the little girls tightly as he left the bed, so they wouldn't miss his warmth. He pulled pants on over his nightshirt and added the sweater Mandy had knit for him. By the time he pulled on boots and overcoat, Michael had the fire stirred up and a pot of water at the boil. He'd eased the bloody bedding out from beneath Violet, replacing it with clean linens, and he'd given her the roll of rags to pack herself as best she could. He instructed her firmly to lie still.

Too terrified to move, Violet lay motionless.

Jeremy lifted the latch and pulled open the door to reveal a wall of snow. "Good grief! It's going to take me a while just to get to the barn in this," he said. "I don't doubt it'll take twice as long as usual to get to Ma's place. Maybe longer."

"Do your best. We'll hold down the fort."

"I'll get back soon as I can."

"Thanks!"

Jeremy slogged his way through the waist-high drifts to saddle up Patsy. She wasn't going to like being thrust into this nose-freezing cold. "Hope the old girl can take it," he mumbled.

It took Jeremy an hour-and-a-half to make the usual thirty-minute trip to the Hawkins' place—he and his faithful old horse both badly spent. By the time he woke the household and Ma had herself ready to ride, more than two hours had slipped away.

Willie had taken Patsy into his barn and given her a thorough rub-down. "She'll never make it back to your place tonight," he told his brother-in-law. "I'll saddle Freddie. He's big enough to carry you both, and he's fresh. Patsy's done in."

"Thanks, Willie. I'm about done in, myself. But I have to fetch Ma back. We don't know what we're apt to find once we get there."

"I hope everything's all right." Sadie hugged her brother.

With two bodies to carry, Freddie struggled his way through the drifts for the next hour-and-a-half. It neared 6 a.m. when Jeremy returned—both he and Ma nearly frozen to the bone.

He dropped Ma at the porch, helping her in the door, then immediately took Willie's horse to the barn, gave him a firm rubdown, and covered him with the wool blanket. After breaking up ice in the watering trough, he gave Freddie a long drink. By the time Jeremy dragged himself back into the cabin, he barely had enough strength left in his legs to stand. He pushed the door shut behind himself and sank to the floor.

When he finally looked up, the scene that greeted him sent shudders down his spine—not shivers from the cold, but tremors of heart-wrenching grief.

Michael sat beside Violet, staring straight ahead, holding the tiniest, bluest babe he'd ever seen. And Ma, on the other side of the bed, gently pulled the sheet over Violet's waif-like face, a pile of bloody linens stacked at her feet.

Dear Libby,

Hope you and youren wintered fair. Me and Katrina had us a cozy time with Jason and Mary Sue over the cold months. I can tell you I sure did take pleasure in spending time with those grandbabies. Josie talks up a storm now that she has turned four. Still calls her little brother He-He. Harley that would be. That boy turned one year just last month. Took his first step on his birthday, he did.

I guess it should come as no surprise that Mary Sue is setting on the nest with number 3. She is due to hatch some time in early summer. Katrina stayed on there to help out. I came back here to open up Riverstop after the ice broke free. Once river traffic took to running again. Josie dotes on her Aunt Katrina. And Katrina is good with the little ones. So it suited for her to stay and help Mary Sue as her legs are already swelling. But being my youngest Katrina knows nothing of births. I am fixing to trade places with her when Mary Sue's time draws near. Let her run our business while I help the new babe into this world.

Truth is I will worry more about Katrina here on her own than about Jason's wife hatching out another chick. But my youngest has her feet planted firm on this one. She says I got to learn to treat her like a full partner. Not a daughter. I did not let on, Libby. But that tickled me to no end. I saw my young self in her so strong right then.

At Christmas time Flora Jean got hitched up with Wheatly Coulter. Never did know his full name until the Justice spoke it out with the I-do's. Funny sounding moniker. I still just call him that Coulter Boy. Flora Jean seems right happy with her pick. I pray she stays happy with him.

The sad news here bouts has to do with the Harrisons once more. Michael's wife Violet is dead. So is her baby what come too soon during that wicked blizzard back in Febyary. Edie says it was a miracle she carried the babe as long as she did. Seeing she had so much trouble thataway before. Sad, sad time for Michael and for Jeremy both. The birth was a terrible bloody one. Brought back dreadful memories for Jeremy. Of when Amanda lost her babe at that kicking bee.

Michael is beside himself with grief. Sadie said he was working on a nice bake oven for Violet. He was fixing up the kitchen fireplace for her special. But he took a hammer to the whole thing after she went and died on him. Smashed it to smithereens.

Jeremy did not say a word. Just commenced to clean up the mess and fix up the old fireplace by hisself. Sadie has the twins for the time being. The Harrison house is no fit place for them right now. Michael has took to the drink to drown his sorrow. Jeremy just sits and smokes his pipe. Fretting for his addled wife to come home to him. A-feared that she will not.

I worry more for my sister. She has took Violet's death awful hard. She was the first mother Edie ever lost. And the second babe. Says she is losing her touch and should give up midwifing for good. Let Sadie take over for her. I say she is just tired and needs a rest. She will be her old self soon enough. Seeing as she has another grandchild to dote on. Tom and Clara's first babe that would be. A boy name of Thomas Anson. Born end of March. They named him after his daddy and after Clara's daddy.

Edie did not handle his birth. She turned Sadie loose for that one. Just stood by to give orders when needed. Edie said the birth went easy enough. But Clara hollered her fool head off the whole time. The babe brought a honest to goodness smile out of Winifred. Anson Guthrie still cannot talk more than a few words, most of them bad ones. But he looked pleased as punch to have a living boy babe in the house at long last.

How go plans for your new house, Lib? I bet you can not wait to see it built. Please write to me when you get a chance. I am still your friend. Though it has been most of a year since we have laid eyes on each other. Over 6 month since I last had any word from you. Hope all is well up there in them Fire lands.

your friend,

Ellie Mae

Chapter 10

"This kind we pull out, leibchein." Lottie showed Amanda the difference between the broad-leafed weeds and green-bean shoots, as the women worked at weeding the Asylum garden. With spring upon them, the patients spent plenty of time out-doors tending to necessary garden chores. The Friends' doctors believed that, aside from the benefit of healthy work, which helped to keep the hospital inmates fed, being outdoors in the sunshine supplied a needed therapy of its own.

"These we let grow, make beans for to eat." Lottie instruct-ed. "Good. Now you vershtain."

Amanda said not a word, but worked her way down the row, Lottie keeping pace with her in the next row over. Most of the other women weeded at the far end of the garden. Amanda and Lottie worked in their usual, companionable silence, with Lottie commenting now and again on the birds nesting in nearby trees, the lilacs in bloom next to the fence, the joy of a lovely spring.

"My last baby born in spring," Lottie said. "Lovely leib-chein, she. Light hair, eyes blue. My Rudi so happy to have girl. After three dark-haired boys born in row. His heart melt at sight of little Greta." Lottie kept quiet for several more minutes, then said, "We lost her in spring, too. When lilacs bloom. Put lilacs all over grave." Lottie wiped away a tear. "Scent makes me to cry still."

"How did you ever stand losing *all* of your children?"

For a moment, Lottie stood dumbstruck, hardly believing she'd heard the tiny woman-child finally speak.

"You weep for them. You cry out to God. Then go on you must."

"The going on part is what I find so difficult," came the quiet, southern drawl. "How ever did you manage it?"

"Must believe, leibchein. Believe that tomorrow bring better things. Must see to business of living, no matter how hard the day."

They continued their weeding in silence to the end of the row. When they started on the next two rows over, Amanda spoke again.

"I lost my Little Ben in a fire. It was so cold. I only wanted to warm up the cabin, finish pouring off the lard." She weeded for a few more minutes; Lottie kept her peace, waiting. "I killed my baby, as surely as if I'd deliberately set that fire," Amanda said, shaking her head.

"Must not think such a way. Accidents happen. You not do on purpose."

"I finally did come to understand that. But it took such a long time," Amanda said. "Jeremiah was so forgiving. He never blamed me."

"Good man."

"He's a very good man. But he must hate me by now."

"Hate? Why hate?"

"I betrayed him," Amanda said with trembling chin. She took a deep breath and forged ahead. "I lost another baby before I came here. I fell, and the baby came too soon. I know God was punishing me."

"For falling? No, no! God not punish so."

"You don't understand. Another man took me against my will," Amanda hung her head in shame, "and Jeremiah never knew... until the boy was stillborn. I wanted to die then, too." She took a deep breath. "My Lord, I lost so much blood, I *should* have died. I honestly don't know what kept me alive."

"Not your time to go, leibchein. God still gives work to do for you," Lottie said with conviction. "Never, never choose to die. Must choose to *live!*"

Amanda weeded quietly for a time. "You are so wise."

"Not wise, leibchein. Crazy, yes. Not wise."

"Nonsense. You're the most rational person I've ever met. How in the world did you come to be in this place?"

"Here, I belong," Lottie said simply. "Rudi good man. He fear for my safety, for my life. I miss him bad. But here I need to be."

"I don't understand."

"No need, leibchein. In this place God has work for me now. This is enough."

The noontime bell rang to call the inmates for dinner, and they marched through the remainder of their regimented day. That night, for the first time in more weeks than she could remember, Amanda finally slept the deep, deep slumber of dreams…

…two little boys. She saw two little boys playing in an apple tree—the very same apple tree beneath which two headstones marked the graves of her two lost babes. Carved upon each stone, a small hand held a broken rose—two young lives, nipped in the bud. Funny, she'd never seen those stones before. Didn't know where they'd come from. But that was definitely Jeremiah's apple tree, only much larger than before. The boys sat in branches on opposite sides of the tree, their giggles ringing like the tinkle of bells. Each time they kicked their feet, apple blossoms rained down upon the grave stones.

She saw herself standing under the tree, beckoning the barefoot boys to come down to her.

"We're coming, Mama," the older one responded. He looked so much like Little Ben, only more grown up—perhaps four years old now. "Come on, Joey," he called to his younger, web-toed playmate. "Mama's calling!"

"Ben? Joey?"

"We're coming, Mama!" The boys jumped down and ran to Amanda, one on either side, hugging her knees.

"It's really you, Ben? And Joey, too?" She ruffed the smaller, toddler's hair. He looked to be just over one, but he managed to keep up with his older brother just fine.

"We're here, Mama. We're always here, you know that."

"I so wanted to see you, to hug you, to tell you how much I miss holding you."

"It's all right, Mama. Hug us any time you want. Just come to the apple tree to find us… "

…Amanda woke with a start. For the first time in months her head felt clear. She'd seen her boys. She'd hugged them! Her arms no longer felt empty.

* * * * *

The next morning, Lottie Mueller did not come to breakfast. Amanda felt lost without her, they'd become so close over the past six months. She ate her porridge in silence, waiting. But no Lottie. After morning examinations and exercise, the attendant marched the women to the garden for more weeding—today in the pea patch. When the dinner bell rang for their noon meal, and still no Lottie, Amanda grew more apprehensive. What could have happened to her?

Mrs. Tetherwood guided the women through the serving line, as usual, but when Amanda reached the head matron, she stopped. "Did something happen to Lottie Mueller? Where is she?"

"Praise be to heaven, child! Thou hast spoken at last." Mrs. Tetherwood came as close to being excited as she could get. "What has kept thee silent so long?"

"I didn't have anything to say," Amanda stated simply. She waited for an answer to her question, eyebrows uplifted in punctuation.

"My dear, last night Mrs. Mueller suffered a Grand Mal seizure that sent her home to our Lord," the head matron replied.

Amanda's eyes began to water; with a hitch in her breath she held back a sob. "Grand Mal?"

"A very serious convulsion. She has endured lesser fits for

years, but this particular one finally claimed her life. Her troubled time on this earth has finally come to a close."

"Her work is done," Amanda reiterated. In her heart, she knew Lottie Muller had been sent as her own, special guardian, to ease her back into the business of life.

Amanda walked through the dinner line on wooden legs. She ate very little. Before retiring to her room for afternoon rest period, Amanda sought out Mrs. Tetherwood with a request. "May I see her? Mrs. Muller?"

"Whatever for?" the head matron wanted to know.

"I'd like to pay my respects. Tell her goodbye."

"The doctor will have to give consent," she said. "I'll see what can be arranged."

Amanda trudged through the remainder of her day, weeping quietly now and then as she pulled weeds, thinking of Lottie's steadfast kindness. Before the supper bell called everyone for the evening meal, Amanda walked to the lilac bushes and picked a small nosegay, carefully easing the flowers into her apron pocket so as not to crush the tender blossoms.

When evening recreation time arrived, Mrs. Tetherwood pulled Amanda aside.

"Come with me, child. Thee may pay thy respects to Mrs. Muller." The head matron led her into the wing that housed the examination rooms. "The attendants laid her out in here," Mrs. Tetherwood said, pushing open the door to a darkened room, where one tiny window let in the last rays of sunset. "Thee may have fifteen minutes, then thou must return to recreation until vespers," the head matron said, as she set the lamp she carried on a small table just inside the doorway. She closed the door behind her, leaving Amanda with instructions to knock when she had finished.

Amanda eased the lilacs from her pocket, walked to the examination table, and gently tucked the fragrant flowers into Lottie's cold hands. "For you," she said in a raspy voice, "and for your little leibchein." Amanda bowed her head. "How can I ever thank you for all you've done for me?" she began. "You showed me how to forgive myself so I could face living again. I'll never be able to repay such kindness."

As Amanda stood there, contemplating the ironies life hands out, the evening sunset took on a bright, pink radiance that refracted through the wavy glass of the room's tiny window. Crimson light fell upon Lottie's face, making it appear to glow.

Amanda shivered. "Dear Lord in Heaven, please give this dear woman peace." She leaned down and placed a kiss on the icy cheek. "I shall never forget thee, friend."

When Amanda returned to the recreation room for the second hour of personal amusement, she wrote her first, and only, letter to Jeremiah:

14 May, 1819

Dear husband,

I would very much like to come home, if you still want me. I regret it has taken so long for me to come to my senses—to begin to understand how fortunate a woman I am to have such a caring man in my life.

I hope you can forgive the way I have failed you as a wife and failed our children as mother. I would be most grateful for an opportunity to make a fresh start in our life together.

If you would rather not claim me again, I completely understand completely.

I remain your most loving wife,
Amanda Jane

* * * * *

Jeremiah reread the letter for the tenth time. "She's ready to come home!" He repeated it over again. He could hardly make himself believe the words swimming before his eyes. "My Mandy wants to come *home*."

Jeremiah wasted no time in arranging for a hurried trip to

Pennsylvania. The doctor's letter, which had accompanied Amanda's short missive, explained her sudden turnaround and cleared her for release. So, with Michael on hand to look after spring chores, though still recovering from his own grief, and with the twins slated to stay with Aunt Sadie, Jeremy took to the road East without delay.

He would bring his little yellow bird home.

End June, 1819

By the time Amanda and Jeremiah crossed the Ohio River on their homeward trip, they'd spent hours talking, getting reacquainted, and catching up on the past year's happenings in and around Justice.

"You mean to tell me Sadie actually got married? And she has a *baby*?"

"Yup. She and Willie make quite a pair. Their little Tadpole looks the spitting image of his daddy. Red hair and all."

"Who could have guessed Sadie, of all people, would find herself a husband out here… have her own family!"

"That's not all. Clara Guthrie and Tom Hawkins got hitched up on the very same day. Surprised everybody good and proper when she marched right up to that Justice and called out for Tom to come and make her a respectable wife," Jeremy recalled. "They have a little boy, now, too. Name of Tommy."

"I can see I've missed so much, Jeremiah. How will I ever manage to face all those people again?"

"You'll do just fine, my little yellow bird," he said, shifting Patsy's reins in order to take Amanda's hand and give it a

squeeze. "You can hold your head up high and be proud of how far you've come. We almost lost you, you know."

"I never could have found my way back without Lottie Mueller," she said, laying her head against Jeremy's shoulder. "She saved my life, Jeremiah. And now she's gone."

They rode in silence for quite some time, enjoying the companionable ease they'd rediscovered over the past fortnight. By the time evening shadows fell, they found a suitable spot to camp for the night and had a fire going to heat water for tea.

Amanda took charge of the simple supper of journey cakes and chamomile tea, while Jeremy lit his pipe and sat back against a rock to watch her efficient movements. "You've changed, Mandy," he said with a contented smile. "You seem more sure of yourself now… more confident."

"I've learned so much these past months. Things I should have known before coming out to this wilderness," she said with a sigh. "Things you've been doing for me all this time. I'm so sorry I've been such a burden to you."

"You haven't been a burden. You're my wife. I'd go through all of it again, just to have you with me like this right now," he said, motioning for her to come sit beside him. She sat, and he folded his arm around her, pulling her close.

"Jeremiah. There's something I need to tell you. Something I think you must already suspect, but–"

"There's no need to go on, Mandy. What's past is past. We're starting out fresh, remember?"

"But I need to tell you this… to ask your forgiveness. It's the only way we can make amends and go forward."

"All right. I'm listening."

"The last baby… Joey. The one born dead. He was not your son," she said, swallowing hard. "Reverend Longbottom made himself… he made me–"

"You don't need to say it, Mandy. I already know."

"He forced himself on me, Jeremiah. While you were gone. He tricked me into trusting him. I couldn't stop him from… he was so insistent… and so much larger. I… I couldn't get away… no matter how hard I tried!" She was silent for a few moments, struggling to regain her composure. "I'm afraid that's what put me out of my head before you came home. It reminded me too much of that first violation… when Ben was conceived.

I just couldn't face the aftermath of such an encounter again."

Jeremy sat quietly, puffing on his pipe.

"I'm so sorry I betrayed you, Jeremiah. I didn't know how to tell you. I just couldn't. I thought I'd end up losing you, too."

"You didn't betray me, Mandy. How could you even think such a thing?" Jeremy pulled her closer in a protective embrace. "None of it was your fault. That devil in sheep's clothing is the one I blame. Not you, my little yellow bird." He drew slowly on his pipe. "For a long time *I* felt responsible for your breakdown... by not being there to protect you," he admitted. "I never should have gone away and left you alone for so long."

"He came again, to that kicking bee... at least I thought it was him. And I had to get out of there, before he saw me... and then I fell, and–"

"Shhhhh." Jeremy put his fingers softly over her mouth. "None of that matters any more, Mandy. *None* of it."

"But how can you even look at me, after so much has happened between us?"

"I love you, Mandy. I've loved you ever since the first time I laid eyes on you, scared to death, clutching onto that wadded-up letter." He gave her a long, passionate kiss. "I'll always love you, my little yellow bird. No matter what happens. Don't ever doubt that again."

"I didn't realize how much you meant to me, Jeremiah," she whispered. "Not until all that cotton finally cleared from my head... just before Lottie died."

They sat, arms wrapped around one another, afraid to let go.

"I don't understand how a man of God can do such a thing."

"I don't believe God was the one driving that one," Jeremy answered. "Else he wouldn't have got passion so mixed up with *com*passion."

"No one has a right to hurt another person so. I don't know if I'll ever be able to forgive the man, Jeremiah."

"Well, you won't have to worry about facing that one again.

He's gone on to his just reward." Jeremy turned to look her square in the eye. "But you know, Mandy, it's not him you need to forgive, so much as yourself," Jeremy said.

She sat silent for a few moments. "I know," she finally said. "Lottie helped me come to understand that. But I'm afraid I still have a long way to go before I can put it all behind me."

"You will, in time. When you can finally let it all go."

"I'll have to take your word for that," she said, giving him a squeeze, then rising to go check on the tea, steeping by the fire. "Meantimes, we must see to this business of living." Amanda thought intently of Lottie's way with that very thought. *Thank you, my special angel, for showing me the way back into life.*

* * * * *

Jeremiah and Amanda arrived home on the evening of Sunday, July 4th, their fourth anniversary. First thing after climbing down from the wagon, Amanda ran to the apple tree. There they stood—the two stones she'd seen in her dream. "Where did those come from?" she asked her husband.

"Michael carved 'em for the boys," Jeremy answered. "He hasn't been able to face making a stone for Violet and his own little babe yet. But he will… in time."

"I saw those very gravestones in my dream, Jeremiah! Broken rosebuds and all." A soft wind rustled the branches, and

Amanda heard a bell-like tinkle. *Her boys' laughter!* She looked up into the tree. "*Chimes!*"

"Violet made those just after she got here," Jeremy said. "While Michael carved on the stones, Violet worked at making the chimes. She gathered up all sorts of things to create just the sounds she wanted. Bent spoons, arrow tips, pieces of that old, broken mirror. They had a wonderful time working side-by-side."

"I wish I could have met her. She sounds like a lovely person."

"She was," Jeremy said. "It's too bad she didn't get to enjoy life a little longer. Lord knows she earned every ounce of joy she finally did find."

Amanda gazed around the orchard. "They're here, Jeremiah," she said, walking up to the apple tree and giving it a big hug. "The boys told me I could always find them right here."

He pulled Amanda close and folded her into his arms. "I'm here, too, Mandy." They stood in the comforting embrace. "Why don't we go inside," he said. "Looks like Michael already did chores. I reckon he's gone to Willie and Sadie's for Sunday supper." He gave her a sly smile. "We can have this evening of homecoming all to ourselves." He gave her a long, passionate kiss. "Tomorrow I'll ride over and bring back our girls."

They headed for the cabin, hand in hand. But before Amanda could walk through the front door, Jeremy swept her off her feet and up, into his arms. "We're starting fresh, so we better do this thing up right!" He gave her a peck on the cheek and carried his wife over the threshold.

* * * * *

Jeremy's assumption about Michael had been correct. His brother had taken to eating and sleeping over at Willie and Sadie's quite often, for the silence of the Harrison cabin echoed too loudly for his liking. Mike would finish evening chores, then head to Sadie's for supper, spending many a night sleeping on the Hawkins' front porch. At dawn he'd head back to do his own morning chores and another day of farm work. But when evening rolled around again, off he'd head, back to Sadie's—to listen to the childhood giggles of Lilly, Millie and little Tad, which managed to considerably buoy his sagging spirits. The routine they'd fallen into seemed a comfort to them all.

Even though he still grieved his own double loss, Michael Harrison had begun to embrace life once more. Outside of farm work, he kept his hands busy with the familiar therapy of working stone.

Willie and Sadie now had their own, outdoor bread oven,

shaped like a bee hive. No one in Justice had ever seen anything like it before. Even Ma thought it quite the novelty. They also had a stone watering trough, with the likeness of a horse carved on its side. It sat at the base of Willie's windmill, welcoming thirsty man or beast. Upon its completion, Michael finally began the task of carving a gravestone for Violet and his unnamed babe.

The fact that he had not named the baby bothered him still. The closer he came to finishing the gravestone, the more he brooded about it.

"It just don't seem right to say 'Violet and baby'," he said to Sadie, who was hanging clean laundry on the clothesline.

"Then give her a name, Mike."

"Vi and I never even talked about names. We figured we'd have plenty of time to do that," he said. "I don't have any idea what she wanted."

"You could name her after Violet, you know."

"I gave that some thought. But somehow, I don't think she would have liked it."

"What was her mother's name? She often talked about how much she missed her mother," Sadie mumbled through the clothes peg she held with her teeth, while pinning up another diaper.

"I don't recall that she ever told me."

"Well, think about this," she said, removing the peg from her mouth and pointing it at Michael. "Since we have all these flower names going on for Harrison girls, maybe you could come up with another one of those," Sadie suggested.

"Maybe," Michael answered. "I'll have to study on that some." He went back to work, chipping away at the stone, designing a hand holding a bouquet of violets for his beloved wife. "We already have a Lilly, and a Camellia, and we had a Violet. What other flower names are left?"

"Rose, Dahlia, Angelica, Tulip, Pansy, Laurel, Myrtle," Sadie rattled off. "Iris, Jasmine, Magnolia, Daisy, Holly, Fern,

Marigold, Petunia..."

"Stop! You're driving me round the bend with so many flowers!"

"Just trying to help," Sadie said with her impish smile.

"I do kind of like Laurel. Iris, too. But they sound like such grown-up names. Far too big for that tiny little bundle we laid in Violet's arms." Michael tapped away, thinking for a time longer. "Angelica might suit. She went from being born, to being an angel right quick," he considered. "Angelica Harrison. I think I like it."

"Well, there you go," Sadie said. "Now you can carve it in stone."

* * * * *

Jeremy and Amanda awoke to a warm, hazy day. Before Michael showed up for chores, Jeremy had all the animals fed, watered and turned out to pasture. With Patsy harnessed to the small cart, he aimed to fetch his girls back home before the day's rising heat made the trip too unbearable. He set off on the dirt road leading toward Justice.

Meanwhile, Michael had struck out overland from Sadie's on the shorter, hillier, trail back home. The brothers headed in opposite directions, without knowing they'd crossed paths.

Amanda, not quite ready for social interaction, as of yet, decided she'd wait at home for the return of her twins. "Two years old already," she mused. "How could I have missed so much time with my little girls?"

She puttered around the cabin, getting reacquainted with familiar things. Amanda shook out the counterpane covering the girls' bed, giving it a good airing, then returned it, smoothing out every wrinkle. She brushed down the curtains, hanging over the cabin's two windows and rearranged the dishes on the pantry shelf.

Even though the day promised to turn sultry, she put water on to heat for a cup of tea. Amanda had grown accustomed to drinking her tea hot, regardless of the outside temperature. And, having become the creature of habit the asylum had so meticulously trained, she clung to her customary practice. Sitting at the table, sipping raspberry-leaf tea, she heard footsteps hit the porch the instant before the door burst open.

"You're *home!*" Michael shouted in surprise.

Amanda sat motionless, the electricity emanating from him making her scalp tingle.

"You remember me, don't you?" he asked. "Michael? I stood up with Jems at your wedding?"

"Of course I remember you, *Brother*," Amanda replied, still quite shaken by the effect of his magnetism. She wondered whether he'd felt it, too.

"Where's Jeremy? When did you two get back? You look *wonderful!*"

Amanda gave her head a shake in an attempt to push away her discomfort. "He drove out about half-an-hour ago, to collect the twins," she answered with as much confidence as she could muster. "We pulled in last evening, just before sunset."

"Rats! I just missed you then! I headed to Sadie and Willie's right after evening chores." He stood, staring at Amanda, bewildered by the strange awkwardness he felt.

"Jeremiah suspected as much. He could tell you'd just fed the animals," she said, taking a deep breath. "I was so sorry to hear about your loss, Michael," she said, trying to keep things as formal between them as she could manage. "Jeremiah told me your Violet was a lovely person."

Michael swallowed hard. "Thank you. She... I mean, we–"

"Oh, and thank you *so* much for the lovely headstones you carved for my boys!" she gushed with an enthusiasm she couldn't manage to hide. Immediately she turned scarlet at her sudden show of feeling.

"You're more than welcome, *Sister*," he replied, collecting himself and taking his cue from her. "I'm working on one for Violet and Angel right now."

"Angel, is that what you named your baby?"

"Angelica. Angel for short," he said. "I think of her as my own, guardian angel watching over me the rest of my days."

After Michael headed outdoors to hoe corn rows, Amanda busied herself preparing a light lunch. She wanted to have a meal at the ready when Jeremiah and the girls arrived back home. She took stock of the food supplies on hand, which offered slim pickings, since Michael hadn't eaten there much, of late. She found very little in the way of fresh foodstuffs, mostly staples. She'd need to plant a late kitchen garden right away, she could see that plainly enough.

Amanda began to stir together a bowlful of biscuit dough. She'd found a small block of aged cheese, which she chopped and thought to add to the biscuits in order to make them more nutritious. The sour milk sitting in the crock by the door would make them rise high and fluffy. Amazing what she'd learned in the past six months, without even being fully aware. "Thank you, Lottie," she whispered to her own guardian angel.

While she measured flour and added ash to work against the sour milk for leavening, she heard a horse and cart pull up outside. "My *girls!*" She wiped floury hands on her apron and rushed to the door, still propped open to let in the light, morning breeze.

Standing there, ready to knock on the door frame, beamed Netta Bailey holding a covered basket. "Oh, Amanda, it's *so* good to see you again! I flagged down Jeremy on his way by to Sadie's. He told me you'd come back, so I just *had* to come right over to welcome you home," Netta babbled. "I haven't seen you in such a long time and there's *so* much news to tell! I knew if I didn't get over here right away, I'd hate myself for waiting and letting somebody else tell you what all's happened while you been away." She snatched a breath and barreled on. "I baked sweet biscuits for breakfast and had a heap of 'em left over, so I just said to myself, 'Netta, you take those right on over to Amanda and welcome her back home,'" she said, holding out the basket. "I made some strawberry-rhubarb preserves last week, too. So I brought a crock full along."

"Thank you," Amanda said, gracefully accepting the basket. "Won't you come in and have a cup of tea?" Amanda motioned her toward the kitchen table. "I was just mixing up cheese biscuits for lunch. Michael doesn't have much in the way of fresh provisions. I'm makin' do with what I could find on hand."

"Cheese in biscuits? Whoever wouldda thought? Did you learn how to make those at your... at the...ah–"

"At the asylum? Yes. It's all right Jeanette, you can say it."

"Well, I sure did not want to make you feel bad by bringing *that* up... I mean by sayin' what other folks are talkin' abo... oh, well... I mean..."

"Good grief, Jeanette. I don't remember you ever being so tongue-tied before."

"Guess I'm not quite sure what to say to you, now that you're back from that nuthouse." Netta immediately put her hand over her mouth, realizing she had said too much already.

"Don't ever worry about hurting my feelings by saying what you really think." Amanda smiled at her embarrassed friend. "I know I've come a long way from where I started. It's just taken me quite a while to even begin admitting that to myself," she said. "I've also come to realize that what anyone else thinks means very little, in the grand scheme of things."

"Oh my, you sound so wise. That place did wonders for you!"

"It wasn't the place, so much as the person who helped me learn how to face up to life," she answered with a wistful smile. "So, tell me, Jeannette, what's been happening to you these past many months?"

"Well, my cousin Luella came out to see me last summer, that would be Luella Witherspoon? From back in Maryland? Luther went and got her and brought her all the way back here. Just so's I'd have company in the house whenever he takes to the woods, like he does. Can you believe my Luther being so thoughtful? Why, I could hardly believe it myself. But he fetched her right out here to stay a long spell without even telling me he was going to do it! She's watching my girls right now, so's I could make a quick trip over here to see you," Netta explained. "Sure has been nice to have someone to help out with the babies, now and again. Gives me a chance to go visiting on my own more often.

"And Amanda, you'll never believe it. Luella just up and decided to stay permanent! Can you imagine such a thing? My best friend in all the world has moved out here to live with me! Until she gets married, that is." Netta grabbed a breath and hurried on. "I just *know* she's going marry up with Harmon. No one's snagged that man yet, you know... well, you probably don't know, but I'm telling you, so now you *do* know... and he stops by a lot more often than he has a reason to... sometimes he has no mail to bring at-all! I just know he's sweet on Luella. Mark my words, there's going to be a weddin' right soon, sure as I'm sitting here drinking this tea." She took a quick sip. "Say, this is real good!"

While Amanda quickly finished mixing her biscuits, she dutifully listened to the tales pouring forth from the neighborhood gossip. By the time she had her biscuits laid out in the reflector oven in front of the fire, Netta still hadn't run out of steam.

"...My lands, I can't believe he says that! Every other word is... well, I won't say it myself. That bad 'F' word. But Clara says her pa can't speak hardly any words but bad ones no more—especially that 'effin' one—ever since he had that stroke of his! Can't say as I quite have a handle on what a stroke really is, but from what Ma Hawkins told me, it must have something to do with things not lining up quite right in his mind no more. 'Cuz of a big bleed that happened inside of his head."

"It makes things get all scrambled in a person's mind," Amanda told her. "It also can make a part of the body not work correctly anymore."

"That's what happened to Anson! His right arm just up and quit working! If Luther hadn't been over that-a-way and found him, Lord knows what he would have come to. Luther said he was walking in circles, with his right leg just sort of standin' there doin' nothin'."

"My maternal grandmother, Grandmother Tedrow, suffered an apoplexy several months before she died," Amanda shared. "Her left side no longer served. She had great difficulty swallowing, too, as I recall."

"Clara says Anson can swallow fine. Eats like a horse now. But her Ma has to help him put his pants on every morning, or he'd fall down tryin'."

Before Netta could ramble on, the clop of horse hooves and the crunch of cart wheels announced Jeremy's arrival.

"Excuse me, Netta, but I think that must be Jeremiah with the girls." Amanda pushed the reflector pan away from the fire and hurried out onto the front stoop. There, at their father's gentle push, two little flowers came running toward her with braids flying, to scurry up the step and give great big hugs to welcome their long-lost Mama.

Dear Ellie,

I have not had the heart to put pen to paper before now. Leesha is gone. We lost her to the bilious fever last November. Elijah seemed more ill than she, but he recovered as she did not. And with her went my joy in this life. Spring has come to the land, and in its turn, summer, but my heart remains in the grip of winter. Zach and I look to each other, then turn away. There is no comfort there or elsewhere. For the first time, friend, I know not how to go on.

I shudder to think how, in my last letter to you, I boasted that all of my chicks were alive and well in this new land. I would gladly relinquish the remainder of my worldly possessions to the depths of the Monongahela River to have our Leesha returned to us.

Lizzie has been more mother than sister to Elijah of late. I have not the heart for mothering. The cabin has an unnatural stillness. Likewise, I cannot face the prospect of building a new house, as only Lizzie and Elijah remain with us at present. The new house has been claimed by Nate and Ivy, who still live with the Cleghorns. It will stand near the mill, which is some distance to the north of us, if I have failed to mention this in the past. Since Nate is working the mill with his father, the new house suits their needs best.

Simeon, Christian, and Levi dig at the Erie salt mine, coming home only once a month. When they are here, the boys speak constantly of the canal that has recently opened in New York. According to them, talk centers around building one here. To hear the boys speak of it, Ohio grain could be sold in every port in the world on the strength of their muscles alone, should they choose to help dig such a ditch.

Last weekend, they brought home a friend: Kit, they called him. He seemed as enthusiastic about the canal project as they. This cabin did ring with young voices and laughter once again, though I took little comfort in it. Zach seemed somewhat animated by these conversations, as if he forgot himself and joined the world for a time. But it lasted only until the young people left us, and silence regained its stranglehold once more.

Nate and Ivy were here Sunday to tell us that she is expecting. I did try to be happy for them. My first grandchild, after all. They watched us, Zach poking up the fire while I sat in the rocker, measuring our reaction, I think, exchanging glances. I rose to hug them both, and Zach clapped Nate on the back. But by their expressions, they must have found our enthusiasm sorely lacking.

My Lizzie seems more of herself these days. For a time, my concern for her was great. Still, it is odd that she desires no congress with others her age. The boys begged her to ride to the Merrifield settlement with them while they were home, but she claims to be happy just to sit on the porch of an evening. I like it not, but feel at a loss (in so many ways). I know not how to help her.

My sweet Leesha is gone, before she could grow into those huge front teeth. I must close before I wet this paper through with too many tears.

July 12, 1819

Simeon has returned unexpectedly this midday, and alone. His brother, Levi, had some skirmish with a fighting Irishman, says Simeon, where each struck the other overtop the head with a shovel. To hear the tale, they took turns at it until the Irish did not get back up. At that point, Levi made to rouse him, failed, and began to blather on about having killed a man. He ran off believing himself a murderer, a hunted man, saying that he should become a pirate and sail the seven seas. The truth of the matter was that Simeon revived the fellow with a bucket of water, but by that time, Levi was nowhere to be found.

I cannot bear this further loss. I beg you to keep an eye out for my Levi in your environs, Ellie. Spread the word amongst your river men. I cannot lose another chick. <u>I will not!</u>

Yours, Libby

Chapter 11

Riverstop Revelation
Late July 1819

"Did you get them eggs, Katrina?" Ellie asked as she patted corncakes and laid them on the flat, hot rock to bake in the fire. "We got us a mess of hungry varmints this morning."

"Got 'em right here, Ma. Three for Zeke, and four each for those other fellas. Our chickens barely keep up at this rate." Katrina had to speak loudly to be heard over the animated conversation of three men seated at the table across the room.

"I'm thinkin' we should add on to that coop and double our birds for next year."

"Same thing I was thinking. We'll have time to do more fixing up around here after the waters get low and river traffic slows down."

"I like hearing that, pard'ner."

"And I like hearing you say 'pard'ner', pard'ner. Be right back to fry up the eggs." With a grin, Katrina pulled the coffee pot out of the coals to refill crockery cups all around, starting with Zeke's. He perched on a flour barrel closer to the women.

"Thank you, darlin'. Ah love seein' a prretty lass in action. And the two o' ye lassies 're a sight for a lonely Scotsman."

"Forget about blatherin' us, you old Scots devil, or soon as I turn these corn cakes, I'll deal with the likes of you," Ellie threatened.

"An' here Ah was, aboot offerin' t' tie mysel' to shore a wee bit, to build ye that chickie coop, much as Ah even hate the wieldin' of a hammerr."

"We don't need no favors from a whiskered old goat like you. My pard'ner and me love to hammer. Just for the fun of it sometimes. Whenever we get tired of stoopin' over a cookfire. Makes for a nice change, don'tcha know," Ellie said, turning from her corncakes to stir at the bacon in the frying pan. "What in blue blazes possessed a river rat like you to even think about stayin' ashore?"

"Musta gone daft ferr a wee bit, darrrlin'... blinded by the beauty o' those sweet eyes. Made me lose site o' the current, they did."

"Don't you darlin' me. I seen you in your altogether at that last revival. Enough to scare dogs and small children, it was. So don't think you can get me all dreamy-eyed with your 'darlin' talk."

"Ochhh, and ye're a hard one, El. Truly ye are."

"You about done with that frying pan, Ma? So I can cook up these eggs?"

"Almost. Next year I aim to make sure we have more than one paltry fry-pan and cook pot betwixt us, pard'ner."

Katrina, returning the coffee pot to the fire, shot back. "No sir, Ma. We almost have enough saved up for Uncle Jonathan to get us a good set of iron pots this year on his next trip East. If we save up just a little bit more, maybe we could even get him to bring us one of those reflectors, like Grandmama had back in Philadelphia."

"Don't you think that's gettin' a mite uppity?" Ellie glanced over to the table of men, then said under her breath, "Loose talk in front of strangers can come to no good, Katrina."

"Sorry, Ma. I wasn't thinking. I'll set the eggs to frying, and we'll get these varmints fed and back on the water before they can give it another thought."

At that moment, the largest of the three men began to shout. "You call this swill coffee? Tastes like a fella washed a winter's worth of socks in this hot water."

"If it's good enough for our friend Zeke, here, mister, it's good enough for you," Katrina shouted back. "Besides, I only washed out one pair of my stockin's in it, 's'all." The other two men began to laugh, and Katrina gave them a wink.

"Good idea, lass. Get them buckos fed and off, so yer Mither an' me can 'ave us a wee bit o' prii-vacy."

Ignoring Zeke's comment, Ellie pulled chunks of bacon from the large, iron fry pan, flinging pieces onto each wooden trencher already filled with two corncakes a piece. She moved aside, setting the trenchers on the wide board mounted near the fire, which served as a place to ready food and keep it warm. As Katrina took her place before the hearth and began to crack eggs into the hot grease, Ellie moved nearer to the group of men to reassure herself that their conversation did not regard The Riverstop, its owners, nor their cook-pot savings. Ellie cocked an ear in their direction.

"I'm telling you, I won hard cash money on that boy. He did it, and that's a fact."

"You're a liar, Bart. Ain't nobody ever walked a wheel on a paddle wheeler and lived to tell the tale." The big man missing two front teeth pounded a gnarled fist on the table to emphasize his words.

"Well, this fella did it. In broad daylight. Not like I couldn't see ev'ry step he took. Ev'ry hop and jump to it. And ever'one else seen it, too."

"You was in the drink. Seeing double, I'll wager. I'd bet *two* fellas done it together, right, Cyrus?" He poked the third man who gave a silly giggle.

"You shut up, Ferd. I don't have to take that from the likes o' you. If you keep it up, I can knock out any teeth Cyrus left you after that last too-rang. Now, listen. This here boy stowed away on that paddle wheeler, and when he got found out and brought up on deck to the captain, he made a wager. Said if he could walk the wheel, the captain should let him ride for free. Well, other passengers was bored and anxious for some entertainment, so they commenced to shoutin' out that the captain ought to take the boy up on it. That's when all the bettin' started up."

"But what moved you to bet he'd make it?" Ferd was careful to be respectful this time, as he needed the rest of his teeth to eat his breakfast, which did smell good, even if it wasn't in front of him yet.

"He was a cocky fella. Short and wiry. Seemed awful sure

217

he could do it, too. And by God, he did. Earned me a handful of hard cash. None of them worthless shin-plasters. But coin, sure's you're born. Boy got to ride for free, clean down to New Orleens, too."

Ferd spat on the floor to show his continued skepticism.

"Do that outside, mister. Not on my clean floor," Ellie said in a stern tone.

Ferd grunted and pushed his chair back, but before he could move any further, Katrina set the overflowing trencher before him. "'Bout time." He scooted his chair back up to the table, hunger winning out over temper. He pulled the chaw from his cheek, sat it on the edge of the trencher, and began stuffing corn cake, eggs, and side-pork into his mouth.

"So, this wheel-walkin' fella, what did he look like, 'zactly?" Ellie asked, bringing salt to the table. "I know a youngster apt to pull a prank like that. Was he about this high, and a towhead?"

"Shore 'nough, ma'am. Hair yaller as this here purty table-cloth," Bart said between bites.

"Any other marks or such, as you'd notice?"

"Yep. Had him one mark I did note. A scar acrosst his ankle. Saw it plain when he took his boots off. Wouldda been his left, no, his right. My left, or so I b'lieve."

"Shut up, you fool. We know you can't tell port from star-board." Ferd continued to empty his trencher even as he spoke.

"I knew it, I just knew it," Ellie said, rushing over to Zeke. "Can't nobody but Levi Howard be up to such monkey shines. Listen here, you river-runnin' scallywag. You knock the notion of shore duty clean outta that head of yours. You're gettin' in that tub and headin' south."

"Ah am?"

"If you value your limbs, you sure enough better," she said, eyeing the vicinity of one, particular appendage that did not come in a pair.

"And why, pray tell, am Ah takin' back to the water so soon, lass?" Zeke asked, gingerly crossing his legs.

"'Cause you're gonna fetch that misguided boy back home to his mama before he gets hisself in bigger trouble than he's already stirred up."

"If Ah run after every lad makin' a wee bit o' trrrouble, lass, mah craft 'd sink to the bottom of the grand Mississip, it would."

"Well you better find this one. My best friend is nursing a broken heart on account of him, and I aim to mend it by seeing her boy gets home to her in one piece."

"How, in the divil do you think *Ah* c'n find 'im, when ah niver e'en laid eyes on the lad, El?"

"Shouldn't be hard. Just look for a toe-head in the midst of some trouble."

"If Ah'm to set off on a wild goose chase, lass, ye should at least have the heart to come along wi' me," he said, draining the last dregs from his coffee cup. "Then one of us might stand a chance of pickin' oot the lad."

"Me? Go with the likes of you? You got to be joshin'."

"Why would Ah josh wi' ye, now, lass?"

"I can't go traipsin' off, just like that. I got me a business to run."

"Things will be slowing down here soon, Ma, what with the river falling off the way it is already. Why don't you go? It'd do you good to get away from here for a while."

"And leave you to fend all alone?"

"If ye have any hope at-all of findin' the lad, Ah need ye wi' me, El," Zeke said, giving Ellie his best hang-dog face.

"Well, mebbe I should. But I'll only go on one condition."

"Darrrlin' lass, Ah knew me charms would smote yerrr heart one day."

"Don't make me hurt you, you old goat. I got no time for nonsense. No romantic tom-foolery, neither. You got that?" Ellie said with a cold stare. "Katrina, I need to pen a quick line to

Lib. Let her know what I'm about. You give it to your cousin Harmon on his rounds. Have him bring someone by to help you out here, too. Whoever can be spared. I won't go less'n I know you won't have to fend all alone. Mebbe Aunt Edie could even come for a spell. She could use a change. Just might perk her up, some."

"I *am* a woman grown, Ma. I can handle my end just fine."

"I know that, girl. But here I am, leavin' you high and dry, which ain't holdin' up *my* end. So you get somebody in here to carry my share of the work load, you hear? I'll come back, soon as can be. With Levi in tow, I'm-a hopin'," Ellie said, as she began to scrub out her frying pan with a handful of sand. "By the time we get rid of this here crowd of river rats, we best be off, then, Zeke. We got to reach New Orleens quick and find Levi Howard 'fore he goes and disappears on us again."

July 24, 1819
Riverstop

Dear Libby,

I can not tell how sorry I am to hear about you losing that sweet girl of yours. You have give up so much in the last year. But this sure is the worst. When I did not hear from you for so long I had me a idee something went wrong. I know nothing can stop your grief, Lib. But I got news that may help sidestep it some.

I heard tell of Levi. I know it has to be him. Right after Mary Sue delivered early of a boy on June 19. They named him Jay. Katrina was still there. So now she has experience in this business of birth. Mary Sue got back on her feet right quick. And my Jason just brought his sister back to The Riverstop when I got your message about Levi's scrape.

Why it was not more than a day or two later when I heard some river rats tell of a boy walking the wheel of a paddle wheeler on a dare. I asked what did he look like. They told of a skinny towhead boy with a scar across his ankle.

It is him, Lib. I know it is.

Zeke will take me downriver to go look for him. Those river rats said he went clean down to New Orleens. Zeke and me leave at daybreak. Katrina will run things here while I am gone. It could be some time till I get back. I told her to get in some help. But she is hard headed enough to try an run this place herself. Too much like her Ma!

I will do my best to find Levi for you, friend.

Meantimes think about this. Jeremy Harrison's brother. That would be Michael. The one what carves and lays up stone? He is heading up to your neck of the woods to work on some new courthouse up that-a-way. Harmon brought news about commissioners up North searching for stone masons to do the work. So Michael took him a notion to try his hand at laying up a fancy stone building. Told Harmon he cannot stay on with Jeremy no more. Now that Amanda is home from the nuthouse. Says he feels like a fifth wheel with his little wife gone on to her reward. So he made up his mind to go away a spell. Think things out.

Now here is why I tell you this. Long as Michael is up in your environs, why Zach should have him lay up a fancy fireplace in that new house he is building for Nate and Ivy. Make them a bake oven and all. What do you think?

I know it is hard for you to think on anything besides losing your girl. But keep in mind that many have suffered like you suffer. In time it will not hurt so deep. So try to get back to the business of living as much as you can, Lib.

I hope you will find some comfort in Nate and Ivy's coming babe. And in knowing that your Levi is still alive and well. And God willing staying out of trouble!

I will find him for you, Lib. I will!

Your true friend, Ellie.

Now took up with river runner Zeke.

I told him no tom foolery. We have a job to do.

Chapter 12

Riverstop Rescue
Mid August 1819

"Where's our food, gal? We got us a powerful hunger goin' here," said the crusty, riverman who stopped every week or so for dinner with his two, bedraggled cohorts. "Ain't that stew done cookin' yet?"

"If you want to eat your potatoes raw and your meat bloody, I'd be happy to serve it up right now for you, boys," Katrina shot back. "But you'd have too much trouble chewing it that way, Ferd," she said with a decided edge to her voice. Though Katrina handled the majority of rivermen frequenting her establishment with light-hearted ease, this particular bunch usually managed to raise her hackles.

"She's gettin' as feisty as that ma of hers, ain't she, Bart?"

"No, Ferd. I b'lieve her ma is one contrary female what has this little filly beat by a good river-mile." Bart gave her a wink he thought to be good-natured, but taken along with the transverse scar on his cheek, it came across as revolting.

"Ain't ya got nothin' we can jaw on till that stew gets ready, gal? We're starvin' to death, here."

"All I have cooked is this apple pie," she said, "but–"

Ferd made a grab for the pie, cooling on the windowsill. Katrina smacked the back of his hand with the wooden spoon she held. "Whoa, right there, mister!"

He pulled his hand away, rubbing at the sting with the other. "Godalmighty! What'd ya go an' do that for?"

A loud giggle escaped from Cyrus, the third man sitting quietly at the table. Ferd reached out and smacked the side of his head. "Quit laughin', Cyrus. T'ain't funny."

"That pie just came out of the Dutch oven! Would you rather I let you grab a red-hot pie pan?"

Ferd stood his ground, fuming with humiliation, but unsure

as to how far he dare push this gutsy gal. "I only wanted a little taste," he grumbled.

"Go ahead, burn your tongue, then. See if I care." Katrina turned her back on him and busied herself stirring up a batch of dumplings to drop into the stew after it cooked for a bit longer.

Ferd shuffled back to the table, where Cyrus and Bart pulled out a deck of cards to pass the time. "Want us to deal you in,?"

"Naw. Don't feel much like card playin'," he grumbled.

"Suit yourself." Bart dealt the hand and the two began play.

Ferd sat there, pouting like a two-year-old, fussing every now and again to see if he could get a rise out of Katrina. "Don't know why we even keep stoppin' here to eat," he mumbled loud enough for Katrina to hear. "Vittles just keep getting' skimpier an' skimpier." He fussed with a loose tooth—the last one left to him on top. "Your ma always gives us our money's worth," he muttered again in her direction. "She would never whack me for tryin' to taste a pie."

"You got something to say to me, say it to my face." Katrina said, turning around and walking to the table. "I don't need no shikepokes talking behind my back." She waved the spoon in his face to emphasize her point.

"I said your vittles is gettin' too skimpy for the price you charge, that's what."

"I never asked you to stop here, you know. You're the ones keep comin' back."

"Aw, hell, woman. I'm starvin'! When are you gonna serve up somethin' to fill my belly?"

"'Case you didn't notice, Ferd gets awful testy when he's hungry," Bart said, laying down his hand. "Rummy!"

"Want me to go squeeze the chickens? See if I can come up with any more eggs to fry, hold you over till the stew's done? Eggs don't take that long."

"I'll go check the coop my own self," Ferd said, stalking out of the cabin in a huff.

Katrina proceeded to drop dumplings onto the bubbling stew, setting the lid back on tight after she'd emptied the mixing bowl of all its dough. By the time she had the bowl washed up, Ferd came walking back in, holding a dead chicken by the neck. "What in blazes did you do to my chicken?" Katrina demanded.

"Blasted bird tried to peck my eyes out. Had to wring its neck in self-defense!"

"Those happen to be the most peaceable birds I ever raised, mister. What did you do to get 'em riled enough to come at you?"

"I only pushed 'em off their nests to look for eggs," Ferd said. "That's what Ma always did."

"Pushing helpless birds around," Katrina said. "It figures. Don't you know you're supposed to ease the eggs out gently from underneath a bird?" She shook her head in frustration. "Why in the world I should expect anything gentle from a bully like you, I haven't got a clue."

"Who you callin' a bully?" Ferd dropped the bird and started toward Katrina."

"You like pushin' helpless women around, too, do you?"

"Watch that mouth, gal. I've took about as much blather from you as I aim to." He made a grab for her arm. But just as quickly, Katrina pulled her cast-iron frying pan off the shelf and swung it around to give Ferd a wallop on the side of the head.

"I'm not helpless by a long shot, mister!"

He staggered backward, stunned for a few moments, then stood there shaking his head. In a trice he gathered himself and came back roaring mad. He raised his arm preparing to give Katrina a good, hard whack, when, from behind, someone grabbed that arm in mid-swing.

"You aim to wring her neck, too?" asked a steady voice coming from a stocky young man with dark hair and large, muscular hands. He slowly pulled the arm back down, then around, forcing Ferd into a kneeling position on the floor in front of himself. "Hello, Katrina. Looks like I got here just in time."

"Simeon! Is that really you?"

"In the flesh, my dear."

"Well, it's about time! I've been waiting nigh on to a year for you to show up. What took you so long?"

"You aim to keep Ferd down there till he expires, mister?" Bart asked. "He's turnin' purple."

Simeon addressed the man whose arm he held twisted tightly behind his back. "You ready to behave yourself? Treat the lady with respect?"

Ferd grunted an incomprehensible answer.

"All right, then," he said, letting go the arm. "Just remember, I aim to stay and keep things peaceable. You got that?"

"Got it." Ferd rubbed circulation back into his aching shoulder, muttering expletives under his breath.

"What-do-you-say we all just sit ourselves down and wait for the lady to dish up some stew, now, shall we?"

Chairs scraped across the floor, as the men seated themselves quietly around the trestle table. Bart and Cyrus continued with their card game, while Ferd sat in silence, massaging his arm and shoulder.

Katrina leaned down to pick the lifeless bird off the floor. Holding it aloft, she said, "Well boys, looks like tomorrow's chicken stew!"

20 August 1819
Riverstop

Dear Mother Howard,

Guess I will just say it. Your son and me got hitched. I hope you take it well, because I know how much Simeon loves his mama. He is pretty fond of me too, but you're the one who has him worried right now.

My ma, she will just pop her buttons to find out she has such a fine son-in-law and got related to her best friend to boot. When she gets back from this crazy mission of hers hunting for your Levi, that is.

Although we have not really met, I sure do feel like I know you after hearing Ma talk about you all these years, and now, after listening to Simeon. It would mean a lot to us both to have you and his daddy's blessing on our hasty union. And also on our plan for Simmie to stay here and help run The Riverstop.

I am sorry for the shock of it, but it was the kind of a thing that called for haste or shame. And we love each other too well to put any shame to it. As a woman, I know you will take my meaning. Also, I have read your old letters to my ma these past weeks since she left, before Simeon arrived in time to save me from the river rats. The passion you have for your Zach, I feel for your son. It could not be otherwise.

So, dear Mother, please send us your blessing.

Your new daughter

Katrina

Dear Son and Daughter-in-law,

To the happy couple, Father and I send our love and best wishes. As to the surprise, I think that was yours alone, Katrina.

After receiving word of your mother's departure, did you not suspect why I related to Simeon that you were on your own amongst those river men? He has been smitten these last three years since the first time he laid eyes on you. I must say, he was more than passing moody while you were in Philadelphia with your grandmother, fearing you would find yourself a husband among the city men. Ever since your return to these environs, he has been working up the courage to come and claim you. So I make no apology for seeing the opportunity to step in and hasten destiny along.

My only uncertainty was in how you would receive him, the depth of your feelings for him. That you conveyed quite frankly in your letter, which relieves my mind considerably.

You take after your mother with your plain speaking, a trait which I have long admired in her. I am gratified to know that my son has found in you his helpmeet, and that the two of you have begun your new life together.

Would that I could travel there myself, to congratulate the two of you and to be on hand if Levi is returned to us, but Ivy grows quite ripe. Lizzie will not go to her, insisting that all will be better served if I myself go to Ivy while Lizzie tends to things here. On this she will not budge.

For now, our love and congratulations we send to you both!

Love,

Mother Howard

Dear Libby,

Don't it beat all? Can you believe what these kids went and done? And with me way down river and you up north. I sure am glad you approve this match. Cause I am just busted out with joy over it all. Libby, we are related at last! And you should see these two together. It is enough to make a lonely old crow like me bawl.

But now I guess I got to tell it. I am so sorry, friend. I failed you. It sure was Levi walking that paddle wheel just like I thought. And I told him that the fighting Irish was not dead. But he was having a high old time when we caught up with him in New Orleens. He would not come back with Zeke and me. Said that he is a man of 16 years now and wants to see more of this world. I did hatch a plot to have Zeke bop him on the head. So as we could tie him up and cart him home to you. Zeke figgered he would just run off again if he was that dead set on it.

Levi did say to give you all his love and to tell you not to worry. He also said something about his twin that I did not grasp. He said just because Lizzie refuses grow up does not mean that he is going to stay a child. Now what in the devil did he mean by that?

One surprise of events was running into that no account Tobias. My first husband. So called. I can tell you it stretches that word husband more than a mite to use in the same breath as Tobias. Well there he come. Walking up the street big as you please. Like he owned the whole damn town. Beside him strolled a red-haired floozy. I can not credit it to be the same one I heard tell of before. In all my born days I never laid eyes on that color of hair. Right out there in broad daylight she was. Wearing satin and laces and more flounces to her skirt than I could begin to count.

I thought then of them hard days trying to scratch out a living from the dirt. After that poor excuse of a man left me and his children high and dry. Only myself and my boy to do the field work. And Jason barely big enough to grasp a hoe.

Well I felt this kind of a click inside my head. Then next thing I knew Zeke was pulling me off of her. Tobias had skedaddled by then. I looked down and saw I had two fist fulls of red-hair. Zeke threw me over his shoulder and would not set me down on my own feet till we got all the way back to his boat. Laughed all the way upriver about it, he did. Kept saying he never knew me for such a spitfire. In truth I came to laugh about it myself after a while. Specially remembering the look on Tobias when I rushed at them. And on the sight of them spots where I snatched that floozy bald.

I got to say the time I spent with Zeke did go by fast. That man is right full of stories. He did his derndest to keep any romantic notions out of his head, too. Treated me so fine. I hardly knew how to abide such high regard from a man. Being so used to the kind of misuse Harvey and Tobias always dished out. I hardly know how to talk civil to a man after them. I know how to give back insults. But to talk straight honest with a man can leave a woman like me at a loss.

Zeke did not seem to mind. In fact he pretty near carried all the talk by his own self. I can tell you he does not like paddle wheelers one bit. If you think he does not swear, think again. He could swear up a storm when one of them churning wonders passed by and set our boat to rocking! Course him speaking Scots I could not make out a single word of it. Just as well, I say.

Listen to me carry on so over a man. And after I vowed to give the whole breed no never mind again. I guess my sister is right when she calls me a infernal optimist. I would like to think this man could be different from the rest of them varmints. But to tell the truth it scares the stuffing out of me to think about it too hard.

This whole man and woman business has me bamboozled. But these kids seem to have it figured out. Katrina showed me the letter you wrote her. And tickled to death she was. They did not worry about how I would take it. But the kids was scared you might think you was losing a son more than gaining a daughter. Knowing what all you been through of late. To be sure I think you will be gaining more than that, Lib.

This morning as Katrina was frying up some eggs for a customer. I saw her run right outside and get sick on the ground. She come back in saying that them eggs smelled bad and she threw them out. They was fresh out of the nest just this morning. But I did not say a word. So mark this, Lib. It looks like you and me are going to be grandmamas of the same babe come next summer!

At this rate I will be related to the whole dern territory! Funny how it all goes together like a good weave, ain't it?

You got to snap out of it, friend. New life is all round us. And it will not wait on us old women to catch up.

Your friend and new relation,

Ellie Mae

Chapter 13

February 1820

"Baby, baby, baby," Millie babbled away. "Mama's getting a baby!"

"We must keep this news to ourselves, Camellia. No one need know anything about it until spring. By then, it can no longer stay hidden."

"Why, Mama?" asked Lilly. At nearly three years old, the twins asked that question relentlessly—especially Lilly.

"This news needs to stay in our own family. To make it very special."

"Oh. Special is good, right?"

"Yes, dear. It will make your daddy very happy. But you girls must let me tell him, is that clear?"

"Yes, Mama," they repeated in unison. Over the past six months, the girls had learned that their mama could be quite insistent upon certain points. She made them toe the line with-out fail. Lilly, of course, had to keep testing that line, just to make sure it remained where she'd left it the last time she needed reminding. With constant 'testing,' came repeated conflict bet-ween Amanda and her most inquisitive daughter.

Amanda wrapped the scarf around Lilly's head and ears, crossed the ties under her chin, and tied it securely behind her neck. "Stand quietly until I get your sister bundled," she instructed. She proceeded to wrap another scarf around Millie to keep out the cold, then checked the buttons of the child's over-coat to make sure all were secure. Amanda shrugged into her own coat, wrapping the last scarf around her head and pul-ling on her mittens. When she looked back to where she'd left Lilly standing, the child had disappeared.

"Lillian! Where have you gone?"

"Here, Mama!" Lilly had her nose pasted to the window.

"Daddy coming!"

"Didn't I tell you to stay put?"

"Yes, Mama. I stay put right here!"

She gave Lilly's bottom a swat, then took each daughter by a hand and led the girls onto the porch. Jeremy pulled up beside them with Patsy harnessed to the sledge.

"My girls all ready for a ride?"

Dropping their mother's hands, both ran to their daddy, full of excitement at the prospect of accompanying him on his rounds to empty sap buckets. Jeremy found this chore much easier to carry out with the aid of his newly built sledge.

"Sleigh ride! Sleigh ride!" Lilly repeated in excitement.

Jeremy lifted his girls aboard, sitting them on the narrow bench he'd fashioned in front of the spot where he stood to hold the reins. He took Amanda's hand and helped her step onto the sledge, getting her seated with a twin on either side. Then he tucked the heavy bear-skin blanket over all three, securing it tightly around their feet to keep biting drafts from blowing up their skirts. That skin had come from the very bear who'd left Jeremy with scar marks down his cheek.

He took his place behind his girls. "Ready?"

"Ready!"

He gave the reins a snap, and the horse trotted off at a brisk pace on the familiar, snow-covered pathway to the woods.

"Too bad we don't have any bells for Pasty," Jeremy called out. "It would make this a festive ride!"

The girls whooped and hollered, enjoying the sunny, February day. Nighttime temperatures still fell below freezing, but strengthening rays of sunshine brought hope of an early spring, along with the sap flow—which meant maple syrup!

Jeremiah began to sing, and soon his girls joined in. He smiled the smile of a contented man.

"Baby, baby, baby," Millie sang away. "Mama's getting a baby!"

"Shhhhh," Amanda shushed, holding her mittened hand to Millie's mouth. She looked behind to see if Jeremiah had heard. He continued to sing in his booming, baritone voice, oblivious to anything but the scope of his own happiness.

* * * * *

Late that afternoon, with evening chores completed early, Willie, Sadie and little Tad arrived at the Harrisons, prepared to stay for the night, so Willie could help boil down sap to make maple sugar for the two households. The men planned to spell one another throughout the nighttime hours to keep the fire burning hot under the big mapleing pot Jeremy had set up outdoors.

While they emptied buckets of sap into the cauldron and got the boiling process underway, Amanda and Sadie laid out supper and proceeded to feed hungry children.

Eighteen-month-old Tad sat in the twin's outgrown high chair, banging his fists on the table. "Eat, eat, eat!"

"He's hungry, Aunt Sadie," Millie reported.

"I know, dear. His food is coming." She turned to give his noodles and mashed-up squash a stir. "It needs to cool off so he doesn't burn his mouth."

"Oh."

Unbeknownst to Sadie, Lilly, sitting on the opposite side of the table from Tad, had handed her chicken leg over to the toddler. Tad sat happily gnawing away at the crusty appendage.

Amanda turned from pouring hot water into the tea pot and immediately reprimanded her intractable daughter, after noticing what she'd done. "Lillian Jane Harrison, did you give that chicken leg to your cousin?"

"Yes, Mama. He's hungry!"

"Aunt Sadie knows he's hungry, darling. She's getting his food right now."

"I just helping."

"Thank you, Lilly," Sadie said with a smile. "I'll take care of him now." She laid the chicken leg back on Lilly's plate. "Here, you can eat this, sweetheart."

"All right." She picked up the leg and began to chew on it herself.

Amanda cringed, but said nothing to Sadie. She did, however, give her daughter a formidable look. Amanda's tendency toward cleanliness had not changed during her tenure at the Asylum. If anything, she had become even more fastidious about its observance.

"Let me have that, Lillian," she said, taking the leg from her daughter, while holding it gingerly between two fingers. "Mother will give you a different piece that hasn't been rubbed all over the table." She set the leg on a dirty plate over on the sideboard, then handed Lilly a thigh from the serving platter. "This one has more meat on it, dear. You like this kind, too."

Without arguing Lilly accepted the thigh and began to eat once more.

Willie walked in, rubbing his hands. "It's getting nippy out there." He headed over to the sideboard and nabbed the rejected chicken leg Amanda had deposited there. "Hmmm, good," he said, between bites. "I'm starving."

"I'll fix a plate for you," Amanda said, shaking her head.

Willie leaned down and planted a kiss on Tad's head, then gave Sadie a peck on her cheek. "Looks like my little Tadpole's enjoying his dinner," he observed of his squash-covered son. Willie patted Sadie on the shoulder. "You feelin' all right, sweetheart?"

"I'm fine. A little queasy, but that salty chicken seems to help."

"Queasy?" Amanda commented.

"Didn't she tell you?" Willie asked surprised.

"Tell me what?"

"She's sittin' on the nest again. We're gonna have us another little chick."

"Oh, Sadie, that's wonderful!" Amanda gushed. "When do you expect it?"

"Sometime in July, I'm guessing," she said. "Just about the time Tad turns two."

"I'm so happy for you," Amanda said. "Nothing like the arrival of a new baby to brighten up a household."

"Baby, baby, baby!" Millie chanted. "Mama's getting a baby!"

"Camellia! Hush!" Amanda waved the serving spoon from the noodles in the air.

"You too?" Sadie asked.

Amanda blushed. "Me, too," she said. "You weren't supposed to tell, you little dickens," she scolded Millie, as she handed Willie a plate filled with chicken, noodles, squash and a big chunk of bread.

"Well, we got us a double reason to celebrate, then," Willie said. "I just told Jeremy about our little bundle in the hopper. He's tickled for us." Willie pondered, "Funny, he didn't say a word about your coming addition."

"He doesn't know yet," Amanda admitted. "I just confirmed it for myself today, when I felt life for the first time. I'm afraid the movement startled me so, I exclaimed out loud. Naturally the girls heard, so I had to make explanations," she said. "Ordinarily, I would tell Jeremiah first, you understand. But all these little ears around here have big mouths, I'm afraid," she said, giving the girls' braids a soft tug. "I'd appreciate it if you could keep this news quiet until I have a chance to tell him myself."

Willie put his hand to his lips and twisted his fingers to mimic a key locking them up tight. "My lips are sealed."

The little girls got such a kick out of their uncle's action, they proceeded to lock up their own lips, too.

"Good dinner, Amanda," Willie said, digging into his food. "Soon as I finish, I'll spell Jeremy so he can come an' eat."

As Willie enjoyed his meal, Amanda wiped off the girls'

hands and faces. "You can go play for a little while until your daddy comes in," she said. "Then it's bedtime."

The girls ran to the other side of the cabin, where their play area sat between their bed and the fireplace. Tad, shoving the last pieces of bread into his mouth all at once, clamored to be set free from the high chair so he could join them.

"Chew up that big bite first. Then I'll let you down," Sadie told him. She wiped off his hands, face, shirt, and the mess he had all over the table. "I don't know how you can spread one piece of bread so far," his mama said. When he swallowed, she untied him from the chair and stood him on his feet. He made a wobbly beeline for the girls.

"Sure is fine, watching those three play," Willie noted. "Pretty soon, we'll be running after five of 'em!" He sopped up the last of the chicken gravy with his bread crust, then excused himself from the table. "Thanks for a fine dinner, Amanda. I'll go fetch Jeremy so he can eat." He pulled on his coat as he headed for the door.

"I'll have some hot coffee ready in a little while," Amanda said.

"Thanks That'd be great."

A few minutes after Willie left the cabin, Jeremy entered. He stomped the snow from his boots, then doffed his hat, coat, and gloves. "It's going to be a beautiful night. Lots of stars out," he commented.

"I have a supper plate warm for you, Jeremiah."

"Thanks. I'm famished." He sat at the table, and Amanda put his plate in front of him. "Thank you, Lord," he prayed succinctly, "and thank you for the new little babe on its way to us from heaven." He dug into the plate of food, chewed a mouthful, then swallowed. "Willie told me your news, Pipsqueak. You feeling all right?"

"Fine, Jems. Just a little green now and then."

"That'll pass." He grabbed another bite. "So when is this little bundle of joy due to land?"

"Midsummer, I calculate."

"Wonderful news, sister of mine. Nothing like a new baby to liven up a household."

"That's just what Amanda said."

"Baby, baby, baby," Millie babbled away from her place near the hearth. "Mama's getting a baby!"

"Aunt Sadie's getting a baby," Jeremy corrected.

"*Mama's* getting a baby!"

"What?" His fork stopped in midair. "Mandy?"

"I had *hoped* to tell you when we were alone, Jeremiah. But since the beans have already been spilled," she glared at Millie, "yes, us too."

"When?"

"About the same time Sadie's due, perhaps a little later."

Jeremy jumped up from the table, grabbed Amanda in a big, bear hug and planted a big, sloppy kiss, smack on her lips. "We're having us a baby, too!" he crowed. "No news could be more welcome than that."

Dear Ellie

Ivy was delivered of a daughter November last. They have christened her Annabelle Olivia. Ivy labored through the night, and at mid-morning Lizzie arrived with some baby things which she had found in my cedar chest.

I almost shed tears upon seeing them, friend, as they were our own Buddy's tiny things, outgrown by him before he left us, and all embroidered with roses in every hue by our dear sweet, Zannah's hand. But I could not spare the attention to reminisce just then, as Ivy's moment to deliver was near at hand.

Lizzie thought not to be pressed to service in the matter. In my impatience, I spoke to her harshly. In the end, the event was simple enough, and I was gladdened that she could bear witness to that fact. It was Lizzie who wrapped the babe and placed her in her father's arms. And the look on his face, so proud and full of love for his child.

We shed our tears onto each other's shoulders, did my daughter and I, as parents marveled over new life. A strange mix, those tears. I could not help but think of Zannah and her son, of my sweet Leesha, and even back to the birth of my Lucy, that first, terrible loss.

But still, they were tears of relief and joy at this happy outcome. Ivy did call me to her bedside then, to put her arms around me and kiss my cheek. I have lost much, friend, but much has also been gained. I have new daughters in Ivy and Katrina, and now here is dear Annabelle, my first lovely grandchild.

It seems that I did not know the full extent of Lizzie's fears after that awful night when we lost Zannah and her babe. In a rush, she revealed that a vow was made by her that night that she would never find herself in childbed. No man would ever claim her, for she thought the ordeal to be a death knell.

And through the sobs, I heard a familiar name—Kit. She's

loved him from the first moment she laid eyes on him, but she turned him away out of fear.

The only daughter of my blood left to me, and she, living with all this pain, while I, abiding in the same house, have been none the wiser, wrapped so securely in my own sorrow have I continued to be. It was that bloodline of which we spoke then. What we share in it, she and I. It was a talk that I never imagined having.

I told her that she has more than just my father's red hair and Irish ancestors; in her veins runs a hot blood. I then told her of the pleasures of the marriage bed, and that her warm blood would assuredly draw her there one day, with or without the sanctity of another vow, one much larger than the one she might have made in a moment of fear.

She pointed out that I have been as guilty as she, absenting myself from my husband and family. And so we have made a pact, Lizzie and I. We cannot hide from life, either one. We must come back to this world and live in it.

I am renewed, Ellie. The spring that has come to the land has long been growing in my heart. Through the long, dark months, my husband and I have been as one being, sharing one space, we were that close. Zach also is full of life, now that I have returned to him; he plans to build a new home for us.

First he will begin sawing and drying the lumber. It will be a project for his spare time only, as this year we have no sons for farming, with Nate now running the mill, Simeon the Riverstop, Levi the whole Mississippi River mayhap, and our Christian readying to make an explore westward.

Of course Elijah, who just turned six, assures his father that he can take the place of all his brothers, so hard will he labor at Zach's side. But my baby's education must begin and is not to be neglected. Lizzie and I have taken over milking of the cow and care of the livestock, things I held myself incapable of doing previously.

I had word from Cait in the fall. She and Will Skillicorn are settled into their new home and are excited that her husband's uncle, a Mr. Lewis Fetter, has given them a heifer as well. Buddy is walking and talking and now has a little sister named—what else? Rosie.

My niece sounds so happy, friend, to be settled at last with her love. She related how at the birth of this daughter, her husband did cry out that he had let her down so, she having birthed their first child while he was out wandering and none the wiser, and how he will never again be torn from her side. All there is as it should be.

And how is our daughter Katrina, friend? Is her condition confirmed? Does she ripen? How was Simeon's first winter at the Riverstop? What news of your friends and old neighbors? I am so eager for news!

Are we to meet this year, Ellie? Write as you are able.

Your old friend, Libby

Renewed at last!

Dear Lib,

Hope you wintered fair. I have not heard from you in such a long time, I pray you are still among the living.

Our Katrina is fattening right up. Thing is I just got a visit from Jason. He says Mary Sue is in the family way once again and her legs are swelling up bad already. Those two waste no time. I am going to her and help with those two children and baby Jay. She has none of her people hereabouts to help out.

Now Simmie and Katrina say they can handle things here just fine. Though I notice she does tire easy these days. I reckon my girl for popping sometime early July. But I do not want her down here alone when her time comes. Specially on a first birth. Or working herself to death cooking for these varmints.

I do not know how it is with you, Lib. But we are in a fix here. So how bout it? Can you come down to stay with these two? Help them out here while I go to Mary Sue? Edie could come for the birth. But she does not stay around to help out much after. Nor before lessen there is trouble. It would be a long ride for Simmie to bring Edie down here at a time when he would not want to leave the girl laboring all alone. I will get word to Edie that Katrina and Simmie may be on their own. In case that you cannot come to help with the birth.

I dare not wait to hear your answer. I got to get over there to Jason's before Mary Sue cannot walk no more. Please come down, Lib. We need you!

Your friend and now relative,
Ellie

June 9, 1820
Jerometown on Muddy Fork

Dear Lib,

I have just got your spring letter. Made my heart glad, it did. Welcome back to the world, girl. Harmon knew I was out at his cousin Jason's. So he brung it to me here. He told me you come down, Lib. Said you had your boy Christian bring you and stopped at Edie's to let her know you was going down to Katrina and Simmie. That is a big load off my mind.

So your first grandbaby got here fine. And now you are going to make sure the second one gets here safe. A body could almost think we got it all figured out!

I am kept right busy here. Jay is a happy babe. But that Harley says nothing but NO! Being that he is now 2. And talk about move? That child never stops. Puts me in mind of your Levi. I been having the best time with Josie. She is growing right up. Thinks she is big stuff, she does. Likes to help with cooking. Course that will change. Easy to get them to help when they are little. When they get big enough to really help they disappear!

Sure wish I could be with my girl about now. But you being there is durn near as good. I reckon her time will be drawing close come another month.

Jay has woke up from his nap. And he went and woke Harley besides. Looks like my rest is done for the time being. Soon as this new one comes I will head home. Mary Sue needs little time to recoup once the swelling goes down in her legs after birth. But that is likely still a ways off.

Send me word, friend, when our new grandpup gets here.

Your friend,
Ellie Mae

Chapter 14

Early July 1820

"Hello the house!"

Amanda brushed hands on her apron as she made her way to the door to see who had ridden up. "Jonathan! What brings you around this time of day?"

He tipped his hat. "On my way back from a supply run up to Uniontown. Thought I'd stop off to say 'howdy'. See if Jeremy needs any help the next few days."

"He's down at the Jarvis place helping Henry clear a new piece of land. I expected Jeremiah back hours ago. I don't know what could be keeping him so long."

"Maybe Lucy already cooked up evenin' vittles for 'em."

"He told me he'd be back in time to do evening chores and eat supper with his girls. It's just not like him to stay away this late."

"I can stop on my way. See what's keepin' him," Jonathan offered.

"I'd be grateful. I truly would."

"No trouble," Jonathan said. "I'm headin' that way to the Hawkins', anyway. Got a package here for sister Edie."

"I thought Harmon delivered all the letters and packages in these parts."

"Generally does. But I reckon he wuz too busy payin' court to some female round abouts to pick up this one."

"Be sure to tell Jeremiah I have supper waiting, will you? I can't keep the girls up much later. It's almost their bed time."

"You want help with evenin' chorin' 'fore I head out?"

"No, Jeremiah can see to the feeding when he gets home," she said. "Bertha's due to drop a calf in the next couple weeks, so there's no milking to tend to right now."

"Suit yourself." Jonathan turned his horse and began to trot back out the lane.

"Thank you!" Amanda called to his disappearing back.

After another hour, Amanda gave up and put the girls to bed with the fading sun. She wrapped Jeremy's supper and stored it in the cold box he'd built in the hillside next to the water pump.

Another hour and a half ticked by, and still no Jeremiah. She decided she'd better feed the animals herself. Fireflies and a full moon lit up the night sky, as she made her way out to the barn.

Amanda had begun to worry.

* * * * *

Jonathan found nary a soul in the Jarvis cabin with supper ready and untouched on the table. With that prickly feeling crawling up the back of his neck, he headed out behind the barn, assuming that's where Henry had wanted another field cleared.

Nearly a dozen trees lay felled and stacked to burn, their branches piled up to act as tinder for the bonfire they'd start in a few months' time, once the green wood had dried out enough to catch. Beside the woodpile sat Jeremy's cart, parked; Little Hank in its small bed, sat playing quietly with blocks. The cart had sides high enough to keep the three-year-old secure inside. No worry of his escape for the moment.

Further afield stood Lucy, beside and to the rear of Jeremy's Patsy and Henry's Clyde, hitched together for the day's work. She held the reins, attempting to get the team to pull another huge tree attached to their traces with two, long ropes. Lucy tried to guide the horses to pull the tree a little at a time, so as not to jerk it loose all at once. Two smaller limbs, wedged underneath, gave the larger tree something to crawl up and onto as the horses pulled.

Jonathan took in the whole scene in an instant. What he discovered made his blood run cold. Underneath that tree lay Jeremy on his stomach—pinned. Further up the trunk, lay Henry, with head bloodied. Neither man moved a muscle.

Obviously Lucy had dug beneath the huge log in order to wedge in those two sled branches. Not many men would have come up with such a solution, yet, there stood levelheaded Lucy, working as hard and ingeniously as any man to free those two men.

"Lucy! I'm here! Let me help!"

Lucy turned and noticed Jonathan advancing toward her. "Jeremy's still alive. But I can't pull him out," she said. "I tried digging underneath to free him, but it's no good. He's pinned between the tree and a big rock."

"Henry?"

"Dead."

"How long have they been like this?"

"I figure at least two hours. More, by now," she said. "I found 'em when I came out to see why they hadn't come in for supper. Jeremy's conscious off and on. He couldn't tell me how long ago it happened. I've been working at this log for over an hour."

Jonathan went straight to Jeremy without another word. The man lay unconscious, but still breathing. By the looks of Henry's crushed head, there was no hope of seeing him alive in this world again. "You keep doin' what you got started, Lucy," he called. "When the log gives enough, I'll pull him out."

Together, Lucy and Jonathan worked to free Jeremiah. When Jonathan had him pulled clear, he called for Lucy to stop the team and hold them steady, until he could lever in a stop to keep the log from rolling back on top of Henry. For now, Henry's body would have to wait. They needed to fetch help for Jeremy—and fast.

While Jonathan rode for Ma Hawkins, Lucy sat vigil with Jeremiah. He lay in an odd position, his back unquestionably broken. They hadn't tried to move him to the cabin without Ma there, out of fear they'd do more damage than had already been done. Lucy brought a blanket out to cover him, as well as another one to cover little Hank, now sound asleep in the cart. She also put a feed sack over Henry's ruined head, holding back an urge to be sick at the sight.

While she sat wiping Jeremy's brow with a damp cloth, she shed the requisite tears for her own lost husband.

Just before Jonathan's return, Jeremy regained consciousness, and during his brief time of awareness, he apologized to Lucy for failing to push Henry clear of the falling tree.

"I saw it going the wrong way," he said, taking a shallow breath and grimacing at the pain.

"You don't have to talk," Lucy replied gently. "Just rest."

"I want you to know," he breathed again. "It wasn't his fault. I thought the tree would fall the other way." Jeremy lay quietly for a few more, shallow breaths. "I hollered. Tried to get to him... to push him out of the way, but..." he breathed shallowly again for a time. "Branch clipped me... took me down before I could reach him," Jeremy said. "Henry never saw it coming."

"Then, he was blessed to have it happen so quick," Lucy replied.

"I'm so sorry," Jeremy said, "I... I...." Before he could finish his thought, Jeremiah felt a wave of excruciating pain. "Mandy...," he breathed. "My little yellow bird... Will you break this to her easy, Lucy?"

"Of course. You know I will."

"She's had so much loss ... so much–"

"Don't worry. We'll manage together, Amanda and I," Lucy tried to reassure him. "Rest, now, if you can."

"Sadie!" Jeremy began to get agitated all over again. His breaths came faster, and before he could put his thought into words, he blacked out once more.

"And it's a blessing you can escape from the pain. At least for a time, my friend."

* * * * *

The moon had reached its pinnacle in the night sky by the time Jonathan returned with his sister Edie and her Harmon, just back home from keeping company with his new love interest at the Bailey household. Sadie, ready to pop her next babe any day, remained behind with Willie for the time being. Ma didn't want to cause premature labor by having her jolted over bumpy roads, if there was no immediate need to do so. She wanted to assess things first, saying she'd send for them in the morning, if the situation warranted.

Harmon brought along a flat plank to use for moving the injured man. Jeremy could speak to them when they arrived, but when they rolled him onto that transport board, he passed out again. Ma insisted they take him no farther than Lucy's cabin. She oversaw the process of getting Jeremy settled into Lucy and Henry's bed with as little jostling as possible.

"I need to check that spine while he's still unconscious," Ma said. "With those broke ribs, it won't be easy on him any time, I'm a'feared." She rolled him gently onto his side, and he groaned even in his unconscious state. Gingerly, she walked her fingers over his twisted back. "Broke for sure," she said. "Don't know as there's any way to set a back broke this bad and have it take," she said, shaking her head. "Jonathan, you better gather up Amanda and get her over here. No tellin' how long he's apt to hang on. I can tell you one thing… it don't look good at-all."

Lucy spoke up. "I'll go," she said. "I promised Jeremy I'd tell her easy."

"You sure you're up to it, gal?" Ma asked.

"I'm still running on nerves," she said, easing her sleeping son into his own bed. "I'll be fine."

"That ain't what I'm talkin' about, an' you know it."

"It's all right," Lucy said, with a knowing nod. "I'm used to working hard. The baby's fine."

Jonathan's head jerked up at this revelation. "You're in the family way? *Now?*"

She nodded in the affirmative, then touched Jonathan's shoulder. "I'll be fine," she said. "I have to be."

"Harmon, go hitch that cart up to your horse and take Lucy over to Amanda's," Ma instructed. "This gal ain't pushin' herself any more'n need be this night, if'n I have ary a thing to say about it."

Lucy gracefully acquiesced to Ma's directive. "Thank you," she said. "It'll be a comfort to have a man along."

While Lucy made a trip to the backhouse, Jonathan told his sister, "I'll see to Henry while she's gone."

By the time Lucy cleaned herself up a bit, Ma had a large pot of coffee boiling to keep everyone going for the long night ahead.

* * * * *

Back at the Harrison cabin, Amanda tried to prepare herself for the worst. She knew something terrible had happened to Jeremy, or Henry, or both. She kept a light burning in the window, while she sat wrapped in a shawl against the late-night chill, rocking on the porch to keep watch for anyone bringing news. She tried valiantly to stay alert, but the fuzz of sleep slowly began to engulf her. Whenever her head fell forward, she'd jerk herself awake. At last, she gave in to the insistence of slumber…

…she felt herself floating in the air, hovering over the trees, watching the landscape fly by beneath her. In an instant, she came to a cleared area where trees lay stacked to burn, with one, large log lying apart from the others. When she drew in closer, she could see a man lying there, his head covered with a sack.

She recognized the face of death.

"This you will survive, leibchein," said a familiar voice beside her ear. "You must be strong. For yourself. For your little girls. For your unborn babe. Your kinders, they need a mama who can comfort them. Love them. See them grow. This, you *will* have strength to do."

The voice faded, as did the vision, evaporating into the fog of early morning haze. Amanda heard the clop of horse hooves and the creak of a cart, and she roused at its approach. When

Harmon and Lucy pulled up to the porch, Amanda stood and stepped down. Lucy descended from the cart, and the two came together in a long, understanding hug.

"He's dead, isn't he," Amanda said, "Jeremiah."

"Jeremy's alive. But he's in a bad way," Lucy answered. "His back's broken."

Amanda shuddered. "Henry?"

"Henry's dead."

Amanda and Lucy hugged again, holding each other tight in combined anguish.

After getting her sleeping girls settled in the back of the cart, Harmon sat Amanda and Lucy together on the seat, then he took a place standing behind them to drive back to the Jarvis place. Amanda and Lucy held one another the entire way. By the time they neared Lucy's, the moon had nearly reached the western horizon, and the faint light of early dawn began to streak the eastern sky.

Candles and lanterns burned brightly in the Jarvis cabin. Ma had made Jeremy as comfortable as she could, and she'd mixed one of her potions to help take the edge off his pain. Nothing could come close to relieving the deep agony he suffered.

"I can't move my legs," he told her when he'd taken stock of himself after regaining consciousness once more. "Arms work. But I can barely lift 'em for the pain in my chest," he said between shallow breaths. "Head hurts, too. Funny kind of hurt."

"Don't try to move," Ma said. "Your back's busted. About smack dab in the middle. You have broken ribs, too. Not sure how many. There's nary a thing I can do to make any of it better, neither," she stated simply. "Wished I knew something to do...'sides just givin' powders for pain. But there ain't nothin' for it." She pulled a chair up to his bedside and sat down. "You got a terrible fight to pull through this," she said. "An' even if you do, you'll likely never use them legs again."

Jeremy lay silent, tears streaming down his cheeks, wetting his beard. "What's my Mandy gonna do, now?" he whispered.

"She'll survive. Like all of us have to when calamity strikes," Ma said. "We pull together to get through it."

The cabin door opened, and Lucy and Amanda entered, still holding one another's hands. Harmon came in behind, giving his ma a nod in acknowledgement.

"Jeremiah?" Amanda hurried to the bed and knelt beside her husband. "I knew something terrible happened. I just *knew*."

"I'm so sorry," he said, catching a hitch in his breath, trying his best to deal with the pain. He breathed slowly, more deliberately, before trying to talk again.

"Send for Michael," he said. "We're gonna need him."

"I'll see to it," Harmon offered. "Aimed to head up North in a couple days, anyhow. I'll set out today."

"Does Sadie know?" Amanda asked Ma.

"She knows her brother needed help, that's all. I told her she better stay put for the night, till I could take stock an' see how bad it was," she said. "That babe's so close, and Sadie's been havin' so much trouble this time, didn't want her bouncing no bumpy roads if it warn't needed. But I can see we'll have to fetch her."

"Where's Jonathan?" Lucy asked, as she settled herself on a kitchen chair, propped her elbows on the table, then dropped her head into her hands.

"You need to lie down, gal," Ma said, going to her side and brushing the loose hair back from her face. "I'll make up a pallet by the fire for you. Sleep while you can, 'fore that little pup o' yours wakes."

"Thanks. I do feel done in," Lucy answered.

Ma got her settled on a pile of blankets by the hearthstone, then returned to Jeremy's bedside, at a complete loss for any way to help him. Amanda sat on the floor, propped against the bed, holding onto his hand.

* * * * *

After Lucy and Harmon had gone to fetch Amanda, Jona-

251

than took it upon himself to move Henry's body into the barn. He laid him out on the old bedstead in the corner, where Henry had lived before he married Lucy. He'd seen to the spent horses, still harnessed in their traces, waiting patiently for food and care. Then Jonathan began building a coffin. He aimed to get Henry boxed up and out of site, before Lucy got back with Amanda. She shouldn't have to lay eyes on that ruined face again, especially not in her condition.

He worked the rest of the night through, cutting, hammering, fashioning a final resting place for the man he never thought deserving enough of an incredible woman like Lucy. Jonathan had never known anyone as courageous as this plucky gal, who'd come out here all by herself to become the wife of a total stranger. And a stranger man than Henry, he never had known. Well, not strange, really. Misguided, maybe. Henry did have his good qualities, but he sure had funny ideas about how to treat a woman.

By the time Jonathan finished the coffin, Lucy and Harmon had just returned with Amanda. He laid Henry in the box, leaving the sack in place that covered his ruined head. "Bye, Henry," he said, nailing the lid down, tight. "I'll see to it Lucy's taken care of."

* * * * *

Dawn broke with the golden haze of summer. Birds sang, cicadas clicked, and farm animals and little children clamored for their breakfast. Inside the Jarvis cabin, the routine of morning pushed ahead, despite the inadequate sleep attained by any of its adult occupants.

Ma made the coffee strong and hot. Lucy busied herself fixing a simple breakfast of cornmeal mush and smoked side pork. And Amanda saw to the needs of three, bouncing three-year-olds. She got them all dressed, washed up and seated at table, then Lucy dished bowls of mush all around. The three little ones chattered while they ate.

"We're visiting Ha-ank, we're visiting Ha-ank" Lilly sang out.

"Lillian, eat your mush, please," Amanda instructed.

"Yes, Mama."

"Why is daddy in bed?"

"He hurt himself, Camellia."

"Can't you kiss it and make it better?"

"Daddy's hurt is much too deep for a kiss to fix it, darling."

"Oh."

The three ate in silence for a few moments. Then Lilly poked Hank with her spoon. He let out a howl.

"Lillian Jane, why on earth did you poke Hank that way?"

"He kicked me!"

"He always kicks, Lilly," said Lucy. "I'll just move his chair over so he can't touch you, all right?"

"Mama, why won't Daddy get up?"

"I told you, Camellia, he's badly hurt. His legs don't work right now, darling."

"Oh." Camellia thought deeply, her eyebrows furrowed in concentration. "Can't Gran'ma Hawkins fix them?"

"I wish I could, Millie. I truly do," Ma answered the child, as she dished up a bowlful of mush for Jeremy.

"Where's Papa?" Hank asked his Mother.

"He's out in the barn, Pun'kin," answered Lucy. "Mr. Jonathan's out there with him, seeing to morning chores."

"Oh." Hank said with a full mouth, continuing to shovel in his breakfast.

Amanda gave Lucy a questioning look, and Lucy mouthed back "not yet." She wasn't ready to break the news of his father's death to little Hank in the middle of breakfast.

Ma tried to spoon some sustenance into Jeremy, but all he managed to get down were a few swallows, along with a little hot, comfrey tea. She needed her laudanum to help him manage this kind of pain. As soon as Harmon had returned just before dawn with Amanda and the girls, she'd sent him on home to tell

Willie and Sadie to come right over after morning chore time. She knew her determined daughter-in-law would wait no longer for news, even if it meant hobbling clear over here by her own self and having the baby on the way.

Ma told Harmon to send her strongest medicines along with them. She also asked for her knitting—a strange request coming from her. Ma seldom ever sat down when she took care of someone. Sadie would understand that Ma intended to stay by Jeremy's side for the long haul, if she aimed to sit and knit.

Ma just wanted something to keep herself busy, so she could try to get her mind off how inadequate she felt at not having some way to fix this mess. With two other women already in the cabin, who needed to remain busy to manage their grief, Ma knew they'd all be tripping over one another. So she'd just sit right here by Jeremy, keep her hands busy, and stay out of their way, as much as possible.

Willie and Sadie arrived by midmorning. This time she allowed Willie to help her down from the wagon. Willie longed for one of those new-fangled buggies with special springs,

rather than this bone-shaking buckboard for Sadie to ride in. Needs must they make do with the transport at hand.

Once she stood upon the ground, Sadie gingerly found her footing. With this pregnancy, she never knew whether or not her right leg would hold her when she stood up. The way this little tyke sat against her pelvis, her hip gave out more than it held, whenever she put weight on it. So she'd taken to walking with a cane. It looked strange to see spry, little Sadie making her way around like an old woman. But there was no help for it.

By the time she had herself walking toward the cabin on semi-steady legs, Willie had two-year-old Tad unloaded. He ran circles around his mama, barking and howling like a dog.

"He's Rover today," Willie explained to Lucy and Amanda and the girls, all coming out to welcome the newcomers. "He wants a puppy so bad, he's taken to pretending he is one." Willie turned back to the wagon, and began unhitching Freddie, so he could tie him over in the shade.

"Tadpole! Tadpole! You're here, too!" Millie exclaimed, as she ran off the porch and tried to give him a hug. Tad, not wanting anything to do with a hug, pretended to bite her ankle.

Lilly, following close on Millie's heels, smacked Tad soundly on the head. "Bad dog!" she scolded. "Must not bite Millie!"

At her reprimand, Hank decided to join the fray and came to Tadpole's aid. "Here, doggie, doggie. Come to Hank," he said, patting Tad on the head. Tad licked his hand. "Let's go play catch!"

The mothers shook their heads in helpless wonder at the resilience of little children in the midst of catastrophe. After breakfast, Lucy had told Hank that his Daddy's spirit went to Heaven last night to be with Jesus, and that they'd have to plant his body in the ground today.

Hank wanted to know what kind of plant grew from a Daddy.

Ma appeared on the porch, following everyone else outdoors. "You take the trip all right?" she asked Sadie, giving her a good look up and down.

"I'm a little shook up, but managing well enough," she said.

"Harmon get on his way North yet, to fetch Michael?"

"He's taking a catnap first, so he won't fall off his horse," Sadie told her. "Aims to head out around noon."

"Just so's he gets on his way," Ma said, shaking her head. "The sooner we get Michael back here, the better."

"Is Jems that bad? Harmon did say he's in terrible pain."

"Did you bring the laudanum? He sure enough needs it."

"Willie has your bag of strong medicines. He'll bring it in after he tends to Freddie," she said. "Is it all right to leave Tad playing out here for a while?"

"You go on in," Lucy told Amanda and Sadie. "I'll keep an eye on all of 'em. I could use some sunshine, myself."

Sadie eased her way up each step, then went inside the cabin door, now propped open to let in some fresh air. She went straight to Jeremy's bedside and sat on the chair.

"What on earth did you go and do now, Jems?"

"Thought I'd try splitting a tree with my back," he said in shallow breaths. "The tree won." He tried to keep it light for the sake of the women, but they could see how badly he suffered.

"We brought Ma's special medicine kit. She's got some potions in there to help with the pain, Jems."

"It's doing a fine job of hurtin' all by itself," he said. "It sure don't need help."

"You *know* what I mean," Sadie whined. "It'll help to ease the pain."

"Good. For a while there, you had me worried."

"Well, you've done a good enough job of keeping everyone else worried all by yourself," she scolded.

"I'm sorry, Pipsqueak. I never would've wished this burden on any of you. Not for all the world."

"It's not your fault, Jems. Accidents happen, just like with Father. We all know that," she said, patting his hand.

"But it *is* my fault," he breathed slowly for a brief time. "I thought I had that tree set to fall the other way... but it fooled me... whipped around and went backwards on us." He closed his eyes as a throbbing wave overtook him. "I killed Henry, sure as if I pulled a trigger and shot him dead."

"But you tried to *save* Henry!" Sadie argued. "You wouldn't be in such a fix yourself, otherwise."

After having a private talk on the porch, Amanda and Ma came inside. Ma dumped her medicine bag onto the table and shuffled through its contents, while Amanda went over to the bed and took Jeremy's hand. He lay flanked by his wife and sister, both pale with worry.

"You two need someone to tickle you silly... put some

smiles back on your faces," Jeremy teased. "I'd be happy to oblige. But at the moment, I don't seem to have the energy to even lift my arms."

"Just rest, brother," Sadie said. "You can tickle us when you're feeling better. We'll be right here, waiting."

Amanda took the cloth out of the basin, wrung it out, and gently wiped down Jeremy's face and neck and shoulders. "We'll do everything we can to get you back on your feet again, won't we, Sadie."

"You BET we will!" Sadie said. "You're gonna have a new niece or nephew to hold real soon, so you better get those arms in shape right quick, Jems, you hear?"

"I'll do my best," Jeremy said, closing his eyes, obviously getting tired out again.

"You two go on out and set a spell by Lucy," Ma told the women. "I got some pain killer to give him, so he can sleep more peaceful for a while." She took the bottle and poured out a generous spoonful. "Open up and swallow this down," she directed him.

Jeremy did as told, making a face at the taste.

"You rest," Ma said, feeling his head to assess the progress of the fever just beginning to set in. "All your girls are here, now, an' doin' fine. So don't you worry your head over any of your people."

"Michael?"

"Harmon's on his way to fetch him. Should be back inside of a week." Ma answered. *Sure hope you can hold on that long,* she thought.

Amanda sat underneath the sycamore tree with Lucy; Sadie eased herself onto an upturned barrel beside them. All three watched their children frolic and play.

"Are you doing all right, Lucy?" Amanda asked. "What can we do to help you?"

"You're already doing it," she answered. "Having you here

right now is the best medicine I can think of. For Hank and me both. I just wish there was something more I could do for Jeremy," she fretted. "If he hadn't tried to save Henry, he'd still be on his feet right now. I feel guilty he got hurt on his account."

"That's Jems," Sadie said. "You know he couldn't have done otherwise."

"I know. But I still feel responsible," said Lucy.

"You can't torture yourself over such things," Amanda told her. "I had to learn that lesson the hard way. I almost let guilt destroy me. You have to let it go, Lucy. It's not your fault. Nor was it Henry's fault, either. Jeremiah made his decision in a split second, and all our lives are changing because of it."

"Listen to you, grown so wise," Sadie said.

"It's a wisdom hard won, sister."

"What did Ma say to you before you came in?" Sadie asked.

"She told me not to be surprised if Jeremy's arms quit working all together. That the swelling in his back would begin to affect more than just his legs," Amanda related. "She also said his insides could start to give him trouble, too… especially if fever sets in bad."

All three sat silently for a spell, listening to the children giggle and squeal.

"I bet by the time Michael gets here, Jems will be back on his feet," said Sadie. "Just wait and see. He's strong. He can beat this thing," she said with conviction. "Once the swelling goes down, Ma can set those bones proper. He'll heal good as new."

Amanda and Lucy just looked at one another, shaking their heads at Sadie's unrealistic point of view. Jeremy could not last much longer in this world. Both women understood that certainty to the depths of their souls.

* * * * *

Before Willie and Sadie had arrived at the Jarvis place, and after finishing up Lucy's chores, Jonathan headed over to Jeremy's to take care of all his animals. This would prove to be a long day, after an already strenuous night, for when he finished up the Harrison's chores, Jonathan intended to start digging Henry's grave.

Henry. What would poor Henry think of Lucy, all alone with a three-year-old and another child on the way? He probably wouldn't give it another thought, just go about his own, oblivious, self-righteous way. Jonathan always did have a hard time watching how Henry treated Lucy—from the time she arrived as his mail-order bride, until he watched her driving that team, struggling to free Jeremiah. Damn, she deserved better than she'd got.

If he could make a difference in her life now, he surely would try, as soon as she'd let him, that is. It had taken Jonathan nearly half a lifetime to find the woman he wanted, only to have to watch someone else claim her and treat her badly in the name of his holier-than-thou duty. Well, her days of suffering that kind of neglect and abuse were through.

Jonathan fed and watered all the animals, then he turned them loose in the south pasture. With the Honey Creek running through the bottoms, he knew they'd get along fine for a spell. That way no one would have to make two trips over every day, just to feed and water the stock. No doubt it'd be a good while before anyone returned to keep the home fires burning here, so Jonathan tied up all the loose ends he could find at the Harrison's.

Jonathan's own hogs knew how to fend for themselves for long stretches at a time, rooting loose in the woods the way they did. He didn't even bother checking on his own place right now. Just headed straight back to Lucy's.

When he arrived after nooning, he found Willie already hard at work digging Henry's grave. Being the middle of hot summer, they knew they had to get Henry planted as soon as possible, even without the services of a real minister to preside, as Henry would have preferred. Were the tables reversed, no one had any doubt that Henry would leave Lucy's body to ripen in the heat, awaiting an official man of the cloth to conduct a bona fide funeral service.

In other circumstances, when a circuit-preacher was not in the vicinity, Jeremy often became the stand-in at a graveside. This time, they'd have to do their best without the comfort of his words. Lord knew, they most likely would have to dig his bury hole next.

With Willie hard at the task, Jonathan took the opportunity to eat a quick bite and take a much needed nap underneath the buckeye tree. The women had already fed children and bedded them down for afternoon slumber beneath the big sycamore. Little bodies sprawled every which way, arms and legs intertwined on the blanket.

Sadie rested on a nearby quilt, propped up by pillows to make her more comfortable. Lucy napped on her pallet back inside, and Amanda lay on the rug beside Jeremy's bed.

While everyone else took advantage of much deserved afternoon sleep, after a most exhausting night of activity, Ma sat vigil at Jeremiah's bedside.

That evening, after a simple dinner of fresh, green beans with ham and biscuits, they gathered to commit Henry Jarvis to the ground. With somber faces all around, Jonathan and Willie eased the wooden box into the grave. Even the children stood quietly, trying to understand the whole process in their innocent fashion. Lucy had taken a few moments alone in the barn with Henry, before the men carried the coffin to his gravesite at the edge of the field Henry had been clearing. Lucy thought it a fitting resting place.

They all stood, looking at one another, waiting for someone to take the lead in saying a few words. Jonathan cleared his throat, but said nothing. Willie, kicking his feet in the dirt, finally stepped forward.

"Seein' as we don't have any preacher here, and Jeremy's laid up, I reckon I'll say a few words over Henry."

No one moved a muscle.

"Henry was... well, he worked hard, he did, to improve his

land and raise a God-fearin' family." He stood a few moments, trying to think of something else to say.

Lucy stepped forward. "Henry did the best he could, with what the Good Lord gave him. His family will miss him." She stepped back, standing tall, nuzzling Hank.

"Ashes to ashes, dust to dust," Willie added. "May the Lord give Henry his rest."

Lucy stooped down, took a handful of dirt, and threw it on top of the coffin. Amanda, Sadie and Ma did likewise. The twins, closely watching their elders, followed suit, as did Tad. But Little Hank stood motionless, painstakingly studying the whole situation, while Jonathan and Willie began to shovel dirt back into the hole to fill up Henry's grave.

"Daddy says the seed splits open to die before the Lord can grow a new bean," he expounded. "Will a new daddy grow from the split-open head of my dead daddy?"

No one said a word. Then Jonathan stooped down to the boy, put a hand on his shoulder and looked him straight in the eye. "The Lord will not grow you a new daddy from the old one, Hank. But he may send a new daddy to see that the job of raisin' up his family gets finished."

Hank thought that through carefully. "Maybe the Lord wants you to be my new daddy." With that simple statement, he turned and followed Tad and the twins back to the cabin, under the shepherding care of Amanda Jane and Sadie.

Lucy remained behind. Quietly, without comment, she picked up a shovel, dug into the pile of dirt, and proceeded to help the men fill in Henry's grave.

* * * * *

Five days, and no sign of Harmon or Michael, yet. Ma didn't really expect them for another two or three days, but knowing Michael, it wouldn't surprise her to see him ride in at any time—especially if Harmon managed to track him down right off.

Jeremy's condition worsened. Despite Ma's comfrey and knitbone compresses, the swelling had not subsided. His fever raged, causing disorientation and delirium. Once in a while he'd awaken coherent, and at those times, he'd give instructions and make his wishes known.

"Mandy, I signed over half the farm to Michael and Violet, before she died," he said in a breathy voice. His breathing had gotten shallower. And to Ma's experienced ear, his bruised lungs were beginning to sound waterlogged. She feared blood clots and pneumonia. "If I can't hold on till Mike gets here…"

"You're hanging on, Jeremiah. You will!"

"…sign the rest over to him. Then you can go back home to Charleston."

"But this is my home, Jeremiah. You are my anchor here."

"I'm afraid this anchor won't hold much longer, my little yellow bird."

"You can't give up … You *can't!*"

"I'm not giving up, Mandy. I'm fighting for all I'm worth. Just don't have a whole lot of fight left in me."

Tears leaked down Amanda's cheeks, despite her resolve not to cry in front of Jeremiah. He could no longer move his arms nor feel his hands; still, she continued to hold them.

Willie had gone back home to take care of his own chores and farm work. Every day Jonathan took care of Lucy's chores, making an occasional trip to his own place to check on his hogs, then check things over at the Harrisons. Other neighbors gathered to take on the Harrison's farm work until Michael returned. The wheat needed harvesting, so Tom Hawkins, Sam Justice and Frank Putnam worked to cut it and tie up the shocks.

At the Jarvis cabin, Lucy and Amanda kept the children fed and well cared for, while Sadie did her best to continue growing the newest little Hawkins. Willie insisted she not try to make the trip back home but remain on at Lucy's. With four women and four children in residence, the cabin felt stifling at times. Luckily, the balmy summer weather afforded plenty of outdoor activity to keep children occupied and happy.

Feeding everyone proved an ongoing challenge. Lucy had put out a good-sized, kitchen garden, and she worked in it constantly—not necessarily because she had to, but because the therapy of pulling weeds and harvesting vegetables gave her great comfort. Her efforts went a long way toward satisfying

everyone's hunger, as well. Jonathan also butchered a hog for them, so they had fresh pork. What they didn't use up immediately, they salted down to help it keep.

Lucy continued to sleep on her pallet by the hearth, now plumped up by the tick from Henry's old bed in the barn, freshened now and re-filled with clean straw. Ma and Amanda took turns sleeping on another pallet they'd fashioned beside Jeremy's bed (formerly Lucy and Henry's) by stacking several rugs to soften the floor. One would sleep, while the other sat vigil. Jonathan made a temporary bedstead in the corner for Sadie, and Willie brought over an extra feather tick for her use. She had such a hard time getting up and down, no one wanted to see her have to sleep on the floor.

The children all slumbered in a pile in the loft. Jonathan fashioned a barricade across its entrance, so no little bodies could fall out. The children thought this "camp out" great fun. They built happy memories: playing, sleeping, and living together during this time of upheaval for the adults.

Two days later Michael arrived in the heat of the afternoon. He'd ridden long and hard, and both he and his horse looked the worse for wear. Jonathan met them near the barn and took the horse to give it a long drink and a rubdown. Michael headed straight for the pump, stuck his head underneath and doused himself with cool water. When he came up sputtering, he shook his head, pushing wet hair back from his eyes.

"Unka Mikey! Unka Mikey!" The twins, playing with the boys by the buckeye tree, saw him and came running.

"Mama, Mama! Unka Mikey's here!" Millie scurried to her mother with the news; Lilly wrapped herself around Michael's leg, hugging tight, and Tad attached himself to the other leg. Hank stood watching with sober expression, looking Michael up and down, then went to the garden to stand by his mother.

"Hello, Lilly," Michael never got the girls mixed up the way most adults did. "How's my little flower?"

"Papa's sick, Unka Mikey. He can't get up."

"I know, sweetheart. That's why I came."

"Mama's real upset. She cries a lot when Papa don't see," she reported. "I try to make her laugh, but Millie just tattles."

"Don't you worry that little head about your mama. We'll all take care of her."

Lilly nodded in the affirmative.

"Let me go, now, so I can go see your papa," Michael said, unwrapping little arms and legs. "Go on over and play by Aunt Sadie, till I come back out." He waved to his sister in acknowledgement, then headed toward the cabin. The children ran off to the little fort they'd fashioned out of branches and sticks underneath the buckeye tree.

Michael brushed off his shirt and pants with his hat, then climbed the steps onto the porch. Amanda walked through the doorway and straight into Michael's outstretched arms, Millie holding fast to her mama's skirts all the while.

"He's so weak and in so much pain," she began to cry softly against his shoulder.

He held her close for a few moments, then eased her away. "Come on, now, Sister, you can't let him see you've been crying," he wiped the tears from her eyes with the dusty handkerchief he pulled from his shirt pocket. "Take me in there, and let's see if we can't cheer him up."

Amanda stepped back, shooed Millie down with the other children, then took Michael by the hand and led him in to Jeremy's bedside.

"What in the world have you gone and done now, Jems?"

"Reckon I've ruined things this time, Mike," Jeremy answered in a raspy voice. "Can't move a thing but my head, and even that hurts like a son-of-a-gun."

"Well, don't move it, then."

"Case you hadn't noticed, I'm stuck here in this bed."

Michael sat in the chair next to Jeremy and touched his shoulder. "What can I do, Jems? Anything, you know that."

"Take me home, Mike. I want to die at home."

On the other side of the bed, Amanda caught her breath.

"You sure?"

"Dead sure."

"Bad joke, brother," Michael shook his head.

"I want to lie underneath the apple tree... by the boys."

"We'll see to that, brother. Dig your resting place right there between the boys and Violet, if you're that set on kicking the bucket," he said in a teasing effort to raise Jeremy's spirits.

"No, I mean I want to draw my last breath under that tree," Jeremy wheezed. "I want to die watching the leaves blow... smelling my crops... hearing the birds sing."

Michael thought to continue with the banter to try and boost Jeremy out of his hopelessness. But he could see precious little life-spark left in his brother. "All right, Jems. No sense tryin' to talk you out of it. We'll do as you wish."

"One more thing... take care of Mandy and the girls?"

"You don't even need to ask. You know I will."

"I can die peaceful, now."

"If it's all the same to you, Jems. I'd kind of like you to stick around, if you can manage it," Michael said, giving his shoulder a squeeze.

"I'd love to oblige. Really I would... but I'm afraid there's not much sand left in my hourglass, brother."

Amanda sat crying quietly, with Ma standing over her, patting her shoulder. Uncharacteristic tears streaked down Edith Hawkins' weathered cheeks unchecked.

* * * * *

Moving Jeremy back to the Harrison's place turned into a major event; trying to decide how to manage it became an even bigger challenge. Ma wouldn't hear of moving him in a bumpy wagon. Jonathan suggested laying him on a travois pulled behind a horse, but Willie said that would give no better cushion than a springless wagon.

Michael finally came up with the solution. They fashioned a hammock suspended by ropes that attached to posts anchored into the four corners of the wagon bed. The hammock hung inside the wagon itself, without touching anything solid, thereby creating as smooth a ride as possible for the injured man.

Ma dosed Jeremy liberally with laudanum and directed settling him into the hammock. Amanda sat in the wagon at his side. The girls wanted to ride with Hank and Tad, so Jonathan drove Lucy's wagon loaded with all the children and their supplies. Despite Willie's and Ma's objections, Sadie flatly refused to be left behind.

"Maybe we should make another hammock for you," Michael said, giving her a wink and a pat on the head."

"Not on your life, brother of mine. I'll sit right up where I belong, at my husband's side, thank you very much."

"Don't like this one bit," Ma voice her disapproval, "don't like it at-all."

"I'll be fine," Sadie tried to reassure. In her heart of hearts, she knew this trip might very well bring on labor. But there was no help for it. She wouldn't leave Jems, and that was that. Ma finally settled herself in the same wagon with Amanda, so she could keep a constant watch over Jeremy.

Lucy had thought to remain behind with Hank, but Amanda insisted they come along. After all that she'd been through— trying to save Jeremy, burying Henry, giving up her own bed for an injured man, not to mention hosting a crowd of people in her home for over a week—Amanda would not hear of Lucy staying on alone.

Early-afternoon set in by the time the entourage had everything packed and ready to leave. Their procession started out slowly: Jeremy's wagon led the way with Michael at the reins; Jonathan and Lucy came next with the wagon full of children and their makeshift playthings; Willie and Sadie brought up the rear, their wagon loaded with blankets, pillows, feather tics, and a variety of foodstuffs for the stay at the Harrisons.

The hammock seemed to cushion Jeremy fairly well. It swayed with the rhythm of the horse. Any time Michael's speed exceeded what Ma thought judicious, she'd smack his back with the walking stick she always kept at hand when she traveled. Immediately he'd slow the horse, to keep the procession crawling at a snail's pace.

"I can walk faster than this," Michael grumbled after the fifth whack.

"Then maybe you should just get out an' walk!" Ma didn't give him an inch of compassion. Over the past week she'd used up all her patience. "Go on up there and lead that horse, 'stead of drivin' it. Give us both a break."

Michael did exactly that. He needed to expend some of the anxious energy building inside him, and for the moment, walking seemed as likely an outlet as any.

It took nearly an hour for the little parade to make its way as far as Justice. By now most folks had heard about Jeremy's accident, and their high regard for this steadfast man brought many people out to pay their respects, as the procession passed by. They'd walk along side Jeremy's wagon for a ways, then give Amanda's hand a pat before they'd drop back to wave at the occupants in the other wagons. The children thought this great fun. The adults, on the other hand, found it most disconcerting.

"Look at this, would you," Willie said. "We got us a regular funeral procession going here."

"Don't *say* such things!" Sadie poked Willie's side. "Jems isn't dead! Don't you even joke about that!"

"I *mean*, look how folks are paying their respects," he tried to appease his upset wife. "They think a lot of him, you know."

He sat quietly for a spell. "We all think a lot of him, Sadie."

"I know," she said, taking a deep breath and letting out a great sigh. "I'm having a really hard time with all this, Willie."

"I know, my love. Wish I could make it better, but I can't."

Sadie snuggled closer to him and let her tears wet his sleeve.

When they neared the blacksmith shop, Sam stood somberly outside his door, holding hat over heart. He nodded at Ma, giving her a meaningful look. Ma nodded back, acknowledging his gesture. Quite the departure for her. They continued to stare at one another as the wagons continued out of Justice.

After another half hour, the procession drew near the Bailey place. They could see Netta and her girls standing at the end of their lane with Luella, waiting for the procession to pass by. Leave it to Netta to know of all the goings-on in the vicinity. The wagons still had a quarter-mile to go before they would reach the women, and already Ma could hear Netta's chatter.

"Just what we need, that blatherin' fool to get everybody worked up," Ma said.

As they came closer, Netta ran to the wagons with four-year-old Rosanna trailing behind her. "I don't know how in the world you're managing Amanda, I really don't. Harmon stopped by to tell us what happened on his way to fetch Michael, an' I've been a nervous wreck ever since! I wanted to come right down to Lucy's to help, but Luella—that's my cousin you know—well Luella said, what with all the trouble youens already had, you sure had no need for two more women and two more children under foot."

"I appreciate the thought, Netta," Amanda said. "But your cousin was right. We've got our hands full right now."

"Whatever are you going to do? Will Jeremy recover? Will he walk again? How will you manage? What are you and your girls going to do if he dies?"

"Michael's here to help out, and Lucy's been such a rock, despite her own terrible loss," Amanda said. "You really should say something to her, you know. She's had so much more to deal with than I have."

"I nearly forgot that Henry went and got his self killed. A tree bashed his head right open, that's what Harmon told Luella. He's sweet on her, you know. She has a hard time when he's off on his mail runs. He told her he'd be back after he sent Michael home. Had him some other deliveries to make while he was up thataway, so she's not to expect him for another week or two at least. She's just sure he's got him another girlfriend up there in them Fire Lands. Makes her crazy to think about it, it does…"

Michael had eased the horse into a faster gait, in the hope that they could bypass the Bailey place as quickly as possible. But the faster they walked, the faster Netta talked, trotting along beside the wagon in an attempt to keep up.

"…I'll come by in a few days to bring over some vittles for y'all," Netta said, losing ground as the wagon pulled ahead. She continued to talk louder. "I know you like my sweet buns. I'll bring some sweet buns, Amanda. You keep strong, now! We sure don't need you going back to the nuthouse over all this!" She immediately clapped her hand over her mouth. "I didn't mean… You *know* what I meant! I hope you can stay brave through this calamity!" She stood waving.

Just before suppertime the wagons pulled up to the Harrison cabin. Everyone piled out: children running and hollering, adults unloading bedding and foodstuffs, to get things settled in.

Ma wanted to put Jeremy to bed in the old part of the cabin, but he refused to be taken inside. "Lay me under the apple tree."

"You have no business on the ground in your condition. You're already burnin' up with fever," Ma huffed. "The night chill will do you no good at-all."

"It won't hurt me any more than I already am," he wheezed. "Besides, I can't feel a thing, except for my head. What difference will a little hard ground make?" His breathing had become shallower and more labored.

"I don't like this one little bit," she grumbled.

"It's out of your hands, Ma... We both know... I don't have much time... I won't... waste it arguing," he managed between shallow breaths.

She gave in to his resolve. With Michael at one end of the hammock and Willie at the other, they carried him over to the orchard and laid him beneath his favorite apple tree—the one holding the wind chimes Violet had made in remembrance of the little Harrison boys.

"Thanks..." Jeremy gasped. He heaved as great a sigh as he could manage.

Sadie lay down as soon as she made it into the cabin. Her hip would barely hold her when she climbed down from the wagon, so Willie scooped her up and carried her inside, where he put her into her old bed in the corner of the main cabin. Immediately she fell into a fitful sleep.

Amanda and Lucy got busy pulling together a hurried supper of biscuits and cheese, fresh tomatoes and early sweet corn for everyone. Michael and Willie took their plates out to the orchard, along with a plate for Ma. Jeremy refused any sustenance, other than a few sips of comfrey tea.

Once the women had all the children seated and served, they took their own plates out onto the porch, sitting on the floor and dangling their feet over the side.

"You doing all right?" Lucy asked Amanda. "It's been quite a day for everyone, but I think most especially for you."

"I have to admit, it has been quite upsetting. Coming back home. All those people, paying respects... knowing Jeremy's—" She couldn't go on.

Lucy put her arm around Amanda and pulled her close in a reassuring hug. "We'll make it through this together. We *will*."

"You've been such a rock," Amanda said. "How are *you* doing? You've had more than your share of upset. Are you still feeling so queasy?"

"I think I'm pretty well past all that," Lucy said. "Once I start feelin' life, it gets better. What about you? How much longer do you have to go?"

"Another month, I imagine. I hope Jeremiah can hold on till..." She fell silent once again.

"We'll all get through this," Lucy said. "We will."

When Sadie awoke about an hour later, she declined any supper. Though she'd never said a word to anyone, her labor pains had begun on their journey, about the time they'd reached Justice. The contractions came sporadically—nothing regular enough to time, as of yet. Sadie knew this babe would not make its way into the world as fast and easily as little Tad. It still sat sideways, pushing harder against her hip than ever, making it nearly impossible for her to stand—especially during a contraction. With Tad, she had puttered around the cabin throughout a good portion of her labor. This time, the pains felt completely different; she felt tethered to the bed.

"Lord, why did they have to start today?" she muttered to herself. "Why couldn't this babe wait a little bit longer?"

"You say something?" Willie had just gotten Tad settled for the night with all the other children in the bedroom over the kitchen. Lucy and Amanda still tended them upstairs, as Willie stopped to check on Sadie before heading back outdoors.

"Don't mind me. I'm just fussing over this whole crazy day," Sadie said, still keeping the contractions to herself. "How's Jeremy? Would you take me out there to sit with him for a spell?"

"You sure you're up to it?"

"I'll be fine. I just don't have the ability to walk myself out there, at the moment."

Willie got her up and steadied with her cane. Then holding tightly to her right arm, he guided, and mostly carried, her out to the orchard. Ma sat vigil with Jeremy, as did Michael. Jonathan had already headed back to Lucy's to tend her animals.

Willie lowered Sadie onto a blanket laid out next to her brother. Jeremy lay quietly, eyes closed, barely breathing.

"Jems? You in there?"

"I'm still here," he said, opening his eyes.

"You're not fixing to go and expire on me, are you?"

"Don't know as I have… a whole lot of choice," he struggled to talk and breathe.

"You've got to hang on, Jems. You've *got* to!"

"Doin' my best… Pipsqueak."

They sat in silence for a time, Sadie holding his hand, though he didn't know it.

"Jems–" she caught her breath as a harder contraction tightened its grip.

"It's coming?" he asked.

"It's coming."

"Get that girl back into the cabin, right now!" Ma instructed.

"Let me sit here a little longer," Sadie begged. "Please. I *need* to stay with Jems as long as I can manage."

"Well, I reckon it won't hurt too much," Ma gave in. She seemed much less sure of things, as if the fight had gone out of her the same way it was draining away from Jeremy.

"You stay strong," Jeremy said to his sister. "For Mandy."

"You know I'll do whatever needs done," Sadie answered in a snippy tone. "But I refuse to make any deathbed promises." She held her breath for a few beats, waiting on the contraction to ease. "You can't die on me, Jems. You *can't!*" She sat in silence, knowing the inevitable, but refusing to acknowledge it.

Amanda walked toward the group settled under the apple tree. Lucy remained behind, keeping watch until all the children fell asleep.

"Mandy…" Jeremy breathed, when she came into his line of sight. She sat on the edge of Sadie's blanket, where Jeremy could see her face. "I love you, my little yellow bird…" he wheezed. "Don't you ever doubt that."

She leaned down and kissed his forehead, his cheeks, his

lips. "I'll always love you, Jeremiah. You've given me so much."

Michael rose from his place at Jeremy's feet and began to pace. He could not sit and watch this—and remember. He'd never had the chance to tell Violet goodbye, in the midst of that distressing birth. It all happened so quickly, so unexpectedly. But this drawn-out agony felt ten times worse—especially with Jeremy; *most* especially with Amanda.

Sadie felt another contraction tighten. Only about ten minutes this time. Things were beginning to accelerate. "I've got to go, Jems. This babe's getting insistent. Don't you dare leave until I get back, you hear?"

"I'll do my best…"

"I'll see you later, Jems."

"See you later, Pipsqueak."

Willie helped Sadie up and carried her back to the cabin. Ma, after checking Jeremy's forehead again, calculating the strength of his fever, left Amanda in charge in the orchard and followed along into the cabin with a slow, heavy step. She'd felt a foreboding all day; it wouldn't let up one bit.

* * * * *

The next morning dawned in a haze. Amanda woke beside Jeremiah, their blanket covered with dew. She reached over to feel his forehead. Cold. He'd left her in the night. She buried her head against his shoulder to shed tears of her goodbye.

When she gathered herself sufficiently, she eased away from him, stood to shake herself, then pulled the blanket over Jeremiah's face. "Goodbye, my love," she whispered. "You and the boys take good care of each other."

Chimes on the branch above her head rustled in the gentle, morning breeze.

On her way back to the cabin, Amanda rounded the corner of the barn just as Michael emerged, holding a still wet, newborn calf. She stopped in her tracks.

"He's gone?" Michael asked.

"He's gone."

Michael's head dropped, and he turned away to find his own solace back in the barn. Amanda continued on to the cabin, knowing the children would most likely still be sleeping under Lucy's watchful care. She quietly pushed open the door, so as not to waken anyone. The sight that greeted her made Amanda wish she still lay beside her husband, dreaming all this misfortune, rather than living it.

Willie sat beside an exhausted, pasty-white Sadie, wiping her brow with a cloth, drying her tears. Ma, sitting on the floor beside the bed, staring straight ahead, held her tiny, still-born, baby granddaughter.

Dear Libby,

Mary Sue had her another little boy. Toby they called him. After Jason's own father. That varmint Tobias who run off on me. I have to say I was a mite put out at the name they picked. But Mary Sue said that a man with sons should name one for his own father. No matter what kind of a man he turned into. If not for Tobias there would be no Jason to give her children of her own, says she. Well what could I say to that? So Toby it is.

I hope our Katrina is delivered by now. I am going right barmy waiting to hear news of <u>our</u> new grandbabe. What is taking the girl so long, Lib?

I am sorry to say that calamity has struck in these parts. Jeremy Harrison got his self trapped under a tree and busted his back. He was helping Henry Jarvis to clear more land for corn. That tree fell wrong and pinned both men. Kilt Henry right off. Jeremy hung on for over a week. Till after Harmon tracked down his brother Michael up in them Fire Lands. In your neck of the woods. He was up thataway setting stone for that new court house.

Edie said Jeremy suffered dreadful bad. Could not move his legs nor even lift his arms at the end. Busted ribs, too. Spent most of that terrible week down at Lucy's holding on to his little wife's hand. Amanda that would be. The one who come back from the nut house.

Jeremy's sister Sadie had her own misery. If you recall she is the wife of my own nephew Willie. She went into labor on account of riding in the wagon train what took Jeremy home to die. She had lots of trouble carrying this babe. Hardly could walk by the end. Edie is in terrible shape. Lost her own grand-babe. A little girl. She blames herself.

Lucy said Sadie had a terrible time with the birth. She sent me a note to let me know about Sadie and Henry and Jeremy. I thought that was rite nice of her. What with her own grief to bear. She said Sadie's babe wanted to come out sideways.

Edie tried to turn it. Was powerful hard on little Sadie. But she could not manage to get it turned right. Came out back ass wards with that cord wrapped around its neck. Babe never took a breath.

Our strong Edie has fell clean apart over it all. First losing Jeremy. She thought so much of that man. And you know how little she thinks of ANY man. Then losing Sadie's girl. Her own blood kin. Says she will give up birthins for good. No more doctoring of nobody. She got so down hearted over the whole thing she even let Sam Justice come to comfort her. Now who would believe that? Let me tell you Sam jumped at the chance. Says she finally needs him. Bout time he said. My own sister, gone and took up with a man after all these years.

Lucy said they buried Jeremy holding Sadie and Willie's little girl. Underneath that same apple tree where they planted Violet and her babe. Right by Amanda's two boys. Getting to be quite the bury ground that. Jeremy's brother Michael was so broke up he could not talk for three days. Willie wanted him to say some words at the grave. But he could not say a thing. Amanda was the one to step up and speak. If you can credit that. That frail little Southern gal has turned into a hearty woman at last. She gave comfort to Michael and to Sadie. Not them to her. Who could guess such a turn. Edie falling to pieces and Amanda become the strong one.

Sadie is rite upset about losing her baby. But she is more upset about not getting to tell her brother goodbye. He died the night she labored to give birth to that poor little girl. Lucy says she is still mad at him for up and dying on her. Once Sadie gets back on her feet she aims to see to any birthins in Edie's stead. Sadie is awful wrung out from her own ordeal. What with Edie having to turn that babe and all. Might take a goodly spell for her to recoup.

Now you may wonder why Lucy of all people would send a letter to me. Seems she will soon become my very own sister-in-law. Brother Jonathan has been sweet on her ever since she come out here from back East. Jonathan aims to become daddy to her children. Now that Henry has passed on and left Lucy alone with a tyke and another babe on the way.

She says she loved Henry well enough. But Jonathan has always looked out for her all these years. Folks might talk that she is moving on too fast. But hard times call for hard choices she says. So let them talk. Lucy will move to his place come fall. Once he gets that pig sty of a cabin fixed up for her. They will keep Henry's place for little Hank. For when he gets big enough to work it. Meantimes Jonathan will run hogs down there. Keep it from getting over growed too bad.

My baby brother a family man at last. I say good for them! And my oldest sister now took up with a man. Who ever would guess such goins on?

That is about all the news from these parts. I cannot wait to meet our own new grandbabe, Lib. You and me related by blood!

Please write soon. As I can hardly stand the wait.

Yours, Ellie

Dear Ellie,

The baby has finally arrived, friend, and all is well. I will not keep you in suspense as to the outcome. We have a boy, and he is called Simon. Katrina went much later than we all had anticipated, which is why you have heard nary word from me until now.

Katrina's slim hips were not a blessing to her, as she did labor all of yesterday and into this very afternoon. The event itself was without complication, but she is quite weak with the strain of it. It is meet that Simeon added these private quarters, as there has been quite the traffic of persons coming and going. He did tend to them, but with such distraction that I heard male voices begging him to go to his dear wife and stop ruining good food. And when next I went for hot water, there was Zeke dishing out stew and serving customers. He pines for you, Ellie.

We are indeed blessed.

Christian has returned for me with news of home. I must travel immediately. Kit has come for Lizzie. She is to marry him, and awaits only my arrival.

I had thought to stop with you a while before my journey back north, but time will no longer allow this. Katrina is regaining her strength quickly. My days here have been filled getting to know this new daughter and coming to appreciate the love she has for my son.

And Christian says that he is glad he postponed his western sojourn to aid us here, as he aims to stand up with Kit at the nuptials, quite the novelty for him.

Oh, a riverman has also left a post for you, old and yellowed though it be. Katrina thinks it looks to be Johannah's

hand, but leaves it for you to open. You will be excited to have word from your last chick, we think. It will be waiting for you here, upon your return.

Take care of little Simon and these love birds for me, friend.

Yours, Libby

Chapter 15

Birthin'
August 1820

"Would you get that bowl down for me, Brother?" Amanda had grown so large with child, she had trouble reaching anything on the top shelf of her pantry cupboard.

"I'm here to serve, *Sister*," Michael said, easing his way beside her and handing down the wooden bowl she indicated, all the while carefully avoiding the temptation to brush against her.

"Thank you." Amanda took the bowl and set it on the table, where she had the ingredients laid out to mix up biscuits. She felt so awkward of late. And not just because of the ponderous size of her belly. She hardly knew how to act around Michael any more. The electricity between them had grown so great, it practically crackled the air around them both.

"When will you get our new baby, Mama?" Camellia asked, carrying around her own baby doll, patting its back to dislodge the pretend burp.

"Soon, darling. Very soon."

Michael blanched at the thought. His fear of childbirth weighed so heavily upon him, that he had a physical reaction at any mention of the process. He had yet to experience a happy outcome at any birth he could remember in his own family. His mother had died giving birth to Sadie, his wife died along with his own, little Angelica, and he'd almost lost his only sister, giving birth to a babe that never drew breath. The whole prospect of facing another birth terrified him.

"Come on, Lilly. Uncle Mikey needs your help milking big Bertha," he said, walking toward the cabin door.

Lilly jumped at the chance to help Uncle Mikey out in the barn. She loved everything about Uncle Mikey—especially when he included her in his day.

"Can I pull her spigots all by myself this time?"

"Sure you can! You're learning fast. Those hands of yours are getting mighty strong for a little girl."

Amanda shook her head at the tomboy emerging in Lilly. The differences between her two girls seemed to intensify every day. Camellia was quite happy to remain inside with her, helping to cook and clean and take care of her baby doll. She couldn't wait to have the real thing here to cuddle and help her mama care for.

Lillian, on the other hand, could not spend enough time outdoors with Uncle Mikey. Michael figured that if Amanda knew half of what they did out in that barn, she'd never let the child come out with him again.

"Can I climb up high, Unka Mikey?"

"Shhhhh," he shushed her, then looked up to see if Amanda had heard. She stood facing the table, counting her measures of flour. "We'll keep that our little secret," he whispered, "all right Pipsqueak?"

"All right."

The two disappeared outdoors, while Amanda and Camellia remained behind, patting out biscuits and laying them in the reflector pan. Once they had their biscuits baking by the fire, they turned their attention to cooking a chicken.

"You should have seen the first chicken I ever tried to cook for your daddy," Amanda told her attentive daughter. "We laughed about that chicken for years!" She felt more comfortable talking about Jeremy of late. She knew she had to keep his memory alive for their girls.

Those first few weeks after he'd died seemed like a dream to Amanda: dealing with his burial, getting Sadie well enough to travel home, helping Ma Hawkins find the will to go on. Amanda couldn't thank Sam Justice enough, for all his help in persuading Ma not to give up for good, although she flatly refused to doctor anyone, ever again. Now that he'd finally convinced Edie how much she needed him, Sam thought that was just fine.

Amanda heard a knock, then the door pushed open and Lucy stuck in her head. "You here, Amanda?"

"Lucy! How wonderful to see you! Come in." Amanda set the chicken aside, quickly washed her hands off in the dishpan, and hurried over to give Lucy a big hug. "What brings you all the way up here?"

"I was over to Jonathan's helping him clean. So I thought I'd come for a visit," she said, "seeing he lives so close by here."

"I can't tell you how much I've missed you," Amanda said. "Can I get you a cup of tea or something?"

"Just a glass of water. That hike through the woods made me thirsty."

"Hi, Aunt Lucy," Millie said. The girls had taken to calling her aunt, over the two weeks they'd spent together. Since they called Sadie aunt, they didn't understand why they shouldn't call Lucy aunt, too. "Where's Hank?"

"He wanted to stay with Jonathan. Seems they've struck up quite a friendship."

"How wonderful for you. It's nice he has a man around once in a while. Little boys need that," Amanda said.

"I reckon he'll be around more than once in a while," Lucy said. "I aim to move in with him, soon as we get his place fixed up enough to hold all my things."

"Oh, Lucy! What wonderful news!"

"You're 'bout the only one who feels that way," she said with a shake of her head. "You wouldn't believe how folks are talking. They think I'm taking up with Jonathan way too quick after Henry died."

"Well, I'll give you horsefeathers for what everyone thinks." Amanda gave her another hug. "I think it's wonderful."

"Horsefeathers!" Millie mimicked.

"Camellia, why don't you go put your baby to bed over in the other room?"

"Yes, Mama." She paddled to the play area in the main cabin.

"I knew I could count on you to support us," Lucy told Amanda.

"Don't worry a hair on your head over what anyone else says. If you feel it's right, then that's all that matters." Amanda poured a glass of water from the pitcher and handed it to Lucy. "They don't know what all you've been through... how hard it is to go it alone out here."

"I'm sure I could manage well enough on my own. Least-wise until this baby comes," Lucy said. "But I don't *want* to be alone. And I really do like Jonathan. Always have. He makes me feel special."

"You are special, Lucy. There's not another person in the world as big-hearted as you are."

The two looked at each other in appreciation. "We're lucky, you and me," she said. "I feel the same way about you."

"Can you stay for supper with us?"

"I'd best get back. Jonathan's good with Hank, but he doesn't know a whole lot about how to take care of a three-year-old for the long haul, yet."

"I understand. Michael's good with the girls, too. But he sure does let Lilly get away with a lot. He doesn't realize I know the mischief they're up to, out there in that barn. I let them think they're having quite the secret time of it."

"How is it between you and Michael?" Lucy asked. "I don't mean to pry. I just know how hard it can be... living with some-one who's not...who's–"

"We're making out all right. He seems awfully jumpy at times. And I have to admit, I feel pretty strange around him lately. But we're managing to carry on with life well enough," she said. "I do have to say that when I look at him, I don't think about Jeremiah as much anymore. Does that sound terrible?"

"Not a bit. I know exactly what you mean. It's the same way I feel around Jonathan. He makes me forget Henry ever existed. Not that I want to forget, mind you. I need to keep his memory alive for little Hank."

"I'm trying to do the same for my girls. They need to remember their daddy."

"We *are* going to make it, Amanda. You and I."

"I know we are," she said, touching grandmother's brooch at her throat.

"I'd better be on my way. Takes a little while to make that hike back," Lucy said. "If I don't show up before dinner time, I'm sure Jonathan will come looking for me."

"It must feel nice to have someone care that much."

"It does." They gave each other another big hug, then Lucy headed for the door. "See you soon! Be sure to send Michael for me when you feel the pains start. Sadie still doesn't have much energy back, yet. You know I'd be glad to help out," she said. "I'll be at Jonathan's a good bit of the time from now on."

"Thanks."

* * * * *

Two days later, Amanda awoke in the middle of the night in a puddle. Her water broke. She didn't want to waken anyone at this hour, so she changed her gown and her bed, got herself cleaned up, then lay back down in her upstairs bedroom to wait for morning's light. She'd been through this often enough to know it took a goodly amount of time before any babe would be making its grand entrance. She felt no need to rouse the rest of the household just yet.

She lay in the early morning silence, sorrowing over the prospect of giving birth without Jeremiah's comforting presence, thinking of that first, traumatic birth long ago....

December 1815, Vermillion Township

"She's been laboring fifteen hours already, Ma. When's this baby going to get here?" Jeremy paced as he spoke to Ma.

"Now don't you go gettin' your cock feathers in a ruff. These things take time—'specially a first birth." With familiar ease, Edith lifted an iron pot off the trammel, put on a soup kettle, then swung it back over the open fire. "Why don't you go put those hands to useful work, like mendin' harness or splittin' wood or some such."

Jeremy hesitated, then donned coat and hat. "You'll call if anything happens?"

"Course I will. Now scoot." Edith turned back to the fire, muttering under her breath. "No place for a man at a time like this."

Jeremy stopped at the door. "Did you say something?"

"No. Just get yourself out from under foot, now. This here is woman's work."

"Woman's work—Ha! I've done woman's work for years. Now's a fine time to get kicked out of my own house," he grumbled. He turned with resolve to face Ma Hawkins. "Before you try and hustle me out of here, I've got to tell you I aim to stay with Mandy till this thing is all over."

"Birthin's no place for a man–"

"I'm staying. So that's that." He hung his coat and hat back on the peg behind the door with an air of finality.

Confounded by this turn of events, Edith Hawkins gave a grunt and glared at him. "Well then, you better wash up good and clean."

He took the bar of lye soap and worked up a thick lather. "How's she doing?"

"Resting right now, so keep your voice down."

"Are the pains any closer yet?"

"Nope."

"Still around ten minutes apart?"

"Near's I can tell."

"Look, Ma. I know you're not happy about having me in here, but I *can* help."

"Never saw a man yet who was any real help to a woman. Just makes more work and causes a whole lot of grief."

"Think what you like, but I intend to be at Mandy's side when this baby comes."

"You ever help at a birthin' before?"

"No, but I know all about taking care of babies."

"How do you know anything about babies?"

"'Cause I raised my own little sister from the time she was born." Jeremy rinsed his long arms and sloshed water on his face.

"That so?" With new interest, Edith handed him the drying cloth.

"There were nine of us boys all together, not counting the ones Ma lost. She all but gave up on having a girl. But number thirteen turned out to be little Sadie. She was my shadow for a lot of years."

"Bet your ma was glad for some help after all those boys."

"She never had the chance to know Sadie. Mother died giving birth to her only daughter."

Edith stood in silence.

"Father put me in charge of the house and all the 'woman's work,' as you call it. I raised Sadie from the time she was just a squirming little bit-of-a pup."

"Well then," she paused, considering. "I reckon you can stay." Edith turned to the fire and gave the soup a stir, and the rich aroma of venison and vegetables filled the cabin. "Want some soup? It's ready."

"Sure do. It smells real good. Maybe Mandy'd take a little bit. She hasn't eaten a thing since last evening."

"We'll see." Edith ladled up a bowl full. "Not always a good idea to give a laborin' woman anything solid. Just some tea, or a little broth, maybe."

Jeremy blew across a spoonful of the steaming soup, then put it back in the bowl. "Won't you sit and eat, too? I'd be honored to share my table with you."

Edith Hawkins reached for the other bowl and filled it for herself. "Thank you kindly." She sat across from Jeremy and started to eat.

"Do you mind if I ask a blessing?"

"Go right ahead, if you've a mind to. But I don't take much to all that God talkin'. I say them that's strong and able don't need a God. Them that ain't, don't belong out here."

"I'm not asking you to pray. I'd like to give thanks, is all."

"Well, it's your roof we're under." Edith Hawkins stiffened and grimaced, as if anticipating a bitter tonic.

Jeremy bowed his head. "Father in Heaven, thank You for this food and this day. I'm mighty glad you sent Ma Hawkins, here, to look after Mandy. I don't mind telling you, I'm worried. She's so little and helpless. Please give her strength to get through this, and to bless her with a healthy baby. Thank you, Father. Amen."

Edith took up her spoon and began to eat in silence, studying on the tiny woman-child huddled in bed beyond the fireplace—a petite little southern belle thrust into the role of a settler's wife here in this Ohio country.

"Mighty good soup, Ma." Jeremy soon emptied his bowl. "Mind if I have some more?" Just as Ma Hawkins pushed her chair away from the table, Jeremy jumped up. "Don't disturb yourself, I can get it. You sit and eat."

Jeremy went over to the fireplace in the center of the cabin, pulled the trammel away from the fire, and dipped out another bowl full of soup.

Ma watched with an unbelieving stare as he sauntered back to the table. A man who didn't expect to be waited on. "Now I've seen it all," she muttered between bites.

From the bed behind the fireplace, Mandy roused when another spasm of pain gripped her. "Oh, help me. I can't do this. I can't–"

"Mandy? You all right?" Jeremy jumped up from the table, knocking over his chair. He hurried around to the bed. She grabbed his hand and squeezed, as her contraction tightened. When it finally began to subside, she loosened her grip, but she wouldn't let go of his hand.

"Jeremiah?"

"Don't talk, Mandy. Save your strength." He took a damp cloth and wiped her forehead. "Take it easy, my little yellow bird. It'll be over with real soon."

"I don't know if I can do this, Jeremiah," she whispered.

"You're doing fine. Try and relax between the pains if you can." He cradled her hand until she closed her eyes, but as he placed it back under the cover she stirred.

"I'm thirsty." He rose to fetch her a drink, but before he could take a step, she caught his arm. "Jeremiah! Don't leave me. Please don't leave me!"

"I'm right here." He knelt back down so he could look into her eyes. "I won't leave, Mandy. I promise. I'll go fetch you a drink. Would you like broth maybe?"

"No. Just water."

Ma Hawkins rounded the fireplace at the very instant Jeremy turned, almost spilling the cup of water she carried.

"Sorry, Ma. Didn't mean to get in your way."

Ma grumbled, "Men are always in the way."

After twenty-four hours, Amanda's pains still came at ten-minute intervals. Jeremy and Ma Hawkins had taken turns sitting up with Amanda through the night, but the longer her labor continued, the weaker she became. By morning she'd begun to babble, apparently reliving a part of her life back in Charleston.

"Papa? Where are you Papa? Down by the ships? I want to see the ships... such pretty sails. No! Go away, you. Get away from me! Don't touch me! Don't *do* that!"

Amanda heaved and gasped; Jeremy held her hand tighter.

"Take it easy, Mandy. You'll be fine." But Jeremy didn't believe his own words of encouragement any more. He turned to Edith Hawkins, "How much longer can she take this?

"Couldn't rightly say for sure. 'T'ain't easy for small ones."

Once again aware of her surroundings, Amanda whispered,

"Jeremiah, if I die in this, promise me–"

"You're *not* going to die, Mandy," he cut her off. "I won't let you die!" Jeremy trembled and held her hand tighter. "Isn't there something we can do to help her, Ma?"

"Well, there is one thing we can try to get the pains movin'. You got a feather?"

"A feather? What good's a feather?"

"Never mind what for, it's too hard to explain. If you want to help, just go get one."

Jeremy eased Amanda's hand under the cover. "You try to rest a few minutes, Mandy. I'll be right back." He hurried around to the door and disappeared outside.

Ma Hawkins dipped a cloth in cold water, then squeezed out the excess moisture. As she wiped the beads of perspiration from the tiny forehead, Amanda caught her wrist. "I don't know if... if I can keep on..."

"Now shush. You're doin' just fine. You're not the first woman to go through this, you know." Her gnarled fingers wrung the cloth again, and she continued to wipe down Amanda's neck and arms. "It'll be over with soon, you'll see. If you can work with the pains instead of fightin' agi'n 'em, it'll go down a lot easier for you."

Jeremy rushed back into the cabin, slamming the door. He bounded around the fireplace to Amanda's bedside. "Here's the feather you wanted, Ma. Don't know how it's gonna help, but here it is." He thrust the feather toward her.

"Where'd you get this?"

"Out in the barnyard—tail feather from Ol' Jake."

"Then you better go wash yourself up again. And wash that feather good, too."

He walked back around to the wash basin. Once he'd scrubbed himself and the feather, considerable time had passed.

"I'm clean... *again*. So's the feather." He handed her the dripping plume.

"That thing's awful wet."

"Well, course it's wet. I just dipped it into that hot water."

"Can't use it wet. Got to be dry to do what we need."

Jeremy grabbed the feather and headed back around to the fireplace, mumbling. "Wash the feather, dry the feather. Horse-feathers! She's just using this blasted thing to keep me out of the way." He waved the feather over the fire until it dried.

"Here's the clean, *dry* feather, Ma."

"All right, you hold Amanda's head up." She handed Jeremy a small bowl. "And keep this bowl close by. She'll need it." Ma placed her hand gently on Amanda's forehead. "Amanda, honey, we're gonna try and get things movin' along, if we can. Set her up a little more there, Jeremy. Good. Now, I've got this here feather. I'm gonna tickle the back of your throat with it and see what happens. Open your mouth now."

Amanda shook her head and made a face. Jeremy looked quizzically at Ma. She gave him a stern stare, as if to say, *'don't you dare question what I'm doing.'*

"Come on, Mandy. Ma's trying to help. Open up."

Amanda opened her mouth. After the feather did its work, she gagged, and Jeremy held the bowl as she retched into it. Im-mediately another pain struck with increased force. She grabbed his arm and strained. "Pull on me, Mandy. Pull!"

That pain had barely eased when another one began to tighten its grip. The intensity pushed Amanda back... back...

... into the present—and the immediate pain of Jeremiah's last child, working toward its own entrance into this world.

Almost daybreak. She heard Michael rustling around in the kitchen below. She called to him.

"Michael? Can you hear me? Would you come up here?"

Michael bounded up the stairs two at a time. "Mandy?"

"We're getting a baby today, Brother. I think it's already too late to go for Lucy. Things seem to be moving along much more quickly than they ever did with the rest of my babies. Pains are less than five minutes apart."

"Lord have mercy! What are we going to do?"

"Don't panic. We'll be fine," she encouraged. "We're going to need some towels and some blankets. Also the sewing kit. Would you fetch those things?"

He raced down the steps, tripping on the last step and nearly falling headlong into the pantry cupboard.

"Are you all right?" Amanda called from upstairs.

"I'm fine. Just clumsy as a cross-eyed ox," he called back.

The noise had roused the girls in the next room. They padded into the kitchen to see who was making all the racket. "Unka Mikey?" They rubbed at sleepy eyes and yawned.

"Go back to bed for a while, girls. It's too early to get up." He turned them around and gave them a boost, back toward their bed.

"Can we have the Lucky cat in bed with us?"

"Sure. Take her with you."

That thrilled Lilly to no end, as their mother seldom let them sleep with the cat. She picked her up off the rocking chair and hauled her into the other room, with Millie trailing behind in a sleepy daze.

"You girls stay over there till I call you to get up, you hear?"

"We will, Unka Mikey."

He gathered the supplies Amanda required, then bounded back upstairs. "You all right? Are you in bad pain? You're not going to up and die on me, too, are you?"

"*Relax!* I'm just fine. A little preoccupied at the moment, but doing fine," Amanda said, gritting her teeth and riding out another contraction. "I'm going to need you to catch this little person. Do you think you can manage that?"

"Oh, Lordy, Lordy, why didn't you call me sooner? Why isn't Lucy here? Why isn't *someone* here!"

"I didn't realize things would move along quite this fast,"

Amanda said, holding on to the bed post for all she was worth, as the next pain hit before the last one had completely released its grip. She breathed hard, fighting the urge to push.

"Go back down and bring up some water. No time to boil it now."

"I already put water on for tea. I'll bring that." He bolted back down, grabbed the tea kettle, then raced back upstairs without stopping even for breath.

"Slow down, Michael! You're going to keel over from apoplexy if you keep up this pace."

"How on earth can you expect me to *relax* at a time like *this?*"

"Right now I just need you to concentrate on what I tell you, all right?"

"I will. I can do this… I can *do* this…, I *can* do this," he urged himself on.

"Push my gown up and put one of those old blankets underneath to catch the worst of the mess," she panted.

He did as told.

"Can you see the head yet?" she asked through breaths.

"I see a round circle of wet, black hair."

"Good!" She gave in to her overwhelming urge to push, grunting with all the strength she had in her.

"It's moving! It's getting bigger!"

"Get ready," she squeaked out, taking a big breath and pushing again.

"I see the whole head!" He put his hands in place, as if ready to catch a ball. "Here come the shoulders!" He clamped his fingers around the little shoulders, heels of his hands supporting the head as the rest of the tiny body slipped out into the world."

"It's a *boy!*" The baby let out a strong, startled cry.

Amanda lay panting, trying to catch her breath. "Turn him… upside down."

Michael held the boy around his middle with one hand, head down, and gave his bottom a smack. His cry didn't let up; he continued to protest this rude arrival into the bright light.

"He's alive! He's really *alive!*" Michael looked at Amanda in absolute wonder. "But he's still hooked on."

"Scissors... in sewing kit," she said. "Lay him on my stomach first."

He did as told, then retrieved the sewing kit.

"Pour some hot water in that basin and put the scissors in for a minute."

He did that, too.

"Now, take the thread. Tie two knots around the cord. One close to his belly. Another a couple inches away from the first one."

Michael complied.

"Get the scissors. Don't touch the blades," she coached. "Cut between those knots."

When Michael had the cord severed, bright red blood dripped for just a moment, then stopped. "He's free."

"Good," she breathed another sigh. Her contractions had begun again. "The sac comes next. Get ready for that." She put her hands up to touch the babe, tears streaming down her face. "Oh, Jeremiah, you finally have a son," she cried. She couldn't help the sudden outpouring of emotion.

Michael gave her a meaningful look, tears sliding down his cheeks, too. He tried to focus his attention back on the task at hand. When he'd delivered the afterbirth, he wrapped it in an old rag towel and laid it aside on the floor for the time being.

"Now pack another rag between my legs for a time. Good." They both breathed a huge sigh of relief.

"We did it!" Michael crowed.

"We did it."

Michael picked up the babe, wrapped him in a blanket, and took him to Amanda's side. "Here's your son. What are you going to call him?"

They looked at each other, and in the same instant, said the very same thing.

"Jems."

"You know there's no way I can continue to call you Sister, after all this, don't you?" Michael told her, giving her an intimate look.

"I know," she said simply.

"Maybe we better get hitched."

"I wondered how long it would take you to figure that out."

"Really? You knew?"

"Of course I did. How could I not know, with so many sparks flying between us around here all this time."

"Mandy... do you mind me calling you that? I know Jems..." he choked up for a moment. "I know that was Jeremy's special name for you. But I don't know what else to call you besides 'Sister'."

"Mandy's just fine," she breathed. "And Michael?"

"Yes..."

"Don't ever feel bad about mentioning Jeremy's name. I loved him dearly, you know. He helped me to grow up."

"He helped us all grow up."

They both sat there, crying tears of grief and tears of joy, all mixed up together.

Soon they heard little giggles on the steps.

"Millie? Lilly?" Michael called.

Girls scurried into the room, then stopped in their tracks at the side of the bed.

"Come over here and meet your new, baby brother," Mandy said, easing the swaddled baby over so the girls could see his face.

Camellia held the Lucky cat, wrapped tight in a blanket. "Here's my baby, too!"

"Will my brother scratch like the Lucky cat does?" Lilly

asked, holding up a bleeding arm.

"If you treat him nicely, he shouldn't hurt you, Lillian. But you can't pull his hair the way you do the Lucky cat's and expect him to do nothing about it."

"All right, Mama. Will you fix my ouchie, Unka Mikey?"

"In a minute, Pipsqueak."

"Why don't you girls go back downstairs and wait for Uncle Mikey to come and fix you some breakfast."

"Will you be all right up here?" he asked, sudden concern in his voice at the prospect of leaving her alone.

"We'll be fine," she smiled, snuggling the tiny babe in her arms. "From now on, we'll *all* be just fine."

The End of Book II

Teaser for Book III of the Hearthstones Series

Excerpt Chapter 1

Letter from the Solicitor
October 1820, Justice, Ohio

Last Will and Testament
Dated February 27, 1818

I, Olympia Lillian Wallingsford Bently, of the Borough of Charleston, in the great State of South Carolina of these United States of America, do make, publish and declare this to be my Last Will and Testament, hereby revoking and annulling any and all wills and codicils by me, heretofore disposed in any way, shape or form...

Amanda Jane looked up from the official-looking document she held, giving Michael a puzzled expression. "They sent me Grandmother Bently's will? What do you suppose it means?"

"Keep reading, or we'll never find out."

She held the page more closely to the cabin's south-facing window, squinting to make sure she didn't miss a single word in the fading, late-afternoon light of autumn.

ITEM I: RESIDUARY ESTATE

At the time of my demise, I leave the entire estate and legacy—real, personal and exceptional—which I now own, to Amanda Jane Bently r.e. Harrison, lineal descendant of afore designated personage, hereby circumventing any and all descendants of the first and second degrees to this previously named grantor who are living at the date of execution of this will.

To Amanda Jane, I entrust all things connected with Wallingsford Plantation and Orchard, both earthly and ethereal, practicable and unexpected.

ITEM II: STIPULATION

I specifically make no provision in this my Last Will and Testament for Joseph Alexander Bently (lately designated III), nor for either one of the younger, empty-headed fruit of his loins. They no doubt will make suitable enough matches to please their social-climbing mother and be adequately looked after for the duration of their inconsequential lives.

To the only true descendant carrying the soul-marker of the great Chickasaw, Bent Leaf, I leave the key to his birthright. Although at present this may appear unusually perplexing to most, in due time, Amanda Jane, and only she, will have the necessary fortitude to come to understand the full scope of this bequest.

"I certainly don't understand any of this now," Amanda said, waving the document in the air. "What did Grandmother mean? What key is she talking about? And why on earth did this take so long to reach me?" she asked, turning the document over and over again in her hand.

"What else does it say?" Michael asked.

"Only a little more legal doubletalk before all the signatures… grandmother's and the people who witnessed for her.

…In witness whereof, I have heretofore set my hand to this, my Last Will and Testament, cast at Wallingsford Plantation and Orchard, Edisto Island, South Carolina, this 27th day of February, the One Thousand Eight Hundred and Eighteenth year of our Lord.

Signed by Olympia Lillian Wallingsford Bently, a.k.a. Woman Who Sings to Bent Leaf, and by her acknowledged to be her Last Will and Testament, before us and in our presence, by us subscribed as attesting witnesses in her presence and at her request.

2

"Oh my Lord, that was the day before I saw her... in my dream!" Amanda dropped the document to her lap and her hand flew to the heirloom brooch she constantly wore at her throat—the treasure Great Grandmother Bently had pressed upon her when Amanda left the only life she'd ever known in Charleston, on her way North to marry a stranger.

Michael picked up the paper and examined it carefully, reading all the way through once again, slowly. "These people who signed... this Winston Horatio Applebaum, a Douglas B. Hornsby and Pitney Doubleday Bower. Who are they? Do you know them?"

"Winston is Grandmother's Manager. He's run Wallingsford for years. Mr. Hornsby's her barrister. He has an office in Charleston, and he's always taken care of Grandmother's legal dealings. Lord knows, she had enough of those over the years. But I can't believe Pitney Bower ever signed a thing! As far as I know, she never learned to read or write."

Amanda rose from the bench under the window and walked over to check the baby, beginning to stir in his bentwood crib beside the hearth. "Three or four years before I left home, Grandmother brought Pitney in the house to ease her workload. As I recall, Pitney threw a hissy fit about having to give up her work in the orchard. That woman had to be nearly 90 back then. No one left alive knows how old she is for sure."

"A woman? Isn't that peculiar? I didn't think women could sign anything legal."

"As a rule they don't. Especially not Negro women."

"She's a slave, then."

"Grandmother never kept slaves. She freed all the people who came to her when she inherited Wallingsford from her father. Caused quite a stir in the low country, I can tell you that. Grandmother didn't believe in slavery, after being kept in servitude."

"Your grandmother, a slave? How?"

"She was 14 when Redskins took her from her father. After a time of hard work, she acquired a place of high standing among them. She used to tell me stories about her time with 'The

People," as they called themselves. Other folks call them Chickasaws."

The baby began to fuss, and Amanda picked him up to cuddle as he came fully awake, rooting for his next meal. Little Jems. Jeremiah's last child. What would his daddy think of this precious boy? If only her husband could be here to see his namesake grow. But no, she dare not let herself go down that road. It still brought too many tears.

Keep moving forward. Never look back.

"Do you want me to read this other letter while you feed Jems?" Michael asked, waving the second paper from the packet. "Maybe it'll give some explanation."

"Go ahead. I'll sit by the fire," Amanda said, taking her place in the rocker Jeremiah had made for her three, short years ago— years that held a lifetime. She put the baby to her breast, discretely covering herself from view with the receiving blanket as he nursed.

Michael unfolded the document. "It's from that Hornsby, written last winter…

29 February, 18 and 20

To Amanda Jane Bently, r.e. Harrison:

As you no doubt surmise by the inclusion of your great-grandmother's Last Will and Testament in this posting, Olympia Bently made her exit from our earthly sphere on the last day of February, 18 and 18. The day before she died, she called me to her bedside to execute this most recent of changes to her Will, naming you sole beneficiary of her entire estate.

I forewarned that it would undoubtedly cause a rift among the living relatives, knowing that her grandson, your father, would contest such a last-minute change completely removing him from the line of inheritance. To that warning she made reply, but being a gentleman born and bred, I shall not pass along her retort, to you a lady— and now one of independent means, I might add. In all her years your grandmother never claimed the status of

4

gentle woman. She was, however, a formidable person without equal—one far advanced for her time.

Joseph Alexander Bently, your father, has done exactly as predicted, forcing the execution of this Last Will and Testament into such a legal dispute, that it has delayed notification to you of your bequest, to the point of complete ignorance on your part that your grandmother had even died. By the time you do receive this missive, she will no doubt have been gone more than two years.

"I don't understand," Michael scratched his head. "If they just now sent word your grandmother died, how did you know already?"

"From the dream. I saw her on the very day she died," Amanda said. "Some things may have gotten muddled in my head over the past two years, Brother, but never that. I'll remember it to my dying day. Grandmother came to give me her last words of wisdom before she left this earth. To tell me goodbye." Amanda put Jems over her shoulder, patting to dislodge a burp. "Does the letter contain anything more?"

"Just a few paragraphs…

Let me be the first to offer you my sincere condolences, Miss Amanda Jane. And at the same time, may I offer my services as barrister in the battle you now face in settling the estate of your great grandmother Olympia. I am afraid there is nothing else for it than to request you make the trip back to Charleston in order to see to the administration of our current legal dispute with Joseph Alexander Bently III. Without your presence, there can be no resolution to this dilemma, which keeps all assets tied up ad infinitum, causing undue distress—most especially for the free people of color currently employed on Wallingsford.

Since Olympia's demise, Winston H. Applebaum has continued to oversee the management of aforementioned plantation in your stead. On her death bed, Olympia empowered me to continue handling all banking and financial affairs for the plantation, as I have done for the past fifteen years—with her blessing, I might add. She also requested that Winston remain in charge of any details pertaining to the supervision and safeguarding of all the workers at Wallingsford, until which time you should take over in her stead.

I hope to hear from you as soon as is humanly possible, Mrs. Harrison. Until such time as you make your wishes otherwise known, Winston and I shall carry on with business as usual, to the best of our combined abilities, insofar as these legal entanglements allow us so to do.

Most sincerely,

Douglas B. Hornsby, Barrister of the 1st Degree

"Well, Sister. Looks like you're making a trip to Charleston!"

"How on earth can I be expected to travel in the cold of winter with a tiny infant?" She cradled the two-month old closer in a protective embrace. "I flatly refuse to lose another boy! I will NOT put Jeremiah's only son at risk over some legal wrangle I care nothing about." She set her chin and stomped her tiny foot.

"Wait a minute. Let me get this straight," Michael said. "You mean to tell me you don't care about inheriting a plantation, lock, stock and peach pits?"

"That's *not* what I said, *Brother*." Her voice had a decided edge to it. "I don't want to even *think* about getting involved in litigation of any kind. Especially with my own family."

"I've got news for you, *Sister*, you're already involved. Wanna be or not."

"Oh *horsefeather*s!" At her agitation, the baby began to fuss in Amanda's arms. She rose from her rocker to pace the floor in an effort to quiet them both.

"You'd better listen to that boy," Michael said, nodding toward the baby. "He knows land is worth fighting for."

"Well, what am I supposed to do about it?"

"Send word you'll come after spring thaw. Once Jems makes it through his first winter, you'll feel better about taking him out."

"Do I really need to go?"

"You really need to go."

"Couldn't you go for me?"

"You know I would if I could, Mandy," he said, gently touching her arm. "I'd do anything for you."

She blushed at the change in his tone of voice and flinched at his touch. Quickly he pulled his hand back to his side. "They wouldn't let me represent you, anyway... seein's we're not married. I'm just your dead husband's brother. No way any judge will take my word for anything concerning you and yours... not until you marry me, that is."

"I know that. I'm just having trouble thinking about marrying so soon after... well, Jeremiah's only been gone for three months! I still expect to hear his footsteps on the porch and see him walk through that door after milking time–" she caught her breath in an involuntary sob that surprised her; tears slid down her cheeks unchecked.

"We'll always miss him," Michael said, pulling her into his arms and holding her and the baby to himself while she cried softly onto his shoulder. "We don't have to rush into anything, Mandy. Not until you're good and ready."

"I just need some time," she sniffled, wiping her nose with the edge of the baby blanket. "Time to grieve. And time to heal, before I can move on."

"I don't plan on going anywhere. I promised Jeremy I'd take care of you and the girls, and that's exactly what I intend to do. Nothing short of dying myself will keep me from it."

"Don't you even *joke* about a thing like that!"

"I'm not joking! I won't leave you, Mandy, not unless you send me away or the Lord sees fit to take me away. So until you're ready to have me as husband, I'll just have to be content being Brother to you... Uncle Mikey to the children." He took his handkerchief and wiped her tear-streaked cheeks. "Now blow," he instructed. She blew. "And when you're ready to head to Charleston, I'll make sure you get down there safe and sound."

"Thank you, *Brother*."

"Don't mention it, *Sister* of mine."

ABOUT THE AUTHORS

Sheryl Drake Lawrence
(as Libby Howard)

MaryLee Marilee
(as Ellie Mae)

MaryLee Marilee, published Humor Columnist (15 years in *The Holmes County Bargain Hunter*), former Editor & Feature Writer (Graphic Publications), Motivational Speaker, and retired Bed & Breakfast Owner/Innkeeper, ML currently devotes most of her time to writing. She splits her life between in a 'Tiny House' at *Wit's End* near Loudonville, OH, in summer, and at her 'Writer's Getaway' in a deer camp near the edge of *Sumter National Forest* in South Carolina during winters. In spring and fall she does her best to keep up with a passel of grandkids all over the country (mostly grown), who try their best to keep her out of trouble.

Sheryl Lawrence, retired Office Finance Coordinator, former English Teacher, and Short-Story Author, has published stories in *"Girls To The Rescue"* series, printed by *Meadowbrook Press*. In addition to keeping multiple offices running smoothly (at the same time!), Sheryl most recently spent the last several years breeding *Sweet Sheepadoodles* and currently lives with her husband of 37 years, while staying current with their children, grandchildren and great-grands!

"ML and I met in a creative-writing class nearly 40 years ago and haven't stopped talking since! We encourage and motivate one another at a time in history just as challenging as that of our frontier sisters."